WRATH OF THE FURIES

WRATH OF THE FURIES

A Novel of the Ancient World

STEVEN SAYLOR

MINOTAUR BOOKS
NEW YORK

WRATH OF THE FURIES. Copyright © 2015 by Steven Saylor. All rights reserved. Printed in the United States of America. For information, address St. Martin's Press, 175 Fifth Avenue, New York, N.Y. 10010.

www.minotaurbooks.com

The Library of Congress has cataloged the hardcover edition as follows:

Saylor, Steven, 1956–
    Wrath of the furies : a novel of the ancient world / Steven Saylor.—First edition.
        p. cm. — (Novels of ancient Rome ; 15)
    ISBN 978-1-250-01598-3 (hardcover)
    ISBN 978-1-250-02607-1 (e-book)
    1. Gordianus, the Finder (Fictitious character), 110 B.C.—Fiction.   2. Rome—History—Republic, 265–30 B.C.—Fiction.   3. Egypt—History—332–30 B.C.—Fiction.   I. Title.
    PS3569.A96W73 2015
    813'.54—dc23
                                                                        2015022081

ISBN 978-1-250-10578-3 (trade paperback)

Our books may be purchased in bulk for promotional, educational, or business use. Please contact your local bookseller or the Macmillan Corporate and Premium Sales Department at 1-800-221-7945, extension 5442, or by e-mail at MacmillanSpecial Markets@macmillan.com.

First Minotaur Books Paperback Edition: September 2016

10 9 8 7 6 5 4 3 2 1

For the wrath of the Furies who keep watch upon mortals will not follow deeds, but I will let loose death in every form.
—Aeschylus, *The Eumenides*

The war with the Romans has begun. . . .
How will our glorious king
Mithradates Dionysus Eupator
find time to listen to Greek poetry now?
—C. P. Cavafy, "Darius"

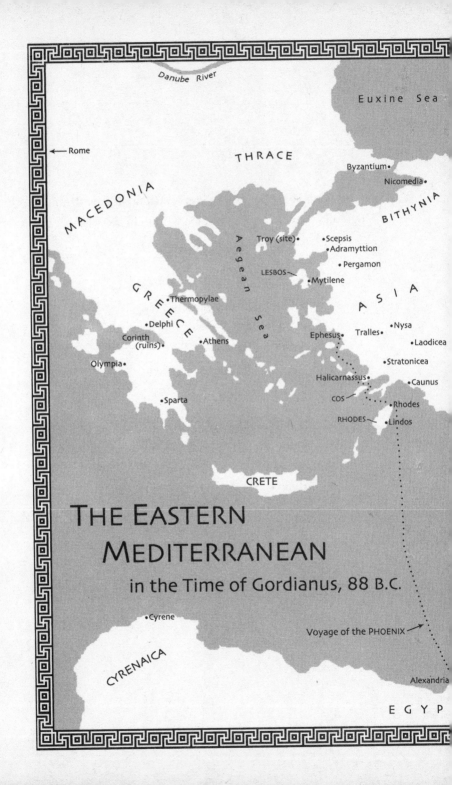

THE EASTERN
MEDITERRANEAN
in the Time of Gordianus, 88 B.C.

Danube River

Euxine Sea

Rome

THRACE

Byzantium

Nicomedia

MACEDONIA

BITHYNIA

Troy (site)

Scepsis

Adramyttion

Pergamon

LESBOS

Mytilene

ASIA

Aegean Sea

GREECE

Thermopylae

Delphi

Tralles

Nysa

Corinth
(ruins)

Athens

Ephesus

Laodicea

Olympia

Stratonicea

Halicarnassus

Caunus

COS

Rhodes

Sparta

RHODES

Lindos

CRETE

Cyrene

Voyage of the PHOENIX

CYRENAICA

Alexandria

E G Y P

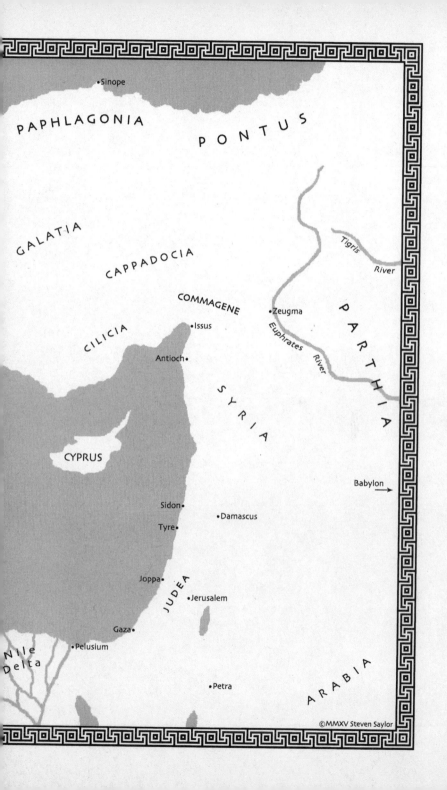

Sinope

PAPHLAGONIA

PONTUS

GALATIA

CAPPADOCIA

COMMAGENE

CILICIA

Issus

Antioch

Tigris River

Zeugma

Euphrates River

PARTHIA

SYRIA

CYPRUS

Babylon →

Sidon

Damascus

Tyre

Joppa

JUDEA

Jerusalem

Gaza

Nile Delta

Pelusium

Petra

ARABIA

©MMXV Steven Saylor

Prologue: From the Secret Diary
of Antipater of Sidon

[The fragmentary text begins in mid-sentence.]

. . . *not even allowed me to keep my own name! Instead the king insists that I continue to use that absurd pseudonym (which he himself suggested) that I took when I agreed to fake my own death and travel the world as a spy for him. So everyone here in Ephesus knows me not as the venerable Antipater of Sidon, greatest of all living poets in the Greek language, but instead as gray-bearded Zoticus of Zeugma, itinerant tutor of wayward Roman boys and all-around nonentity. The humiliation!*

But oh, how I wish that were the only humiliation I have been made to suffer, or even the worst.

I would challenge him in this matter, but I have seen what happens to those who dare to cross the Shahansha—King of Kings!—as he now styles himself in the barbaric tongue of the Persians. Part Greek the king may be, but part Persian as well—and since I joined his traveling court I have seen far too much of the barbarian and far too little of the Greek!

His execution of the captured Roman general Aquillius, which I was made to witness at Pergamon, is a case in point. I have no doubt that Aquillius was a scoundrel, one of the very worst of the Roman overlords who have subjugated the Greek-speaking world. He deserved to be tried for his crimes, and punished for them. But did even Aquillius deserve the horrible death the king devised? What sort of fiend could invent such a cruel punishment, and make a public spectacle of it? I was close enough to smell the sizzling flesh. The sounds Aquillius made—his convulsions of agony—I grow faint when I think of it. . . . Perhaps at some later date I will describe what happened, but I cannot bear to do so now.

I wonder sometimes if such a horrible fate lies in store for me—or some death even worse, devised by the king's boundless imagination.

When I remember the life I had in Rome, only a few years ago—recognized and respected by all the best people, well paid and well fed for my recitations, the envy of every poet in the city . . . Then the agents of the king approached me, and whispered in my ear: "What are you doing among these people? A Greek you are, not a Roman! The Roman conquerors have overrun your homeland. They empty our treasuries. They loot our temples. The rich they make poor with taxes. The poor they make into slaves. Any who dare to protest, they strike down with a sword. Yet here you live in luxury, reciting pretty verses to tickle their ears!"

"But what can I do to stop the Romans?" I asked them. "What can anyone do?"

"Have you not heard?" they answered. "King Mithridates of Pontus is on the march! He has taken up the mantle of Alexander, and that of Cyrus the Great as well—heir to the greatness of both Greece and Persia. Mithridates is the world's only hope to stop these infernal Romans!"

So I was seduced into the service of the king—and once I dispatched my first secret report to his agents, there could be no turning back. Even the most cultured and Greek-loving of my patrons in Rome would have had me crucified if they knew of my activities on behalf of the king.

But I was careless. The veil of secrecy grew thin. To escape discovery, I was obliged to fake my own death and to leave Rome. As the clouds of war gathered, I traveled all over the Greek-speaking world—not as Antipater the poet, but incognito, as Zoticus the nobody—carrying messages and secretly rallying support for the king. To Olympia I journeyed, and to the ruins of Corinth, and even as far as Babylon to the east and Alexandria to the south.

Sometimes I adopted a disguise, but this was rarely necessary. Antipater might be the world's most famous poet, but it was my words that people knew, not my face. I had been living in Rome a long time, and there I was known by sight, but in Greece and Asia and even in my hometowns of Sidon and Tyre, no one knew what Antipater looked like. When an old man introduced himself as Zoticus of Zeugma, no one gave him a second glance.

Then, at last, the war began in earnest. Some say Manius Aquillius initiated the hostilities, on his own initiative and without the approval of the Roman Senate. Whoever started the war, Mithridates quickly enjoyed a string of victories in and around the province the Romans called Asia, liberating city after city—liberating them from Roman control, that is, and placing them under his own control, or that of his appointed overseers.

To celebrate his victories, Mithridates staged a triumphal tour of the liberated cities of Asia—and I received a message, written in our secret code, inviting me to join him. As I made my way from Alexandria to Pergamon, I thought: He will reward me now. The King of Kings will make me his court poet. In return for my faithful service, a grateful Mithridates will crown me with glory!

Instead, at our first meeting, before I could even begin to recite the poem I had composed for the occasion—the meeting of the world's greatest poet and the world's greatest king—Mithridates told me that I must continue to play the role of Zoticus. "Antipater is useless to me," he said, "but Zoticus— oh, as wily Zoticus you have served me well! I may yet have need of your secret services, so Zoticus you shall remain."

For a long moment, I was dumbfounded. "But surely," I said, "I am more valuable to you as Antipater than as Zoticus. When it becomes known that the greatest of all living poets has joined your retinue, and is eager to dedicate his art to your service, all the world will see that you are the champion of Greek culture."

I thought this would make him smile. Instead he scowled. "I am already the champion of Greek culture, as everyone already knows—everyone except you, perhaps!"

I stammered, unused to being at a loss for words. "Ah, yes, widely known your achievements may be, but my words will make those achievements immortal."

His scowl deepened. "My achievements will be immortal with or without your words—Zoticus!"

It is hard for an old man with a stiff back to bow, but I bowed even lower before him. "Please, King Mithridates. For whatever time I have left in this world, I would live not behind a mask, but openly and proudly as myself."

The king grew furious. "You will address me as Shahansha, King of Kings! And all men shall address you as Zoticus!"

"But . . . for how long, O King of Kings?" I managed to utter, ashamed at the mouse-squeak that came out of my mouth.

"For as long as I say. Or for as long as you continue to live—and that, too, is for the King of Kings to decide!"

I dared to look into his eyes. I could bear his gaze for only an instant—but in that brief moment I caught a glimpse of madness behind those fiery eyes. This was the man for whom I had given up everything, in whose service I had become a wandering nobody, a vagrant, a liar, a spy!

Zoticus I had become, and Zoticus I would remain.

And so, in his victory march across the liberated lands, I followed in the king's retinue, but not among the luminaries of his court. Instead of taking my rightful place alongside the famous scholars, philosophers, astrologers, and Magi, I, Antipater of Sidon, was relegated to the outermost circle of the court. I found myself surrounded by jugglers and acrobats, sniveling sycophants and hangers-on of the lowest sort!

Then there is the matter of my relations with the king's wife, a sly young minx called Monime. Hardly more that a child she looks, but what a schemer! The little queen bends the will of the king this way and that, as if he were her plaything, and he doesn't even realize it. Worst of all, she took an instant disliking to me. No doubt she saw the look of reciprocal loathing on my face, and marked me at once as her enemy. And those whom Monime dislikes have a way of leaving this world sooner rather than later.

Now we have arrived in Ephesus, where with great pomp and ceremony *the king has appointed Monime's father, Philopoemen, royal overseer of the city. While the king is busy plotting his next military campaign, the little queen and her father wield absolute power over Ephesus. As long as I remain here, I know . . .*

[This fragment ends in mid-sentence. A portion of the diary appears to be missing, after which the text resumes, again in mid-sentence.]

. . . is in an even worse dilemma than myself, it would be the Romans who remain in Ephesus. Thousands already lived here, and thousands more fled to this city ahead of the king's arrival, hoping to escape by ship to the island of Rhodes, which remains loyal to the Romans. But even with their decks crammed to overflowing, there were not enough ships to carry so many refugees. Many Romans—thousands of them—remain in Ephesus. Some are longtime residents who go about their business as best they can, but many are homeless. They fill the temples to overflowing, seeking sanctuary and crying out for the protection of the gods.

So it is, not just in Ephesus but in all the cities up and down the coast. Where Roman magistrates and merchants once held sway, they now find themselves stripped of their power and at the mercy of Mithridates. How low our former masters have fallen! What shall become of them now?

Eutropius, my host here in Ephesus, has just given me shocking news.

He says he has been approached by one of the king's agents, who swore him to secrecy upon pain of death. According to this agent, the king is determined to exterminate every remaining Roman under his control—not just in Ephesus, but in all the liberated cities, and not in stages, but in a single, vast slaughter, occurring everywhere on the same day. Eutropius, as one of the leading citizens of Ephesus, is to be enlisted in this secret enterprise.

The magnitude of such a massacre is almost unimaginable. There must be tens of thousands of Romans remaining in the lands King Mithridates has liberated from Roman control. Eutropius estimates the number to be as high as eighty or even a hundred thousand! Is it even possible those eighty thousand unsuspecting human beings, living hundreds of miles apart, could all be slaughtered in a single day, upon the order of a single man?

I thank the gods that my erstwhile traveling companion, young Gordianus, is not here with me—any time he spoke a word of Greek, his atrocious Latin accent always gave him away as a Roman! His friendship with myself and with Eutropius would afford him no protection if this butchery takes place, for no Roman is to be spared. Men and women, the old and the young—if the king has his way, all will be killed, without exception and without mercy. And all in a single day!

Ah, Gordianus, as much as I miss you, how glad I am that you are far from this place, safe in Alexandria where I left you, or perhaps even back in Rome with your father. Tonight I shall go to the Temple of Artemis and sacrifice to the goddess, with a prayer that you may remain far, far away from the catastrophe about to occur here in Ephesus. . . .

[Here ends this fragment from the secret diary
of Antipater of Sidon.]

I

I, Gordianus of Rome, was living a few miles to the west of Alexandria that summer, in a house on the beach next to a small fishing village.

My hosts were the owners of the house, two eunuchs who had retired from the Egyptian royal court, Kettel and Berynus. When King Ptolemy lost control of Alexandria and the city became too wild and lawless even for a footloose young Roman like me, the eunuchs invited me to stay with them for a while, and I gladly accepted. I shared a room with my slave, Bethesda. The room was quite small, but the bed was just large enough for two.

From the rooftop terrace of the house, looking east over the sand dunes and up the coastline, we had a clear view of the skyline of Alexandria in the distance. Most prominent was the towering Pharos Lighthouse in the harbor; its fiery beacon was visible for many miles, both day and night. The Temple of Serapis, situated atop the city's highest hill in the quarter nearest to us, was also easy to make out. The rest was all a jumble of obelisks and rooftops surrounded by the high city wall.

"No smoke today," noted Kettel, whose massive bulk threatened to overflow even his commodious dining couch. It seemed to me that he had gained even more weight since his retirement. His appetite was certainly as voracious as ever. When Bethesda mounted the stairs from the kitchen and approached carrying a steaming platter of grilled fish, he eagerly took a helping.

Berynus, who was as slender as Kettel was fat, looked toward the skyline and squinted. "There's been no smoke—and so presumably no rioters—since the day King Ptolemy sailed off, even as his brother, our new king, marched into town with that huge army of his." He turned up his nose at the fish and waved Bethesda on. "Are we to conclude that the chaos is ended and the civil war is really, truly over?"

"Hardly!" Kettel chomped and snorted. "The old king will still have some fight in him. Just because he's fled into exile doesn't mean he's given up the throne. If he can somehow raise an army, he'll be back. Unless, of course, he loses his head in the meantime."

"Always a possibility," said Berynus, nodding grimly.

"They say the city has calmed down considerably since the new king's arrival," I said. "It may actually be safe to walk the streets again." Bethesda stepped toward me and held forth the platter of fish, from which I took a modest portion. Her back was to my hosts, who could not see as she dared to lift a morsel to her own lips and nibble at it, giving me a sly smile as she did so. I sighed. What a poor excuse for a Roman I was, unable to control the only slave I possessed.

"I was thinking I might venture into the city tomorrow," I said.

"Whatever for, Gordianus?" asked Kettel, smacking his lips. "Do you not have all that you need here? Good food, good company, long walks on the beach to pass the day, and the murmur of the surf to lull you to sleep at night."

"If indeed our bearded young friend gets much sleep," Berynus muttered under his breath, raising an eyebrow and casting a sidelong glance at Bethesda as she retreated down the steps to the kitchen to fetch more food and drink. Her black hair, glistening in the sunlight, was so long that it almost reached her hips, which swayed provocatively as she descended out of sight.

"The harbor seems to be rather busy again, since the old king fled,"

I said. "With all those ships coming and going, I was thinking a letter might have arrived for me."

"A letter?" With his fleshy forefinger Kettel poked at a bit of fish that threatened to escape from between his lips.

"Yes, perhaps there's a letter . . . from my father."

"Ah, yes, your father—back in Rome." Kettel licked his fingertips. "How long has it been since you last heard from him?"

"Months," I said.

"Such a long time," said Berynus.

"Yes." I frowned. "Of course, it may be that he's written, but his letters were lost or went astray." This was true. Travel by land and sea had been greatly disrupted in recent months, not just by the civil war in Egypt, but by events in Asia, where King Mithridates was said to be driving the Romans out of one province after another, and in Italy as well, where Rome's subject cities had rebelled against her. The whole world was at war. The days when one could exchange regular letters across great distances—as I had done with my father after I first arrived in Alexandria three years ago—now seemed a distant memory.

So it was entirely possible that my father had written any number of letters to me in recent months, but for one reason or another none of them had reached me. But there was another possibility. It might be that no letters had come from my father because my father was no longer among the living.

The little news that had arrived from Italy was grim. For rebelling against Rome, entire cities have been massacred, and the Roman Senate itself had descended into a kind of civil war. Growing up in Rome, I had observed that my father was always careful to tread a middle path, allying himself with no particular family or faction. This independence allowed him to work for any man who sought out his services. But could even my father remain neutral—and safe—amid the chaos in Italy?

In reality, just how neutral was my father? And how loyal was he to Rome? He had seen trouble coming in Italy—that was one of the reasons he sent me off with my old tutor Antipater on our journey to see the Seven Wonders, to get me far from Rome and away from the looming danger. I had been more naive than a young Roman of eighteen should be. I had thought our trip was merely for pleasure. Even Antipater's faked death and assumption of a false identity—Zoticus of Zeugma—had not alerted my suspicion. I accepted at face value Antipater's explanation that he simply wanted a fresh start, a last chance for an old man to see the world through new eyes.

But there was much more to Antipater's deceit than that. As I learned only at the end of our journey, Antipater had been a spy for King Mithridates all along—and thus an enemy of Rome. Our trip to the Wonders had been a grand reconnaissance mission for him, as he carried messages for the king's agents from Olympia to Babylon and to many cities between. No sooner did I discover Antipater's deception than he vanished from Alexandria, before I could get any sort of explanation from him.

What role had I played in his scheme? Had I simply been a traveling companion, sent along by my father to get me out of harm's way? And what role had my father played? He helped Antipater fake his death; had he done so knowing the old poet's true purpose? Could it be that my father was himself an agent of Mithridates?

Such a possibility was unthinkable. Or so I would have said once upon a time, when I was naive and untraveled and knew little about the ways of men. But now, in a world turned upside down by treachery and war, anything seemed possible—even that my father could be a traitor to Rome.

What if he was? Where, then, should my own loyalties lie? With Rome? With my father? With neither?

Before I could answer that question, I needed to discover the truth about my father, but that was not possible. "Are you a traitor to Rome, Father?" Such a dangerous question could never be posed in a letter, which might be read by anyone who opened it. Perhaps Antipater could have told me the truth, but I had no idea where the old poet went after he left Alexandria. I might have solved the problem by going back to Rome, to confront my father face-to-face—provided that he was still alive—but that journey I had put off time and again, either because of the danger, or the expense, or the impossibility of doing so as the seas were emptied of passenger ships by the threat of war from all sides.

But there was another reason that kept me from returning home, eclipsing all others: I simply had no taste for the journey. Was it any wonder that I preferred to dawdle in Egypt, basking in the warm sunshine of the rooftop terrace, feasting on fish and pomegranates and dates at the eunuchs' expense, taking long walks on the beach with Bethesda to find secluded places where we might lie together on a blanket between heat-shimmering dunes?

I had all a young man needed to be content. Yet, in my heart of hearts, what I wanted more than anything was to pay a visit to the banker in Alexandria who received correspondence for me and to find that a letter had arrived from Rome, a letter from my father telling me that he was alive and well.

"Well then, by all means, you must take a trip into the city to see if there are any letters for you," said Berynus, as if he had read my thoughts. This apparent ability to read minds was a trait I had noticed in both of the eunuchs. No doubt it was one of the attributes that had kept them alive through treacherous times, and had made them such well-rewarded servants in the royal bureaucracy.

"And take the girl with you," said Kettel, chewing with his mouth open, then swallowing the last of his fish with an audible gulp. "You'll want to do a bit of shopping, I imagine—if the shops are open again— and the slave can carry your purchases."

I nodded, thinking that any money I spent would more likely be on Bethesda than on myself, and that she would probably wear any such purchase rather than carry it. As she re-emerged on the rooftop bearing a tray of fresh delicacies, I noticed, not for the first time, how even the smallest adornments to her beauty gave pleasure to my eyes—the ivory pin in her lustrous black hair, the simple wooden bracelet on her wrist, and the copper brooch that decorated her green dress, a garment I had recently bought for her to celebrate my twenty-second birthday.

"Very well, then," I said. "Tomorrow, first thing, I'll head into Alexandria, and take Bethesda with me."

She raised her eyebrows at this information, then looked over her shoulder, toward the city, turning her body in such a way that the sinuous line running over one hip and up to her breast took my breath away. The eunuchs paid her no attention at all.

In the end it was decided that I should drive a donkey cart into the city, since the eunuchs kept thinking of various provisions they wanted me to buy, provided that such were available, "and not too outrageously expensive!" as Berynus cautioned. The eunuchs had retired with considerable wealth, but wartime prices threatened to make beggars even of rich men. How wise it seemed in retrospect that they had retired to the fishing village. For food, one could practically pluck fish from the sea. For entertainment, the setting sun and the sound of waves lapping the shore provided a spectacle that cost nothing, and that never grew stale.

There was no way of knowing what we might encounter in the city, so it seemed a good idea to make ourselves as inconspicuous as possible. I wore a faded tunic with a few tears that needed mending. Bethesda wore a modest, loose-fitting garment that did more to hide her beauty than to show it off.

The coast road was much traveled and well maintained. The two donkeys made good time, and we arrived at the city's western gate well before noon. The document attesting our affiliation with the eunuchs got us through the gates with no problem—the seals of Kettel and Berynus still carried weight, despite the fact that they had served under the deposed king. Inside the walls, the city was more orderly than I had expected. The new king's men were out in force, patrolling the streets with swords sheathed but with wooden cudgels in hand, and no one seemed in a mood to challenge them.

We headed down the broad avenue that runs the whole length of the city from west to east, lined with palm trees and decorated with statues and obelisks. In some areas I saw the results of riots and street fights—damaged buildings with broken doors and shutters hanging askew, dry fountains littered with rubbish and debris, and even whole blocks that had been gutted by fire—but many of the neighborhoods seemed to have returned to normal, with open storefronts and street merchants hawking their wares.

At one of the grand intersections along the way we turned left, toward the waterfront, and took the quickest and most direct route to the offices of the banker who sometimes held money for me and also received any letters that arrived in Alexandria addressed to me.

While Bethesda waited outside in the cart, I stepped into the little reception room. It was crammed with people, some wanting to leave bags of coins with the banker, others wanting to make a withdrawal. It required considerable persistence just to make my way to the counter, where I was given a wooden disk with a Greek letter carved on it— λ—and told to wait and listen.

At last a high-pitched voice called, "Lambda," and I elbowed my way to the counter, disk in hand, where I was met by a frazzled eunuch with a stubbly head and three chins.

"Well, what is it?" he snapped. "Deposit, withdrawal, inquiry?"

"My name is Gordianus, of Rome. I'm wondering if there might be a letter for me."

He turned and called to a clerk behind him, who called to yet another clerk in another room. Behind me, newcomers clamored for attention, but the clerk studiously ignored them, training his expressionless stare on my forehead while we waited for a reply.

A voice called from the next room. "Gordianus, did you say?"

My heart leaped. "Yes," I answered. "That's me."

The clerk who had called from the other room appeared. This one seemed almost a twin of the other, except that his head was smooth and freshly shaved, and he had not three chins but four. "Can you write your name?"

"Of course I can."

"Then you'll need to sign for this." He held a rolled and sealed scrap of parchment in one hand, and placed another piece of parchment on the counter before me. "Sign here, here, and here."

I picked up a stylus from the counter and quickly scribbled my name three times, not bothering to read the document I was signing. Who knows what becomes of all these forms that bankers require? Egyptian bankers are even madder for record-keeping than the ones in Rome.

There was a fee to be paid. It seemed rather steep, compared to the fees I had paid for previous letters, but these were wartime prices, I told myself, as I gave the clerk a handful of coins.

My heart sped up and my fingers trembled as the clerk handed me the tiny scroll. The seal was of red beeswax. My father usually used a cheaper wax, without pigment. Nor did the seal bear the stamp of his iron citizen's ring. The seal bore no stamp at all.

As I turned from the counter, I broke the seal and unrolled the parchment. I knew at once that it was not a letter from my father, for the letters were Greek, and my father always wrote to me in Latin. The handwriting looked familiar, but there was no salutation at the top and no signature at the bottom. A quick look at the page gave me little sense of what it was about. It seemed to be taken from some larger document, since it appeared to begin in mid-sentence and ended that way as well.

"There must be some mistake," I said, turning back to the clerk. He was already waiting on another customer, but turned to look at me with a sour expression.

"Mistake?" he said.

"This isn't a letter. I'm not sure what it is. A page from someone's diary, perhaps—"

"So? It arrived addressed to you."

"But who sent it? There's no indication—"

"How should I know?" said the clerk.

"But where did it come from? How did it get here?"

The clerk sighed wearily, then turned to a table behind him to reach for a ledger. The customer he was ignoring gave me a nasty look.

The clerk unrolled the scroll and ran a well-manicured fingernail down a column with scribbled names and dates, then tapped at the scroll with a flourish of authority. "There it is. Your letter arrived five days ago, on a ship that sailed here from Ephesus."

"Ephesus?"

"That's what I said."

"Is that where the letter originated?"

"So it says here. The document was taken aboard at Ephesus, for delivery to Gordianus of Rome, residing in or around Alexandria."

"But who sent it?"

"It doesn't say."

"But who do I know in Ephesus?" I said, thinking aloud. In fact, I did know a few people in Ephesus, having stayed briefly in the house of Antipater's old pupil Eutropius during our journey. But who among them would—

"How should I know?" snapped the clerk. "Figure it out for yourself. You've signed the receipt, paid the fee, and taken possession of the document. So now, if you have no further business with this establishment, I must ask you to move along. I have a great many other customers to wait on, as you can see."

I backed away from the counter, clutching the mysterious scrap of parchment. I stepped outside and walked to the donkey cart.

Bethesda saw the look on my face. "Bad news, Master?"

"No. I mean . . . I'm not sure."

She glanced at the parchment. Having never learned to read, all documents were mysterious to her. "Is it from your father?"

"I don't think so. I'm not sure who sent it, or why. I'm not even sure what it is." I climbed up beside her on the cart and unrolled the parchment.

"The letters are pretty," said Bethesda, peering over my shoulder.

"Yes, Greek letters are prettier than Roman ones. But wait—I *do* know this handwriting." My heart raced. My fingers trembled.

"Master?" said Bethesda, with concern in her voice. She laid a hand on my arm.

"This was written by Antipater," I whispered.

"Your old tutor?" Bethesda had never met Antipater, for I acquired her long after he and I parted ways, but she had heard me speak of him from time to time. I had not told her that he was a spy and an enemy of Rome—that was a secret I kept to myself—but she knew that we had parted under a cloud.

"Yes, my old tutor." I peered at the elegantly made letters and began to move my lips. It was not exactly my intention to read the letter to Bethesda, but in effect that was what I did, for it was easier for me to read Greek if I spoke the words aloud. When I came to the parts about myself, my face turned hot, but I kept reading:

> . . . I am in great danger. I fear for my life every hour of every day.
>
> For the time being, at least, I am allowed to reside away from the royal court, in the home of my old pupil and friend, Eutropius. Removed from the constant gaze of the king and his vicious little queen, perhaps I am out of their thoughts as well, and thus in less danger of incurring their wrath. But as a part of my living arrangements, I have been assigned two male servants from the royal household to look after my personal needs, ostensibly so that I should impose no burden on Eutropius. But who knows if I can trust these fellows? They might be assassins, for all I know!
>
> No man was happier than my host Eutropius to see the Romans driven from power, or more pleased at the king's arrival in Ephesus. Yet Eutropius is not such a Roman-hater as some. It was Roman abuses Eutropius detested, not every Roman who happened to settle in Ephesus or have business in the city. Apparently Eutropius was even arranging for his daughter Anthea to marry a wealthy Roman, before the man fled for his life, like so many of his countrymen.
>
> When I was last in Ephesus—then as now posing as Zoticus!— it was in the company of young Gordianus, at the very beginning of the journey that would take us to see the Seven Wonders. "And how is that young Roman?" asked Eutropius. "Faring well, I hope!" For it was Gordianus who saved his daughter's life during our visit. If only for that, Eutropius does not judge all Romans harshly.
>
> Ah, Gordianus! How I miss that youth—his steadfastness, his courage, his cleverness. How I could use a companion with those

qualities now, if I am to have any hope of escaping the parlous pre-
dicament in which I find myself. Instead I am alone, with no one to
turn to.

And if anybody . . .

My voice trailed away. Bethesda clutched my arm. "Then what does
it say?"

"That's it. There is no more."

"But there must be. That can't be the end of it."

I nodded and sighed. "You're right. Something tells me this is just
the beginning."

II

"That final, incomplete sentence—how do you suppose it would end?" asked Berynus.

I was back at the eunuchs' house after a long, busy day in the city. The hour was late, but my hosts often stayed up well past sunset, talking and dining by starlight and the soft glow of lamps on the roof terrace. With the sound of waves gently lapping the beach as backdrop, the setting could not have been more serene, even as my own state of mind could not have been more turbulent. In my distress, I had taken both of them into my confidence, explaining the circumstances of my parting with Antipater and reading the fragment aloud to them.

Holding the scrap of parchment in my hand, by the light of a nearby lamp I stared at the familiar handwriting. "What comes next? I suppose . . . I suppose it would say: 'If anybody . . . if anybody could help me, it would be . . . Gordianus.'"

"You're certain this was written by Antipater?" asked Kettel, giving me a quizzical look and lacing his pudgy fingers beneath his multiple chins.

"Absolutely. The handwriting is unmistakable."

"And that's all that arrived, that single scrap of parchment?" said Berynus, pursing his thin lips.

"Yes. The fragment begins and ends in mid-sentence. Clearly, it's been taken from some longer piece of writing."

"From a letter, perhaps?" said Kettel.

"Not a letter addressed to me, obviously, since he refers to me in the third person. Not a letter at all, I suspect. And certainly not an official document of any sort, or something meant for publication; that would have been dictated to a scribe, while this is in his own hand. It seems to have been written more to himself than to someone else. Or written for posterity. It's as if Antipater wanted to record the events going on around him."

"But why?" asked Berynus.

"Because he has a story to tell, but fears that he may not be around to tell it much longer. These words were written by a frightened man. A man who fears for his life." I sighed and lowered the piece of parchment. "And here I am in Egypt, frittering away my time, unable to help him."

"I thought you parted on bad terms with the old fellow," said Kettel.

"What if I did? He still thinks of me fondly. He says so in this fragment. He wishes that I were with him."

"He doesn't actually say *that*." This came from Bethesda, who sat on a rug before me, massaging my feet, which were sore from so much walking that day. My hosts had grown used to my slave's unruly manners and my tendency to indulge her, and hardly raised an eyebrow when she made bold to enter the conversation.

"He doesn't say what?" I asked.

Bethesda raised an eyebrow and resumed massaging my feet. "He doesn't say that he wishes you were with him, Master. What he actually says is that he could use someone with certain of your qualities. That is not exactly the same thing." Like many who cannot read, Bethesda was a careful listener and had a sharp memory.

I laughed. "You sound like a Roman lawyer, splitting hairs! Though you hardly look like one." The soft light of the lamps picked out glints of many colors amid her black tresses, and the creamy smoothness of her forehead and cheeks shone like ivory. "The point is clear: Antipater desperately needs someone to help him, someone he can trust. Instead, he finds himself alone, and in terrible danger."

"Whose fault is that?" asked Kettel. "From what you've told us, Gordianus, the whole time the two of you traveled together, your old tutor was secretly spying for King Mithridates. And no sooner did he reveal the truth to you here in Alexandria than he vanished, leaving you to fend for yourself. Well, now you know where he ended up. He's in Ephesus, residing with this old pupil of his, Eutropius—another supporter of Mithridates, from the way Antipater describes him. So he's hardly alone, is he? He and his host should both be happy, since the king has virtually driven the Romans out of Asia."

"And yet," I said, "Antipater doesn't feel safe, even in the house of Eutropius. He fears for his life, and the source of his fear appears to be the king himself—or else the 'vicious little queen,' as Antipater calls her. Somehow Antipater must have offended them, and now he fears he may be killed at any moment."

"If your old tutor has been swept up in the dangers of court intrigue, that's not your fault, Gordianus," said Kettel. "Spying is a dangerous profession. It requires deceiving people. What is a spy, but a master of deception—and who can trust such a man, or ever be certain where his loyalties lie? Believe me, no one is more suspicious and distrustful than a king. When Berynus and I served in the royal palace under King Ptolemy, we saw many a shady character come and go. Some received great rewards at the whim of our master. Others lost their heads. Not a few met with both fates—first the reward, then the beheading."

An image flashed in my mind: Antipater with his neck on an executioner's chopping block, and the blade descending, hewing his head from his shoulders, sending his white-bearded, white-haired head tumbling off in one direction while blood spurted from his decapitated neck. I gasped and gave such a jerk that Bethesda clutched my feet to steady me.

"There are other questions that need to be asked," said Berynus, frowning and training his beady gaze on me. "If this 'fragment,' as you call it, wasn't sent to you by Antipater, then who did send it, and how did the sender come into possession of it? And why was it sent to you, here in Egypt? This odd, orphaned scrap of parchment was sent to you by an unknown person with an unknown agenda. There's court intrigue behind this, I'll wager. And you, Gordianus, would do well to stay clear of it."

Kettel nodded sagely, compressing his multiple chins. "Or it may be that this scrap comes not from a secret diary but from a letter written by Antipater—a letter *not* addressed to you, Gordianus, and therefore none of your business. Or . . ." He narrowed his eyes until they were almost lost between his fat cheeks and the furrows of his forehead, and his pupils glinted like shards of glass reflecting the starlight. "Or could it be that Antipater is behind the whole thing—that the master spy contrived this 'fragment' as ruse to stir your sympathy, and sent it to you anonymously."

"But for what possible purpose?" I said.

Kettel and Berynus answered in unison: "To lure you to Ephesus!"

I shook my head. "Such an idea is . . . utterly fantastic. If Antipater wanted me to join him, he would simply write to me and say so."

"After the things he did to you?" said Kettel.

"Lying to you, betraying you, making a fool of you?" added Berynus.

"I wouldn't exactly say that Antipater made a . . ." I shook my head. What they said was true. If Antipater had written to me openly, I would have broken the seal on such a letter with my guard up, bristling with resentment before I read a single word. The fragment had effected quite a different response; it caught me off-guard and sent me reeling with puzzlement and alarm. If Antipater wanted to elicit my sympathy rather than my suspicion, sending such a contrived document in place of a letter would be one way to do it. But was Antipater that devious?

"Either your old tutor wants to lure you to Ephesus, or someone else does," said Berynus. "What other result could the sender be hoping for?"

"Perhaps this was sent by someone who cares about Antipater, some-one who wants to help him," I said.

"In that case, why did this person not write to you directly, and ask for your help?" Kettel shook his head. "No, for such a 'fragment' to land in your lap, without any explanation, with no clue as to who sent it or why—someone is up to no good."

Had I been as old and experienced as the two retired eunuchs, I prob-ably would have been as cautious and suspicious as they were. But I was still young and not as wise in the ways of the world as I one day would be.

I looked again at the fragment.

I am in great danger, I read. *I fear for my life every hour of every day.*

I lowered the scrap of parchment and stared beyond the parapet of the roof terrace. At the distant horizon, the night sky met the sea—two endless voids of darkness pricked with countless tiny stars and the reflections of stars. Somewhere in that direction lay Ephesus.

"I must go to Ephesus," I said.

Both eunuchs sighed and threw up their hands. Bethesda dropped my feet, which fell to the rug with a thump.

"Gordianus, do you not understand the danger?" said Berynus. "You're a Roman, and there's no disguising the fact. Your Greek is quite good—for someone who didn't grow up speaking it. But your Latin accent will always give you away. You know what they say: 'You can take the boy out of Rome . . .' "

"Yes, I'm a Roman. What of it?"

"Do you not understand the situation in the cities and provinces that Mithridates has liberated from Roman control? In those places, to be a Roman is no longer a guarantee of privilege. Quite the opposite. Across much of Asia, many people hate the Romans and were glad to see them toppled from power."

"But not every Greek hates every Roman. Antipater says as much in this fragment. Eutropius, for example—"

"An Ephesian who hates the Romans *less* than some, and why? Be-cause you, a Roman, saved his daughter's life! This Eutropius is hardly a representative example, Gordianus."

What Berynus said was true. In my travels with Antipater, many a native Greek-speaker had shown resentment and unfriendliness toward me, for no other reason than because I was a Roman. This anti-Roman sentiment had been especially evident in Ephesus.

"But not every Roman has been driven out of Asia," I said. "The Roman legions have been defeated and pushed back, and one hears that many Romans have fled—some of them have sailed here to Alexandria as refugees. But many a Roman citizen, along with his family and dependents, must still reside in the cities taken by Mithridates. All those Roman bankers and merchants, and the Romans who oversee the slave markets, and the Romans who run mines and farms—"

"Yes, Gordianus, thousands of Romans, or perhaps tens of thousands, may yet remain in Ephesus and the other cities of Asia," said Berynus. "But they are no longer in control of the banks or running the marketplaces. Mithridates has stripped them of their power and their possessions. Their situation is quite precarious."

"But I'm not a banker or a greedy merchant," I said. "I've never hurt or exploited any of those people."

"But you are a Roman, nonetheless. And this is not a time for any Roman to plan a trip to Ephesus!"

I frowned, then raised an eyebrow. "If it's my accent that always gives me away, then perhaps I can simply keep my mouth shut."

Kettel smiled. "That hardly seems practical. How would you pull that off, by pretending to be a mute?"

I gazed at the dark horizon and blinked. "Why not?"

"But how would you make your way, or ask directions, or accomplish anything else you needed to do? Absurd!" Kettel laughed and slapped a meaty hand against his knee.

Berynus made a sour face. "I fear our young Roman friend has made up his mind not only to go to Ephesus, but to travel under pretense of being mute. A Roman who lacks the power of speech—a double handicap!"

They were right. I was letting my imagination run ahead of me. A trip to Ephesus inevitably would entail unforeseen difficulties and some degree of danger. To make my way without ever uttering a word would likely be impossible. Unless . . .

"What if I traveled with someone?" I said. "Someone who could speak for me?"

"Who would that be?" asked Kettel, pursing his lips at my foolishness. "Some urchin hired at the waterfront, who's likely to steal your money and run off the first chance he gets—or worse, betray you to some petty official the moment you get to Ephesus, and laugh while they lock you in a cell and throw away the key?"

I shook my head. "It would have to be someone I trust, of course. Someone I already know. Someone who knows me, well enough to speak for me if we should find ourselves in a tight spot. But who?"

I had made numerous acquaintances during my months in Alexandria, but who among them was suited to be my traveling companion on such a journey, and would be willing to do so?

Another man's slave, young Djet, had accompanied me on my recent journey into the wilds of the Nile Delta. Sometimes Djet had been a great help to me; at other times, a handicap. At any rate, it was unlikely that his master would allow me to take the boy on such a long journey, so soon after our return.

The two eunuchs were among the more respectable people I knew, and had become my closest friends, but they certainly had no intention of going with me. Most of my contacts in the city were not nearly as reputable or trustworthy. As I went down the list in my head, I was struck by the number of actors and street mimes with whom I was acquainted, not to mention professional informers and poison merchants, purse-snatching street urchins and tattletale slaves. To be sure, I knew a few philosophers and scholars as well, but I could hardly expect those men to accompany me on such an uncertain journey.

Bethesda cleared her throat. I looked down at my feet on the rug— she had not picked them up after letting them drop—and then past my feet, to see her sitting back with her head cocked to one side, staring at me with that indecipherable catlike expression of hers.

I looked at the eunuchs. They, too, were staring at me with curious expressions. They seemed to be amused at my confusion.

"Did I miss something?" I said.

"Only the most obvious solution to your dilemma," said Berynus. "The answer is right in front of you."

I frowned and shook my head. What was he talking about?

Berynus looked at me askance, with the haughty, exasperated expression typical of royal bureaucrats everywhere. "Literally: right in front of you. Oh, come now, Gordianus, must I point at the girl to make you see?" He extended a bony finger in the direction of Bethesda, who was now looking at me with the slightest hint of a smile.

"Take Bethesda with me? Of course not!" Though I had not yet thought that far ahead, in the back of my mind I had assumed that she would stay with the two eunuchs while I was gone. To take her with me would be to put her in danger, and that was the last thing I wanted to do. Bethesda had faced more than enough danger in the last months, thanks to the kidnappers who had taken her off to the Nile Delta. The separation had been painful for me; after finally getting her back I was not eager to be separated again, but to take her with me was surely not a good idea.

Or was it?

All three of them stared at me, and then all three began to laugh. Kettel's chortle was low and rumbling, that of Bethesda was musical, while the laughter of Berynus had a dry, reedy sound. Combined with the sighing of the waves, their amusement made a strange kind of music.

"What are you all laughing about? I was thinking I could leave Bethesda here. I realize it's a bit of an imposition. She can be rather troublesome, I know, but you might get some work out of her, to make it worth your while. I can pay for her to be fed, of course . . ."

I looked from face to face. They seemed not to have heard me.

It was Bethesda who finally spoke. "Master, I have no intention of being left behind."

I blushed a bit, chagrined that the eunuchs should hear my slave speak to me in such a way. "Bethesda, whether you go or not is for *me* to decide."

"Well put, Gordianus!" said Kettel. "And of course you must decide to take her with you."

I shook my head. "I think not."

"Think again! Did you not just hear her? The slave speaks perfectly passable Greek, with an Alexandrian accent. No one in Ephesus will think of Rome when she opens her mouth. And if she says her master— her *mute* master—is a native Egyptian of Greek descent, no one will think to question that, either. As to why you might be traveling with such an interpreter . . . well, no one who sees Bethesda will wonder why you wish to keep her by your side." Kettel cast a sidelong glance at Bethesda, and I was reminded that even eunuchs are not entirely immune to the allure of a voluptuous young female.

Bethesda narrowed her eyes and gave me an inquisitive look. "Well, Master, how soon shall we leave for Ephesus?"

III

―――――

"You'll need a pseudonym." Kettel stood in the doorway of the little room I shared with Bethesda and watched me pack. His bulk filled the passageway, making it hard for him to move his arms freely, so that as he nibbled at a handful of dates his fleshy elbows repeatedly struck the doorframe.

"When he traveled into the Delta, looking for the Cuckoo's Gang, the Master called himself Marcus Pecunius," said Bethesda. She was helping me look through my small wardrobe of well-worn tunics to see which ones needed mending, if I were to be presentable on my journey.

"But that's a Roman name," noted Kettel. "Unsuitable for this occasion. Nor should you take a native Egyptian name, I think, for you haven't the proper complexion. You have the nose of a Roman, that's for sure, but still, with your dark, curly hair and olive skin you could easily pass for a young man of Greek descent."

"It needs to be a simple name—either that, or something very unusual," I said. "Either way, a name that's easy for me to remember, even if I'm half-awake or caught by surprise. And a credible name—something that won't arouse suspicion or disbelief."

"How do you know so much about assuming a false identity?" asked

Berynus, who was so thin that he somehow managed to slide past Kettel to enter the room.

"I learned from my father, back in Rome," I said. "He knows everything there is to know about using disguises and false names, not to mention poisons and antidotes, and how to pick any lock, or follow someone without being seen, or tell if someone is lying to you." I sighed, suddenly missing my father very much and feeling homesick for Rome.

"Ah, yes, your father, who calls himself the Finder." Kettel nodded. "You seem to have learned a great deal from the man, Gordianus."

"Yet I never knew how much, until I was out in the world on my own and needed all those lessons. How would he choose a name for this occasion?" I glanced about the room, until my eyes fell on a scroll from my hosts' library that I was reading at my leisure, an old play called in Greek *Anthos,* or "The Flower." A copy had been among the few scrolls my father owned—the gift of a wealthy, satisfied client when he learned that the Finder's son was studying Greek. Antipater had taught me to quote long passages from the play, to my father's delight. The copy now at my bedside was owned by the eunuchs; during their years of royal service, they had acquired a great many scrolls, laying claim to damaged or redundant copies no longer needed in the great Library of Alexandria.

"Agathon," I said. "I shall call myself Agathon, like the playwright of old Athens who wrote 'The Flower.' "

Berynus glimpsed the scroll at my bedside and clapped his long, narrow hands. "An excellent choice! The name is neither too common nor too uncommon nowadays in Alexandria—we've all met an Agathon or two. And the name in Greek means 'good fellow,' which you certainly are."

"And as I recall," said Kettel, nibbling at a date, " 'The Flower' was especially praised by Aristotle for giving pleasure, despite the fact that everything and everybody in the drama is completely made up— invented wholly from the author's imagination. As shall be this identity under which you'll be traveling, Gordianus—or rather, Agathon."

"In *this* drama, our Agathon is going in search of Antipater," said

Berynus. "A playwright seeks a poet—there you have a mnemonic device that makes it easy to remember."

I nodded, and did not explain that I should hardly forget the connection, since Antipater himself had drilled me in reciting Agathon.

"You'll be needing travel documents, too," noted Berynus.

"Yes, I was just thinking about that." I had traveled widely with Antipater, but always as myself, Gordianus, citizen of Rome, and never using a false name. "Everyone entering Ephesus by ship is questioned, perhaps more closely now than ever. My old documents—the ones I've carried ever since I left Rome—won't do. But I've crossed paths with a forger or two since I came to Egypt. I suppose, for a reasonable sum . . ."

"Nonsense!" said Kettel. "You needn't hire a forger to produce suitable documents for this so-called Agathon of Alexandria. We can take care of that for you. Can't we, Berynus?"

The thin eunuch squeezed his lips together to make a sour expression of displeasure, or so I thought at first; then I realized that his wizened features had compressed into a sly smile. The face of Berynus was not as easy to read as that of Kettel. Behind his tightly shut lips he was silently laughing.

"Oh, yes," he said. "One does not spend a lifetime in the service of the royal palace without learning how to cut a corner here and there, or grant a special favor to a friend—or forge an official document, so expertly that not even the king himself could detect the counterfeit. Kettel and I can whip up documents for you that will fool the port authorities at Ephesus, never fear."

"For such a favor, I would be very grateful," I said. "How long does the journey take, if a ship sails directly from Alexandria to Ephesus?"

"Five days, more or less, depending on the weather and the winds," said Berynus.

"How easy will it be for me to book passage on such a ship?"

"I don't think you should have any trouble. With the new king on the throne, and the new king's soldiers manning the docks and operating the Pharos Lighthouse, the shipping traffic in Alexandria appears to be back to its normal summer pace."

"Yes, but for how long?" said Kettel. "The civil war here in Egypt may not be over. Shipping could be disrupted at any moment by some unforeseen event. If you must go, Gordianus, it will be best to book passage right away."

I nodded, then frowned. "But when I arrive, along with examining my documents, the gatekeepers are sure to ask about the purpose of my visit. What pretext could a mute from Alexandria have for visiting Ephesus?"

"Why, to be cured of his muteness, of course!" said Kettel. "Perhaps you weren't born mute. The affliction came upon you suddenly, as the result of some illness or because you offended some god. You've consulted every physician in Egypt, to no avail, and visited all the temples, seeking the help of any god or goddess willing to listen—"

"But again, to no avail." I nodded, seeing where this tale was leading. "And some omen or oracle here in Egypt has directed me to go to Ephesus in search of a cure. Only the Artemis worshipped in Ephesus can grant me the favor I seek."

Berynus clapped his thin hands. "A splendid excuse, and completely credible! Why do so many pilgrims visit Ephesus, except to seek the blessing of the goddess Artemis in the great temple revered as one of the Seven Wonders? That shall be your reason, Gordianus. Oh, what a clever pair of liars are living in my house!" He clucked his tongue and cast sidelong glances at Kettel and at me. His pursed lips expressed mock-disapproval, but his eyes glimmered with affection.

"And what if some sympathetic Ephesian snatches me up and takes me straight to the temple, and the priests make a great fuss, and a crowd gathers, and there in front of everyone the goddess 'cures' me? As soon as I open my mouth . . ."

"Artemis will have lifted your affliction—but given you a Roman accent!" Kettel laughed heartily, causing various parts of his body to jiggle. "The jests of the gods can be strange indeed!"

"I suppose I'll deal with the problem of being 'cured' when and if it should happen," I said. "Very well, I now have a name, Agathon, and a city of origin, Alexandria. I have an excuse not to speak—the affliction of muteness. And I have a reason for visiting Ephesus—to worship at the Temple of Artemis, seeking to regain the power of speech. And I have someone to speak for me—my faithful slave and traveling companion, Bethesda."

She and I looked at each other and smiled. The eunuchs nodded.

Just how wildly impractical—and dangerous—such a scheme would turn out to be I could not then have imagined. It was the sort of harebrained idea that could only have been concocted by a young wanderer with delusions of invincibility and two sexless courtiers who knew a great deal about palace intrigue but very little about the challenges of traveling from one city to another in a time of chaos and confusion. But, having come up with a plan, I was determined to return to Ephesus.

[From the secret diary of Antipater of Sidon:]

This morning, in a cold sweat, I woke from a nightmare—the nightmare, I should say, for I have been afflicted by this nocturnal terror almost every night since I witnessed the horrible end of Manius Aquillius.

I suppose I should finally write down what I saw that day. Perhaps, by recounting the incident, I can rid myself of this curse of revisiting it over and over in my dreams.

Some say it was Manius Aquillius who started the war. Others say it was Mithridates. Historians will no doubt argue the question for centuries to come. I am no historian, but rather a poet, so I will say that it must have been the meddlesome gods who started this war, looking down on us foolish mortals just as they looked down so long ago on the doomed heroes of Greece and Troy. But the men of this age are lesser men than their ancestors, even as the wars they make are bloodier and more far-flung than Achilles or Hector could ever have imagined.

It hardly matters who started the war. The conflict was inevitable. For years the Romans pushed their empire eastward, subduing one region after another, suborning this or that petty king with gold, taking other cities by armed force. Meanwhile, Mithridates ascended to the throne of Pontus, and he, too, began to increase his kingdom by seizing smaller, weaker kingdoms around him.

Rome and their puppet kings came to rule much of Asia, while Mithridates and his puppets ruled the rest. On the seas, Roman galleys patrolled the Aegean and its countless islands, while the ships of Mithridates dominated the vast Euxine Sea. Like crowded men knocking shoulders, one side had to give way, or else the two must come to blows.

The hostilities began with a puppet war. The Roman general Manius Aquillius pressured a Roman ally, King Nicomedes of Bithynia, to make war on some neighboring port cities ruled by Mithridates. Nicomedes was so deeply in debt to Rome that he could hardly refuse; when he expressed his fear that Mithridates might retaliate, Manius Aquillius assured him that Roman arms would protect Bithynia.

What was Manius Aquillius thinking? Did he imagine that Mithridates would be so intimidated by the prospect of war with Rome that the king would allow his cities to be raped without responding, and become yet another Roman puppet? Or was Aquillius so shortsighted and so greedy for the spoils from those raids that he prodded Nicomedes on with no thought for the consequences? Or—and this is what I think—did Aquillius deliberately hope to provoke a war with Mithridates, in the expectation that Roman arms could subdue Pontus in short order so that he, Manius Aquillius, could return to Rome to celebrate a triumph as conqueror of a new province, riding in a golden chariot to the accolades of the Roman mob while the vanquished Mithridates trudged behind him in chains?

If such was the plan of Aquillius, he was in for a rude surprise.

After Nicomedes attacked the coastal cities, Mithridates struck back, decisively and with far greater force than Aquillius expected. The theater of the war rapidly expanded. In battle after battle, the Romans and their allies were routed. While the panicked Roman generals fled, Mithridates advanced from city to city, at each stop gaining more wealth and prestige, and adding fighting men as well, as thousands of Greek-speaking soldiers deserted the Roman armies.

In the liberated cities, Roman bankers and merchants who once had ruled the roost were stripped of their property and thrown out of their elegant houses. Some of the most hated Romans were hunted down and killed by angry mobs. Other Romans went into hiding, or cowered inside their barricaded homes. Those natives who had been Roman sympathizers were also exposed to the wrath of the Rome-haters. Some followed the retreating Roman armies into exile. Some committed suicide in the hope that their families would be spared from retribution.

Those were joyous days for the Greek-speakers of the world. At last, someone was standing up to the Romans—and not just standing up to them, but pushing them back and putting them in their place. The name of Mithridates, long spoken in whispers, was now shouted in acclamation. Our savior had come at last, and he was unstoppable. Roman rule in Asia had abruptly come to an end.

Having lost his kingdom, the Roman puppet Nicomedes fled by ship to Rome. Gaius Cassius, governor of the Roman province of Asia, abandoned his capitol at Pergamon and made a headlong rush for the island of Rhodes, which remains allied with Rome. One of the Roman generals, Quintus Oppius, took refuge in the city of Laodicea, but the Laodiceans promptly expelled his ragged, half-starved army and handed Oppius over to Mithridates.

But what of Manius Aquillius, who started all this trouble by prodding Nicomedes into a puppet war?

Even before this man appeared on the scene, the name Aquillius was hated by the Greeks. In the previous generation the father of Aquillius was a provincial governor notorious for the harshness of his rule, and in particular for his suppression of the so-called "Citizens of the Sun," a group of Greek rebels who went so far as to preach the abolition of slavery. Tired of besieging their strongholds, the elder Aquillius poisoned their water supplies, causing the deaths of an untold number of women and children along with the men on the barricades. After stamping out all resistance, the elder Aquillius ruthlessly taxed his subjects. Roman bankers defrauded the natives and confiscated family estates. Roman soldiers raped virgin daughters. When the natives sued for redress, the elder Aquillius ordered them to be fined and beaten and thrown into the street. Romans such as this sowed the seeds of further resistance, and drove a man like myself to become a spy.

To be sure, on his return to Rome, the elder Aquillius was accused of maladministration by a fellow Roman senator. Aquillius was even made to stand trial, but he avoided conviction by bribing the judges. So much for Roman justice.

When Manius Aquillius, the son of Aquillius, was posted to command a Roman army, his very appearance on the scene seemed a provocation, a deliberate snub by the Roman Senate against those who had suffered for so many years under Roman rule. Even before Aquillius began his manipulation of Nicomedes and set in train the machinations that would lead to his own destruction, the Greek-speakers of Asia were ready to hate him.

Defeated by Mithridates, Manius Aquillius fled for his life. With a small company of soldiers he reached the coast and commandeered a boat to take him to the island of Lesbos, which was still loyal to Rome—or so Aquillius thought. No sooner had Aquillius taken refuge in the home of a local physician than an angry mob appeared. They broke down the doors of the house, seized Aquillius, and put him in chains. He was thrown in a boat, rowed back to the mainland, and handed over to Mithridates's men.

The soldiers treated him roughly, but not so roughly that he might die, for they knew their master wanted Aquillius alive. This I did not witness, but according to hearsay the various parts of his military garb, including his cape and his greaves and breastplate and other armor, were stripped from his body and claimed by the more aggressive soldiers as souvenirs. Then the soldiers slapped Aquillius about. With his hands chained behind him, Aquillius was helpless to resist. Repeatedly his captors knocked him down, then kicked him, then forced him to stand and be slapped about again. Ripped to shreds, his undergarments hung in tatters from his chained hands and feet. While Aquillius crawled in the dirt, the soldiers stood in a circle and altogether they urinated on him, making a game of it. Some even defecated on him.

Naked and covered with filth, Aquillius was put on a donkey. His fetters were refastened around the neck and belly of the beast so that he could not dismount. Switches were used to drive the donkey forward. As often as not, the whips struck Aquillius instead of the donkey.

The donkey and its rider were driven from town to town. At each stop, crowds gathered, curious to know what sort of criminal had earned such a humiliating punishment. "Say your name!" his captors would shout at Aquillius. "Tell the people who you are, and what you did to deserve this!" I imagine, for a while, Aquillius managed to maintain a stoic silence, as one might expect of a Roman general, but soon enough, with prompting from the switches, he shrieked his name whenever he was ordered to, and admitted his crimes.

Some wit among the captors got the idea that their prisoner should introduce himself not as Manius Aquillius, but as "Maniac" Aquillius, making a Greek pun out of his Latin name. Surely Aquillius resisted—to make an ugly joke of his own name, the name he inherited from countless forefathers, is as low as any Roman could sink—but soon enough Aquillius was babbling on command: "I am Maniac Aquillius, son of Maniac Aquillius! I am a filthy Roman, and like my father I am a murderer and a liar and a thief!"

Those who gathered to watch the captive pass by were invited, indeed encouraged, to spit on him and to throw rotten food at him, but no one was allowed to strike him or throw stones, for fear that Aquillius might be killed before the procession reached Pergamon, where King Mithridates was waiting to receive his captive.

Thus Manius Aquillius entered the city from which his father had once ruled the Roman province of Asia, not in a chariot but chained to a donkey. Covered with bruises and lacerations, and coated with every imaginable kind of filth, he looked hardly human, and emitted such a stench that his captors could hardly stand to be near him. Deprived of food, water, and sleep, he was so dizzy and weak he could hardly hold his head up. His voice was so hoarse that the sounds from his throat were like the croaking of some animal as he was prodded to shout again and again: "I am Maniac Aquillius! I am Maniac Aquillius!"

I was in Pergamon on the day Aquillius arrived. I had only just joined the court of Mithridates. I had been debriefed by various underlings, but had not yet been granted an audience with the king himself. Nevertheless, I was allowed to join the royal entourage on the day the king's victories were to be celebrated with a great spectacle in the Theater of Dionysus, perched on a steep hillside. I happened to be given a spot in the procession not too far behind the king and his new bride, Queen Monime. They rode in a chariot while the rest of us followed on foot. I saw little of them except the back of their heads, and their upraised arms as they waved to the cheering crowds on either side.

As we filed into the theater, I was given a seat in the front row, near the center, and was quite pleased at this stroke of apparent good fortune. Mithridates and Monime were seated on a dais on the stage of the theater, directly in front of me, so that finally, as ten thousand spectators took their seats behind me, I had my first good look at the man whom I had been serving in secret for so many months.

Mithridates looked exactly as I had pictured him from seeing his image on coins, and from a statue I had seen in Rhodes. He wore his hair long, like that of Alexander the Great, and was quite handsome and clean-shaven, in the way that Alexander was handsome, with strong, regular features and bright eyes. Alexander had never reached his late forties as Mithridates had, but this was how he might have appeared, still trim and fit and strongly muscled. Like Alexander, Mithridates wore only a simple diadem, a purple and white fillet of twined wool tied around his head; the head of Monime was likewise adorned with such a fillet.

While other kings often mimicked the extravagance of Persian royal costume, that of Mithridates was relatively simple and recalled that of Alexander, who likewise mixed clothing that was both Greek and Persian. His white tunic, dazzling in the sunlight, was trimmed with purple embroidery and belted with a jewel-encrusted sash. At his hip, fitted to this sash, was the golden scabbard of the dagger he was said to carry always on his person. His legs were covered by Persian-style trousers. On his feet were intricately tooled leather boots with the toes turned up.

Draped over his shoulders, despite the warm weather, was a cape-like cloak, purple with gold embroidery, but faded and worn in places, as if it might be very old. A hand-me-down from the king's forebears, worn for sentimental reasons, I thought. Then, with a gasp, I realized what this garment must be—the purple cloak of Alexander himself! This fabled cloak was said to be among the vast inventory of items seized by Mithridates when he took the island of Cos, a place where a number of kings and nations kept treasuries remote from themselves and therefore thought to be safe, for Cos had long been sacrosanct; even the Romans had never dared to loot any of the treasuries there. But Mithridates had done so, and among the booty had been the treasury of Egypt, which contained not only fabulous jewels and stores of precious metals, but the most sacred heirlooms of the Ptolemy family, including the cloak worn in life by Alexander, which no one since had dared to wear. Now it adorned the shoulders of Mithridates.

I looked at the queen, who appeared hardly older than a child. Indeed, at first glance I thought she might be one of Mithridates's daughters. But the intimate looks and touches they exchanged soon enough dispelled that notion. I suppose the queen is beautiful (clearly the king thinks so), but my first impression was formed by the look in her eyes—the restless, rapacious eyes of some predatory beast, more dangerous than beautiful.

Joining the king on the stage and seated to his right and left were the closest members of the royal circle, including childhood friends who now served as the king's generals, and the most influential stargazers, shamans, seers, and philosophers of the court. The Grand Magus and many lesser Magi were present. There was even a Scythian snake charmer—with a snake around his neck! In search of reliable prophecy and divination, the king reaches to the farthest corners of his kingdom.

How I longed to be a part of that inner circle! The next time such an assembly gathered, surely Antipater of Sidon, the world's most renowned poet and a loyal servant of the king, would be seated among the other luminaries of the court.

At some point I turned and looked behind me, craning my neck to gaze up to the highest tier of seats. The great amphitheater at Pergamon is said to have the steepest seating of any theater in the world, and to accommodate more than ten thousand spectators. On this occasion it was filled to capacity. What wonders and marvels had Mithridates devised to entertain such a huge audience?

At first we were treated to some trifling amusements—parades of jugglers and acrobats, dancing boys, female contortionists, men who swallowed coals and belched out flames, and so on. These entertainers were the finest of their sort, but they only served to warm up the crowd.

The main attraction commenced with a crier who read out the names of the cities that Mithridates had liberated from Roman oppression. Banners representing each city were paraded on the stage before us—Ephesus, Tralles, Adramyttion, Caunus, and many more. The list ended with Pergamon. When a statue of the city's patron goddess, Athena, was wheeled across the stage, ten thousand people rose to their feet, cheering wildly—everyone except the queen and Mithridates, who remained seated on his throne but raised both arms to acknowledge the accolades of the crowd.

There followed a parade of spoils taken in battle from the Romans, including not only weapons and armor, but also catapults and spear-launchers. The crier shouted the details of where each of the spoils had been taken, recounting the number of Roman dead or captured at each battle.

There was also a parade of chariots from Mithridates's own army, notable for the long, sickle-shaped blades that projected from the axles. The scythed chariot was a weapon of legend, invented by Cyrus the Great but not seen for generations. Mithridates had surprised the Romans with his own version of this terrible weapon, which mowed through their lines like a scythe mowing grass.

There followed a parade of captives. This included many notorious collaborators, Greeks who had aided and abetted the Romans. These scoundrels had grown rich, profiting from the misery of their fellow citizens. They were rich no longer, but reduced to rags and bare feet as they trudged before the people of Pergamon, who jeered and shouted curses.

At the end of this parade appeared one of the most striking duos I have ever seen.

The first was a man dressed as a Roman general—an actor, I thought at first—with a plumed helmet and a red cape and a full kit of armor, including a brightly polished breastplate with an image of Medusa and matching greaves with more Gorgon images to cover his shins. I was struck by the man's proud bearing, for he walked with his shoulders back and his chin up.

In fact, the man was no actor but an actual Roman general: Quintus Oppius, captured at Laodicea. And he held his shoulders back and chin up not from pride but because he could not do otherwise. The posture was imposed on him by the fact that his hands were chained together behind his back, and a thick iron collar was snugly fitted around his neck. Bolted to this collar was a thick chain; its further end was clutched in the fist of the largest mortal I have ever seen, a veritable Colossus dressed in animal skins and wearing a necklace made of bones and fangs. He was a grim, hulking figure with straw-colored hair and gaunt features. The barbarian's real name was unpronounceable; Mithridates called him Bastarna, which was the name of his race, the Bastarnae, a tribe on the northern shore of the Euxine Sea who had sworn loyalty to Mithridates.

At the sight of Quintus Oppius, the jeering rose to a deafening pitch. I covered my ears, the din was so great. I glanced up to see that Queen Monime was staring at me with an icy look in her eyes. My face grew hot and I quickly uncovered my ears.

As the roar of the crowd subsided, the crier with great relish detailed the humiliating defeats suffered by Quintus Oppius and the details of his capture. Oppius was led to one side of the stage, where Bastarna handed the chain to another barbarian. The giant then crossed the stage and disappeared in the wings, apparently on his way to bring out another captive.

The crowd grew quiet with anticipation.

It was at this moment that I first smelled smoke. It was not the homey, comforting smell that comes from an oil lamp or a hearth flame. It was the sharper, more disquieting smell that comes from a red-hot oven or kiln. I looked about, slightly alarmed. Behind me I heard an uneasy rustling in the crowd.

The sight that suddenly bolted onto the stage was so unexpected and so bizarre that many in the audience gasped. Others shrieked with laughter. Then all other sounds were surpassed by the loud braying of the donkey that bounded onto the stage, as if goaded by a sharp and sudden poke.

On the donkey's back was the most wretched excuse for a human being I had ever seen. Following the donkey and rider was Bastarna, who carried a switch in one hand and a spear in the other. To drive the donkey, he alternately beat it with the switch and poked it with the spear. He did the same to the rider, who barely responded to this mistreatment.

King Mithridates rose to his feet. He put his hands on his hips and made *a show of looking perplexed. He spoke at an orator's pitch, so that everyone in the theater could hear him. "Bastarna, what is this sorry sight you've brought to show us? Who rides on the back of this braying donkey?"*

"He can tell you his name, Your Majesty." Bastarna spoke with a thick barbarian accent.

"Can he? Speak up, then, wretch. Who are you? What is your name? Surely even a creature like you has a name!"

Bastarna planted his spear in the stage. He grabbed the prisoner's hair and jerked up head up. "Speak!" he commanded. "Answer the King of Kings!"

The man on the donkey emitted a weak, unintelligible series of croaks. The crowd laughed uproariously.

"Speak louder!" commanded Bastarna, pulling the man's hair and striking him with the switch.

"I am Maniac . . . Maniac Aquillius, son of Maniac Aquillius!"

"Did you hear that?" shouted the crier. "He calls himself Maniac!*" There were screams of laughter.*

"What else are you?" said Bastarna.

"I am a filthy Roman!" the man croaked.

"Have you ever seen anyone filthier?" asked the crier. The crowd roared.

"What else are you?" demanded Bastarna.

"I am a murderer! And a liar! And a thief!"

"And so was your father?" Bastarna prompted. The switch whistled through the air and struck flesh.

"And so was my father!" The words emerged in such a hoarse, plaintive wail, it was hard to imagine that another word could be forced from that distended throat.

The crier stepped forth and began a long recitation of the crimes committed by both father and son.

Meanwhile, Bastarna removed the shackles of Manius Aquillius and pulled him from the donkey. Too weak to stand, Aquillius collapsed at the giant's feet. Bastarna pulled the chain taut, forcing Aquillius to hold up his head.

At the same time, from the wings at either side, slaves wearing only loincloths wheeled two curious contraptions onto the stage. One of these devices was a rack for securing a prisoner, made of iron bars with manacles attached. The other was a sort of furnace on wheels, its iron bottom filled with coals. Nestled in the coals, mounted so that it could be tilted, was a red-hot crucible. The slaves who pushed this infernal conveyance onto the stage were sweating profusely. Sitting in the front row, I could feel the heat that radiated from the crucible on my face, so hot was the thing. Then another conveyance was wheeled onto the stage, a small pushcart containing a heap of golden coins.

The crier reached the end of his recitation of the crimes of the Aquillii, but by this time I was no longer listening. My attention was focused entirely on the red-hot crucible, the rack, and the heap of gold. What in the name of Hades was about to take place on that stage?

The slaves used a long-handled shovel to scoop up the coins and pour them into the crucible. At the same time, Bastarna dragged Aquillius to the rack and bound him to it in such a way that the Roman was made to kneel with his arms outstretched and his head bent back, his eyes staring upward. Into his gaping mouth Bastarna inserted a hollow bit. Into this cavity Bastarna inserted a large funnel.

It now became evident to everyone what was about to happen, including Aquillius, who began to scream, or at least to scream as best he could with the bit and the funnel shoved into his mouth. The sound that came out sounded strained and distant, like the squeak of a mouse. From the side of the stage his fellow Roman, Quintus Oppius, stared in wide-eyed horror. Mithridates smiled. Queen Monime leaned forward to get a better view.

A strange noise arose from the many-tiered seats behind me. It was like the roar of the sea heard inside a shell—all those screams and jeers and laughs and gasps melded into a sort of sigh, like an intake of breath, or the hissing of wind in tall grass. It was not so loud that the voice of Mithridates could not be heard above it as he rose from his throne and began to speak.

"*People of Pergamon, you are the witnesses to this act of justice. As he has lived by greed—committed crimes, killed the innocent, corrupted all those around him for the sake of greed—let this Roman die by greed. Look at him there, with his mouth gaping open. Even now, he hungers for gold! Shall we satisfy his craving? Shall we feed him the gold?*"

The crowd of ten thousand roared their assent.

With three slaves managing the long handle, the scoop was inserted into the tilted crucible, and then withdrawn, brimming with molten gold. Bastarna strode forth and took hold of the long handle, waving the others aside. He carried the scoop to the rack and positioned the molten contents directly above the funnel fitted into Aquillius's gaping mouth. Aquillius's staring eyes were so wide I thought they might pop from their sockets. His mouse-squeal of a scream rose even higher. He clenched and unclenched his bound fists, and wriggled his body as much as he could within the constraints of his bondage.

Bastarna held the scoop in place, but it was Mithridates who took hold of the end of the handle and gave it a turn, so that the contents were emptied into the funnel.

What happened then—

It is this moment that haunts my nightmares. I feel the heat of the crucible on my face. I smell the burning flesh and the sizzling blood. I hear the popping and exploding of the vital organs inside Aquillius. Behind me I hear the din of the crowd, a bellowing roar filled with hate.

Every part of Aquillius convulses in agony. Unable to bear the sight, I turn about, only to confront ten thousand faces contorted with fury and derision.

In my nightmare, I look from face to face, but they are all the same. Not one shows the slightest hint of pity or revulsion. Are these the people whom I dreamed of saving from the Romans?

I turn back, and on the stage I see Mithridates with his arms raised and a smug smile on his face. He has put on a show for the people, and the people love it. Their roar of hatred for Rome gradually turns to cheering, becoming a roar of adoration for their Shahansha, *their King of Kings. Is this the man for whom I became a liar and a spy, for whom I sacrificed everything, even my name?*

I lower my face and cover my ears, unable to bear the sights and sounds around me. When I dare to look up again, I see Queen Monime staring back at me, her pretty mouth misshapen by a scowl of contempt.

[Here ends this fragment from the secret diary
of Antipater of Sidon.]

IV

It was Bethesda's idea that we should consult a fortune-teller before our departure for Ephesus. Indeed, she insisted on it.

How Bethesda chose this particular fortune-teller, I didn't know. I had never heard of the woman, despite my network of contacts among the lowlifes and shady characters of Alexandria. Yet somehow Bethesda had chosen this fortune-teller above all others, and insisted that only she would do. I sometimes think there is a secret web, invisible to men, that links all the women of the world.

However that may be, very early on the morning we were to board ship, when a soft light pervaded the sky but the sun had not yet risen, and pockets of pitch-dark night still darkened doorways and the space between buildings, I found myself in a narrow street in the Rhakotis district, the oldest part of Alexandria. Before Alexander drew the boundaries for the great city that would bear his name, and laid out its grid of broad boulevards intersecting at right angles, Rhakotis was a ramshackle fishing village on a barren stretch of coast. Unlike the rest of the city that grew up around it, Rhakotis remains a network of narrow, winding alleyways, so mazelike that a visitor can easily become lost. Rhakotis seems quaint when one visits by daylight, but dangerous after dark.

Rhakotis reminds me of the Subura district in Rome, but is much more cosmopolitan. In the Subura, the stranger who might offer to sell you stolen goods, or invite you to have sex with his sister, or knife you in the back, is almost certain to be a Roman and to speak Latin, but in Rhakotis such a fellow might come from anywhere in the world, have skin of a color never seen in Rome, and speak any of a hundred different languages. The Subura, for all its seedy reputation, seems a rather tame and homey place compared to the exotic seep of vice and menace that is Rhakotis.

The alley down which we ventured that morning was particularly winding and narrow, and stank of cat urine. We arrived at a squat, mud-brick building with a black door upon which was carved the Egyptian symbol called an ankh. Here, according to Bethesda's information, we would find a fortune-teller called Ameretat. The name sounded neither Greek nor Egyptian; perhaps it was Persian. I knocked on the door. In the predawn stillness, the noise sounded very loud.

The door seemed to open by itself, for I saw no one on the other side. Then I lowered my eyes and perceived a small, shadowy figure no taller than my waist. The child—though I could not see him clearly, I presumed it was a little boy—took a good look at both of us, then without a word let us in.

"Follow," he said, in a high-pitched but peculiarly husky voice. He carried a small lamp, which provided the only illumination as he led us down a hallway so narrow I banged my elbows against the walls. The place had a peculiar smell, a mixture of incense and stewed onions. We came to a room at the back of the building where the shutters of a high window had been opened to admit the first feeble light of morning. The boy told us to sit, which we did on the rug beneath us, since the room had no furniture. Because she sat on the floor below the window, with the light in her visitors' eyes, the woman before us appeared as little more than a patch of gray against a field of black. At least I presumed the patch of gray to be a woman, though thus far she had not said a word.

The boy disappeared for a moment, then brought us each a cup of something to drink. The brew was slightly tepid and smelled like the fermented beverage the Egyptians make from grain, a beer with aromatic spices added. It was an old charlatan's trick, to intoxicate a customer with drugged food or wine—so my father had taught me—and this act of suspect hospitality immediately put me on my guard. When I lowered my cup to the floor without drinking from it, and gestured for Bethesda to do the same, I expected the woman to encourage us to drink, but instead she remained silent. The vague outline amid the shadows seemed less certain than ever. I thought I could make out the shape of a dark cloak and a cowl, but peer as I might, I could see no face within the shadowy folds of cloth. I couldn't tell if she looked at us or not, or even if she was awake.

Bethesda had arranged ahead of time, with an agent who worked for the fortune-teller, that we should visit Ameretat on this day and at this hour, so of course she knew who we were. Still, it was startling to hear a strange voice from the shadows suddenly speak my name, loudly and with a peculiar accent.

"Gordianus of Rome!" she said. "And you, the slave girl called Bethesda. You come to Ameretat seeking knowledge of what lies ahead, yes?"

Before I could answer, Bethesda whispered, "Yes, Ameretat, we do." I was about to chide her for speaking out of turn, when Ameretat interrupted me with a laugh.

"You might as well get used to it, Gordianus of Rome," she said. "Soon enough the slave girl will be doing all the talking, and you will be mute!"

I wrinkled my brow. Just how much had Bethesda told this woman's agent about my plans and the purpose for my journey? The more a fortune-teller knows about you, the more easily she can spin a tale so as to make herself appear more prescient than she is. So my father had told me.

"First, the payment," she said. That seemed straightforward enough. I produced a small bag that contained the agreed-upon amount. The boy appeared from the shadows and snatched it from my hand. He emptied the bag onto his cupped palm, counted the coins out loud, and gave the woman a nod.

"Something else I must have, some article of clothing or other item close to you. Your shoes, I think. Yes, each of you, give me a shoe, since it is on a journey of many steps that you are about to embark."

I slipped off a shoe, and so did Bethesda. The little boy collected them and gave them to the woman. I still couldn't see her clearly amid the shadows. If anything, as the light from outside very gradually grew stronger, the shadows across from us seemed to grow deeper.

I heard her draw a sharp breath—of surprise, I assumed, for Bethesda and I both were wearing finely crafted footwear of supple leather, with brass buckles for the narrow straps and tiny brass hobnails to secure the soles. Such shoes were far better than anything I would normally have possessed; they had come from the booty of the Nile bandits with whom we both had resided for a while. The woman sighed—with regret, I thought, for she must be thinking that the owner of such fine shoes could have afforded to pay considerably more for her services.

"I see a long journey," she said. "A journey of many days. Most of your travel will be by sea. Still, many a step each of you will take in these shoes. Friends and foes . . . but the friend is sometimes not a friend, and the foe not always a foe . . . a loved one from the past . . . a trusted teacher . . . danger . . . a sacrifice—"

"Danger?" whispered Bethesda.

I shook my head. The woman was speaking gibberish. She could have uttered the same words to any two people going on a long trip, and left it up to her listeners to make out a meaning.

"Danger?" Bethesda repeated. "Who is in danger?"

"I see . . . a beautiful young girl," the fortune-teller said.

So do I, I almost said, casting a sidelong glance at Bethesda.

"A virgin girl . . ."

Ah, well, *not* Bethesda, then—who looked a bit peeved, I thought, at the mention of this other beautiful girl looming mysteriously in my future. *Think nothing of it,* I wanted to tell her. *These fortune-tellers always throw in a beautiful virgin, don't they, just to get one's attention?*

Ameretat gasped, and heaved a sigh. "The virgin is soon to be in terrible danger . . ."

Of losing her virginity, no doubt! I thought these words, but did not speak them. I was finding Ameretat's performance to be less than impressive, but Bethesda gazed raptly at the shadowy figure, hanging on every word.

"And someone else I see . . ."

"Who?" I said, growing impatient. "Who else do you see besides the virgin?"

"An old man. Close to you, or close to your thoughts. Not your grandfather, I think. But old, yes. And dear to you—despite the rift between you . . ."

I shook my head. It was obvious that Bethesda must have given too much information to the so-called fortune-teller's agent. Such intermediaries were trained to elicit useful details, even from the canniest customer. Having been briefed ahead of time, Ameretat was simply repeating back to me what I already knew.

"I suppose that next you'll tell me the dear old man is in danger, too?" I said.

"He most certainly is."

"And that he wants me to come and help him?"

"Most certainly not! For you to join him is the last thing he desires. It is his wish that you should stay far away from him."

I shook my head. Somewhere between Bethesda and the agent and the fortune-teller, the story must have become garbled, or else Ameretat's memory had failed her. If anything had been clear to me from the words written by Antipater, it was that he greatly needed and desired my help.

"I intend to go to him, nonetheless," I said. "I leave this very day—

as I'm sure you know. What else awaits me on this journey, besides a
virgin in peril and an old man who's bitten off more than he can chew?"
I almost laughed, for it sounded as if I were describing a plot from
Plautus.

"If you think a comedy lies ahead of you, young man, think again!"
Ameretat seemed to pull the thought from my mind with such preci-
sion that I was taken aback.

Suddenly thirsty, I reached for the cup I had earlier put down. I took
a cautious sip of the tepid beer and tasted nothing suspicious. I drank
the whole cup, thinking I might as well get some value for the money
I had spent.

The woman appeared to stir uneasily. It was as if a bundle of rags
suddenly became animated and rearranged themselves in the dark corner beneath the window. The feeble light of approaching dawn had
grown just bright enough to acquire a pale blue tinge.

When she spoke again, her voice seemed like that of another woman,
so strained and unnatural did it sound. "Fool of a Roman, you have no
idea what awaits you!" she whispered. "Blood! Fountains of blood, lakes
of blood, a sea of blood! The streets will be filled with rejoicing. The
temples will be filled with corpses!"

Bethesda gazed at the darkness below the window. Could her eyes
discern what mine could not, a face amid the shadow? She gripped my
arm, so hard that I winced at the bite of her fingernails.

"Are we among those rejoicing?" Bethesda whispered. "Or are we
among the dead?"

"Neither, I should hope," I mumbled, feeling a bit unnerved, and
not liking the feeling. I shouldn't have drunk the beer, I thought. The
fortune-teller had seen me do it, and had taken it for a sign of weakness. Now she would make her prophecy as alarming as possible, hoping to scare me into giving her more money in the hope that I might
avoid some vague catastrophe.

"Where are these streets you speak of?" I asked. "Where are these
temples filled with bodies? Are you describing Ephesus—or some other

place?" I thought of my father in Rome, and the awful stories I had heard about the fighting and slaughter there. I thought of the death and destruction I had seen with my own eyes in Alexandria during the recent upheaval. Was no place safe?

Again, she seemed to read my thoughts. "Danger is everywhere, yes—but the danger ahead of you is more terrible than you can imagine, you fool of a Roman! The mightiest mortal on earth is about to inflict death and destruction on a scale the world has never seen before. The wrath of those whose very name the ancient poets feared to speak—yes, the wrath of the Furies!—will be unleashed, before which all men flee in terror. Even you, fool of a Roman!"

My head felt light. A chill ran up my spine. Freeing my arm from Bethesda's grip, I reached for her untouched cup, thinking another drink might settle my nerves. After I drank it down, the chill subsided, but the growing light from the window hurt my eyes. The light was no longer faint blue, but pale yellow. The sun must have just peeked above the eastern horizon.

"What should I do, fortune-teller? Should I go to Ephesus, or not? Will Antipater die if I don't go? Will he—will he—" The words caught in my throat. Try as I might, I could not speak them aloud. *Will he die anyway, whether I go to him or not?*

I took a deep breath, and tried to speak again, but the words would not come out.

With a start, I realized that I had been rendered speechless. It was my plan, hatched in a reckless moment, to masquerade as mute—and suddenly I had become so. I felt as if the words themselves were stuffed down my throat. I could not spit them out. I experienced a thrill of panic. The pulse of my heartbeat was loud in my ears. Had the fortune-teller bewitched me? Had I been put under some spell by the contents of the two cups?

I clutched my throat, and squeezed it, striving somehow to loosen the words lodged inside. At last a strangled noise came forth, and all the words piled up behind it came rushing out. "Will Antipater die anyway? Will he die whether I go to him or not?"

Ameretat laughed. "Of course he'll die! All men die. Did you not know that, Roman?"

"You mock me, fortune-teller! You serve me a strange brew, you take my money, you tell me nothing I don't already know, and now you mock me!"

She sighed. "You have a tongue to speak, it seems, but you have no ears to hear. This is a waste of my time and yours."

From the patch of darkness came a slithering sound, and my squinting eyes perceived a vague movement. I decided the fortune-teller had remained unseen for long enough. I rose to my feet and stepped toward her, intending to pull her into the light. I shielded my eyes from the glow of the window, thinking to see her more clearly, but when I reached for what I took to be the cowl of her cloak my hands encountered only a pile of empty cloth with no person inside.

"It's only a pile of rags!" I said, tossing aside the various pieces until nothing remained and the corner was empty.

"How in Hades . . . ?" I whispered, looking about the room. With my back to the window I could now see Bethesda quite clearly, and the rug on which she sat, and the empty cups on the rug—but nothing else. Except for the two of us, the room was empty. The only way into or out of the room was through the door by which we had entered, or else through the window, and the fortune-teller had exited by neither route, for we would have seen her do so. Unless the room had a trap-door . . .

Before I could set about examining the wall and floor beneath the window, a voice called out from the doorway.

"Time to go!"

It was the little boy who had shown us in—or so I thought. But when I looked at the person in the doorway I saw not a boy but a very small woman, her wizened features starkly lit by the morning light from the window.

"Time to go!" she said again.

I frowned. "Who are you? You can't be the person who greeted us at the door . . ."

Bethesda, rising from the rug, turned to look at the woman. "Of course it's the same person, Master. She opened the door for us and showed us in, and brought the two cups."

"You recognize her?"

"Of course, Master. Do you not?"

"The voice is the same, yes. But I thought . . ."

"Perhaps you were mistaken. Would it be the first time, Roman?" The dwarfish woman's wrinkled features were drawn into a smile. I drew a sharp breath. Now she sounded like the fortune-teller!

"Time for you to go!" she said again, clapping her hands for emphasis. She ushered us down the narrow hallway, which was now light enough so that I could avoid banging my elbows. She opened the door and shooed us into the street.

I put my hand on the door before she could close it.

"Who are you?" I said. "What happened here?"

The little woman looked up at me. She sighed. "Alas, Roman, sometimes things are not what they seem."

"So I've discovered. But I would see things as they are."

"Would you, Roman? Is that truly your desire?"

"Always."

"Always?" She laughed. "To always and everywhere see things as they truly are—that is not a blessing, Roman, but a curse, and only a handful of mortals must bear it. They are called fortune-tellers."

"Or finders," I said, thinking of my father, who strove always to see things as they were. It was from him that I had inherited the same curse, if a curse it was. . . .

The little woman took advantage of the lapse in my concentration to push the door shut. I heard a bolt fall, and knew she had locked the door.

So ended my visit to Ameretat the fortune-teller.

V

"Look, Master! Is that a dolphin, swimming alongside the ship? I've seen pictures of them in mosaics, and statues in fountains, but never a *real* dolphin. Look, there's another! And listen—do you hear? They seem to be chattering to each other. Or laughing! Do dolphins speak? Do they laugh? I wonder, are those two a couple? Do dolphins pair, as mortals do?"

Bethesda looked at me with raised eyebrows, feigning innocence—for she knew how much her pestering questions had come to irritate me, since I could answer only with a nod, or a shrug, or a grunt. I tried to make a sour face, but probably failed, for I found myself thinking how beautiful she looked with her long black hair fluttering in the salty breeze.

Four days before that sighting of the dolphins, we had boarded the *Phoenix* as planned, despite Bethesda's protests.

To her, the fortune-teller's words had been a clear warning that we should not take the trip. I was more skeptical. What, after all, had Ameretat said that I did not know already, or could not have imagined on my own? She had said something about "the mightiest mortal on earth" causing destruction unlike anything the world had ever seen, unleashing the Furies themselves. Given his recent victories, the mightiest mortal might be King Mithridates, but it seemed to me more likely that the mightiest of mortals surely must be some Roman general or other, though perhaps that was only my bias as a Roman. As for unprecedented destruction, the world had seen a great deal of bloodshed and horror since Prometheus first created mankind, and it seemed to me unlikely that there could be anything new looming in that regard. As for the Furies being unleashed on earth . . . well, just as Bethesda had never before seen a real dolphin, I had lived twenty-two years on earth and traveled many hundreds of miles without encountering a Fury, except in statues and paintings and mosaics, and it seemed unlikely that I would meet one of those fierce, snake-haired, winged crones in Ephesus.

The one thing Ameretat had said that gnawed at my equanimity was that Antipater did *not* want me to come to his aid—indeed, that he wanted me to stay away from Ephesus. This contradicted the words of Antipater that I had read with my own eyes, so it seemed to me this utterance proved either that the fortune-teller was a fraud, or that she did in fact know something I did not—a disturbing notion. But I inclined toward the first conclusion, reasoning that Bethesda, intentionally or not, had revealed to the fortune-teller's agent her own desire that we should not go, inspiring Ameretat to weave this invented detail into her narrative.

So, despite the fortune-teller's words and Bethesda's objections, we set sail from Alexandria aboard the *Phoenix,* bound for Ephesus by way of Rhodes with a cargo of papyrus, grain, perfumes, and spices in the hold, and a handful of passengers on deck, almost all of them men. Fortunately, there had been no one on the waterfront that day, or among those who boarded the ship, who recognized me as Gordianus of Rome, so I successfully managed to depart from Egypt under the guise of Agathon of Alexandria, recently stricken mute, bound for Ephesus and attended by a single slave.

Bethesda had boarded the ship with trepidation. Her misgivings mounted when we set sail. She had been on board a ship only once in her life, and briefly, as a captive of the Nile bandits, but in that instance had been kept locked away; also, the bandits' ship had hugged the coastline, never venturing out of sight of land. Standing on board the *Phoenix,* watching the skyline of Alexandria and the towering Pharos Lighthouse slowly dwindle and finally vanish from sight, she grew so agitated, pacing and biting her knuckles, that I feared she might burst into tears and say something to give me away.

Then, before my eyes, a transformation took place. She looked at a seagull overhead—a rather intrepid creature, to be venturing so far from shore. She breathed in the fresh, salt-scented air. She gazed at the endless expanse of the sea, an undulating blanket of lapis-blue spangled with sparkling points of golden sunlight. Far to the east we could see the red-and-white-striped sail of another ship, and far to the west was another sail, this one bright yellow. Aboard the *Phoenix* there was nowhere to go and very little to do, but with the sun shining and a steady breeze in our sail, what place on earth could be more beautiful? The detached languor of travel by sea settled over Bethesda, calming and soothing her. When I caught her chin and turned her face toward me so I could look in her eyes, I saw not trepidation but the placid, catlike contentment I had grown used to seeing there, and had come to love.

"Perhaps," she said, "this trip will not be so awful after all."

It was hard for me at that moment to remain mute, and merely nod. It was harder still not to kiss her, in full view of the sailors and the other passengers. Instead, remembering my roles as both mute and master, I allowed myself only to look into her eyes for a long, lingering moment before returning my gaze to the sea.

For the next four days the weather was mild and the sky mostly clear, with only occasional clouds affording welcome patches of shade. We quickly grew used to the tilting and rocking of the ship. At night we lay side by side on a blanket on the deck, letting the gentle motion rock us to sleep.

Passing as a mute presented challenges. My days on board the

Phoenix would give me a chance to practice my role, so to speak, before I arrived in Ephesus. I soon discovered that having Bethesda serve as my mouthpiece afforded an advantage I had not anticipated: as long as she did the talking, no one seemed to take much notice of me. All eyes were drawn to the beautiful Bethesda, and mute Agathon faded into the background.

But having no way to speak my own mind, and having to rely on Bethesda to speak for me, did sometimes present problems.

Many of the passengers passed the time by playing games of various sorts, often with small wagers attached. One of the most popular of these games was Pharaoh's Beard, played with dice and a wooden board upon which pegs were moved forward or back. When I was invited to play, I declined with a shake of my head, and thought that would be the end of the matter. But when the others badgered me to join with some good-natured jibes, and still I declined, Bethesda spoke up.

"My master does not play Pharaoh's Beard," she said, stepping forward to take a closer look at the playing board. "Nor does he ever gamble."

"Why not?" asked a big, brusque Jew. The man had been conspicuous among the other passengers from the first day because of his striking features; he had shoulders like a bricklayer, shoulder-length hair, and a long, plaited beard. I didn't know his real name. Bethesda had teasingly nicknamed him Samson, after some legendary strongman in the stories her mother told her, and nobody on the *Phoenix* called him anything else.

"Because," Bethesda began, circling around to get a better look at the board, "it was not long ago, while playing Pharaoh's Beard, that he gambled away everything he possessed, and then—"

"I think, young woman," said Samson, "there must be some reason your master is scurrying this way, frantically shaking his head!" He grinned as I took hold of Bethesda's arm and drew her aside. "Poor Agathon. Lost his voice, and apparently lost his fortune as well, by playing Pharaoh's Beard. I wonder which he lost first."

"And which he'll get back first!" joked another of the passengers.

"Just as well he won't play," muttered another. "I don't like to stand too close to a fellow who's gotten on the wrong side of Fortuna."

"Oh, really?" said Samson. "That's just the sort of fellow I like to play against! Sure you won't join us, Agathon?" he asked, raising his voice as I retreated to the far side of the deck. I shook my head and pulled Bethesda along with me.

The others laughed and commenced playing the game, while I silently vowed to keep a tighter rein on Bethesda.

Along with games, conversations filled the idle hours. Men talked about what they did for a living, where they had traveled or wanted to travel next, which cities had the most beautiful women, and that sort of thing. Having been to see all the Seven Wonders of the World, I could have regaled the others for hours, and I regretted my inability to correct some of the ill-informed ideas I heard about places I had seen with my own eyes, like Babylon. But when the conversation inevitably turned to war and politics, I was glad I had a reason to keep my mouth shut.

It quickly became evident that some of the travelers favored the cause of Mithridates, while others did not, and another small group (mostly Egyptians and Syrians, who lived beyond the sway of both Rome and Mithridates) claimed to favor neither side. Our first port of call would be the island of Rhodes, which was independent but had sided with Rome, and most of the passengers planning to disembark there were pro-Roman as well. They expressed anxiety that Rhodes might become the next theater of war, unless Mithridates intended to turn his attention instead to the Greek mainland, perhaps with an invasion of Athens.

After Rhodes, our next stop would be Ephesus, and the passengers who would disembark there mostly seemed to be partisans of Mithridates. They, too, wondered whether Mithridates would turn next to Rhodes or to Greece.

"Why not attack both at once?" quipped Samson, which sparked a heated debate. As an Alexandrian Jew without a drop of Greek or

Roman blood, Samson claimed to be completely impartial. Still, it seemed to amuse him to stir up an argument.

For the most part these conversations remained civil, with no curses or threats uttered and only mild insults exchanged, no matter how controversial the topic. Men on board a ship tend naturally to keep cooler heads than men on land, sensing instinctively that, unlike a tavern or gymnasium, on board a ship there is no street outside—no "outside" at all—where one may go to cool off. Crew and passengers are stuck with one another for the duration of the voyage, and must strive to get along.

Some passengers spoke of the purpose of their journey, but some did not. I found myself wondering how many of them were not what they appeared to be, but a spy, or a war profiteer, or a mercenary, or set to go about some other business best left unspoken—just as my purpose was, literally, unspoken.

Hours passed, days passed, and at last, at dawn on the fifth day, we sighted land—the craggy coast of the island of Rhodes. We sailed past the city of Lindos on the island's southeast coast and continued northward. As we drew near to the capital city, which bears the same name as the island, I stood with the other passengers along the port side of the ship, enjoying the view of the coast on such a bright, sunny day, until Bethesda took my arm and pulled me to the starboard side.

"Look, Master!" She pointed at a silvery shape beneath the waves. "Is that a dolphin, swimming alongside the ship?"

So it was, and not one dolphin, but two. As Bethesda continued to ask one question after another, none of which I could answer in my role as a mute, the two dolphins swam along our starboard side, zigzagging through the glittering green water and sometimes leaping into the air. Other passengers joined us in watching them, and as the ship made a wide turn to the west, it seemed as if the dolphins were herding us in that direction. The port of Rhodes came into view, and the dolphins continued to swim and leap alongside us, as if acting as honor guards for our arrival in Rhodes.

We came to the great mole that projects into the harbor, at the tip of which lay the ruins of the famous Colossus. More than a hundred years ago an earthquake caused the towering bronze statue of Helios to come tumbling down, but the broken remains were still a marvel to behold, made even stranger by their grotesque condition. The two feet were still firmly connected to a high pedestal, but were broken off at the ankles. A massive forearm lay half-submerged amid the lapping waves, as if the hand at its terminus might be reaching out to touch the underside of our ship. Farther on, the gigantic head lay on its side, with one eye appearing to stare at all who entered the harbor. Tiny-looking mortals wandering amid the ruins gave an idea of the staggering scale of the statue.

"Oh, Master!" cried Bethesda, with an awed expression on her face. "Is this the great Colossus of Rhodes?"

I nodded.

"Which you've seen already, when you traveled here?"

I nodded. The sight of the monumental ruins stirred fond memories, and some darker ones.

"Will we be going ashore in Rhodes?"

I nodded again.

"Oh, Master, I have a thousand questions to ask—but not now." She smiled demurely and lowered her voice to a whisper. "Later, when we can be alone. Oh, there are so many things I want to ask!"

I longed to take her in my arms, but did not. If indeed we soon had a chance to be alone and unobserved, talking was not how I imagined we would spend that precious time together. Before she could utter the first word of the first of her thousand questions, I would cover her mouth with a kiss, and go on kissing her. . . .

The dolphins made a final leap in the air, side by side, then plunged into the waves and vanished. We sailed past the last of the scattered ruins of the Colossus and headed for the docks. Like a jumble of rooftops spread across the cupped palm of a giant's hand, the city of Rhodes lay before us.

The moment held a dreamlike beauty, until it was broken by a voice behind me. "What's that on the mole?" said Samson. "All those people, and tents? Is it some sort of festival?"

"Can't be a festival," someone answered. "The people all look too glum. See, how no one waves back to us? They avert their eyes. It's as if they dread the arrival of another ship."

There were indeed a great many ships already in the harbor, of every size and type, and as we sailed closer I could see that the waterfront, like the mole, was thronged with people and tents and lean-tos and other makeshift shelters.

"Refugees," said Samson. "Rhodes must be full of them. How tiny they look, at this distance."

"Like lice!" said someone. "Mithridates drove them out of the mainland, and now they infest the Colossus!"

Amid those "lice," as we sailed closer, I could see a great many women and children, and men of all ages. Was that how the partisans of Mithridates saw a Roman like myself, as vermin to be shaken off—or exterminated?

VI

With the harbor so busy, it took a long time for the *Phoenix* to dock and begin disgorging its passengers. When it came our turn to step off, the captain asked me how long I intended to stay ashore. I held up one finger.

"An hour?" The grizzled old seaman nodded. "That's probably all you need to stretch you legs. I don't expect you'll have much chance to spend your money. The shops will all be picked clean. Anything left worth buying will cost a small fortune."

I frowned and shook my head, then mimed the act of laying my head to rest for the night.

"You plan to spend the night? With all these refugees, you're unlikely to find lodgings. If you're intending to sleep under the stars, you can do that just as comfortably here on the ship, and with less chance of being picked clean by some sneak thief."

"Perhaps young Agathon has a host here in Rhodes, as I do," said Samson, who was next in line to disembark. "Don't expect me back until tomorrow morning, Captain. And don't sail without me!" He laughed and stroked his long, plaited beard.

As soon as we stepped onto the dock, a harried-looking port official demanded to see my travel documents and to state my purpose for visiting and how long I intended to stay. When Bethesda told him I intended to spend the night in the house of Posidonius, the official gave me a reappraising look; the name Posidonius carried much weight in Rhodes. The man handed me a small blue piece of fired clay that had been stamped with a crude image of the standing Colossus.

"Produce that if anyone demands to see your permission to be in the city. The color means it was issued today, and the numeral stamped on the back means you can stay one night—and one night only. Stay any longer without obtaining permission, and you'll be hurled over the city wall. Even if your host is Posidonius."

I nodded to show I understood, and smiled. The official did not smile back.

I hurried into the crowd, trying to get well ahead of Samson and away from anyone else from the ship. As I wandered through the multitude, all around me I heard people speaking Latin, and felt a pang of homesickness, but the looks on their faces and the strain in their voices were disturbing. A crying mother called for a lost child, an elderly couple begged for food, and all around I heard squabbling and complaining. I had never seen so many people so crowded together, and all looking so wretched. They were of all ages and of all social ranks, to judge by their dress—I saw everything from rags to togas, the distinctive garb of the Roman citizen at home and abroad—but there was not a smile to be seen. On their faces I saw weariness, anxiety, anger, and confusion.

Suddenly I found myself looking at another face, expressing quite the opposite of those things—serenity, confidence, pride. It was the face of the man who had caused all this chaos. I was looking at a statue of King Mithridates of Pontus.

The statue had been erected in the main square of Rhodes at about the time I was born, and portrayed the king at about the age I now was. As a young ruler he had taken a grand tour of various provinces and cities and kingdoms, including Rhodes, where he had been well received and in return had lavished many gifts on the city. The Rhodians had shown their gratitude by putting up this statue of him. I only vaguely remembered seeing it on my previous visit to Rhodes. Now chance had guided me to a spot in the crowded square directly before the statue, where I could not help but notice it.

The king was portrayed in garments more Greek than Roman, which showed off his fine physique, including his muscular arms and brawny legs. His face was quite handsome, and more than a little reminiscent of images I had seen of Alexander the Great, with a smooth brow, broad nose, and thick mane of windswept hair. It was a bit odd, seeing him at roughly my age, and knowing he must now be close to fifty, more my father's age.

The king's name was inscribed on the pedestal. Bethesda could not read it, of course, but somehow she knew whom the statue portrayed.

"King Mithridates?" she asked, standing beside me and peering up. I nodded.

"So this is the fellow who's causing so much trouble for Rome," she said quietly.

As if to give action to her thoughts, a rotten piece of fruit hurtled through the air and struck the statue's face. Bethesda and I jumped back as the person who had thrown the fruit rushed up to the statue. It was a woman with gray hair, dressed in a matronly Roman stola that badly needed mending. She glared up at the statue and shook her fist.

"Murderer!" she screamed. "Liar! Traitor! Fiend!"

Others rushed toward the statue, and more objects were hurled at it: fruit, vegetables, horse dung, small stones, and bits of broken tile.

Soldiers appeared, brandishing spears and swords to drive the crowd back. They formed a cordon around the statue.

"Every blasted day!" I heard one of the soldiers mutter. "Why don't they just take the statue down? Or else let these poor people pull it down themselves?"

"It's not for Romans to decide which statues stand in the agora of Rhodes," one of his companions reminded him. "We're not at war with the king. Not yet."

Bethesda and I moved on. With the streets so crowded, it took a long time to cross the heart of the city. As I began to walk up the hill,

into one of the better residential districts, I intentionally took a circuitous route and occasionally doubled back to make sure that no one was
following us. I communicated with Bethesda using nods and hand sig-
nals, and did not speak a word, in case someone from the *Phoenix*
should happen to cross our path.

The long summer day was almost done when we finally arrived at
Posidonius's house. A handsome young slave answered the door. Before I could speak, I had to cough and clear my throat. My own voice
sounded a bit odd to me as I uttered the first words I had spoken aloud
in days, stating my name and asking to see the master of the house.

We were admitted into the very crowded vestibule and told to wait.
Here I saw no people in rags, but I did see a number of men in togas,
and overheard snatches of Latin, mingled with the elevated Greek spoken by well-educated Romans.

"One keeps hearing rumors of warships spotted on the horizon—"

"They say Mithridates could invade any day now—"

"Certainly before the end of the sailing season, so perhaps we still
have some time to get ready—"

"If anyone will know the truth of the situation, it's Posidonius. The
man's been a marvel, rallying the Rhodians, taking in us Romans—"

"I hear that Gaius Cassius is staying here—you know, the Roman
governor. They say he's afraid to sail back to Rome, for fear of the thrashing he'll get from the Senate for losing Asia—"

"At least Gaius Cassius is still alive. Quintus Oppius was captured,
they say—"

"Nothing compared to what was done to Manius Aquillius! What,
you've not heard the news? Horrible, horrible . . ."

I pricked up my ears, but at that moment the slave returned. I half-
expected him to turn me away; the house of Posidonius was obviously
full to bursting with guests, and who was I to expect hospitality from
a man of such importance, at such a crucial time? True, I had once been
his houseguest for a whole winter, sitting out the stormy months when
no ships would sail, but that had been four years ago, and as traveling

companion to his old friend Antipater. Posidonius would certainly remember me, but would he be happy to see me?

Apparently he was, for when the slave led us across the garden—as crowded with togas as the vestibule—and up a flight of stairs, Posidonius greeted me on the landing with open arms and an affectionate hug.

"Gordianus! Truly, you are the last person I expected to see today. Yet here you are, looking quite fit and well, I must say. Did you and Antipater manage to see all seven of the Wonders, as you intended?"

"We did."

"Marvelous! Is he with you?"

"Not any longer."

Posidonius frowned. "Oh, dear, the old fellow isn't . . . ?"

"Not as far as I know."

"Then where is he? Ah, but you shall tell me everything over a cup of wine." He raised an eyebrow. "And who is this?"

"This is my slave, Bethesda. If you wish, she can stay in the vestibule—"

"And have all those old lechers in togas gawking at her? Much better to have such a beautiful creature ornament my private study while you and I catch up."

Posidonius ran his fingers through his thick locks, which showed a bit more gray than when I had last been a guest in his house, then led us down a short hallway to a room of which I had fond memories. The study of Posidonius was filled with scrolls and scientific instruments and curious souvenirs from his many travels.

While Bethesda withdrew to a corner, Posidonius and I sat facing each other in elegant chairs carved from ebony with inlays of ivory. A slave appeared and poured us each a cup of wine, then quickly vanished.

"How long have you been in Rhodes?" said Posidonius.

"I've only just arrived, by ship from Alexandria."

"Where are you staying?"

"I was hoping . . ."

"I see. Oh, yes, you must stay here, of course. At least, I *think* there's a spare room left. How long do you intend to stay?" He made a face and clucked his tongue. "That's a very rude question for a host to ask, I know, but with things as they are—"

"No need to apologize," I said. "I'm very grateful for your hospitality, Posidonius. I'll only stay the night. Tomorrow we sail on to Ephesus."

He looked at me, aghast. "Ephesus? Are you out of your mind?"

"I think I still had my wits about me, the last time I checked for them."

"Gordianus, this is no joke. Sail for Ephesus, tomorrow? Oh, no, you must think again. Reconsider, I beg you!"

"But I—"

"On your way here from the waterfront, Gordianus, did you not see all the Romans who've fled from Ephesus, as well as from Pergamon and Mytilene and so many other cities? Not just Romans, but friends of Rome—Rome-lovers, Mithridates calls them, all fleeing as far and as fast as they can."

"See them?" I said. "I could barely squeeze past them! They're all along the waterfront, and fill the main square and all the streets around it for blocks. A great many seem to be camped out in that big sporting complex just down the hill from here—"

"It's called a gymnasium," said Posidonius, in that weary tone that even friendly Greeks often adopt when speaking to us uncouth Romans.

"Yes, well, it's full of refugees. The track of the foot-racing stadium is crowded with tents. The viewing stands have been covered with canvas and turned into shelters. The people all look miserable."

Posidonius cocked an eyebrow. "Miserable, no doubt, but also sensible. You do understand that all those people are *fleeing* from the storm—not rushing straight into it?"

"From what some passengers on the ship are saying, the storm you speak of is likely to follow those refugees and come crashing into Rhodes."

"And if it does, we shall be ready for it!" Posidonius was not just a scientist and scholar and world traveler, but also one of the city fathers of Rhodes. From the proud confidence in his voice, I assumed he played some role in organizing the defense of the city.

I had managed so far to avoid telling him my purpose for traveling to Ephesus, wanting first to get some sense of where his loyalty lay. To all appearances Posidonius was firmly allied with Rome, along with his fellow Rhodians, yet I knew him to be a close friend of Antipater, and Antipater had turned out to be a spy for Mithridates. During our long stay on Rhodes, had Antipater sought to recruit Posidonius in the anti-Roman fold—and might he have succeeded?

Across the room, Bethesda was sitting in a chair beside a table upon which a number of scrolls had been unrolled. She seemed more interested in the decorative bronze weights that were used to hold the scrolls open. One was fashioned as a Gorgon's head, another as a sphinx. Bethesda fiddled with them as a curious child might fiddle with dolls.

"Bethesda!" I said. "You mustn't touch anything in this room."

She drew back her hands and sat on them, then cast her eyes to the floor and pouted her lips.

Posidonius glanced at her, briefly amused. "But back to the matter at hand," he said briskly. "This nonsense about sailing to Ephesus to-morrow. What possible reason could you have for going to such a dangerous place?"

"I received a certain document."

"This was in Alexandria?"

"Yes."

"A letter?"

"Not exactly. An excerpt from a private journal, I think."

"Not so private if it was shared with you. Who was the author?"

"It was written in the hand of Antipater."

"Ah! When did the two of you part ways?"

"Three years ago, after we saw the last of the Seven Wonders—the Great Pyramid in Egypt. I stayed in Alexandria. Antipater . . . moved on. He didn't come here, did he?"

"No. I've neither seen him nor received a letter from him in all the months since the two of you stayed here."

I studied his face for any sign of guile, and saw none. "The document I received caused me to believe that Antipater is in grave danger . . . and in Ephesus."

Posidonius frowned. "I see. And that's why you're going there?"

"Yes."

"In grave danger, you say?"

" 'Every hour of every day,' " I quoted.

"Is he still traveling under that ridiculous assumed name—Zoticus of Zeugma?"

"Apparently he is."

"But why? I never really believed that feeble excuse he gave me for remaining incognito the whole time he was here on Rhodes—something about fleeing from his fame and being freed from all the expectations people had of him."

"Antipater assumed that false name . . . because he was a spy," I said.

Posidonius frowned. "For Rome? But if that were the case, then why—"

I shook my head. "For Mithridates."

I had thought Posidonius looked aghast when I told him of my intention to go to Ephesus, but that expression was mild compared to the one that now spread across his face. Patches of bright red appeared on his forehead and cheeks, and his ears turned a shade that was almost purple.

He stood up from his chair, then staggered to one side. He dropped the empty wine cup and grabbed the back of the chair to steady himself, then fell to the floor, pulling the chair with him.

The chair and the cup made such a clatter that a slave or a bodyguard would surely come running at any moment. What would they think when they saw the master of the house lying lifeless at my feet?

VII

As it turned out, Posidonius was not dead.

He had simply stood up too fast while blood was rushing to his head, suffered a dizzy spell, and lost his balance. He must have been unconscious for a moment, for he lay there as motionless as a stone while I stared blankly at Bethesda, who stared back blankly at me. By the time a pair of slaves came running into the room, their master was groaning and shuddering and on his way to all-fours. As they helped him up and pushed the chair beneath him, I realized that I was feeling rather light-headed myself, from the scare he had given me.

Posidonius called for more wine, and insisted that I match him cup for cup while he interrogated me with a long series of questions. Where exactly had Antipater and I traveled before and after our stay on Rhodes? With whom had we stayed, and for how long? What side trips had we taken? How and why had Antipater confessed the truth to me before we parted ways in Alexandria? How, once in Ephesus, did I intend to hide the fact that I was Roman?

Posidonius insisted that I produce the scrap of parchment that had set me on my journey to Ephesus, and he sat poring over it for a long time, not merely reading the words but examining the parchment from

various angles, holding it up to the light and sniffing at the ink, as if it
might contain some secret message.

Eventually he handed the document back to me and sat for a long
moment with his hands folded on his lap, staring at nothing.

At last he slapped his knees and stood. "But what sort of host must
you think me, Gordianus, that I've not yet shown you to your room,
or offered you a chance to wash your face and hands? Here, follow me.
I think the little room at the southwest corner is still unoccupied. The
door's too narrow and the bed's too hard for most of those big-bellied
Roman merchants downstairs—it's just a storage pantry really, that's
had the shelves taken out and a bed put in. Yes, here it is. Room enough
for both you *and* your slave, I suspect." He raised an eyebrow and smiled
at Bethesda; he clearly took it for granted that we would both sleep in
the bed, for there was no room on the floor for a person to lie down.
"That little window up there doesn't give you a view, but it should let
in a bit of fresh air. There's a basin of water and a cloth in that little
niche there. Freshen up a bit, and I'll see you at dinner."

"Dinner?" I had hardly expected to merit the honor of dining with
my host, with so many other and surely more distinguished guests in
the house.

"Yes. There are some people staying here that I think you should
meet. And I'm sure they'll want to meet you, Gordianus."

With that, he left the narrow room and closed the door behind him.
I heard a curious clicking noise and reflexively reached for the door-
knob.

Posidonius had locked us inside.

I looked up at the little window he had mentioned. I could reach it if
I stood on the bed, but it was too small for a grown man to climb through.
With the door locked, I was now the guest of Posidonius whether I
wished to be or not. Had it been a mistake to tell him of Antipater's du-
plicity? At least I had determined that Posidonius was not in league with
Antipater. His shock at the news had been genuine. A good actor can
fake a fainting spell, but no man can will his ears to turn purple.

I sighed at my predicament, then decided to do as my host suggested, and splash a bit of water on my face. With two people in such a small, narrow room, maneuvering proved to be a challenge—a comical challenge, for soon Bethesda and I were both laughing at the contortions we were forced into when stepping past each other. As I brushed against her, various parts of our bodies made contact, and I became aroused. On the crowded ship, sleeping alongside other passengers, we had never had a private moment. This was the first time in days that I had been truly alone with her, and not only alone, but with a bed that proved to be not nearly as uncomfortable as my host had suggested.

Bethesda appeared to be as eager as I was, for she made quick work of pulling my tunic over my head, then undoing the loincloth from my hips. The happy task of removing her clothes she left to me.

The room was warm. Soon we were both covered with a sheen of sweat; our bodies slid against each other as if we had been oiled like athletes. But every now and then the high window admitted a breeze from the sea, and the occasional drafts of cool air raised delicious goose bumps on my back and buttocks, causing me to grin and shout with laughter even as I was gripped by the most sublime ecstasy.

As we lay curled together on the bed, dozing, our limbs entangled, the light from the high window slowly faded. I found myself staring up at the simple clay lamp suspended from a chain in the ceiling; as yet, no slave had come to light it. Had Posidonius forgotten about me? Even as this thought crossed my mind, I heard a noise at the door—a metallic clanking as the door was unlocked, then a voice calling through the wood.

"The master invites you to dinner, at your earliest convenience."

Bethesda was soundly asleep, and remained so, her lips slightly parted and her breasts gently rising and falling, as I extricated myself from her and pulled on my clothes. I covered her with the thin sheet, then opened the door as little as I could, stepped into the hallway, and closed the door behind me, thinking to shield her from the gaze of the slave who had made the summons and was waiting to escort me to his master's dining room. But in a house as well regulated as that of Posidonius, the servants were trained to be circumspect. The slave, a man perhaps twice my age, stood some distance from the door and made no attempt to peek inside.

Over one arm he held a folded garment of white wool.

"A toga?" I said. "Is that for me?"

The slave nodded.

I laughed. "I haven't worn a toga in ages. I'm not sure I can remember how to put it on. And if you expect me to do it myself, in that tiny room—"

"Oh, no, the master sent me especially to help you. We may do so in the master's study. If you'll follow me. . . ."

The slave proved to be an expert in the art of donning the toga. He put to shame old Damon, my father's slave, who had assisted me in putting on my first toga when I turned seventeen. In no time, with a bit of tugging here and a bit of gathering there, the toga lay just as it should, falling in proper folds from my shoulders and forearms.

Smiling with prim satisfaction at his handiwork, the slave led me down the hall to a different stairway from the one I had ascended earlier. For a moment I felt lost in that rambling house, despite the months I had spent there with Antipater, then I found my bearings again as the slave led me to Posidonius's elegant dining room, which was brightly lit. There were lamps set in sconces in the wall, lamps on bronze stands with griffin heads, and more lamps hanging from the ceiling. One side of the room was open to a garden from which radiated the last faint light of day. The three walls of the room were painted with flowers and trees and butterflies, so that the room seemed a natural continuation of the garden, but while the real garden grew dim, here the soft glow of twilight lingered.

There were six couches, with two set against each wall. The two closest to the garden, and farthest from our host, were unoccupied; it appeared I was the last but one to arrive. The slave indicated which of these was for me. Next to Posidonius, in the place of honor, was another guest in a toga, a stout Roman with a grim expression. The two other guests, dressed like our host in more colorful, loose-fitting garments, were not much older than me and alike enough to be brothers, which in fact they were.

From the way the four of them looked at me, I knew that Posidonius had already explained who I was. As I settled myself on my couch, a slave placed a cup of wine in my hand, and Posidonius introduced them to me.

"Gordianus, this is Gaius Cassius, the governor of Asia."

Deposed governor, I thought. The stout Roman gave me a nod.

Posidonius gestured to his left and right. "This is Pythion of Nysa. Across from him, his brother, Pythodorus."

"Nysa," I said, "where the hero Lycurgus 'drove the nursing mothers of wine-crazed Dionysus over the sacred mountains.'" Greeks are always impressed if you can quote an appropriate bit of Homer.

Pythion—whom I took to be the older brother, since he did most of the talking—gave me a piercing look. "Was it your treacherous tutor who taught you that—this Zoticus of Zeugma?"

I glanced at Posidonius. Clearly he had told them something of my situation, but for reasons of his own he had decided not to reveal Antipater's true identity. It occurred to me that Posidonius would prefer his guests to think he had been duped by a nobody—the obscure Zoticus—rather than let it be known that his old friend, the famous poet Antipater of Sidon, had operated as spy for Mithridates under this very roof.

I cleared my throat. "As a matter of fact—yes, it was my old tutor who taught me those lines of Homer. He's . . . something of a poet himself."

"Is he?" said Gaius Cassius. "Can't have been much good, if I've never heard of him."

"You have a fondness for Greek poetry, Governor?" I said.

"I put up with it." Cassius's voice was as flat and dry as parchment. "But there's not a living poet, Greek or Latin, who can compare with Ennius. He was the only true heir to Homer." His voice, so lifeless speaking Greek, took on an orator's lilt as he recited the Latin:

"In sleep, blind Homer appeared at my side.
'Wake now, poet, and sing!' he cried."

Python trained his gaze on me. "Perhaps Gordianus could recite something by this Zoticus."

"Yes, let's hear something by Mithridates's spy," said his brother, his voice dripping with malice.

My mind went blank for a moment. I didn't dare to quote anything by Antipater, for they might recognize it. Then I recalled something Antipater had come up with after we left Rome. I tried to speak with perfect Greek diction:

> *"Two widows of Halicarnassus lived under the same roof,*
> *One beautiful, young, and shy, the other stern and aloof."*

Python pursed his lips. "That's not bad, actually. How does the rest of it go?"

"I . . . I'm not sure. I don't think . . . Zoticus . . . ever actually finished that poem."

"Perhaps he's working on it right now, while he dines in Ephesus with his master, Mithridates," said Gaius Cassius, reverting to lifeless Greek.

"You must be wondering, Gordianus, exactly what I've told these others about you," said Posidonius. "I've explained that you arrived by ship from Alexandria today, and intend to sail on to Ephesus tomorrow; that a few years back you spent a winter under this roof, along with . . . Zoticus . . . whom I knew from my time in Rome; and it turns out that all along, without your knowledge or mine, Zoticus was traveling as a spy for Mithridates, and now seems to be in Ephesus, along with the king's court; and that, having received information that Zoticus is in danger, you intend to go to him and offer your assistance—despite that fact that he duped you as well as me, and many others."

Python raised an eyebrow. "Unless, of course, Gordianus is himself a spy for Mithridates."

Posidonius sighed. "Putting aside my lapse of judgment in the case of Zoticus, I still think I'm a good judge of character, and I can't believe that Gordianus is a traitor to Rome. This young man values truth and honesty above all other virtues. He's not the stuff that spies are made of."

"And yet," said Gaius Cassius, "a spy is exactly what we would like him to be." Before I could ask what this meant, he went on. "Tell me, Gordianus, how do you intend to operate in Ephesus, as a Roman among so many Roman-hating Greeks? What makes you think they'll even let you off the ship?"

"Or that you won't be torn limb from limb the moment you set foot on Ephesian soil?" said Pythion.

"Whatever happens, you'd better be wearing a toga when you step off the ship," added his brother.

"A toga?" I managed a small laugh. "Until this evening, I hadn't worn a toga in years. Posidonius kindly provided this one. I don't even own one."

"Then you'd better ask Posidonius if you can take that one with you," said Pythion. "According to reports from the latest refugees, signs were posted overnight in every village and city under Mithridates's control. The signs are in both Latin and Greek: 'By decree of the king and on pain of death, all Romans must wear the toga at all times.'"

"But why?" I asked. The toga was worn when conducting business or religious rituals, or—as on this occasion—when dining in a rich man's house, but even senators didn't wear a toga all the time.

"So that they can be recognized, of course," said Pythion. "If all the Romans are in togas, it will be easier to shun them. Easier to drive them off—or round them up."

"Round them up?" I frowned.

"The king's decree also has the perverse effect of making something you Romans are so proud of—your distinctive form of dress—into something more like a mark of shame," Pythion added.

"Never!" declared Gaius Cassius, clutching the folds of his toga.

Our host cleared his throat. "Ah, but we have strayed from the original question: How is Gordianus to operate freely in Ephesus? That's the really clever part. Since leaving Egypt, Gordianus has been posing not as a Roman but as a native Alexandrian, a young man of Greek descent—"

"But his accent!" protested Pythion.

"—who's lost the power of speech. The slave girl traveling with him will do all the talking, at least in public. A rather brilliant ruse, I think."

"Provided he can maintain such a pretense," said Gaius Cassius. "But don't you see, Posidonius, that you've just demolished your own argument for trusting this young man? First you say he's completely honest, then you tell us he's traveling under a false identity, pretending to be something he's not. Which is it? Is Gordianus a man incapable of deception, or is he a master deceiver, capable of fooling even Mithridates's minions?"

Posidonius shook his head. "You Romans *do* always insist that the answer to every question must be one thing or its opposite. Sometimes the answer lies in the middle, or elsewhere altogether. The world is rather more complicated and unpredictable than any of us thought, as we've learned in the last year or so. Can we trust Gordianus to be loyal to Rome? I think we can. Can he deceive those who wish harm to Rome? I hope he can, for all our sakes. It was you, Cassius, who suggested that Gordianus might be suitable for our purpose."

"What purpose?" I asked. "And what did you mean a moment ago, Governor, when you said, 'A spy is exactly what we would like him to be'?"

Gaius Cassius looked at me sternly. "If you possess even half your father's talents, I think you might serve Rome very well indeed."

"You know my father?" I felt a stab of homesickness.

"Of course I do. Everyone in Rome knows the Finder. Well, anyone who's ever had to dig up dirt on a rival, or clear himself of some trumped-up charge. I've been to your house more than once, young man, seeking your father's help. To be sure, my last visit was a number of years ago; you must have been hardly more than a child, which explains why we never met. Your father is the man who can pick any lock, yet never steals; the man who can follow anyone anywhere without being seen, yet never stabs a man in the back; the man who knows every secret, yet who never whispers a word of them. If you're made of the same stuff, I think you just might be able to pull off this masquerade of being mute, at least long enough to be of some use to us."

"What is he talking about?" I looked at Posidonius, who answered.

"Think, Gordianus! While every other Roman is desperately attempting to get *out* of Ephesus, you're determined to get *in*. That could make you very valuable to us, especially if you manage to reach your old tutor. That would bring you into the king's court, perhaps even give you access to his inner circle. Eyes and ears are what we lack in Ephesus. Eyes to see what Mithridates is up to, ears to overhear his plans."

"But no mouth to give yourself away," added Gaius Cassius, with a mirthless laugh.

"You want me to be a spy for you?"

"A spy for *Rome*," said Gaius Cassius.

I shook my head. "I have no training for that sort of thing. I don't know secret codes, or how to put on disguises. I have no military experience. How would I know which bits of information are valuable, and which bits are worthless?"

"You wouldn't need to know any of those things," said Gaius Cassius. "You would merely be the sand-gatherer, not the sieve."

"I don't understand."

"You will simply report what you observe; another will determine what details are important, and relay the information back to us. Perhaps"—he smiled—"even using a secret code, as you suggest."

"I would 'report'? Report to whom?"

"To the agent above you, of course. The man assigned to monitor you and your activities."

"And who would that be?" I looked from Posidonius to Gaius Cassius, then at Pythion and Pythodorus, and finally at the empty couch across from mine. It occurred to me that the sixth guest had yet to arrive.

At that moment a large, shadowy figure came bustling across the garden, his features obscured by the gathering shadows of nightfall.

"Apologies, Posidonius, for being late," he called out. I gave a start, for his voice was familiar. As he emerged into the artificial twilight of the dining room, I recognized Samson, the Alexandrian Jew from the *Phoenix*.

VIII

"Samson!" I exclaimed.

The newly arrived dinner guest went about settling his oversized physique on a dining couch that was too small for him. "So you *can* speak," he said.

I turned to Posidonius. "What is Samson doing here?"

My host laughed. "Samson? Is that the name he's traveling under? Appropriate, I suppose, if not very original. At least it will be easy to remember."

The big Jew shrugged. "I didn't choose the name. This young Roman's slave calls me that." He smiled. "She's a bit of a flirt."

I didn't like the sound of that, but I bit my tongue.

"It seems rather impertinent, for a slave to be assigning nicknames," said Gaius Cassius. He was clearly one of those Romans who believed the world would be a better place if only everyone would stop coddling their slaves.

Samson grinned. "As far as I'm concerned, Governor, that lovely girl can call me anything she likes—as long as she doesn't try to play barber."

The others laughed, apparently at some joke that went over my head.

"'Samson' let it be, then," said Posidonius. "We shall call you nothing else, at least not until you return from Ephesus."

The man called Samson nodded. He appeared to already know and be known to everyone present, since he addressed them by name. "Is it true, Pythion, what they're saying down at the waterfront—that Mithridates has put a bounty on your head?"

Pythion choked on the wine he was drinking. "A bounty?"

"Proclamations have gone out far and wide. Some refugees who just arrived from Caunus were talking about it."

"What sort of proclamations?"

"You're a wanted man, dead or alive. So is Pythodorus, and your father, too."

"How much is the king offering?" asked Pythion.

"Mithridates will pay forty talents for each of you, if brought to him alive. Only twenty talents if it's just your head."

While the two brothers impulsively touched their throats, Gaius Cassius whistled. "How in Hades can Mithridates offer such extravagant rewards?"

"When he captured the island of Cos, he opened the foreign treasuries kept there and seized all the contents," said Posidonius. "Added to all his other recent acquisitions, that must make him the richest man in the world. The king has more money than he knows what to do with. Money for troops, for weapons, for bounties."

"He had no right to plunder the treasuries at Cos," said Samson. All trace of amusement vanished from his face. "Those riches belonged to neutral parties, to men and nations with whom Mithridates has no quarrel."

"You speak of Egypt," I said, remembering that the loss of the Egyptian treasury on the island of Cos had done much to turn the Egyptian people against the deposed king. Along with the tangible assets in the Egyptian treasury, Mithridates had taken into his custody the son of King Ptolemy as well. The young prince had been sent to the faraway island to keep him safe from the palace intrigues of Alexandria, only to fall into Mithridates's hands. Protective custody, Mithridates called it. Kidnapping, said others.

"Yes, there was an Egyptian treasury on Cos," said Samson. "And also, among others, a treasury belonging to the Jews of Alexandria. Mithridates had no right to take those riches. The man is no better than a common thief. He should have both hands cut off!"

Gaius Cassius pursed his lips shrewdly. "What a lovely idea. I'll keep that in mind, when we finally defeat the son of a whore. I should quite like to see Mithridates paraded through the streets of Rome with a chain around his neck and both hands cut off." He narrowed his eyes and smiled grimly.

"About this bounty," I said. "If I may ask, what makes the king desire your capture so much?"

"When the war broke out, our father remained loyal to Rome," said Pythion. "He donated a great deal of grain to feed the Roman troops, and offered other assistance."

"No man was ever a better friend to Rome than Chaeremon," declared Gaius Cassius.

"But when Mithridates defeated the Romans, we had to flee from Nysa," said Pythion. "We headed for Ephesus. We had no idea how much the Romans are hated there. The Ephesians were overjoyed at the prospect of being 'freed from the Roman yoke,' as they put it. It was only a matter of time before Mithridates would arrive, and the Ephesians would open their gates to him. Our father managed to book passage for my brother and me on a ship bound for Rhodes."

"And Chaeremon?" I asked.

"Father stayed behind. We've had no word from him since," said Pythion.

I nodded, knowing how it felt to be separated from a father and to have no news of him.

"So the bounty is actually a hopeful sign," said his brother. "If Mithridates is offering a reward for Father's capture, that means he's still alive. And the fact that Mithridates is offering a bounty for us means he doesn't know that we've escaped to Rhodes."

"Unless he means to take Rhodes next," said Samson. The others looked at him sharply. "If your father is still in Ephesus, he's very likely taken sanctuary in the Temple of Artemis. If that's the case, Mithridates knows exactly where Chaeremon is, and the bounty is meant to encourage the most rabid of the Rome-haters in Ephesus to storm the sanctuary and capture everyone inside, never mind the laws of gods and men."

Python and Pythodorus both turned pale. The younger brother covered his face.

More food was brought, a fish course garnished with bitter radishes and salted olives. No one touched it except Samson. I had noticed that he always displayed a hearty appetite on board the *Phoenix*. He took his time, relishing each bite as the rest of us watched.

"This treacherous tutor, this Zoticus of Zeugma," he finally said, wiping the corners of his mouth. He saw the look on my face. "Oh, yes, Posidonius has already told me everything." *Everything but Antipater's true name,* I thought. "We know he didn't seduce *you* into betraying Rome, Posidonius, but what about your students? They come here every day, and they include all sorts. Zoticus must have had contact with them. How are we to know that the old fellow didn't lure some budding young philosopher into playing spy for Mithridates, right under your own roof?"

Python threw up his hands. "How are we to trust anyone, anywhere?"

"My point exactly," said Samson.

Posidonius nodded. "The question you raise has already occurred to me. That's why we six are the only guests at this dinner. Every man in this room can be trusted. We all come from different places, but we all have the same goal: to stop Mithridates."

"Is that *your* goal, Gordianus?" asked Samson.

"I want to stop Mithridates from harming Zoticus, yes."

"But is that enough? The rest of us in this room want to see Mithridates destroyed. From what Posidonius told me, you merely want to save the life of a single man, and an enemy at that—a worthless scoundrel whom the rest of us would like to see paraded in chains along with Mithridates through the streets of Rome someday."

Posidonius raised his hand. "Enough of that, Samson! Gordianus will stand with us. Of that I'm sure."

"But is Gordianus sure? I should like to hear him say it aloud."

"So should I," said Gaius Cassius, staring at me.

"And so should we," said the two brothers, not quite in unison, so that one sounded like the echo of the other.

I looked from face to face. I had come to the house of Posidonius merely seeking shelter for the night, and perhaps a bit of conversation with someone who knew Antipater. What had I gotten myself into?

"What exactly do you want from me?" I asked.

"We've already told you!" snapped Gaius Cassius. "While in Ephesus, or anywhere else under the control of Mithridates, you will act as eyes and ears for Rome. No action is required of you; you need only to watch and to listen, and pass on what you've observed to Samson here, who is embarking on his own mission, but who is a friend of Rome. Any information of value will find its way back here to me."

It would never turn out to be that simple, I thought.

He scowled at my hesitation. "Well? What do you say?"

"Why should I—"

"Because you are a Roman!" Gaius Cassius rose to his feet and gathered the folds of his toga. "Because you are the son of your father! If the Finder were here, what would he say to you?"

Without realizing it, Gaius Cassius had touched on one of the reasons for my uncertainty. My father had helped Antipater to fake his own death in Rome and to set out on his journey under a new name. Had my father known of Antipater's intentions, and of his loyalty to Mithridates? Had he shared that loyalty? The idea was shocking, but anything seemed possible. By helping Rome, would I be doing what he would wish me to do, or would I be betraying my father?

"How I wish my father were here," I said aloud.

"Since he's not, I will speak for him," said Gaius Cassius. "As he is a Roman, and so am I, I am the nearest thing you have to a father in this place, so far from Rome. Are you not a Roman, Gordianus? Are you not a son of Rome?"

I stared at the governor. No man could be more different from my father. Gaius Cassius struck me as a gruff, scowling bully of a man, quite the opposite of my father. And yet . . .

"I am a Roman," I said.

"Then you will do what Rome requires of you!" he shouted.

Still I hesitated.

"And if you don't," said Posidonius, almost in a whisper, "then Samson here will see to it that you're exposed as an imposter and a Roman the moment you set foot in Ephesus. That will be the end of any plan you may have to save Zoticus."

"And the end of you," added Samson. "And of that pretty slave girl, as well."

For a long moment they all looked at me in silence.

"How shall we go about this?" I asked.

IX

[From the secret diary of Antipater of Sidon:]

... *having just locked myself in this room after enduring a most disturbing dinner with the king.*

As always I was obliged to maintain my identity as nonentity, posing as Zoticus of Zeugma. A poet unable to recite his own verses might as well be mute! Instead, when asked about my life and work, I stutter and stammer and inevitably come off as an old fool who's risen above his station. They must all think: What in Hades is that fellow doing among us? Is he here to play the fool in the king's court!?

Of course, the court has plenty of fools already. The Shahansha has a weakness for fawning underlings who happen to possess some paltry talent. A juggler named Sosipater is probably the worst of the lot. "Juggle this!" says the king, pointing at a stool. "Now juggle that!" he says, throwing a cup or a bowl at the poor wretch. "Poor," I say, but Sosipater owns vineyards and ships and mines and pastures and vast herds of livestock. Not bad for a man who began as a street urchin in a village on the Euxine Sea, and now dines with the King of Kings, even if he must juggle for his supper.

I was forced to sit next to this creature at the banquet, which was in honor of the father of Queen Monime, Philopoemen, marking his investiture as Episcopus of Ephesus. Philopoemen has been running Ephesus for some time, but Mithridates has only now decided the title by which his royal overseer should be addressed, what rank he should have in the court, what sort of regalia he may wear, and so on.

There is a great deal of pomp and ceremony at these banquets, which wear on for hours. In between the boring parts the guests are treated to an endless parade of acrobats, contortionists, singers, dancers, musicians, and actors. These are the people I am forced to sit with, with whom I have nothing in common.

This banquet was held in what surely must be the largest dining chamber in all of Ephesus. Half of the guests reclined on couches along one long wall, while the other half reclined across from us, with the space between open for recitations and other entertainments. Thus I was kept at a distance from anyone with whom I could possibly have enjoyed an intelligent conversation.

Across the way, I could see young Prince Ptolemy, formerly resident on the island of Cos but now, through no choice of his own, a member of the royal retinue. Does the king have designs on Egypt as well as Rome? One hears that all of Egypt is in chaos, and thus vulnerable to invasion, but surely Mithridates is not so mad that he wants to try his hand at ruling that unruly land!

Also across the way—he might as well have been across the sea—I spotted Metrodorus of Scepsis, a man with whom I would dearly love to converse. Everyone here calls him Misorhomaios, *"Rome-Hater," as if that were his official title. Metrodorus is famous for inventing a scientific method of memorization and perfect recollection—he does this somehow by assigning one of the 360 degrees contained in the twelve houses of the zodiac to whatever detail needs to be remembered. It is said that 360 random words can be recited to him, and he can recite them back in precisely the same order, or even in reverse order. Such a thing hardly seems possible, yet Metrodorus is famed for it. He is also famed for his eloquent and unrelenting diatribes against the Romans, from which has arisen his title of Rome-Hater. He and* the king are said to regard each other almost as father and son, so great is their mutual fondness and their accord on matters of state. I'm lucky to say two words to the man—much less 360 words!—at these interminable royal banquets, where men infinitely more important than Zoticus of Zeugma are all eager to have the ear of the esteemed Misorhomaios.

Also present were a great many of the Persian wise men called Magi, dressed in exotic robes and colorful turbans. They tend to keep to themselves and to cluster about their leader, a half-blind old man whom they address as the Grand Magus. The Magi are neither philosophers nor priests, at least not in the Greek sense. I think they draw wisdom from the stars. Mithridates thinks very highly of them.

An equal number of the Megabyzoi were present, the priests of Artemis who dress in yellow and wear towering yellow headdresses, the tallest of which is worn by the Great Megabyzus, a tall, slender fellow. From across the room he looks like a yellow stick insect. His predecessor disappeared some years ago—young Gordianus was involved in that affair, during our visit to Ephesus—leaving this fellow to rise to the foremost place among the Megabyzoi. He treads a rather delicate course these days, obliged on the one hand to genuflect before the King of Kings, and on the other to fulfill his sacred duty to offer sanctuary to all who seek it at the Temple of Artemis. The temple and the sacred precinct around it are filled to overflowing with Romans and others fleeing the wrath of Mithridates. They say that Chaeremon of Nysa is in the temple even now, and that Mithridates will not rest until he sees the fellow's head on a stick, with or without the blessing of Artemis. Shall the sanctity of the temple remain inviolate, or shall the priests expel the asylum seekers and consign them to certain death? With such a choice facing him, it was no wonder the Great Megabyzus was the only guest at the banquet with a gloomier expression than mine.

No, I take that back. For also in attendance was the captured Roman general Quintus Oppius, dressed in a spotless white toga and seated very near the king, as if he were a guest of honor. But next to him sat the giant Bastarna, holding a chain connected to an iron collar around Oppius's neck. Every now and then, either at his own whim or at some secret signal from Mithridates, Bastarna would give the chain a hard yank, causing Oppius

to spit out a mouthful of wine or half-chewed food, then sit there, morti-
fied and red-faced, not daring to wipe his chin or dab the drivel from his
toga while everyone laughed, with the Shahansha laughing loudest of all.
Yes, Quintus Oppius wore an expression even gloomier than that of the
Great Megabyzus.

And what is one to make of the other Roman in attendance, a former
consul named Publius Rutilius Rufus? He sat on the other side of the king
and in even greater proximity—at the right hand of Mithridates, in fact.
When we were both in Rome, somehow I never made the acquaintance of
Rutilius, though I knew his reputation as one of the more generous and
cultured patrons of the Greek arts. His recent tenure as a provincial legate
in Anatolia is recalled by the natives as a kind of golden age—for once, a
Roman seemed more interested in cultivating good will and fostering pros-
perity than in filling his private treasury. Such exemplary behavior made
the other Roman officials look bad, so it was no surprise that when Rutilius returned to Rome four years ago he was immediately put on trial, accused of doing the very things he did not do—pilfer tax revenues and extort
the locals. All too predictably, he was found guilty of these trumped-up
charges. Even after selling all his properties, Rutilius lacked sufficient funds
to pay the fine imposed on him by the court—that fact in itself was proof
that the charges were false, for if Rutilius had committed the crimes of which
he was accused, he could easily have paid the fine and had a fortune left
over.

A handful of Romans of the better sort helped Rutilius to pay the fine,
after which, now in his seventies, he went into voluntary exile, returning
to the very region he had been accused of plundering—yet another proof of
his innocence, for the locals gave him a hero's welcome. Apparently he was
able to lead a comfortable life, being kept in funds by his friends in both
Rome and Asia, including heads of state whom he had befriended. He was
in Mytilene, on Lesbos, when Mithridates's troops took the island and captured Manius Aquillius. Rutilius was "captured" at the same time, if that
is the word for it, for he gave himself up voluntarily and was treated by his
captors as an honored guest. I have heard a rumor to the effect that Rutilius
actually colluded in the capture of Manius Aquillius, leading Mithridates's

men to the place where that doomed wretch was hiding, but I am not sure I believe this story. Perhaps there was bad blood between them. Still, Rutilius is a Stoic of great integrity, hardly the sort of fellow to betray a fellow Roman citizen.

Unlike Quintus Oppius—and in flagrant violation of the king's recent decree that all Romans must at all time wear their national garment—Rutilius was not wearing a toga. He was dressed in a rather simple green and yellow robe and slippers. At first glance, no one would have taken him for a Roman, but simply as another member of the king's court. For a Roman of consular rank to be seen out of toga at a dinner with a head of state is almost unthinkable, whatever the circumstances; a Roman without his toga is not quite a Roman. And despite the royal decree regarding Romans and togas, the king clearly approved of Rutilius's appearance. So it would appear that Rutilius has cut his ties to Rome completely. What role does Mithridates intend for this renegade Roman? I have no idea, for I had no chance to speak to Rutilius, being relegated to a place among the actors and contortionists.

Of course Queen Monime was there, looking as pleased as a cat with a bird in its mouth to see her father invested with the rank of episcopus. Mithridates clucked his tongue and kissed her dainty fingers and doted on her as if she were a child, which she is, completely lacking in the mature refinement and dignity one wishes to see in a queen. Of course, refinement and dignity were not the attributes that induced Mithridates to marry the little vixen and seat her on a throne next to his.

Mithridates himself was more splendidly adorned than I had previously seen him. He literally sparkled, so covered with jewels and precious metals was every garment he wore, from his curl-toed shoes to his necklace-laden breast. But for a crown, as always, he wore only a simple fillet of twined purple and white woolen yarn. From his broad shoulders, as if it were his own family heirloom, hung the centuries-old cloak of Alexander the Great.

After the investiture of Philopoemen, amid the feasting, the guests were treated to an entertainment combining dancing with a recitation in verse. The story was based on a century-old legend: the tale of the Syrian warrior Bouplagos, who came back to life to prophesy the end of Rome. No author was credited. The man who recited the poem was clearly a professional actor, not the poet.

Who composed this entertainment? I do not know. Before I describe it, let me admit something. Before I arrived, when I looked forward to taking my rightful place in the king's court, I anticipated that one of my roles would be to compose just this sort of entertainment, providing uplifting verses to be recited for the edification of the king, his household, and his guests. Instead I am made to sit in silence while the verses of some unknown, second-rate poet are inflicted on us.

With the dancers I have no quarrel. In fact, they displayed a great deal of skill and created several memorable tableaux as they acted out the scenes described by the poem. The lighting effects, the costumes, and the various theatrical illusions were all very well done. Nor do I fault the actor who recited the poem, for he did his best with the text he was given.

I will not attempt to quote the entire text. Suffice to say that for the most part the metaphors were unoriginal, the rhythms awkward, and the vocabulary unimaginative. What might I, Antipater of Sidon, have done with the same material? I am tempted to write my own version of the tale of Bouplagos, to show the king what can be achieved when a true poet rises to the occasion. But no, the material is simply too sordid and sensational to inspire a first-rate poem. I suspect it was the king himself who chose the topic, judging by the rapt expression on his face all through the recitation. Perhaps—horrible thought!—he even wrote the poem himself.

The setting of the story was a battle at Thermopylae—not the famous last stand of the three hundred Spartans, but the much later battle that took place only a hundred years ago, between the Romans and King Antiochus of Syria, who was then laying claim to that part of Greece, and who counted among his mercenaries that old "Rome-Hater," Hannibal of Carthage. (Already you can see why this tale fascinates Mithridates, who sees himself as the successor of these noble warriors against Rome.) In this battle, the Romans were triumphant. So devastating was his defeat that King Antiochus was forced to withdraw from Greece entirely, fleeing all the way to Ephesus, leaving behind at Thermopylae a veritable mountain of fallen soldiers.

After the battle, the Romans set about the grisly task of stripping armor and other spoils from the corpses of their enemies. Among these cadavers was the body of Bouplagos, a Syrian cavalry commander held in great esteem by Antiochus. Bouplagos had fought long and nobly against the Romans, suffering twelve ghastly wounds before he fell.

While the Romans were stripping the dead bodies, Bouplagos suddenly got to his feet. Fresh blood began to pour from his twelve wounds. It hardly seemed possible that he could have survived those wounds, yet the alternative—that he had come back to life—seemed even more impossible.

This part of the story was well enacted, I must admit. The dancer playing Bouplagos sent a tremor of fear through the audience. He was dressed in bloodstained armor, his face was made to look waxy and pale, and fluttering streamers of red cloth simulated blood flowing from his wounds.

Bewildered and terrified, the Roman soldiers fell back. Bouplagos marched slowly but steadily through the Roman camp and into the tent of the generals, who were as frightened as their soldiers. Standing before the Roman commanders, Bouplagos spoke. At this point in the recitation, the actor pitched his voice in a manner calculated to chill the blood of everyone in the room:

"Cease despoiling my brave comrades, gone to Hades's lands.
Already Zeus is angry at the slaughter by your hands.
He shall raise up a leader to bring about your fall.
The name of Rome shall be spat upon by all."

As soon as the reciter finished speaking the prophecy, the dancer playing Bouplagos collapsed into a heap of bloody armor, as if his bones had turned to water.

For the next tableau the room was made very dim. This was the visit by the Roman generals to the Oracle of Delphi, asking what the temporary resurrection of Bouplagos signified. The Pythia, the priestess of Apollo's temple at Delphi, was danced by a figure in heavy robes, illuminated by lamps set all about her but seen by the audience only through a screen of

dark veils—an ingenious effect that created a genuine aura of mystery.
From offstage, a female singer provided the voice of the Pythia, making bird-
like, nonsense sounds. At last she fell silent, leaving it to the priests of
Apollo to discern her meaning. The reciter spoke the oracle:

"Restrain yourselves, Romans, let justice abide,
Lest Ares in his anger support the other side.
Your farms and cities will be made a desolation.
Your women to their conquerors will look for consolation."

Such a stark, unambiguous message was something rare from the Ora-
cle of Delphi, but the Romans shrugged off this warning and continued their
war against Antiochus. But no sooner had they returned to the theater of
battle than one of the generals suddenly began to rave and to thrash about,
so violently that the other commanders gave up trying to restrain him and
fell back.

This tableau began with the dancers, dressed in stage armor and red
capes, all gathered in a circle. Then, as the reciter imitated the incompre-
hensible rantings of the possessed Roman general, the dancers gathered more
closely, and at the same time began to whirl about in a circle, causing their
red capes to whip through the air. As the whirling grew more and more
frenzied, one dancer after another flew away from the group, like sparks
from a whetting stone, until, revealed at the center, was none other than . . .
Quintus Oppius!

I looked at the place where Oppius had been sitting, next to the giant
Bastarna. Sure enough, both were gone. It truly was Quintus Oppius be-
fore us, a genuine Roman general playing the role of a Roman general—or
at least it was the head of Oppius, for the oversized body beneath him,
dressed in stage armor and a cape, was some sort of grotesque puppet, with
thrashing limbs that moved in impossible ways. It appeared that Oppius
was somehow restrained inside the costume, along with one or more un-
seen dancers, who operated the arms.

The effect was macabre, and became even more so when the head of

Oppius began to rotate one way, while the puppet body in which he was encased started to rotate in the opposite direction. There must have been some mechanical apparatus beneath the floor, such as those that produce gods from nowhere on the stage.

As well as creating a strangely horrifying effect, the slow rotation also allowed everyone in the room to get a good look at the face of Oppius. Some device inside his mouth forced it to gape open. He could move his lips a bit, but he could not close his jaw. I think the poor man was trying to maintain an expression of grim dignity, which was impossible with his mouth forced open. During one turn he looked quite mad, and at the next turning as if he might burst into tears, and then like a constipated man at the public latrina desperate to relieve himself. There was laughter in the room despite the gravity of the prophetic words being recited by the actor, which we were to imagine coming from Oppius's gaping mouth and trembling lips:

"Oh, my country, what destruction will Ares bring to one
Who dares to ravage Asia and the lands of the rising sun?
From all the East, as far as Babylon, an army will arise
To wreak their vengeance on a land that all despise. . . ."

There was a great deal more in this vein. Then, slowly, both the puppet body and the head of Oppius stopped spinning, until body and head were again properly aligned. Oppius looked pale and queasy. I felt a bit dizzy myself from watching all that spinning and counter-spinning.

The actor uttered another burst of poetry, speaking more quickly and raising the pitch of his voice. I knew, of course, that it was not Oppius speaking. Nevertheless—perhaps it was the genuine look of alarm in Oppius's eyes, and the wormlike writhing of his lips—the words seemed somehow to issue from his open mouth:

"The demon wolf comes! Step back and let him pass, you clods!
He can't be killed. He can't be stopped. He does the work of the gods!
The red wolf comes!"

From a patch of darkness at one end of the room a gigantic wolf—three or four dancers inside another oversized costume—came running toward Oppius and his now motionless puppet body. The reciter cried out:

"I am like the helpless tree before the ax. I cannot move. I cannot run.
The red wolf comes! He looms so large he hides the sun.
Ravenous, he eats me whole. I am Rome. I am dismembered.
I am Rome, eaten alive, vanished, not even remembered."

To achieve this effect, the puppet wolf snapped its jaws as it circled the puppet body, which rapidly began to dwindle—swallowed not by the red wolf but by a trapdoor in the floor. As the puppet body vanished, the head of Oppius sank lower and lower, as his real body was lowered through the same hidden hatch.

By some theatrical effect, the snapping jaws of the wolf turned crimson, as if stained with blood. Sated, the red wolf made a final circuit, then headed back whence it had come, leaving the head of Oppius on the floor, surrounded by a circle of blood-red cloth. The illusion that Oppius had actually been beheaded was so startling that I heard gasps all around me.

The reciter spoke again, now in a thin, reedy voice that seemed to issue from the bodiless head on the floor:

"My body is devoured. Only my head remains. I am asunder.
No head, however swollen, can live without what's under.
The end approaches."

The head began to spin again, and slowly to sink into the floor, sending wave-like billows through the surrounding pool of blood-red cloth. Just before the spinning head vanished, the face of Oppius turned ivory-white. He made a weird sound, and suddenly a stream of vomit erupted from his propped-open mouth. As Oppius spun around, the jet of pale green vomit fell in a spiral pattern upon the scarlet cloth.

An instant later, still vomiting, the head vanished from sight. Then the red cloth began to disappear, from the outside in, like blood running into a drain. A clash of cymbals disguised the noise of the trapdoor snapping shut, then nothing at all remained of Oppius or his puppet body. There was only a bare, spotless floor, looking as if it had been freshly swept.

No poet, dramatist, or even king could have forced such a singular occurrence, or foreseen its effect. The sight of Oppius vomiting capped the presentation with an image as shocking as it was spectacular, as sordid as it was unforgettable. The audience erupted in helpless laughter. There was thunderous applause. Queen Monime was the first to jump to her feet. Everyone else did likewise.

Only one man in the room kept his composure. Barely smiling, the king slowly looked from face to face. He even deigned to look at me, with a blank, unblinking gaze that sent a shiver though me. At last he stood and raised one hand to acknowledge the acclaim of the audience. The rapturous cheering and applause did not abate, but grew louder.

We had seen the enactment of an old legend. We had heard the ancient prophecy. We had witnessed with our own astonished eyes the fulfillment of that prophecy, the devouring of Rome by the red wolf—Rome in the person of Quintus Oppius, not only forced to foretell his own destruction but humiliated in a manner so complete and so spontaneous that no one could have anticipated it, not even Mithridates.

Next to the king, standing along with everyone else, was Rutilius, the Roman without a toga. His applause was more restrained than that of the others—it would hardly have been seemly for any Roman to cheer and stamp his feet at the symbolic annihilation of Rome—but Rutilius applauded nonetheless.

I suddenly thought of the destruction that was closer at hand—the king's imminent plan to kill every Roman still alive in the territories under his control. Would Quintus Oppius be among those killed? Or was he too valuable a hostage, or too precious a plaything for the king? And what of Rutilius? Surely the king would spare a Roman who had seemingly joined the royal court.

At that moment, while I watched, Mithridates turned to Rutilius and spoke in his ear. Rutilius nodded and made some reply. They were of an

age to be father and son, I thought, and that was what they looked like—
two men of different generations but of one accord. Could it be that Ruti-
lius himself had a hand in planning the impending massacre? Who better
than a Roman to root out the hiding places of his fellow Romans?

I looked at the rapturous people around me, who continued to shout
and cheer and applaud. Would this be their reaction to the genuine slaugh-
ter to come? Would they laugh and jeer as women and children were mas-
sacred before their eyes? Would they join in the killing like the wine-maddened
maenads of Bacchus, gouging the eyes from old men and tearing the limbs
off babies?

Suddenly I felt so faint that I could hardly remain standing. Yet, like an
automaton, I kept clapping my hands together until my palms were numb,
and I shouted until I was hoarse. What choice had I, with everyone watch-
ing everyone else across the room, and the gaze of the king or the queen likely
to fall upon me at any moment?

I have learned, in such moments of despair, to purposely turn my mind
to some thought that gives me comfort. Of late only one such thought pro-
vides a respite, and that is the fact that I parted ways with young Gordi-
anus back in Alexandria. I can at least be thankful that he is far away
from this dangerous place. Alas, almost certainly I will never see him again.
But at least I will not see him put to death before my eyes.

[Here ends this fragment from the secret diary
of Antipater of Sidon.]

X

The *Phoenix* rounded a bend in the Cayster River, and there ahead of us lay the city of Ephesus, glittering in the lowering sunlight like a many-faceted jewel set into the scooped-out hillside. Crowning Mount Pion, the city's highest point, and dominating the skyline was the massive semicircular theater, one of the grandest in the world. Antipater had called Ephesus the most cosmopolitan of all Greek cities, the pride of Asia, the jewel of the East.

Above us, to the right, loomed wooded bluffs. Somewhere up there was the sacred Grove of Ortygia, where—on my previous visit to Ephesus—in the dark recesses of a cave I had matched wits with the Great Megabyzus himself, and saved the young daughter of my Ephesian host from a fate worse than death.

I had not rescued the beautiful Anthea by myself. I was helped in that endeavor by Anthea's slave, the equally beautiful Amestris. She was not quite as young as her mistress, and was more darkly complexioned, with skin like burnished bronze and hair the color of a midnight sky in summer—yes, very much like the night sky, for even in darkness her lustrous black hair had seemed to glitter with starlike points of light. Our mission to rescue her mistress had been successful, but had placed

us in terrible danger. The joy and relief we both felt afterward, back at
the house of Eutropius, had only been fully realized when she came to
me that night, and for the first time in my life I knew a woman.

That night had been four years ago, but it lingered vividly in my
memory. Such exquisite moments; such sublime sensations! As I turned
my distracted gaze from the bluffs back to the glittering city ahead of
us, I seemed to see the smiling face of Amestris before me. . . .

With a start, I realized that I was gazing not at a phantom from the
past, but at a female very much present in the flesh.

"Why are you looking at me in such a strange way, Master?" Bethesda
tilted her head to one side and cocked an eyebrow. Passing close by me,
she whispered in my ear, "I suppose I can only wonder what you're
thinking, since it's not possible for you to speak."

She was right. Although we appeared to be out of anyone's earshot,
no one is ever really alone on board a ship, where any spoken word
might be heard by an unseen listener.

For once, I was glad to have assumed the pretense of muteness. I
had never told Bethesda about Amestris. I had no desire to tell her
now.

Besides, with our arrival in Ephesus imminent, I had plenty of other
things to think about. My first challenge would be to gain entry into
the city. I had my story—stricken mute, come to seek a cure from the
city's patron goddess—and I had my counterfeit papers, thanks to the
two eunuchs. I should have no problem—unless, of course, something
went wrong.

What could go wrong?

I was on a secret mission. Samson was on a secret mission. Who else
on board was not what he pretended to be, but was instead a smuggler,
or an assassin—or a spy for Mithridates? And what if this person had
already spotted my deceit, and planned to expose me the moment I
stepped through the city gates? What sort of punishments would King
Mithridates inflict on a young Roman who pretended not to be Roman and who tried to sneak past his guards? These Eastern kings were
said to have devised tortures so intricate and horrific that a Roman could

hardly imagine them. If I were exposed, I would not need to use my imagination—

"*What* must you be thinking now?" whispered Bethesda with a frown.

I blinked and tried to make my face a blank. I endeavored to think more positive thoughts. We would gain entry to Ephesus with no problem and no delay. Before sundown I would be in one of the world's most sophisticated cities, teeming with taverns and temples and everything between. What then?

I knew, in a general way, what I had come to achieve. I wanted to see with my own eyes that Antipater was alive, and well; and if he was in danger, I would try to help him.

Besides my original agenda, I now had another, imposed on me by Gaius Cassius. As the standing Roman governor of the province of Asia, Cassius had every right to impose it on me, since I was after all a citizen of Rome, entitled to all the privileges—and liable to add the obligations—adhering thereto.

There were four main points to this agenda.

First, I was to discover the fate of Rome's stalwart ally, Chaeremon of Nysa, believed by his sons to be in Ephesus. If he was still alive, and if I was able to contact him, I was to render whatever assistance he might require of me.

Second, I was to discover, if I could do so discreetly, the fate of the Roman commander Quintus Oppius, who had last been seen in headlong flight from Mithridates, but who had failed to rendezvous with Gaius Cassius in Rhodes. Was Oppius still a fugitive? Was he being held captive by Mithridates? Had he been horribly executed, as had been reported about Manius Aquillius?

Third, I was to discover, if I could, the whereabouts and circumstances of a certain prince of the Egyptian royal family, the son of the recently deposed King Ptolemy. This young man, about seventeen years of age, had been kidnapped by Mithridates from his dwelling place at Cos, at the same time Mithridates seized the treasuries on the island.

At that time, he had been heir to the throne of Egypt. Now that his uncle had seized the throne, young Ptolemy's position, and his value as a hostage, was more uncertain. Nevertheless, any information about him might be useful to Roman strategists, since Egypt, thus far neutral in the conflict, might not remain so much longer. How Mithridates treated the young prince, and what conditions he placed on his release, might yet play a role in the king's future relations with Egypt, and Egypt's relations with Rome. The multiple diplomatic variables at play (as explained to me by Cassius) were too complicated for me to remember; my only concern would be to gather any information regarding the kidnapped Prince Ptolemy.

Fourth, I was to inquire, again discreetly, about a Roman named Publius Rutilius Rufus, a hero of the long-ago Numantine War who had served a term as consul eighteen years ago. More recently, Rutilius had been a legate in Asia, serving under the Roman governor. Apparently, not long after I left Rome on my travels, this Rutilius had been called on to defend himself against charges of malfeasance in Asia. The trial had created a sensation in Rome. Rutilius had been found guilty and was made a pauper by the fines imposed on him, whereupon he fled back to Asia. "Where he now sponges a living off Greek-speaking royalty," Gaius Cassius had explained in a sarcastic tone that left no doubt that he detested Rutilius.

Posidonius had been more measured. "It may be that Rutilius has been captured by Mithridates and is being held against his will; a Roman of consular rank would make a fine prize. Or it may be that the situation is . . . more complicated."

"What does that mean?" I had asked.

"It means that we don't wish to prejudice you one way or the other," Cassius shot back. "Assess the situation with your own eyes and ears and make of it what you will."

I took this to mean that Rutilius might have "gone Greek," as the saying goes, taking up the cause of Mithridates and his mostly Greek-speaking allies against Rome. Even if that were so, of what use to the

king was a penniless septuagenarian? Then it occurred to me that Antipater was even older than Rutilius, but had managed to cause a great
deal of mischief despite his creaking bones.

All my discoveries and observations I was to report to Samson. Once
we reached Ephesus, I was not to try to contact him, or speak to him
or even give any indication that I recognized him should I see him in a
public place; he would contact me. On the short journey from Rhodes
to Ephesus the two of us kept well apart and did not make eye contact.
Exactly why Gaius Cassius thought the Jew was to be trusted, I did
not know. It seemed to me that Samson must have his own agenda,
but if so, perhaps it coincided with the interests of Rome, at least in the
short term. At any rate, Samson was to be my only conduit to Cassius,
and I was to obey any order he gave me as if it came from the Roman
governor himself.

My original plan, hazy as it was, was of my own choosing. The agenda
imposed on me by Cassius was very much not of my choosing. I cursed
myself for my decision to leave the ship at Rhodes and seek out Posidonius. At the time it had seemed a reasonable thing to do; given their long
relationship, Posidonius might have had news about Antipater, and I
wanted his advice. How could I have anticipated that a Roman governor
would appear, and conscript me to serve as an agent of Rome?

At least I had received something from Cassius in return. First, he
promised to assist me financially, via Samson, in case I ran short of
funds in Ephesus; second, he and the others had shared with me what
they knew about the king and his court, especially Queen Monime, of
whom Antipater had seemed especially fearful in the passage from his
journal. Their intelligence was scant, derived largely from rumor, but
I was glad for any bits of information they could give me.

Just before I left the house of Posidonius, in the predawn hour as I
made ready to head back to the *Phoenix,* Cassius appeared at my door,
slipped into my room, and made me repeat back to him all the orders
he had given me the night before. Satisfied, he gave me a curt nod and
left the room. His place was taken by my host, who yawned—unused

WRATH OF THE FURIES 101

to being up at such an hour—and wished Bethesda and me a safe voyage. As he escorted us to the vestibule, Posidonius gave a grunt.

"Ah, yes, I just remembered—there's a question I've been meaning to ask you. If I understand correctly, Gordianus, you actually made the acquaintance of the king of Egypt—the recently deposed king, I mean—shortly before he fled from Alexandria."

"I saw him in the flesh, and we spoke, if that's what you mean."

"Yes, that's *precisely* what I mean: You have seen with your own eyes this fellow *in the flesh*. Tell me—is he really as incredibly fat as rumor makes him out to be?"

I had been expecting a weightier question. Surprised, I laughed aloud. "I've never seen a fatter man in my life."

"They say—well, this is rather indelicate . . . but they say—oh, now how can I put this . . . ?"

I laughed again, anticipating his question. "Yes, I've heard the story, as has everyone in Alexandria. The man is so fat, he can't take a piss or a shit without servants to help him. He has to be hoisted on and off the latrina, and his arms are too short to aim his manhood in front or wipe himself behind, so others have to do it for him. That vulgar rumor was memorably enacted in a rather rude mime show I saw in Alexandria. But I myself never saw the king tend to his bodily functions, so I can't affirm that it's true."

Posidonius nodded thoughtfully. "They also say that when he's in his cups, he can dance and jump on tables and cavort with the best of them."

"That also I never saw. But yes, that's what the Alexandrian gossips say."

"Ah, yes, I see." Posidonius produced a stylus and wax tablet and began scribbling notes. He was famous for recording the habits of Gauls and Celts and other exotic folk he had observed in his travels. Did he intend to record the appearance and behavior of King Ptolemy for posterity? Such gossip hardly seemed the kind of thing that would be of use to some future historian.

. . .

Because we came from Rhodes, everyone disembarking at Ephesus from the *Phoenix* was herded by port officials into a special queue for passengers arriving from "unfriendly" ports. After an hour or so of waiting in line on the wharf, my turn at last arrived to pass through the city gates. As it turned out, I was not exposed as a Roman spy. Nor was I allowed to simply enter the city, as I had hoped. As so often happens, there was a third possibility that I could not have foreseen.

Before we left Alexandria, the eunuchs and Bethesda and I had rehearsed the scene of my arrival, employing several different scenarios. Kettel and Berynus played the Ephesian entry officials, asking all the many questions that might come up. I had been made to maintain complete silence, while Bethesda had been coached to answer as simply and briefly as she could. ("And if the snooty bureaucrat seems even the least bit susceptible to your charms, my dear, do not hesitate to use them," Kettel had advised her, putting his hands on his hips and batting his eyelashes to demonstrate, at which an unamused Bethesda returned an unblinking sphinxlike stare that was infinitely more provocative.)

As it turned out, the eunuchs had done an excellent job of anticipating the kinds of questions we would be asked, and all the various reactions our answers might elicit—all except one.

Things seemed to be going very well, I thought. The official was a young man, decidedly not a eunuch to judge by his neatly trimmed beard. As he looked over my travel documents, his manner was brisk and efficient, but not unfeeling. He seemed mildly susceptible to Bethesda's charms, and not unsympathetic with the plight of a man in the prime of youth struck dumb and desperately in search of a cure.

"Do you have a place to stay in the city?" he asked.

"The last time my master was in Ephesus," answered Bethesda, "he stayed with a man called Eutropius, who lives up the hill, near the theater."

"Not a cheap neighborhood. This Eutropius must be a man of means."

Bethesda turned to me. I nodded vigorously, and she replied, "Oh, yes, Eutropius is a man of considerable means."

The young bureaucrat cast a skeptical glance at my clothes, obviously wondering what relationship might exist between a man as humble as me and a rich Ephesian.

Bethesda, too, noticed his skepticism. "I believe my master and this Eutropius met through a mutual friend, a traveling tutor by the name of Zoticus. Zoticus of Zeugma—perhaps you've heard of him?"

The young man seemed amused. No one famous ever came from Zeugma. "I don't think so."

"Oh, he's quite widely known," said Bethesda with a sly smile. "He writes poetry, too. My master would recite some lines of it for you, I'm sure, except that . . . well, as I explained . . . my master is dumb."

I bit my tongue and resisted the urge to give her a kick. Giving complete answers was one thing. Spinning needless elaborations was another.

"Dumb, did she say?" Another functionary suddenly appeared—this one a eunuch, to judge by the softness of his downy jowls. He was more senior than the official who had been questioning us, to judge by the ostentatious headdress he wore, a kind of turban from which dangled a great many gewgaws made of cheap metal and colored glass.

The younger official nodded. "Yes, sir. He's an Alexandrian come to seek healing at the Temple of Artemis. I explained that he'd be lucky to get in, with that mob of Romans cramming themselves inside, seeking sanctuary—"

"And mute?" said the older man, giving me a hard look.

"So he says. Or rather, so his slave says—"

"Can't say a word?" The eunuch kept staring at me until I nodded. He snatched my documents from the younger man and gave them a cursory glance. "Well, then—Agathon of Alexandria—this is your lucky day." He swatted his underling with the documents. "Did you forget, Terpsicles, that we're to be on the lookout for specimens exactly such as this one?"

Terpsicles grimaced to acknowledge some oversight. I frowned, not liking the sound of that word: *specimens.*

"Follow me, Agathon of Alexandria," said the eunuch.

Bethesda shot me a questioning glance. I shrugged.

"Is there some problem?" she asked.

"No problem at all," the eunuch called over his shoulder. "Did you not hear me? Not deaf as well, are you? Follow me!"

"Follow you *where*?" insisted Bethesda.

"To the royal palace."

"Royal . . . palace?" Bethesda wrinkled her brow. So did I.

"Yes. You know, the big building where the king stays when he's in residence. You have one of those in Alexandria, don't you?" He clucked his tongue and shook his head. "What a pair the two of you make. A mute master and a simple slave!"

Bethesda's expression turned stormy. She opened her mouth, but I silenced her with a jab from my elbow. I took her by the arm and pulled her after me.

"But why are we going to the palace?" she whispered.

The question was spoken to me, but it was the keen-eared eunuch who answered. "To meet Queen Monime, you silly girl."

Until then I had only been pretending. Now I was genuinely dumb-struck.

XI

"His vicious little queen," Antipater had written about this woman called Monime. What threat did she pose to Antipater, and how great was the danger? For what possible reason had I been summoned to her royal presence? Was such an unexpected privilege the best thing that could happen—or the worst?

Gaius Cassius had been able to give me only a few pieces of information about Monime. Her father was one Philopoemen, a man of Macedonian blood and a person of considerable importance in the city of Stratonicea. When Mithridates laid claim to Stratonicea, he met with the city's most powerful families, and the alluring Monime caught his eye.

It had not, at first, been the king's intention to marry the young woman. Mithridates had been married only once before, to his own sister, Laodice, whom he had executed for sleeping with his friends and plotting against him. Having been given several male heirs already by the late Laodice, and having access to any number of beautiful courtesans for his pleasure, Mithridates had vowed never to marry again. Probably he thought Monime would be flattered to become yet another of his courtesans, but the young woman resisted his advances, and her father stepped in to negotiate. In such cases, money usually sufficed. Flush from his victories and his acquisition of the treasuries on Cos, Mithridates offered an astounding sum—fifteen thousand gold pieces— that Monime refused. She insisted on a marriage contract, a royal diadem, and the title of queen.

Monime had nerve—a quality Mithridates apparently found as appealing as her beauty. Instead of incurring his wrath, her audacity only whetted his appetite for the nuptial bed. Monime's resolve was rewarded with a royal marriage. For his reward, the king's new father-in-law was appointed royal overseer of Ephesus.

These bits of information gave me some idea of the sort of woman I was soon to meet, but no clue as to why she wanted to meet me.

Clucking his tongue and shooing various lesser functionaries out of his way, the eunuch escorted us to a shaded portico just inside the city gate. A great many litters, large and small, were stationed on blocks; the bearers to carry them stood idly by, awaiting orders. The eunuch practically shoved me into one of the two-person litters, then got into it himself, taking the seat across from me. It was a covered litter, with curtains that could either be tucked behind hooks or closed for privacy.

The eunuch unhooked the curtains and let them fall shut, then thrust one arm outside the box and snapped his fingers. I heard the shuffling sounds of a team of bearers taking their stations at the poles on either side of the box.

"The royal palace!" he said.

I grabbed my seat as the bearers lifted us off the blocks.

What of Bethesda? Apparently the eunuch expected her to walk. I did not like the idea. Nor did she. She parted the curtains and peered inside.

"Am I not to ride, as well?" she asked.

"You? A slave?" said the eunuch.

"But I am my master's tongue—the only voice he possesses. Do you not intend to converse with him during the trip?"

The eunuch considered this for a moment, then dismissed her with a wave. "We shall ride in silence," he said. "Follow along behind us, girl. You look fit enough to keep up."

Bethesda pursed her lips, then vanished from sight as the curtain of the litter fell shut and we headed off.

Where exactly was I being taken? That was another question I might have asked the eunuch, had I a voice.

The last time I had been in Ephesus, there had been no such thing as a royal palace, because there had been no royalty. Like many a Greek-speaking city, Ephesus had become a Roman protectorate, having been bequeathed to the Senate and People of Rome in the will of its last ruler, the heirless King Attalus III of Pergamon. As governor of Asia, Gaius Cassius had been in charge of Ephesus, ruling from Pergamon. More locally, the city had been governed by a council of city fathers. Anti-pater had undoubtedly explained the governing structure of Ephesus to me, but I had not paid much attention to the details—I had been too busy saving Anthea, and receiving my reward from Amestris. But I was certain there had been no king or queen running the place. That had changed with the city's "liberation" by Mithridates. He was now the king, Monime was the queen, and Philopoemen was the episco-pus, or royal overseer.

What, then, was this so-called "royal palace" to which I was being taken? As I would later learn, Attalus III had kept a residence in the city—not surprisingly, the grandest dwelling in Ephesus. Subsequently, this dwelling had become the property of the richest Roman banker in the city, who filled it with artworks and furnishings fit for a king—quite literally, as it turned out, for when the Roman banker fled for his life to Rhodes, Mithridates claimed the abandoned property for his royal residence.

As our journey progressed, I quickly grew bored of looking at the eunuch across from me, and parted the curtains of the litter so I could look outside. One waterside market looks much like any other, I thought, until my attention was drawn to a placard posted in a conspicuous spot. It was daubed with red paint that read, in both Latin and Greek:

BY DECREE OF HIS MAJESTY
KING MITHRIDATES, KING OF KINGS,
AND UPON PAIN OF IMMEDIATE DEATH,
ALL ROMANS MUST WEAR THE TOGA
AT ALL TIMES.

Python had told me about this proclamation. But to hear of such a decree is one thing; to see it with my own eyes was another. And I saw it not once, but many times, repeated on placards posted in every available spot, not just in the markets but in the residential streets beyond. Appended to many of these placards was a second decree, apparently added later since the paint was another shade of red and the smaller letters were cramped to fit the remaining space:

IT IS FURTHER DECREED,
ALSO UPON PAIN OF IMMEDIATE DEATH,
THAT ALL ROMANS MUST SURRENDER ALL ARMS,
LARGE AND SMALL, TO THE CIVIL AUTHORITIES.

What made the first decree so sinister? Why did it raise hackles on the back of my neck? It was something about the words "immediate death"—not just death, but *immediate* death, inflicted on the spot—and the coupling of such a frightful punishment with the toga. The donning of his first toga marks every Roman boy's induction into manhood. To wear the toga in Rome is to feel one is a Roman among many Romans, not only the living but the ancestors as well, all sharing centuries of tradition. To wear the toga in foreign lands is to show one's pride at being Roman among those who are not. But there could be no pride in wearing a garment because a king demanded it, knowing that failure to do so would bring immediate death. A mark of pride had been made into something shameful.

Why were the decrees in both Latin and Greek? To a Roman the message would mean one thing. To a Greek it would mean something quite different—that the outsiders had been forced to wear an identifying garment, making them easy to spot at a distance. Easy to shun, or to follow, or to track. Easy to round up, as Pythion had said.

Now these outcasts had been stripped of their weapons, as well.

The placards grew less frequent as the bearers began to ascend one winding street after another, taking us into the district of fine mansions in the vicinity of the theater. This was the neighborhood where Antipater's friend and former pupil Eutropius lived. Studying the passing scene, I recognized certain landmarks, and drew in a sharp breath as we passed directly in front of Eutropius's house.

Antipater had written that he was being allowed to reside away from the royal court, in the house of Eutropius. Was he inside the house at that very moment, perhaps sitting down to dinner with his host and his host's daughter? And was the lovely Anthea being waited upon by her equally lovely slave Amestris, she whose hair was the color of midnight?

Even as my thoughts took a certain turn, I again saw before me, peering into the litter, the face of . . . not Amestris, but Bethesda!

She gave me a blank stare, and then I quickly averted my face, feeling my cheeks grow hot. Simply by looking at me, Bethesda was often able to read my thoughts. This ability had proven useful to a master feigning muteness, but it could also be disconcerting. How did she do it? I suspected sorcery. It seemed to me that her ability had grown stronger since the time she spent as a captive in the Nile Delta, under the protection and possible tutelage of the Corinthian witch, Ismene.

The eunuch shooed Bethesda away, and the litter sped past the house of Eutropius and ascended even higher up the hill, beyond the theater, passing mansions even grander than that of Eutropius. At last we could go no higher, for the street ended.

The eunuch indicated that I should step out of the litter first. I looked for Bethesda and beckoned for her to join me. The eunuch ushered the two of us up the steps that led to the entrance. The massive bronze doors stood wide open, flanked by two of the brawniest guards I had ever seen. By their raven hair, dark skin, and exotic armor I took them to be Persians.

The house before me was one of the grandest I had ever seen, ornamented with fluted marble columns and rimmed with many terraces and balconies. At the top of the steps, I turned and swept my gaze across the city below. To the west, silhouetted by the sinking sun, I saw the wooded bluffs beyond the harbor. Below us were countless rooftops clustered around the concave mass of the theater. To the northeast, dominating the plain beyond the city, stood the Temple of Artemis.

This was my first sight of the temple since I had arrived, and the first time I had seen it from such a lofty vantage point. I drew a sharp breath, amazed that the temple appeared even larger than I remembered, and more beautiful. The temple did not stand in complete isolation, for a number of lesser buildings consecrated for sacred uses were scattered on the surrounding grounds. But these more modest structures only served to highlight the magnificence of the temple. Clad in marble and gold and brightly colored paint, it glittered like some monstrous jewel box—which in a way it was, for the temple was even more spectacular inside than out, a repository of fabulous treasures of every sort, from rubies and emeralds to antique weapons to the famous painting of Alexander the Great that seemed to lunge forward from the wall.

The temple had been the first World Wonder I visited, and none that I saw afterward, not even the Great Pyramid, had impressed me more. Antipater had spoken truly when he wrote his famous poem about it. I silently mouthed the words:

I have seen the walls of Babylon, so lofty and so wide,
And the Gardens of that city, which flower in the skies.
I have seen the ivory Zeus, great Olympia's pride,
And the towering Mausoleum where Artemisia's husband lies.
I have seen the huge Colossus, which lifts its head to heaven,
And taller still, the Pyramids, whose secrets none can tell.
But the house of Artemis at Ephesus, of all the Wonders Seven,
Must surely be the grandest, where a god may rightly dwell.

If Artemis truly dwelled in the temple, she was not alone. I had been told that a great many Romans were seeking sanctuary there, and indeed, I saw many people moving in and out of the temple and milling about, some sitting on the temple steps while others loitered around the great altar. A few of these people were the priests of Artemis, called Megabyzoi, recognizable even at such a great distance by their bright yellow robes and tall yellow headdresses. But many more were obviously Romans, equally recognizable by the white togas they wore. The women I took to be Roman wives and daughters. Others in the crowd were probably household servants and slaves who had accompanied their masters in search of a safe haven.

While I stood staring at the view, the eunuch obtained permission for us to enter. He ushered us onward, through the massive entry and into a large courtyard. Here he stopped to confer with another official, this one even more ostentatiously dressed. The gewgaws dangling from this man's turban appeared to be made of silver and precious stones, rather than base metal and glass, as no doubt suited a chamberlain of the royal household.

"But you will make sure I get the credit for finding this one?" insisted the eunuch. The royal chamberlain gave him a curt, dismissive nod, then, with a simple movement of one eyebrow, indicated that I should follow him.

We left the courtyard and entered one wing of the house. Every space was filled with sumptuous decoration, from the frescoes on the walls and ceilings to the geometric mosaics underfoot. Beside me, I saw Bethesda staring at our surroundings in wonder.

We walked down a long hallway, passing busy slaves and bustling military officers. At last we arrived in a small but dazzling vestibule where every architectural detail and ornament appeared to be covered with gold foil. Mosaic peacocks spread their wings on the floor beneath us. Painted storks and egrets wheeled across the ceiling above us. I could only wonder what sort of fabulous room lay beyond.

The chamberlain at last spoke. "I understand that you are mute."

I nodded.

"But you can hear, and have all your other senses?"

I nodded.

"Good. And this is your slave, who speaks for you?"

Bethesda opened her mouth to speak, but the man silenced her with a raised finger. He hummed and clicked his teeth.

"Ah, not the most ideal situation. Court protocol dictates that a slave may speak directly to Her Majesty only in certain rare circumstances. But . . . I suppose this might be one such circumstance. And yet. . . ." He appeared to weigh his options for a long moment, then nodded. "Yes, I have it! What is your name, slave?"

"Bethesda," she said.

The man made a face. "What sort of name is that?" He grunted, but did not wait for an answer. "Well, then . . . slave," he said, unable or unwilling to pronounce her exotic name, "when a question is asked by Her Majesty of your master, which you are capable of answering, you will whisper the answer to me, and I will convey the answer to Her Majesty. Do you understand, slave?"

Bethesda drew a deep breath. She narrowed her eyes. "Yes, I understand."

"Very good. Well, then, follow me." The man signaled to a servant who stood beside the door, who obediently opened it for us.

XII

We entered a room that seemed to be wrapped in layer upon layer of gauze.

Everywhere, hanging vertically, were translucent veils of soft, lovely colors—lilac and azure, mossy green and buttery yellow. Though they were hard to see, there were openings in these veils, for we passed through one shimmering layer after another. The soft touch of the veils as they slid against my cheeks and the backs of my hands was delightful.

Of what fantastic material were they made? I suddenly realized it had to be the famous silk of Cos, an example of which I had first seen in the home of Antipater's cousin Bitto in Halicarnassus. She had worn a green garment made of the stuff, which clung to her flesh like a rippling sheet of water. No fabric was more costly than the silk of Cos. Had these been sheets of hammered gold they could hardly have been more valuable. I wondered how anyone, even Mithridates, could have got his hands on so much of the stuff. He must have plundered the island's entire store of silk.

From somewhere ahead of me I heard the sound of someone giggling—a boy, I thought, with some surprise. No, it was a girl—or rather, it was both, a boy and a girl laughing together. Slanting sunlight lit the room, passing through some veils and reflecting off others. The queen was able to see me before I could see her.

"Is this the mute?" said a girlish voice, to a background of boyish giggles.

"Yes, Your Majesty."

"And who is the lovely creature with him?" asked the boy, whose shape I was just beginning to discern as we stepped through yet another layer of veils.

"His slave. Because he has been struck mute, she travels with him, to speak when he cannot."

"How tiresome that must be for them both," said the boy.

The chamberlain pushed aside one last veil, and I finally saw the young man, who half-sat, half-reclined on an elegant couch, propped on one elbow. The cut of his long, sleeveless robe was distinctly Egyptian, as was his simple uraeus crown. It looked as if a slender cobra made of gold had wrapped itself around his head, with its flattened, ruby-eyed face poised to strike from the middle of his forehead. The young man had slender arms but a chubby face. Perhaps he was predisposed to fatness, like his famously fat father—for as surely as the fabrics surrounding us were the silks of Cos, this was the son of the deposed king of Egypt.

By rights, I thought, he probably should not be wearing that royal crown. But then again, he was the nephew of the current king, so perhaps, by the rules of the incestuous Ptolemy clan, he still had some claim to a princely crown. Apparently the chamberlain thought so, for after a great deal of bowing—which I did my best to emulate, indicating to Bethesda that she should do likewise—he addressed both young people before me with royal titles. Both, I say, for seated on an adjacent couch, reclining in a similar pose and head to head with the prince, was a curious being who could be none other than Queen Monime.

"Your Majesty, Queen Monime; Your Majesty, Prince Ptolemy—I present to you Agathon of Alexandria, a young man who has lost the power of speech."

I had never seen anyone quite like the young queen. She was so pe-
tite as to be almost dwarfish. Her size made her appear to be almost a
child, but only at first glance, for the curves of her body were decidedly those of a woman. I had always thought that Bethesda was voluptuous, but Monime was even more curvaceous, a fact that her clothing
did nothing to conceal. A nod to modesty was perhaps intended by the
wispy white veils that hung from her gown here and there, but these
were so flimsy they merely accentuated the shimmering white garment
beneath, which clung to her like a second skin.

The flesh of her bare arms was as perfectly white as her gown, and
had a translucent, pearly sheen; moment by moment it seemed to glitter as if reflecting all the various colors of the roomful of veils around
us. Her hair was like red gold, likewise reflecting the colors of the room.
Around her forehead, serving as a royal diadem, was a simple fillet of
twined purple and white wool.

Her features were delicate, and only very subtly enhanced by
cosmetics—a bit of kohl to outline her eyes and some henna to redden
her lips. She looked like a girl made up to pass for a woman. Like the
Egyptian prince, she was still a teenager. She had very large eyes, so it
should have been easy to ascertain their color, but this seemed to change
from moment to moment, at first green, then green verging into blue,
then blue with hints of violet.

Beside me, the chamberlain stood with his face slightly lowered, not
gazing directly at either of the royal personages. I realized I should do
likewise, but found myself staring at the queen, unable to look away.
She stared back at me with a cool, calculating gaze.

I heard the music of a lute. When had it started? The sound was soft,
but not distant. Somewhere in the room there was a musician. Lamps
were being lit, for as reddish twilight faded, rosy lamplight took its
place. Lamplighters and a musician were in the room, then, and surely
there were handmaidens as well, to serve the queen, and there must have
been armed guards to protect her and to keep watch on Prince Ptolemy. But I never saw them. Everyone around us was hidden behind
layers of veils. I saw only the queen and the young prince of Egypt,

reclining head to head. Their couches were atop a dais several steps up from the floor, so that even though they reclined and I stood, our eyes were on the same level.

The queen had a voice to match her giggle, surprisingly girlish from a creature so voluptuous. "So, Agathon of Alexandria, you are a man who once could speak like everyone else, but now you are mute. Is that correct?"

I nodded.

"How is it that you lost your voice?"

The chamberlain turned to Bethesda, who spoke in his ear, not quite loud enough for me to overhear. Eventually the man nodded and turned back to the queen.

"As Her Majesty the Queen may know, and as His Majesty the Prince undoubtedly knows, the inundations of the Nile bring blessings but also curses, for when the waters recede, the muddy ground releases vapors that can cause a multitude of maladies. This man contracted one such illness. He suffered a fever for several days, and afterwards he could not speak. Not a word has passed his lips since then."

"He's not still ill, is he?" said the prince, looking at me warily. "He's not carrying some contagion?"

The chamberlain turned once again to Bethesda. This time she spoke just loud enough for me to overhear. "Tell the fat boy that my master is more fit than he shall ever be."

The chamberlain grimaced slightly, then turned back toward the dais. "The Alexandrian is well, Your Majesty, and his malady is not contagious."

"What is he doing in Ephesus?" asked the queen.

With some hesitation, the chamberlain turned to Bethesda. Again I was just able to overhear her. "Tell the white moth that my master comes to seek a cure for his muteness at the Temple of Artemis. Perhaps you should likewise seek a cure for that bad breath of yours."

The chamberlain was visibly flustered for a moment, then recovered and put on a smile for Her Majesty. "He comes to seek the blessing of Artemis and to ask that she restore his voice."

"Well, he mustn't do that!" said the queen, sounding peeved. "Not yet, anyway. He'll be of no use to us if he gets his voice back. The Magi were quite explicit. The ritual must be 'heard by one who cannot see, seen by one who cannot hear, witnessed by one who cannot speak.' Wait . . . did I get that right?" She frowned, then giggled. "Yes, I think I did. It's a bit of a mouthful, isn't it?"

"You mean a tongue twister," said Prince Ptolemy.

"Not a tongue twister, silly. That's something hard to say because the words sound alike and go all slippery on you."

"Perhaps, but one shouldn't say 'mouthful.' It sounds rude."

"You mean it sounds dirty?" The queen giggled.

"Only to *you*," said the prince, giggling back at her.

Monime rolled her eyes. "Well, we see what comes of being brought up on a remote island by priests and eunuchs. You're such a prude, Ptolemy."

"I am not! I simply have manners. It's something one acquires after ten generations of being royal. Maybe in a couple of centuries, *your* descendants will have learned some manners, Moni."

"If you call me Moni, I *will* call you Ptoly."

"The indignities I must endure! But I *am* your prisoner, after all."

The chamberlain cleared his throat. "If Her Majesty finds the candidate unsatisfactory—"

"Oh, no. He seems satisfactory." The queen looked me up and down. "Quite satisfactory, in every way. Of course the Grand Magus must have a look at him, and the Great Megabyzus as well. But he appears to be whole and unblemished. *Are* you whole and unblemished, Agathon of Alexandria?"

I was not quite sure what she meant by this, but I nodded.

"Well, then, the task my dear husband set me is almost complete. We have the blind man, and the deaf man, and now the mute. Next we must acquire the proper virgin for the sacrifice."

Prince Ptolemy gave her a sidelong glance. "I should think the king had reserved the task of selecting the virgin for himself."

"Oh, I'm sure he would have liked that, but I insisted that he let me choose *all* the necessary participants, including the virgin." Monime looked past me, at Bethesda. "I don't suppose *she's* a virgin?"

The queen returned her gaze to me. I'm not sure what expression crossed my face, but she found her answer.

Monime pursed her lips. "No, I suppose she's not."

"But would a slave do, for the virgin?" said the prince.

"Of course a slave will do. It's customary, in fact, for such sacrifices. Or so I'm told. This sort of thing is more Persian than Greek. It was the Magi's idea, of course, not the Megabyzoi's, though they insist on playing a role as well."

"We Egyptians do *not* practice human sacrifice," said the prince, with an air of superiority. "I didn't think the Greeks did so, either, at least not any longer."

"Oh, yes, it's still done, if rarely. Following the example of Agamemnon with Iphigenia, you know. I'm told that even the Romans practice human sacrifice from time to time, though they don't like to admit it."

I would have liked to protest this slander, but I kept my mouth shut. Not only was I pretending to be mute, I was also pretending not to be a Roman. But what was this talk of human sacrifice, and what sort of role had I been chosen to play? It seemed a cruel joke of the gods that the pretense meant to protect me from scrutiny—my inability to speak—had somehow made me the thing I least wanted to be, an object of interest to the Roman-hating royal household.

Queen Monime gave me another appraising look, then dismissed us all with a flick of her wrist. "Well then, take the mute away. Give him lodging with the others, and arrange for the Magi and the Megabyzoi to have a look at him and give their approval."

"Yes, Your Majesty." The chamberlain gave a low bow and began to back away. I imitated the bow and did likewise, bumping into Bethesda behind me, who made a complaining grunt. If Their Majesties noticed our awkwardness, they showed no sign. They seemed too busy teasing each other.

"It's hard work, being a queen," sighed Monime.

"Ha! You should try ruling Egypt," said the prince. Despite his jovial tone, there was an edge in his voice; his father had been driven from the throne and he himself was a captive of some sort.

"Rule Egypt?" said Monime. "The King of Kings will have to take back all of Greece, first. But then . . . who knows?"

How Prince Ptolemy reacted to this suggestion I did not hear. We retreated though the veils, and then through the door, which closed behind us, leaving the chamberlain, Bethesda, and myself once more in the gilded vestibule outside the queen's reception room.

"Come along, then," said the chamberlain, unbending his back and straightening the bejeweled turban on his head. "I'll show you to your quarters."

XIII

A room of my own, in a royal palace? This was to be a new experience, I thought.

We walked down a broad corridor, passing well-dressed courtiers, pretty serving girls, and swaggering soldiers. Down a side corridor I caught a glimpse of some men dressed in wildly colorful robes and head-dresses whom I took to be Magi, having seen a few on my trip to Babylon with Antipater. The Magi were engaged in a spirited debate, but I was able to catch only a few words of Persian.

I tried to get a good look at every face we passed. Was it possible that Antipater might not be at the house of Eutropius, but here in the royal palace, summoned for a dinner or some other function? And would I know him if I saw him? During our journey he had several times donned disguises, putting on putty noses, stuffing his cheeks, and wearing wigs. Might he be incognito even here, in the court of the man whom he had served, and perhaps still served, as a spy?

I saw a number of gray heads and stooped elders and tried to get a good look at them, but none appeared to be Antipater.

We descended to a lower level. The floor beneath our feet changed as we went down, from marble on the upper landing to plain wood on

the last flight of steps—highly polished wood, to be sure, but no match
for the marble upstairs. Here the hallways were narrower, the decora-
tions sparser, and the people less elegantly dressed. I was no longer sure
who was a household slave and who was not—except that no slave, even
in the most common household, would dare to spit on the floor, as I saw
one man do. He leaned against a wall cleaning his teeth with a silver
pick, dressed in a sleeveless tunic and wearing a great deal of jewelry.
His bearded face registered no emotion as we passed, but I saw him
wink at Bethesda. Then he spat again.

The chamberlain wrinkled his nose. "The things that fellow gets
away with," he muttered. "And only because he can throw things in
the air!"

I glanced back over my shoulder. This was my first look at Sosipater,
whom I would later learn was not only the world's greatest juggler, but
also one of King Mithridates's favorite dinner companions. His muscular arms were adorned by many bands of silver and gold—bands he
had juggled for the king's amusement, as I would later learn, and with
which the king had rewarded him, letting Sosipater keep as many bands
as he could keep in the air at once. How many bands was that? There
were certainly more of them glittering around his arms than I could
count at a glance.

A troupe of giggling, scantily dressed girls swept past us. Normally
they would have set my head spinning, but after gazing at Queen
Monime I found them plain and uninteresting. Walking beside me,
Bethesda noticed my apathetic response and raised an eyebrow, pleased
that I showed no reaction, displeased because she probably guessed the
reason.

"Dancers!" mumbled the chamberlain. He made it sound as if dancing were the only thing more distasteful than juggling.

We rounded a corner and ahead of us I heard the sound of a flute
being played, and not too well. As the shrill music grew louder, I had
a sinking feeling. Sure enough, the chamberlain led me to the doorway of the room from which the music was coming.

"Your quarters," he said.

I had been imagining a spacious chamber that opened onto one of those balconies or terraces I had seen from outside. The room I peered into was dark and dingy. A high window admitted the last faint glow of the long summer day, but afforded no view. The furnishings were sparse. A flickering lamp was set atop a small table, and next to that was a single chair. A rug that had seen better days covered most of the plain wooden floor.

Placed longwise against each of three walls were three narrow beds. On the bed to my left sat the man who was murdering the flute. On the bed to my right sat another man, who gave me a keen look as I stepped inside, then looked at Bethesda as she followed me. The music suddenly stopped. The man on my left lowered the flute and cocked his head. He stared at me with vacant, cloudy eyes.

The two men were neither young nor old, neither handsome nor ugly. Neither had the figure of a dancer or an acrobat. I doubted that either could juggle, and the blind man with the flute was certainly not a musician. Who were they, then, and what were they doing here? I remembered what Monime had said, quoting the Grand Magus: the ritual—whatever that was—must be heard by one who cannot see, seen by one who cannot hear, witnessed by one who cannot speak.

Apparently I was to be the witness who could not speak. The man looking at us so keenly had to be the one who could not hear—how else could he put up with that terrible music?—and the flute player was the one who could not see.

I turned to the chamberlain. I gestured to the room, then looked at Bethesda.

"My master is to sleep here?" she asked.

"Is that a girl I hear?" said the flute player, with a smile that looked at once innocent and lecherous, situated as it was beneath those vacant eyes.

The deaf man had leaned forward on his narrow bed and was staring intently at his blind companion across the room. Apparently he was able to read lips, for he knocked on the wall behind him twice, which, from the blind man's nod, I took to be a code meaning *yes*.

"Is she pretty?" asked the blind man.

The deaf man again knocked twice on the wall, with a bit more enthusiasm than I would have liked, though I saw Bethesda smile.

The chamberlain ignored them. "For the time being, this will be your master's room," he answered.

"For how long?" said Bethesda.

"Your master is to be the guest of His Majesty until his presence is no longer required."

"Days? Months?"

"A few days only, from what I've heard."

"And what have you heard?"

I pursed my lips and gave Bethesda a sidelong glance. She was asking exactly the questions on my mind.

"What I have heard . . ." The chamberlain lowered his voice, smiled, and gestured for Bethesda to lean closer. "What I have heard . . . is that I should keep my mouth shut! That advice applies to your master, as well—and to you, slave."

"Ha! You'll get nothing useful out of that fellow," said the blind man. "But who exactly is joining us, and why is the girl speaking for him? No, let me guess! The fellow is mute, and the slave girl serves as his voice."

The deaf man slapped the wall two times.

"Oh, dear, how are we going to communicate?" said the blind man. "I can't see, you can't hear, this one can't speak. And where is his slave to sleep? There are only three beds, and none is wide enough for two." Again he flashed that lecherous, or perhaps innocent, smile.

"There is a rug on the floor," said the chamberlain.

I put a finger to Bethesda's lips before she could say something rash, and gave the chamberlain a plaintive look.

"I suppose I can have an extra blanket delivered to the room," he said.

I smiled to show my gratitude, then caught a glimpse of a figure passing in the hallway outside—a man of many years, his long white hair and beard illuminated by lamplight.

Could it be—?

At the very instant I moved toward the door, the blind man decided to spring from his bed. I might have avoided colliding with him, but the chamberlain also got in the way. Somehow Bethesda became entangled as well.

The deaf man stayed clear of the jumble, sitting on his bed. He made a strange braying sound, slapped his thigh, and pointed at us. An Alexandrian mime troupe could not have staged a more farcical collision.

When I at last broke free and hurried to the door, there was no one in the hall outside. The passage was lit by lamps set in niches along each wall. I walked to the end of the hall and stuck my head around the corner. No one was in sight, except the bevy of dancing girls, heading back the way they had come, now accompanied by a dwarf who seemed to be on very familiar terms, to judge from the way he kept raising their sheer skirts and peeking under them. The girls giggled and shrieked with laughter.

Had I seen Antipater? I'd had only the briefest glimpse of the man's profile, but I was certain . . . almost certain . . . that it was him.

But how could that be? Surely the world's greatest poet should be upstairs, in the company of other poets, and philosophers and playwrights and sages. What would Antipater be doing below stairs with the dancing girls and acrobats and other riffraff?

The chamberlain came huffing and puffing after me. "You mustn't run off like that," he said. "Not without permission, or someone to look after you. Have you any idea what would happen to me if one of you three went missing before . . ." His voice trailed off. "Come back and let me properly introduce you to the others."

I shrugged and followed him back to the dingy little room.

"And the food is rather good, and there's plenty of it," said the blind man, whose name was Gnossipus. He came from a nearby village and had been able to see until a few years ago, when an illness made him blind. His livelihood as a wagon driver ruined, he had come to Ephesus to beg outside the Temple of Artemis, where he made a better living than before. It was outside the temple that the Great Megabyzus had approached him a few days ago and then brought him to the royal palace.

My stomach growled. Darkness had fallen and we had not yet been fed. I was beginning to wonder if I was expected to fall asleep on an empty stomach. Why did Gnossipus insist on talking about food?

"And at this time of year," he went on, "there are plenty of fruits and vegetables. Oh! The other day, we actually had cherries. Have you ever eaten cherries, Agathon?"

I shook my head, then realized I would need to use the code. I shifted a bit on my narrow bed and knocked once on the wall behind me.

"No? I suppose they're even rarer in Alexandria than they are here. Cherries come from somewhere up north, on the shores of the Euxine Sea. King Mithridates grew up eating them—'Summer isn't summer without cherries,' he says—and a few days ago a wagonload arrived here in Ephesus. All for the royal court, of course, but there were so many that even we nobodies got some. Oh, how delightful! Small and sweet and juicy, and I am told they have the most beautiful red color, the color of blood. I remember red. . . ." He sighed. "Do I exaggerate, Damianus? About the cherries?"

Damianus was the deaf man. He banged the wall once, very hard, to communicate the vehemence of his agreement: *No, Gnossipus, you do not exaggerate!*

But Gnossipus certainly liked to talk. He had been talking nonstop ever since the chamberlain left me in the room. His constant chatter was grating, but marginally more bearable than his flute playing. Had I a voice, I would have yelled at him to shut up. The only voice I had— Bethesda—lay curled on the rug at my feet. She had somehow managed to fall asleep, and began to snore very softly.

Gnossipus paused. "What is that sound? Is there a cat in the room? Cats make me break out in hives!"

Damianus brayed, which was his way of laughing. He drew a breath, then managed to make a passable cat noise, though it sounded as if the cat might be drowning in a well.

"Oh, that's you, Damianus!" said Gnossipus. "Is there a cat in the room or not? Let the slave girl speak. Oh, wait—that's her, isn't it?"

Damianus brayed again and banged the wall twice. I should not have wished to be lodged in the room behind him, with all that banging, though it would have been preferable to the room in which I found myself.

The banging woke Bethesda. She sat up and rubbed her eyes. How delicate she looked in the soft lamplight, leaning back against the bed with her legs tucked beneath her. From where I sat above her on the narrow bed, I had a lovely view of the tops of her breasts and the cleavage between. Oh, if only the two of us had been alone in that room!

The door swung open and the chamberlain stepped inside.

"I hope you're here to call us to dinner," said Gnossipus.

"Is that all you ever think about, being fed?" said the chamberlain. "Your dinner will be late tonight. The priests and the wise men need to have a look at your new roommate first."

"Ah, the same inspection I received, as did our deaf friend, I suspect," said Gnossipus. "I hope you're not bashful, Agathon."

"Shut up, Gnossipus," said the chamberlain. "No one is to speak to the mute until the priests are done with him. Now come along, Agathon, and follow me."

I saw that he was accompanied by two armed guards.

I got up from the bed. Bethesda got up and stood beside me. When I stepped toward the door, she followed, but the chamberlain raised his hand.

"Only the mute witness. No one else."

"But what if they ask questions of my master?" said Bethesda. "How is he to answer? And what if he has questions for them?"

"He will simply have to manage as best he can."

"But surely he should be allowed to have his voice."

The chamberlain gave her a sour look. "Let me explain something to you, slave. I am about to take your master to a room full of Magi and Megabyzoi. In case you do not know, the Megabyzoi are the priests of Artemis. They are sworn to chastity, and there are strict rules regarding any contact between the Megabyzoi and women. In an official proceeding such as this, in a closed room, no female may be present unless she is a virgin. Now tell me slave, are you a virgin?" He gave her a penetrating look, and when she did not answer, turned to me. "Well, Agathon, is your slave a virgin? Ah, you may be mute, but that blush on your face tells me all I need to know. Now come along, and leave the slave girl behind."

I looked at the two men with whom I was leaving her and felt a bit uneasy. Gnossipus seemed harmless enough, but I had learned almost nothing about the deaf man. Bethesda crossed her arms and assumed a posture that announced she could take care of herself. I should have liked to kiss her good-bye, but not in front of this particular audience. I gave her a nod, then turned to follow the chamberlain.

We went up one staircase, exchanging wooden steps for marble, then up another flight of steps, and then another. This uppermost floor of the house was not as grandiose as the main level with its imposing statuary and large reception halls. The hallways were narrower, the rooms smaller, and there were fewer people about, but the fittings and furnishings were exquisite. There was a hush about the place, and an atmosphere of mystery. Perhaps it was just the thick carpets, absorbing every sound, and the faint light from the lamps in sconces on the wall, inadequate to dispel the shadows all around us, but it seemed as if this was a place where secret things were done.

The chamberlain showed me into a room at the end of a long hallway. The room was even more dimly lit than the hall, and for a moment all I could see of the men surrounding me were their faces, peering back at me. There were at least twenty of them. Some were quite old, and only a few were as young as myself. As my eyes adjusted, I began to perceive their costumes.

The Magi were a motley bunch, dressed in many colors, wearing various sorts of head coverings. The jewels in their necklaces and rings glittered brightly, reflecting the lamplight. The Megabyzoi were more alike and austere, dressed entirely in yellow, with tall headdresses that dominated the room.

A number of lamps were brought into the room and placed in a circle on the floor around me. The light blinded me, so that I could barely see the men around me.

One of them stepped forward, inside the ring of lamps, so that I could see him clearly. By the towering audacity of his headdress, I knew he must be the Great Megabyzus. His wizened face looked hard and wily by the harsh lamplight. I recalled some very unpleasant dealings with his predecessor, who had been wicked as well as wily. I would need to keep my wits about me with such a man. That would be no easy task, and it was about to be made harder by the first words he spoke.

"Take off your clothes, Agathon of Alexandria," he said, in a deep, commanding voice. "Everything, including your shoes. We need to see you naked."

XIV

"Naked," he repeated, when he saw me hesitate. "Just as the gods made you."

I took a deep breath.

Greeks, of course, go naked at every possible opportunity. They practically make a religion of it. (I mean the males. The wives and daughters of Greek citizens are kept covered up.) Romans are not quite so eager to strip naked in public; even at the baths, some men modestly conceal their genitals with a towel. I had never been particularly shy about taking off my clothes, at least in suitable circumstances. Being gawked at by a bunch of fully dressed men did not strike me as particularly suitable, but there was nothing conditional about the Great Megabyzus's instruction. It was an order, not a request.

I bent down to unstrap my shoes, and kicked them past the circle of lamps on the floor. I pulled my tunic over my head, folded it, and handed it to the chamberlain. I took another deep breath, undid the loincloth around my hips, folded that as well, and placed it atop the tunic.

I was wearing nothing else, except the necklace I always wore, from which hung a lion's tooth. I began to take that off as well, but the Great Megabyzus stopped me.

"That pendant—is it an amulet of some sort?"

I nodded.

He turned to one of the Magi—the foremost among them, the Grand Magus, to judge by the man's ornate plumage and his prominent placement in the group—and held a whispered conference. He turned back to me. "You may leave on the amulet, for now." He stepped back and slowly looked me up and down. "Raise your arms above your head. Good. Now turn about to face each of the four walls in turn. Slowly."

I did as he said, feeling their eyes all over me. I experienced a curious surge of confidence—I was a fit young man in a room of mostly old men, after all, and had nothing to be embarrassed about as they looked closely at this, that, and the other part of me.

"He appears to have all his parts," noted the Great Megabyzus.

The Grand Magus grunted. "Yes. And I see no blemish." The squinting old man spoke flawless Greek, but with a distinctly Persian accent.

"Have him bend over and touch his toes," said one of the Magi behind me.

"Do so," said the Great Megabyzus.

At this order I almost balked, but the tone of the high priest allowed no dissent. I did as he requested. I was afraid I would be asked to perform the awkward and unseemly task of rotating in this position, but after a cursory inspection, the Magus behind me declared, "No blemish." This seemed to satisfy the others, and I was allowed to stand upright again.

The Grand Magus stepped closer and squinted. "But what is that mark on his forehead?"

"Where?" said the Great Megabyzus.

"There."

"Ah, yes, I see. It looks like a scar. Should that disqualify him?"

"That depends. *Is* it a scar, young man?"

I nodded.

"Not a blemish he's had from birth, then," said the Grand Magus. "So the question must be, how did he obtain this scar?" He looked past me, at the chamberlain, who noisily cleared his throat.

"I must admit, Your Eminence, I didn't notice the scar," he said apologetically. "Had I done so, I would not have bothered Your Eminence—"

"Oh, stop sniveling!" snapped the Grand Magus. "How did the Alexandrian come to have this scar?"

"I have no idea," whimpered the chamberlain. His manner, so haughty with me, was quite the opposite in this room full of frowning religious authorities.

The Grand Magus opened his mouth to further rebuke him, then noticed that I was attempting to communicate something, using my hands. Again he squinted. I realized he must be quite nearsighted.

I repeated the gesture, pointing first at the pendant that hung from my necklace, then at the scar.

"What is that amulet, anyway?" said the Grand Magus, stepping closer.

The Great Megabyzus put his head alongside that of the Grand Magus. "If I'm not mistaken, it's the tooth of some sort of beast. A bear, perhaps?"

I shook my head.

"Or a big cat?"

I nodded.

"An unusually large Egyptian housecat, probably," said the Grand Magus. "The Alexandrians adore such creatures. Is that the tooth of some beloved pet?"

I shook my head and made a gesture of enormity, spreading my hands in the air.

"Bigger than a housecat?" said the Great Megabyzus. "Are you saying this was the tooth of . . . a tiger?"

I shook my head.

"Or a panther?" offered another Megabyzoi.

I shook my head again.

The Grand Magus drew very close, squinting at the tooth. He gasped. "Why, this is the fang of a lion!"

I nodded vigorously. Again I pointed from the tooth to the scar.

"Are you saying, young man, that the mark on your forehead came from that tooth?"

I drew back my shoulders and nodded gravely. The scar had in fact been made by the tooth, but not because the lion bit me. The actual circumstances were rather complicated, and I would have needed a voice to explain. The wise men jumped to their own conclusions.

The Grand Magus stepped back and nodded thoughtfully. "The most ferocious of all animals drew close enough to scar you with its fang—yet here you stand before us, alive and whole, except for that small scar. And the fang that made the scar you wear as a trophy around your neck—an amulet to mark your good fortune, no doubt! You grappled with a lion, and lived to tell the tale—is that correct?"

I held my chin high and nodded. What he had said—the last part, anyway—was the truth, after all.

"Agathon of Alexandria, a fortunate man you must be, indeed," declared the Grand Magus, "despite the infirmity of your muteness— though for a man to be speechless is not always an unfortunate thing, or an unwise thing, as every wise man here knows. I think, my fellows, that we have here a splendid candidate to play mute witness to the ritual. It took us a while to find him, but here he is. Do you agree, Your Eminence?"

The Great Megabyzus made only a small nod, so as not to upset his towering headdress. "I'm not surprised that he was the last of the three to be found. A man who is mute but not also deaf is not so very common, yet that is what was prescribed. But what the gods prescribe, the gods provide, as the saying goes."

One of the younger Magi stepped forward. "But what of his muteness, and the exact nature of it? Was the Alexandrian born without speech, or did he possess the power of speech and then somehow lose it? Might this be a factor in his acceptability?"

The chamberlain answered. "This young man lost the power of speech only recently. In fact, he came to Ephesus for the express purpose of making pilgrimage to the great temple and pleading to have his speech restored by Artemis."

The Grand Magus squinted and hummed. The Great Megabyzus nodded thoughtfully, then spoke.

"It seems to me, Your Eminence, that your fellow Magus raises a pertinent question. Is there more than one kind of muteness, or multiple degrees of muteness, and does this Agathon possess the muteness required for the ritual? We might even ask if he truly is mute at all, since we have only his word for it—so to speak."

The Grand Magus tilted his head to one side. "Do you suggest that we should test his muteness somehow? I suppose we might place him in some extreme situation, and see if he might indeed mutter a word or two, perhaps to save himself or some loved one from physical harm . . ."

I drew a sharp breath, not liking the direction this conversation was taking. Was I to be tortured? If so, could I keep from speaking? If I spoke, my torturers would know that I was not only an imposter, but also a Roman.

"We could stick him with a pin and see if he yells," suggested the Magus who had insisted on examining my backside for blemishes.

The Great Megabyzus saw the look on my face and smiled. "Oh, I hardly think that's called for. Given the circumstances, we have no reason to doubt this young man's identity or his inability to speak. He could hardly have foreseen that upon his arrival in Ephesus he would be called before us for the singular fact of his infirmity. More worrisome to me is the idea that he might be curable, if not by human physicians, then by divine intervention. What if, before the ritual—or worse, in the middle of it!—he should suddenly regain his speech? That is, after all, what he came to Ephesus to do."

The Grand Magus thought about this. "You planned to go to the Temple of Artemis—is that correct, Agathon?"

I nodded.

"Then I say, let him go to the temple. If the goddess sees fit to cure him of his muteness, then this is not the man for us. On the other hand, if he makes propitiation to Artemis but remains mute, then we may take that as a sign that Agathon of Alexandria is indeed the mute witness we seek. Would you agree, Your Eminence?"

"Heartily! As high priest of the goddess, I think it proper that Artemis should have her say in the matter. That will make the ritual all the more definitive. Do you agree, my fellow Megabyzoi?"

A great many yellow headdresses nodded ever so slightly around the room, like long-stalked flowers stirring in a breeze.

"Do you agree also, Magi of the royal court?"

All the Magi nodded. The jewels on their turbans sparkled in the lamplight.

"Then it is agreed. Tomorrow morning, the Grand Magus and I will escort young Agathon of Alexandria to the Temple of Artemis. There, he shall make supplication to the goddess to restore his power of speech. And we shall see the result."

The Great Megabyzus swept his gaze around the room. Satisfied that the agreement of his fellows was unanimous, he looked me up and down a final time, then turned to the chamberlain. "Help the mute witness get dressed, then escort him back to his quarters."

XV

[From the secret diary of Antipater of Sidon:]

Late in the day, a messenger arrived at the house of Eutropius to summon me to the royal palace.

Am I allowed to use the main entrance, so that I may see and be seen by the other dignitaries in the grand vestibule? No! I must come in by the back door, tramping through the lower level where mimes loiter and jugglers practice. I passed a group of giggling dancing girls clad in flimsy gowns that left very little to the imagination. They have no manners. One of them asked me if my beard was real, and gave it a tug. She thought I was an actor!

A chamberlain (I don't remember which one; there are scores of these nameless fellows, all busy running the royal household) escorted me upstairs, not to a ceremonial hall or throne room, but to a small chamber that appeared to be part of the king's private quarters. The king stood on a small balcony, his back to me. He wore a simple tunic, though the white and purple fillet remained on his head. I noticed that the cloak of Alexander was nearby, folded atop a small table. To my surprise there was no one else present, not even a bodyguard or scribe. When the chamberlain withdrew, I was alone with the king.

My heart pounded in my chest—not a pleasant sensation for a fellow as old as I am. Why was there no one else in the room? All sorts of wild ideas raced through my head. Did the king wish to apologize to me for the shameful way I had been treated? That was certainly something he would want no one else to overhear. Yes, that might be it, I thought—or . . . was he for some reason angry with me, so angry he planned to throttle me with his own hands, and wished to have no witnesses?

Killing a man by his own hand was not beyond him. Nor was cold-blooded murder, committed before thousands of witnesses. Everyone knows the old story of how he murdered his own nephew, young King Ariarathes of Cappadocia, when the two were on the brink of war and met face-to-face in front of their troops. First, they both laid down their weapons, so as to meet unarmed, but Ariarathes, sensing treachery, insisted that his uncle be searched. When the man patting him down came near his crotch, Mithridates snidely said, "Take care, lest you should find another sort of weapon down there," and the man drew back—just as Mithridates intended, for concealed next to his genitals was a slender knife. The two kings drew close. Mithridates put his arm around his nephew's shoulders, and before Ariarathes could say a word, Mithridates pulled out the knife and slit his throat. While the young king writhed on the ground and bled to death, Mithridates picked up Ariarathes's crown and placed it on the head of his eight-year-old stepson, and no one, including the army of the murdered king, dared to oppose him. . . .

With such images in my head, you may understand why I was so fearful at being in the king's presence, especially in circumstances that seemed irregular. Night was falling, and the room was dimly lit. As the king turned to face me, I looked first at his hands to see if they held a weapon or some instrument of punishment—they did not—then at his face. His expression was somber, but not angry.

I lowered my face and began to bow.

"You can dispense with the groveling," he said. "There's no one here to see it. Besides, I can hear the cracking of your joints, and the sound is most unpleasant."

I began to apologize for making such a noise, but the king interrupted me. "What do you know about the Furies?" he asked.

"I beg Your Majesty's pardon?"

"The Furies—what do you know about them?"

"I'm not sure . . . I mean . . . Your Majesty is aware that I am not a priest or wise man—"

"Great Zeus, man! I have priests and wise men running out my ears! If I lined them up outside this door and gave each one an hour to talk to me, I'd still be listening to them a month from now. Of course I know you're not a priest. You call yourself a poet, don't you?"

I sighed. "Perhaps, if Your Majesty would give me a chance to recite some of my work, Your Majesty would call me a poet, too."

He laughed. Harsh as it was, the sound of that laughter caused me to relax a bit. "Perhaps I would. But that's not what you're here for. Poets are like priests in a way, aren't they? They know things that others don't—see what others do not. Well, then—have you ever seen a Fury?"

"I have not."

"Ha! Neither have any of the Megabyzoi or Magi I've talked to. Yet they seem to know a great deal about these Furies. What do you know about them, poet?"

I thought about this for a moment.

"For one thing, there are those who believe it's unlucky even to speak of them, or say their names aloud."

"But speak of them you will, because I command you!"

I racked my memory, and recited back to him all I could remember about the Furies. The winged sisters are three in number: Alecto, Megaera, and Tisiphone. They are older than Zeus and the other Olympian gods, having been born from the blood of Uranus when his son Kronos castrated him. They dwell among the dead in Tartarus, but are sometimes drawn to earth to punish certain kinds of wickedness. Once they find the mortal culprit, they hound him relentlessly, circling him and shrieking, striking him with brass-studded scourges. To be forced to see their hideousness is itself a punishment. They have snouts like dogs, bulging, bloodshot eyes, and snakes for hair. Their bodies are as black as coal, and they flit through the air on batlike wings.

I recited for him various lines from the poets and playwrights having to do with the Furies. He paced back and forth on the balcony, not looking at me. When I could recall no more about the subject, I fell silent for a long moment, then dared to speak again.

"Why does Your Majesty wish to know about the Furies, if I may ask?"

"That's none of your business!" he snapped. He stopped his pacing and gazed at the first stars to appear in a sky of darkest blue. "But you'll know soon enough—if you don't know already! It's supposed to be a secret, known only to those who need to know, but with a scheme of this magnitude, there are always rumors flying about."

"Rumors?" I said, as innocently as I could, for I was remembering what Eutropius had told me, about being enlisted to help organize a massacre of unprecedented proportions—the slaughter in a single day of every Roman still alive in the territories conquered by the king. If such a scheme could be realized, tens of thousands of men and women—frightened, unarmed, guilty of no crime—would be murdered in a matter of hours.

"Why do I ask about the Furies? I have been advised by the leading religious authorities—Persian as well as Greek—that a certain ritual sacrifice must be carried out before this . . . secret event . . . takes place. The exact timing of this event was determined by my astrologers. But before the event, there must be the sacrifice. Otherwise . . ."

He was silent for so long that I dared to whisper, "'Otherwise,' Your Majesty?"

"Otherwise, the enormity of the event may rouse the Furies . . . may incur their anger . . . may cause the full, dreadful, unthinkable wrath of the Furies to be unleashed against me, not against my enemies."

"And if the ritual sacrifice is properly carried out?"

"Then the Furies will be propitiated. If their wrath is stirred, it will be in my favor, like a wind against a runner's back. The Furies will be on my side when . . . the event . . . takes place. The wrath of the Furies will be unleashed not against me, but against . . ."

Your victims, *I thought—for surely he was speaking of the tens of thousands of Romans who were to die at his command. By making a sacrifice to the Furies, he intended to harness the very power that might otherwise be directed against the slayer of those victims. Instead of punishing the perpetrator of the slaughter, the Furies would sate their hunger for human suffering by taking part in the slaughter. Mithridates would receive the blessing of the Furies, not their curse.*

Mithridates was an even greater monster than I had imagined. And yet . . . if he could truly harness and direct the terrible rage of the Furies, was he a monster, or something more closely approaching a god? The king turned toward me, saw the awe on my face, and smiled.

"From the look on our face, Zoticus of Zeugma, I think perhaps I've given you the inspiration for a poem."

What sort of poem would that be? I wondered. What epic would celebrate the slaughter of innocents? What words could capture the amazement and horror I felt in the presence of a man who intended to bend the will of the Furies?

He sighed wearily, and suddenly looked not like a god at all, but simply a tired man of middle age at the end of a long day. "You haven't been very helpful to me, poet. Or perhaps you have. This is the first time I've stated out loud what I expect to achieve with the sacrifice in the Grove of the Furies. My mind is clearer than before. Yes, I see my path more plainly now. You may go."

Reflexively, I bowed as I retreated, and saw him wince at the noise made by my creaking joints.

Outside, the chamberlain awaited me in the hallway. Two men were walking toward us. I gasped a little when I recognized Metrodorus of Scepsis, the Rome-Hater. With him was the Roman exile, Rutilius—the Roman without a toga, as I shall always think of him.

The two were deep in conversation. I heard a few scattered words, something to do with "logistics" and "weapons to be used" and—at this my ears pricked up—"the problem of disposing of all those bodies."

Then, quite clearly, I heard Rutilius say, "Burn them, bury them, take them out to sea and dump them overboard! I'm more concerned about what's to be done with all the personal effects—jewelry and coins and such. It mustn't descend to simple looting and chaos—"

Rutilius at last took notice of me, and fell silent. He gave me a quizzical look. Did I look vaguely familiar? Had he seen me across a room on some occasion, back in Rome? I was certain we had never been introduced.

Nor were we to be introduced now. Metrodorus spoke to the chamberlain. "Don't just stand there, man. The king is expecting us. Go in and announce us." He stared at the ceiling for a moment, then turned to look me in the eye.

Without thinking, I spoke his name aloud, as one sometimes does in the presence of a famous man. "Metrodorus the Rome-Hater!"

He smiled rather grimly and nodded. "And who are you?"

"Nobody," I said. "Nobody at all."

The chamberlain showed them into the room and announced them to the king, then withdrew. Without a word he escorted me back the way we had come, all the way out of the palace. I was not even fed dinner with the entertainers and buffoons below stairs.

[Here ends this fragment from the secret diary
of Antipater of Sidon.]

XVI

After the examination by the Magi and Megabyzoi, on the way back to my quarters, again I thought I saw Antipater.

I was following the chamberlain, lost in thought, when I happened to look down a hallway that opened to our left. In the passageway parallel to ours I saw—for only a moment, since they were heading in the opposite direction—another chamberlain escorting a man with a white beard. I was certain this was the man I had seen before. I was almost certain it was Antipater.

I very nearly called his name, but bit my tongue. I tugged at the chamberlain's cloak.

"What are you doing?" he snapped. "Your room is this way."

I gestured with some urgency my desire to go the other way.

"If it's a latrina you need, that's in this direction, as well." He grabbed my arm.

I broke from his grip and headed down the adjoining hall, walking fast. When I reached the spot where I thought I had seen Antipater, I turned and headed in the direction they had been walking. I went for some distance, looking up and down the intersecting hallways. The white-bearded man and his escort were nowhere to be seen.

The chamberlain caught up with me. "If you keep running off like this, I shall assign an armed guard to watch you! What were you thinking, anyway? If only you could speak . . ." He shook his head. "Now, are you going to follow me or not? Your dinner is this way."

Obediently, I followed. Probably it was not Antipater, I told myself. It was only my imagination.

Since she was not merely my slave, but also my voice, Bethesda was allowed to join me in a large room where we dined with a great many others. Some stood about talking. Some sat on chairs or reclined on couches while servants carrying trays passed through the room offering various delicacies. The diners included the juggler Sosipater, who was actually one of the less colorful characters, for in this company eccentric manners and flamboyant dress were the norm. I was reminded of the actors and mimes I had known in Alexandria, and felt quite at ease, especially since I was not required to say anything.

As Gnossipus had promised, the food was excellent. Apparently we were served dishes that had been deemed not quite good enough to serve to the upstairs guests, along with the leftovers they failed to eat. If this was the food deemed second-rate, I could only imagine the quality of the dishes being enjoyed by the king and the more esteemed guests and residents of the royal palace.

There were various kinds of fowl and fish, steamed or broiled or grilled, all served with wonderful sauces. There were a great many vegetables, and ripe summer fruits, including peaches and plums and the much-talked-about cherries, which were indeed delicious.

I heard many languages being spoken, and saw many different sorts of dress. The patchwork kingdom of Mithridates now stretched from the farthermost shores of the Euxine Sea to the Mediterranean, and from the land of the Scythians to the north to that of the Persians to the south. The people around me represented a sampling of the many nationalities now united under the king's sway. Mithridates himself was said to speak two dozen languages. That sort of polyglot virtuosity amazed me, since I often thought that I was still mastering my native tongue and barely fluent in a second. Or as an exasperated Antipater had once said of me, "The boy knows little Latin and less Greek."

Moving about the room, I had a closer look at the dancing girls, who dined in a group and never seemed to stop giggling. Not one of them could compare to Bethesda, I thought. But when Bethesda caught me staring at them, she got the wrong idea, and gave me a withering look. How I longed to tell her—no, show her—what I was truly feeling at that moment. How frustrating it was, that there was no place where we could be alone. Perhaps later, in my quarters, if we waited until both Gnossipus and Damianus were asleep. . . .

A large man brushed by me and spoke so quietly I barely heard him. "Latrina. Bethesda knows and will stay here. Follow me."

With a start, I realized that the speaker was Samson. I turned to see his mane of dark hair and his broad shoulders as he walked toward one of the exits. I glanced at Bethesda, who gave me a barely perceptible nod, then cast a look at Samson perhaps not unlike the looks I had given the dancing girls. Feeling a twinge of jealousy, and annoyed at the interruption to my dinner, I did as Samson asked and followed him at a discreet distance.

He headed in the direction of a latrina that had already been pointed out to me by the chamberlain, but before reaching it he turned about, ascertained that only the two of us were in the hallway, then gestured for me to follow him down a side passage and into a shadowy room. He pulled me inside, then closed the door. There was a simple latch to lock it.

The room was not completely dark. A high window admitted a bit of starlight, so that I could vaguely see the features of his broad face and his plaited beard.

"We're alone," he whispered. "No one will disturb us here. You can speak, but keep your voice low. I'll keep you here as briefly as I can, and I'll ask you to speak as little as possible. From the gossip around the palace, I understand that you were selected to come here because of your muteness. They want you to take part in some sort of ritual."

I didn't speak for a long moment. "Yes," I finally said. "Now you answer a question for me. What are *you* doing in the palace?"

Samson smiled. His white teeth gleamed in the starlight. "Isn't it convenient, that we should both have ended up in the king's household?"

This was no answer at all. "If you won't tell me, I'll have to guess. You're not here as a juggler or an actor. I think you're a diplomat, Samson. Or posing as one."

"A diplomat?"

"An official representative of the Jews of Alexandria."

Even by the faint starlight, I could see the deep furrow that wrinkled his brow. I was right, or right enough to have thrown him off balance.

He made a scoffing noise. "Do you really think a diplomat would be put downstairs to dine with acrobats?"

"Perhaps. If the king wishes to show just how little he values your mission."

The furrow across his brow deepened. "Very well," he finally said. "It's just as you said. My role—one of my roles—here in Ephesus is to speak on behalf of the Jews of Alexandria."

"Because Mithridates seized their treasury on Cos."

"Yes."

"And they want to get it back."

He hesitated. "Some of it. If we can."

"Why would Mithridates give any of it back?"

"There are certain items not of great monetary value, but of . . . sentimental . . . value."

"Here's something I don't understand," I said. "Why on earth would the Jews of Alexandria keep their treasury anywhere but in Egypt, where they could easily lay hands on it?"

"Because of the uncertainty there. I don't have to explain the situation in Alexandria to you, Gordianus."

"But why Cos?"

"We had knowledge of the Cosian treasurers, because of their long-standing service to the Ptolemy family. We felt we could trust them. And we thought that Cos would be a safer place for our gold and silver than Alexandria, where one Ptolemy or another might seize it to pay for troops. Civil wars are expensive."

"All wars are expensive," I said. "Mithridates has to pay his soldiers, too. You thought Alexandria was unsafe, so you moved your treasure to Cos—and promptly lost it to the king."

"Yes, Gordianus, I appreciate the irony."

"How great was this treasure, anyway?"

"The total value was calculated at eight hundred talents."

"Since I've never possessed even a single talent of silver myself, that amount means nothing to me."

"Consider this: the cost of building the Pharos Lighthouse was also said to be eight hundred talents."

I had not only seen the great lighthouse, but had been inside it, more than once, so I had some idea of its size and grandeur. "Yes, that must be a great deal of silver," I said.

"Or put it this way. You know what amphorae are, those big clay jugs used to transport wine?"

"Of course. They have handles on each side, because it takes two men to carry one."

"One talent equals the mass of water required to fill an amphora, or about one cubic foot. Now, imagine eight hundred amphorae all filled with silver."

I whistled. "That would be an awful lot of silver. No wonder the Jews of Alexandria are so pained at the loss."

"I've let you ask a great many questions, Gordianus. Now you answer mine. Have you seen the king?"

"No."

"Or someone else high up in the palace? One of his trusted generals?"

"His queen, actually."

He raised his eyebrows. "Really? The beautiful Monime?"

"It seems the king charged her with making certain arrangements for this ritual that's being planned, the one that I'm to witness but not talk about."

"Not talk about?"

"Because I'm mute, of course. I am the mute witness."

"What sort of ritual?"

"The sacrifice of a virgin. Both the Magi and Megabyzoi are playing roles."

"When is this sacrifice to take place?"

"I'm not sure. Soon, I think. But my role is not yet confirmed."

"No?"

"I'm to go to the Temple of Artemis tomorrow, and beg the goddess to restore my voice. Only if she refuses will I be deemed appropriately mute."

"I see."

"I've half a mind to let the goddess cure me."

"I wouldn't recommend that, considering—"

"I'm only joking, Samson. Of course I won't give myself away, if only for Bethesda's sake. And the sake of . . . Zoticus."

"Ah, yes, your old tutor. Have you spotted him yet?"

I hesitated.

"Well, have you?"

"I'm not sure. Maybe."

"Here in the royal palace?"

"Yes. If it was him, which it probably wasn't."

He nodded. "Have you had any contact with the others you were to watch for? Chaeremon, or Rutilius, or—"

"By Hercules, Samson!" I said, and then laughed, for how often does one say those two names in a single breath? "I've been in Ephesus less than a day, and I've already met the queen."

"Yes, that's something," he said, without much enthusiasm. The queen was not on the list of those I was to watch for. But someone else was. I had been holding back on telling Samson that I had seen Prince Ptolemy, not wanting to give him this information too cheaply. But since he had answered all my questions, I decided to tell him.

"There was someone else, with the queen."

"Yes?"

"The young Ptolemy. The prince who was living on Cos."

"Ah, yes. He was with the queen, you say?"

"They seem to be friends."

"So he wasn't in shackles, or—"

"Nothing of the sort. He and Queen Monime were like . . ." I thought for a moment. "Like brother and sister."

"Did they squabble?"

"Quite the contrary. They were like a brother and sister who like each other perhaps a bit too much." I wasn't sure if young Ptolemy had any sisters, but everyone knew there were many instances of incest in the Ptolemy lineage. Perhaps a sort of fraternal flirtation was the only way he knew to relate to a young woman. As for Monime, finding herself in a court of grizzled warriors and gray-bearded priests, was it any surprise that she was drawn to one of the few people her own age, and the only one close to her in status? Having been born royal instead of ascending to royalty by marriage, Ptolemy was perhaps a sort of role model for the callow queen.

"Their relationship struck me as rather . . . complex," I said.

"Does the king have cause to be jealous?"

"I didn't see them kiss, if that's what you mean."

"Is the queen as beautiful as everyone says?"

"Beautiful? Yes, in the way that certain dangerous animals are beautiful. I didn't desire her, if that's what you mean."

Samson smiled. "I think you're the sort of man who settles on one woman to desire. You're lucky that woman is so beautiful. She's probably missing you now, stuck as she is in a room full of social climbers and actors—and a few minor diplomats, like myself." I heard him unlatch the door. "I'll let you go back to her now. I'll leave first. When

I see the way is clear, I'll knock on the door and you'll know it's safe to come out."

"When will I see you again?"

"You'll see me when you see me," he said, then slipped out the door.

A few moments later I heard a single knock, and stepped into the hallway. Samson was nowhere to be seen. Like Antipater—if it *was* Antipater I had seen—he seemed able to vanish at will.

XVII

"You can't possibly wear that," said the chamberlain, studying me with a glum expression. "Here, put this on."

He handed me a spotless tunic that appeared to be made of the same fine yellow fabric as the robes of the Megabyzoi. I dutifully stripped off my own tunic, though I could see nothing wrong with it, and put on the new one.

He looked me up and down. "I suppose you're presentable. You may wash your face and comb your hair."

From behind the chamberlain two servant girls slipped inside the room, one carrying a basin of water, the other a fine comb that appeared to be made from ivory. While I washed the sleep from my eyes, the girl with the comb set about untangling my hair. She even combed my beard, which hardly needed such attention.

Bethesda also took advantage of the basin of water. But when she took the comb and began running it through her hair, the chamberlain became impatient. "You may bring your slave with you, if you wish. Come along!"

Bethesda and I followed him out the door.

"Good luck!" Gnossipus called after me. The sun was barely up, and he remained in his bed. Damianus, oblivious to the knocking that had awakened me and the noise made by my visitors, continued to snore beneath the coverlet pulled over his head.

At such an early hour, the dim hallways of the palace were very quiet. The chamberlain led us upstairs and into a large courtyard, where the Great Megabyzus and the Grand Magus and a troop of spear-bearers awaited me.

The Great Megabyzus stepped forward. "Well, young man, for better for worse, this is an important day for you. The goddess shall show favor to you, or she shall not. Either way, we will witness her divine will at work."

Three litters appeared, carried by their bearers. Each was set upon blocks, and wooden steps were produced. The first litter, with a canopy of yellow silk festooned with yellow tassels, was for the Great Megabyzus. The compartment was so tall that he had no need to remove his towering headdress. The second litter had an even more elaborate canopy made of many colors. This was for the Grand Magus.

The third and by far plainest litter was much like the simple conveyance that had brought me to the palace the day before. The chamberlain drew back; apparently he was not to accompany me. As I mounted the steps, I turned back to take Bethesda's hand. At this, the chamberlain stepped forward, shaking his head.

Bethesda looked at me, then at the chamberlain. "My master wishes for me to accompany him in the litter."

"That would be most irregular," said the chamberlain.

"My master is quite—*insistent!*" she said with a small gasp, for an instant later I was inside the litter, pulling her after me. The compartment was well padded with cushions, so that she tumbled next to me without mishap.

"Most irregular!" the chamberlain repeated, but too late, for the bearers, falling behind the other litters and eager to catch up, were already off at a trot.

Downhill we went, with a troop of spear-bearers leading the way, through the neighborhood of fine houses and gardens that clung to the hillside below the palace of Mithridates. The fresh morning air and the sensation of movement made me fully awake. On a sudden impulse I set about closing the curtains around us.

"But Master, we can't see out," said Bethesda, who was clearly enjoying the novelty of being carried aloft in a litter.

"Nor can anyone see in," I said, and covered her mouth with a kiss.

How I had longed to be alone with her, ever since the moment we arrived in Ephesus. At last I was able to hold her and to touch her. I ran my fingers through her black hair, so straight and fine it had no need of a comb. When I buried my face in it, all I could see through barely open eyelids were bright spangles of crimson and purple and many other colors, captured by her lustrous hair where bits of filtered sunlight shone through the curtains.

I was ready and eager to couple with her, and I moved to do so.

"But your yellow tunic," she whispered. "We mustn't—"

I pulled it up to my shoulders, well out of the way, while she released me from the confining loincloth.

Our lovemaking was slow and sensual, not acrobatic. Constrained as it was, the telltale to-and-fro motion of two people joining as one must nonetheless have been sensed by the litter-bearers. I thought I heard snatches of laughter from outside, sounding distant and faint beyond the rush of Bethesda's quickened breath in my ear and the pounding of my own heart. The laughter was without malice, light and carefree. The litter-bearers were also exhilarated by the fresh morning air.

The moment of bliss arrived. In the same instant, Bethesda stiffened in my arms. With one hand I held her tight. With the other I covered her mouth. I cried out myself, and felt her hand on my mouth. Then it was all I could do to keep from laughing and crying out at the same time, at the exquisite absurdity of two mortals attempting to stifle the sounds of their mutual ecstasy.

There followed a long moment when I seemed to be cut adrift from the world around me. Slanting sunlight shone vaguely through the curtains, illuminating motes of dust suspended in midair. The air itself seemed heavy, like a blanket pressing me down. My breathing slowed.

My arms dropped away from Bethesda, and hers from me. It might have been the cherubs of Venus who set about rearranging my clothing and smoothing my hair, so strange to me were the motions of my own hands.

The sensation of forward movement abruptly ended. The litter hovered for a moment, then settled. From outside I heard the sighs of the bearers as they were relieved of their burden. Another moment passed, and then someone outside the compartment drew the curtains back. It was the Great Megabyzus, silhouetted by the rising sun but easily recognized by the shape of his headdress.

"By Artemis, did you fall asleep, young man? I should think you would be wide awake with excitement. You have an appointment with the goddess! Stir yourself, and step out of the litter. We shall walk the rest of the way."

With shaky arms and wobbly legs I managed to lift myself and descend the short flight of steps. I helped Bethesda descend. Though her hair was a mess, her breathing was steady and her expression was composed, almost sphinxlike. I did my best to emulate her. Standing there like wooden statues, what a contrast we must have made to the grinning litter-bearers around us.

If the Great Megabyzus noticed anything improper, he did not show it. "Your slave shall walk at the end of the procession, behind the spear-bearers. You will walk at the head, between the Grand Magus and myself, with the spear-bearers following. Come, let's get organized."

We were on a very wide street just inside the high city wall, next to a massive gate, the doors of which were closed. I recognized the location, having passed this way on my previous visit to Ephesus, when Antipater and I took part in a holiday procession. The street was the Sacred Way, one of the grandest in Ephesus, lined with many fine buildings and shops of every sort. We had arrived at the very moment when the gates were to be opened, and as I watched, a group of soldiers set about unbarring the tall bronze doors and pushing them open. All around us, shops began to open and vendors set up their goods.

Suddenly, from the gate, I heard the sound of raised voices, and turned to see a scuffle. A man from outside pushed his way past the guards and ran directly before us, heading for the nearest shop, where the vendor started back at the sight of him. The man's face was gaunt and haggard, his eyes haunted. The shopkeeper yelled and waved his arms, shooing the man away from the vegetables and fruits on display.

So powerful was the impression made on me by the man's desperate face that it took me a moment to realize that he was wearing a toga—a filthy, ragged garment, but a toga nonetheless.

"But I have money!" he shouted, clutching a small bag in his fist.

"Your Roman coins are no good here," said the shopkeeper. "Ephesus mints its own coins now."

"Silver is silver," said the man in the toga. "Take what I have left and give me some food!"

"Buy your goods from the shops outside the gates, like the rest of your lot," said the shopkeeper.

"But those shops have nothing left," pleaded the Roman. "I have a wife and child. They're hungry. They must have food. I beg you!"

A small crowd began to gather. Most were women with baskets, out to do their early shopping.

"Get along with you, filthy Roman!" shouted a woman. "Can't you see you're not wanted here?"

A man stepped forward. "Go back outside the gate! We don't want Roman scum inside the city!"

Others began to jeer and shake their fists. Something hurtled through the air and struck the Roman's shoulder. He cried out and gripped the place where he had been struck. The object, a large onion, tumbled across the paving stones.

"You want food, do you?" shouted someone. "We'll give you more of that, if you like!"

The crowd grew. Some of the onlookers had baskets already full of food. Others ran to nearby shops in search of projectiles. They began pelting the Roman with radishes and turnips. A plum was thrown so hard it exploded, spattering his toga with juice. Another plum struck his forehead and sent him staggering backward. He tried to wipe the pulp from his face, but only smeared it. It looked like gore from some terrible wound.

All of this took place in front of the spear-bearers from the palace, who did nothing to stop it. Nor did the guards at the gate take action. They stood outside the guard post, smirking and laughing.

How I longed to have a voice at that moment, but what could I have said? I trembled with anger, humiliated that I could do nothing to help the man.

"Stop this! Stop this at once!"

The deep, commanding voice was that of a man used to being obeyed. I realized it was the Great Megabyzus, who strode past the spear-bearers and confronted the crowd. They fell back before him.

A man armed with a fistful of radishes dared to step forward. "But Your Eminence, this man is a Roman. A dirty, toga-wearing Roman! He has no business—"

"Be silent!" shouted the priest.

Shamefaced, the man with the radishes stepped back into the crowd.

The Great Megabyzus strode into the crowd and began to pluck items from food baskets. When he could carry no more, he moved toward the Roman, walking slowly and rigidly erect, so as not to disturb his towering headdress.

"Take this," he said to the Roman, who looked dazed for a moment, then made a basket with the folds of his toga and eagerly accepted the jumble of food from the Great Megabyzus.

"Now go back to the place you came from, and don't enter the city again," said the Great Megabyzus. "The Temple of Artemis is your only sanctuary now."

"But there's no food left," pleaded the Roman. "How are we to—"

"Go!"

The Roman lowered his head. Clutching the food, he turned and scurried past the guards at the gate. They stepped back to let him pass, but one of them spat in his face, then laughed when the Roman uttered a last, plaintive whimper before disappearing.

The Great Megabyzus rejoined the retinue. "The interruption is over," he said, addressing the spear-bearers. "You will pay attention to me now. We are about to step through the gate. We will proceed at a normal pace along the Sacred Way to the Temple of Artemis. There, at the great altar in front of the temple steps, a group of Megabyzoi will be awaiting us, with the sacrifice. After the lamb is slaughtered, and a portion has been consecrated to the goddess, the meat will be roasted on the fire, and a piece will be given to every man here. But before that happens, every man here will join in a prayer to the goddess on behalf of this suppliant." He gestured to me. "He is Agathon of Alexandria, and he comes to Artemis seeking to have restored to him the voice he was born with, but which he possesses no longer. We may anticipate . . ."

He paused, looking past the spear-bearers to the place where he had confronted the mob. Most of the angry Ephesians had dispersed. Only a few still lingered, going about their normal business.

"We may anticipate a certain amount of . . . disturbance . . . from those who have sought refuge at the temple. The authority of the Megabyzoi should be enough to discourage any serious hindrance. But if anything untoward should occur, you are armed and authorized, at my command only, to use your weapons. Does every man here understand?"

"Yes, Your Eminence," said the men behind me.

A few moments later, with the Great Megabyzus on one side of me and the Grand Magus on the other, and with the spear-bearers behind us, and Bethesda somewhere behind them, we set out for the temple.

Beyond the gate, there were few buildings and few people. The land tilted gently downward, so that walking was easy. Ahead of us, looming majestically, was the temple. From such a distance, the people swarming around the temple looked very small. Ahead of us on the road I could see the Roman, walking quickly with a crooked gait as he tried not to spill any of the precious food wrapped in the folds of his toga.

The Grand Magus and the Great Megabyzus began to converse in low voices, speaking just behind my head, as if I weren't there.

"Why in Hades did you help the Roman?" asked the Grand Magus.

"Hades has nothing to do with it. I am a priest of Artemis, and the Romans have sought sanctuary in her temple."

"That Roman was not in the temple. He dared to stray into the city, where his kind are not wanted. The people had every right to show their displeasure."

"Displeasure? They'd have been pelting him with stones next. There would have been bloodshed."

"Bloodshed? The Romans have caused enough of that over the years! People want to see if a Roman can bleed like the rest of us."

"They bleed," the Great Megabyzus assured him.

"They also need to eat, it seems," said the Grand Magus. "Stopping the violence was one thing, but you actually gave the man food."

"He has a wife and child."

"Feeding them only postpones the inevitable. It's a waste of food."

"Hunger makes people desperate."

"Hunger makes them weak," said the Grand Magus. "And the weaker they are, the easier . . ."

As his voice trailed off, I felt his gaze on me. He seemed suddenly to remember that while I might be mute I was not deaf. He looked straight ahead, and neither of them said another word as we drew nearer to the temple and the crowded sacred precinct around it.

The sheer magnificence of the structure contrasted sharply with the squalid encampment of makeshift shelters and tents, populated by a throng of miserable-looking people. Seeing them from a distance, I had thought they numbered in the hundreds. Now I realized their number must be much greater than that.

In the shallow valley beyond the city, surrounding the Temple of Artemis, there were thousands of men, women, and children desperate for food and shelter. And we were about to eat a lamb while they watched.

XVIII

First, a great deal of incense was burned.

Incense is said to be pleasing to the gods. It summons their attention, just as a whiff of a perfume piques the attention of mortals.

Incense can also mask other smells, and for my mortal nostrils it gave much-needed distraction from the powerful odors that inevitably follow on the gathering of a large number of people, especially if they vastly outstrip the facilities for washing themselves or disposing of their bodily wastes. While we were still a considerable distance from the temple, I got my first whiff of the smell emanating from the restless, wretched crowd surrounding the Temple of Artemis—a combination of urine, excrement, and unwashed humanity. The closer we came to the temple, the more powerful the smell grew, until I thought it might gag me.

But, once immersed in such a smell, little by little one becomes used to it. I remembered something my father had said: "However horrible, no odor ever killed a man." It also helped that I found myself standing before a broad stone altar, with massive braziers to either side of me belching clouds of smoking incense. The altar was on a raised platform, several steps above the crowd.

When I had last attended a sacrifice in this spot, it had been a day of celebration, and a huge crowd of visitors from all over the world had paraded out of the city to the sound of music and laughter. Cattle, sheep, goats, and oxen too numerous to count had been consecrated to the goddess and slaughtered, after which the entire crowd was treated to the roasted remains, along with a great deal of wine.

What a starkly different experience this was. Our procession consisted only of myself and the two holy men and a troop of spear-bearers to protect us. (And Bethesda, of course, trailing behind. What did she make of this peculiar experience? This was her introduction to one of the world's greatest marvels, the Temple of Artemis, and I feared any wonderment she felt would be forever tainted by the circumstances.)

The shallow valley surrounding the temple is a large open space with scattered trees for shade, grassy in places and trampled to bare dirt in others, suitable for accommodating the huge crowds that attend the festivals at Ephesus. On this occasion the crowd consisted of sullen-looking Roman refugees. They kept their distance as we paraded before them and congregated at the altar. They stared at us with blank expressions. I found it unnerving to look at them. I averted my eyes.

At the great altar a group of Megabyzoi awaited us. They had already washed the altar and were busy stoking the incense braziers and the roasting pyre. The lamb was in a small enclosure nearby, out of sight, but occasionally it bleated, sending a murmur of excitement through the crowd of hungry refugees.

Standing on the raised platform before the altar, I looked over the heads of the crowd to the steps that led up to the colonnaded porch of the temple. Above the porch, the soaring columns supported a triangular pediment. In all the other Greek temples I had seen, the pediment was decorated with statues that filled the entire space, but the Temple of Artemis was different. At its center, where the triangle was highest, the pediment had a circular window, and standing inside this window, as if looking down on those of us gathered at the altar, was an ancient wooden statue of the goddess. The statue was larger than life-size and brightly painted. Standing stiffly upright, the goddess wore a mural crown and a necklace of acorns. A mass of pendulous, gourd-shaped protrusions hung from her upper body, said by some to be multiple breasts and by others to be the testicles of bulls. From this circular window high above the temple porch, the goddess would be able to see everything that took place at the altar.

The hungry, watching crowd unnerved me. So did the watching Artemis. It occurred to me that I was about to be the instigator of a flagrantly impious act, fraudulently calling upon an Olympian goddess to cure a nonexistent ailment. What if the goddess took offense, and by way of revenge forced me to speak? I would be known at once for a Roman. Would I be cast into the crowd of refugees, forced to join them? Or would I face a swifter, more terrible punishment?

If I were killed on the spot, what would become of Bethesda? I looked about, wondering where she had gone, and realized she was standing at the front of the crowd before the raised platform, directly before me. The altar blocked my view; I could see only her face, peering up at me. I tried to give her a smile of reassurance, but whatever crooked semblance of a smile I manage lacked conviction. She did not smile back.

Standing beside me, the Great Megabyzus raised his arms and began an invocation to Artemis, reciting her many names and attributes and acknowledging the many blessings she had bestowed on Ephesus. As he droned on, I looked at Bethesda, and then at the faces in the crowd around her. Who were all these people? The Roman citizens were easily picked out by their togas. I presumed that most of these men were, or had been, merchants or moneymen or managers. With them were their wives and children, including teenaged sons too young to wear the toga, and household slaves. There were other men not dressed in togas, but who did not have the look of slaves. They had to be so-called Rome-lovers who had been driven out of the city along with the Romans.

My gaze wandered to one far edge of the crowd, beyond the temple grounds, where I saw a row of laborers with shovels. They appeared to be digging a very long trench, with a waist-high ridge of excavated dirt alongside it. The reason for all this digging puzzled me for a moment, until it occurred to me that the trench must be intended to give the sanctuary-seekers a place to bury their waste. That would go a long way to relieving the stench that surrounded the temple, which must surely have been offensive to the goddess herself.

The Great Megabyzus suddenly fell silent. Two priests took hold of my arms and pulled me closer to the altar. For a heart-stopping moment, I thought they were going to throw me upon it, but they only wanted me to stand closer to the sacrifice, where Artemis could see me more clearly. The Great Megabyzus was fitted with a sort of apron, to protect his yellow clothing from the blood—for in one hand he now held a slaughtering knife and in the other a small ax, the sacred tools he would use to cut the lamb's throat, skin the creature, and then dismember it.

"Great Artemis of Ephesus!" he shouted, so loudly that I gave a start. "We pray that you will restore the voice of this mortal who has been struck mute! Let the tongue of Agathon of Alexandria speak again, so that he may utter endless paeans of thanksgiving in your honor!"

The bound lamb was brought forth and placed on the altar. At the sight of it, the crowd released a groan the likes of which I had never heard before. It seemed to come from nowhere and everywhere, hardly human but expressing endless human misery. If no smell, however noxious, could kill a man, then surely no sound could kill a man, either. But were there sounds that could drive a man mad? This one, if it continued much longer, might be one of them.

As if to counter the horrible groan, some of the Megabyzoi began to ululate and to shake rattles and tambourines. This frantic music combined with the miserable noise of the crowd to create a discord that set my teeth on edge.

With a single motion, the Great Megabyzus cut the lamb's throat. Blood spurted from the gaping wound, but not a drop of it struck the Great Megabyzus. With sure, steady motions—clearly, he had much experience at this sort of butchery—he proceeded to skin the carcass, and then to slice it open, removing some organs and leaving others in place. The altar was tilted slightly toward him, so that the blood drained into a channel and then into drains on either side. A portion of the sacrifice was offered to Artemis—the heart, perhaps, for it was oozing with blood and still seemed to be pulsing—and was then cast onto the pyre. Smoke alone is said to be the only nourishment the gods need. The grosser, material parts of the animal—the viscera and the flesh— are suitable sustenance for mankind, but not for immortals.

Various parts of the animal were thrown on the pyre. At the smell of roasting flesh, the murmur of the crowd expressed an almost unbearable anguish. The rattles and tambourines of the ululating Megabyzoi grew louder and more frenzied.

"Is some of the meat for us?" cried one man.

"It must be!" cried another.

"But there's only one lamb. One lamb can't feed us all!"

"Maybe there are more animals to be sacrificed. There must be. They can't let us starve!"

The throng before the altar became more compact and crowded, as those on the edge were drawn by the wild music and the commotion and the smell of charred flesh. Bethesda was jostled about. Suddenly I lost sight of her.

The Great Megabyzus set aside his knife and ax. His fellow priests helped him remove his apron, then held a basin of water so that he could wash his hands. He stepped toward me with open arms and startled me with an unexpected embrace.

He whispered in my ear, "May Artemis bless you! May the goddess heal you and make you whole! There is nothing we can do for all these poor wretches—except, perhaps, show them a miracle. Do you understand? If Artemis chooses to cure you, might she not show mercy to these wretches and somehow save them from their suffering? Your cure could give them hope, if nothing else."

His words, and the mercy he had shown to the Roman at the gate, confused me. Did he not hate the Romans as much as every other Ephesian? He stepped back and looked into my eyes, as if he expected the miracle to occur at that very moment. Without thinking I opened my mouth, and I saw his eyes light up.

I bit my lips and shut my mouth. The Great Megabyzus continued to stare at me for a long moment, then took my arm and led me to the roasting pyre.

"You must eat the first portion," he said. He picked up his knife and ax. He chopped a piece of meat, deftly carved it, spitted a piece on the tip of the knife and offered it to me. I took the smoking morsel between my teeth. I felt the ooze of the charred fat on my lips and tasted the bloody flesh on my tongue. From the corner of my eye, I thought I saw the distant statue of Artemis move—but when I turned to look, she stood as stiff as ever in the circular opening of the pediment.

I looked down at the crowd, trying to spot Bethesda. The sea of faces was now in constant motion. Like waves, the crowd surged against the edge of the raised platform. The spear-bearers formed a cordon around the perimeter of the platform, tilting their spears toward the surrounding crowd to hold them back.

The Megabyzoi were now eating their share of the sacrifice, looking anxiously over their shoulders. As I watched them hurriedly chew and champ their jaws and wipe juice from their chins, it struck me that there is no dignified way for a mortal to ingest his food. When others eat, we politely look elsewhere—anywhere but at their mouths, as if the organ were doing something obscene. No wonder the gods prefer to live on smoke!

The spear-bearers were given a share, which they ate in turns, some eating while the others held the crowd in check. The sound of the crowd grew to a roar, drowning out the music of the rattles and tambourines.

The Grand Magus, with a look of alarm on his face, drew close to the Great Megabyzus. Above the noise all around us, I strained to hear what he said.

"You obviously underestimated the reaction of the Roman rabble. We should have brought more men, or else cleared the crowd from the temple grounds beforehand."

"These people came to the temple seeking sanctuary," said the Great Megabyzus. "There is a sacred obligation—"

"Your first obligation is to keep us alive!" snapped the Grand Magus. "I suggest we retreat at once."

The Great Megabyzus looked at the crowd, then at me.

The Grand Magus grabbed his arm. "If you're still waiting for this mute to speak—"

"He must sleep overnight in the temple," said the Great Megabyzus. "I never expected him to speak at once. Suppliants often make prayers and sacrifices first, then spend the night in the sanctuary, awaiting the goddess to visit them in a dream."

"Do you expect us all to stay here overnight?" The Grand Magus looked outraged.

"Of course not. Only the suppliant must do so."

"What's to keep him from wandering off?"

"One of the Megabyzoi will watch over him, as is customary."

"Better to leave some of these spear-bearers."

The Great Megabyzus shook his head. "No man is allowed to carry a weapon into the temple."

"Then have them stand guard outside the door!"

"That would only provoke the crowd. What's to keep these desperate people from overwhelming any guards we leave here, and taking their weapons? No, I shall assign a single priest to accompany the suppliant, and sleep beside him inside the temple. Tomorrow morning, if Agathon of Alexandria can speak again, we shall know that he is not, and never was, the man we need for the ritual. On the other hand, if he's still mute—"

"But either way, he may wander off!"

The Great Megabyzus looked at me shrewdly. "Not if we hold something dear to him."

The Grand Magus pursed his lips. "What manner of surety could we take from him? You've seen the man naked. The only jewelry on his person is that lion's tooth around his neck."

"He has a piece of property he values much more than that."

The Grand Magus looked puzzled, but with a sinking heart I perceived the Great Megabyzus's intent. I looked at the crowd again, searching for Bethesda, and saw her nowhere. She seemed to have vanished. Then I saw that the Great Megabyzus was looking at someone behind me. Bethesda stood on the platform, only a few steps away from me. She had worked her way through the surging crowd, and the spear-bearers had allowed her through the cordon. My heart leaped at the sight of her—and then grew cold when the Great Megabyzus spoke.

"We'll hold the girl for surety," he said, nodding toward Bethesda.

"A slave girl?" The Grand Magus scoffed. "That's no kind of surety!"

"I think, Grand Magus, you have not been very observant. If you doubt the value Agathon places on the slave, just look at his face."

The Grand Magus squinted at me, then at Bethesda. "Ah, yes. I see what you mean. Very well, if the mute must be left to sleep in the sanc-tuary of the goddess, let one of your priests accompany him, to see that all is done properly, while we hold his slave as surety."

The Great Megabyzus nodded. "And in the morning, whatever the goddess decides, the priest will escort Agathon back to the palace—"

"Yes, yes! The matter is settled. Now, let's get out of here. Quickly, before this crowd of Roman filth turns into a howling mob!"

The Megabyzoi set about extinguishing the incense braziers and the roasting pyre.

"They're putting out the fires!" someone in the crowd yelled. "Where is the meat for us? Is there no more meat?"

"Impossible!" cried a woman. "Our children must have food. If not meat, then bread. Anything, to fill their bellies. Priests of Artemis, we beg you! Would the goddess see children starve to death on her door-step?"

I saw the Great Megabyzus cringe, but the Grand Magus only sneered.

One of the priests approached, bearing a silver platter with a piece of meat on it. "Great Megabyzus, a single shank of the lamb remains. Mustn't the entire sacrifice be consumed before we leave the altar?"

Before the Great Megabyzus could answer, the Grand Magus took hold of the shank, raised his arm, and threw the smoking meat as far as he could into the crowd. A mad scramble erupted where the shank landed. People screamed and shoved, trying to get hold of the food.

The Grand Magus smiled. "There, that should throw the Roman dogs off the scent while we make our exit!"

The spear-bearers formed a cordon around the priests and began to force a path through the crowd. In their midst was Bethesda, who looked over her shoulder at me with a stricken expression.

I moved to follow, but the cordon closed behind her, shutting me out.

"Your slave will be well looked after," said a voice in my ear. The tone was calm, almost soothing, in sharp contrast to the uproar all around me. I felt a touch on my arm, and turned to see one of the Megabyzoi—surely the youngest among them, for he looked hardly older than myself.

"My name is Zeuxidemus," he said, again in that impossibly calm voice. "The Great Megabyzus instructed me to look after you. I think we should get inside the temple as soon as possible, don't you?"

Walking slowly and with measured steps, he escorted me away from the altar, off the platform, and into the crowd, which seemed to fall back from us, as if his very presence acted as a shield. He even made a joke of it, gesturing to his clothing and mine and whispering in my ear, "You'd think these Romans had an aversion to the color yellow!"

We walked toward the temple and up the steps. The sheer magnificence of the towering columns and the elaborately ornamented pediment above us overwhelmed me for a moment, making me oblivious of the surging crowd behind us.

"I hope you had enough of the lamb," said Zeuxidemus, with a smile. "As you may have gathered, there is no food to be had, inside the temple or out. But no matter. It's customary for a suppliant to fast once he enters the temple. All the better to prepare you for the visitation of the goddess tonight."

XIX

Sleep was far off, for there were several hours of daylight left. But I had no trouble occupying myself. The Temple of Artemis is a World Wonder not only for what is outside, but also for the splendors it holds within.

Ephesus has long been one of the richest cities in the world, and the Temple of Artemis is its treasure house. Not only does every Ephesian, rich and poor, contribute to the temple's upkeep, but people come from all over the world to worship Ephesian Artemis and ask for her blessing, and they leave behind whatever donations they can afford. This worship, with an annual cycle of massive festivals and celebrations, has been going on for hundreds of years, during which time the Temple of Artemis has become a repository of fabulous wealth.

I had been inside the temple once before, and on that occasion had seen only a fraction of its wonders. The interior space is one of the grandest on earth, with a floor of gleaming marble in a dizzying array of patterns, equally magnificent marble walls, and, far above our heads, a ceiling of massive cedar beams, alternately painted yellow, blue, and red, outlined with gold and studded with gold ornaments. This breathtaking space is decorated with many of the most renowned statues and paintings in the world, including perhaps the most famous painting of

all, the gigantic portrait of Alexander the Great by Apelles. By some astonishing illusion, the conqueror's hand and the thunderbolt he grips
appear to come out of the wall and hover above one's head. It is an unforgettable sight.

But there were many other works of art in the temple that I had seen
only briefly or not at all on my previous visit. Zeuxidemus acted as my
guide, explaining where the paintings and statues had come from, or
recounting the stories they portrayed. He was clearly very proud of the
temple, and what he had to say was actually quite interesting. I knew
already the tale of Actaeon, the young hunter who accidentally gazed
upon Artemis bathing naked in a stream, but Zeuxidemus's version was
nonetheless riveting; several of the paintings depicted this event, as well
as the hunter's subsequent punishment—his transformation by Artemis into a stag, after which the hunter was torn apart by his own frenzied hounds.

I learned a great deal that day from Zeuxidemus, but since I could
not ask questions and the two of us could not converse, he eventually
ran out of things to say, and after that he let me wander about on my
own while he maintained a polite but watchful distance.

As I moved from statue to statue, and painting to painting, I allowed
myself to become lost in a sort of reverie, bemused by images of gods
and heroes, and scenes from legend or history depicting love and deceit, honor and villainy, serenity and horror.

This reverie was frequently broken, however, for there were regular
worshippers inside the temple, mostly women being led in various rituals by the so-called hierodules, the virgin acolytes of Artemis who serve
under the Great Megabyzus. These rituals involved a great deal of incense, chanting, and ecstatic dancing. At any given moment, a ritual
of some sort was always taking place in some part of the temple.

There were also a great many sanctuary-seekers inside the temple.
Some slept huddled against the walls. Others sat on the floor, staring
into space, or wandered about in a sort of daze. A great many were gathered in one corner of the building, where a statue of Artemis in her
Roman guise of Diana stood on a high pedestal. This marble statue,

painted in lifelike colors, had been a gift from the Senate and People of Rome, installed during the tenure of one of the first Roman governors at Pergamon.

How different this Artemis was from the ancient wooden statue that gazed out from the pediment! This goddess looked very young, and wore a short, sleeveless tunic, suitable for a huntress who needed bare legs for running and bare arms for wielding her bow. Fitted over her shoulders was a fawnskin cape and a quiver full of arrows. The only attribute she seemed to have in common with her Ephesian counterpart was a necklace of gilded acorns.

Before this Roman Diana a great many Roman refugees, more women than men, prostrated themselves in worship. Some prayed softly but others more loudly, wailing and begging the goddess to deliver them from their misery and uncertainty. Some worshippers came and went, praying only briefly, but others bowed over and over again, or lay prostrate on the floor.

As shadows thickened, more lamps were lit. The grand interior became even more magical. The gleaming marble floors, reflecting the light of the lamps, looked like the placid surface of a vast lake. Above our heads, the spaces between the cedar beams grew very dark, and the gold ornaments glittered like a multitude of distant suns. The paintings could be seen only dimly, which increased their mystery, and the statues, lit by flickering lamps, seemed to draw breath and come to life.

I was gazing up at just such a statue—a broad-chested Apollo who seemed to look back at me with emerald eyes, on the verge of speaking— when Zeuxidemus spoke in my ear.

"Are you ready to meet the goddess, Agathon of Alexandria?"

I dutifully nodded, and he led me to a hidden doorway behind the pedestal of one of the larger statues, not far from the temple's entrance. We stepped into a small room and he closed the door behind us. Taking a torch from a sconce in the wall, Zeuxidemus indicated that I should ascend a broad, winding stairway while he followed. By the light of his torch the steps ahead of me were visible, but I saw only darkness above, and wondered where the stairway could possibly lead.

Up and up we went, until at last I stepped into a room that seemed to have some opening to the outside, for I faintly heard the sound of the Roman throng and felt a slight breeze on my face. Above and before me I saw a silhouette framed by a round window, and realized I was in the pediment of the temple, standing directly behind the ten-foot-tall wooden statue of Ephesian Artemis that stood at the round opening.

Even though the goddess's back was to me—or so I thought—I felt an uncanny shiver at being so close to her. Then Zeuxidemus followed me into the room, and the light of his torch revealed that Artemis was not looking out the round window, but had somehow turned around and was facing me! The sight of her was so strange—her huge size and stiff posture, her staring eyes, the pendulous orbs clustered like multiple breasts—that I nearly cried out.

For a terrifying moment, I was convinced that Artemis had turned around just before I entered the room, as a mortal would, alerted by the sound of approaching steps and the flicker of torchlight. Then I realized that the statue might have been turned around at any time since I had seen it earlier that day, from the altar outside. Perhaps Zeuxidemus himself had done it, using some clever mechanical device such as one sees in the theater, when gods appear from the sky or out of the earth.

"Do you see, Agathon? The goddess greets you. She welcomes you to her sacred chamber. She invites you to sleep at her feet. Do you see?" He gestured to the base of the statue's pedestal, where pillows and coverlets had been strewn on the floor. "I will sleep nearby. Shall we have a cup of wine, to help us sleep?"

Zeuxidemus fitted his torch into a sconce by the doorway. He removed his headdress and placed it on a table next to the statue's pedestal. I had to smile at the state of his chestnut-colored hair, all mussed and tangled and sweaty—"headdress hair," my father had once called it, noting that the authority imbued on its wearer by an ornamental helmet or headdress was inversely proportional to the look of dishevelment revealed when the headdress comes off. Such was the case with Zeuxidemus.

On the same table where he placed his headdress sat a silver pitcher and two silver cups. With his back to me, he poured a cup of wine for each of us, then stepped to one side and invited me to join him.

I was not so unnerved by the presence of the goddess, nor so amused by the state of the young Megabyzoi's hair, that I forgot something else my father had said: *When you are offered one cup, take the other.* This may seem the stuff of Roman comedy—the poisoned cup and the switching thereof—but the lesson holds, nonetheless. Proof of its wisdom came in that high room, with the goddess looking on.

When I joined him at the small table, Zeuxidemus handed me one of the cups. Pretending to hear some alarming noise from outside, I put the cup down and stepped toward the round window. Just as I had intended, the young priest followed me. We stood beside the goddess for a moment, staying back from the opening so that we should not be easily seen, standing on tiptoes to peer out at the restless crowd that continued to mill about the altar, even though darkness had fallen.

"What did you hear?" asked Zeuxidemus.

I bit my lip and feigned concern, then finally shrugged and shook my head. I returned to the table. Zeuxidemus did not follow at once, but lingered for a moment at the window, peering out and wondering what I might have heard. When he joined me at the table, the pitcher and the cups were just where we had left them—or so it appeared. I picked up the nearest cup—presumably the one I had recently put down—and politely waited for my host to pick up the other. As he did so, the faintest shadow of doubt creased his forehead. He scrutinized me for a moment, detected no guile on my face, and raised his cup.

"May Artemis bring you the gift you most desire. Happy dreams, Agathon of Alexandria."

I nodded to acknowledge his blessing, and brought the cup to my lips. Zeuxidemus did likewise. We drank.

I had switched the cups, and Zeuxidemus was none the wiser. My pantomime had been flawless, and the switching of the cups had been executed quickly and without a sound. My father would have been proud of me.

The wine was much finer than the cheap stuff I was used to. The Megabyzoi owned their own vineyards—yet another source of revenue for the Temple of Artemis—and they reserved the very finest of their vintages for those who most deserved such pleasure, including themselves. After all the many smells I had endured that day, the bouquet of that wine was the best possible tonic. I would have been satisfied just to swirl it in the cup and relish the smell. But even finer than the bouquet was the taste, very refined and complex, quite unlike any other wine I had ever tasted. After I swallowed, almost at once I felt a sweet sense of euphoria. Had I been drugged, after all? No, it was only that I had eaten nothing for hours. My empty, growling stomach eagerly absorbed the wine, and almost at once I felt the glow of inebriation.

So did Zeuxidemus, apparently, for his cheeks turned red and the smile on his face was quite giddy. I decided he must be even younger than me, so boyish did he look with his hopelessly unruly hair. He put down his empty cup and reached for the pitcher.

"Shall we drink the rest? A pity I have no food to offer you. The wine is risky enough. If those Romans knew we had it, they'd break down the door and run up those stairs to take it."

As he spoke, his speech became more and more slurred, until I could hardly understand him. He swayed a bit as he poured the wine, then offered the brimming cup to me.

I showed him that I already had a cup.

"But Agathon, you haven't even finished yours! You must. Drink up! It's very, very good for dreaming. They all say so . . . the next morning."

He put down the brimming cup and staggered toward the pile of pillows at the feet of the goddess.

"I must lie down . . . for just a moment," he said, clutching the pillows and closing his eyes.

He lay very still. His breathing grew slow and steady. He began to quietly snore.

I took a deep breath. I experienced an odd exhilaration. At first I attributed it to the wine, then realized that it was something else. For the first time in many days, I was *alone*—not by myself, strictly speaking, but with the only other person present completely unconscious. Alone! How luxurious that suddenly felt—to be unseen, unheard, unwatched by anyone. I could stop pretending to be something I was not. I could even speak out loud if I wanted to, and in Latin, not Greek. What would I have said?

I am not mute! I am not Agathon of Alexandria! I am Gordianus, a citizen of Rome, son of the Finder, pupil of Antipater of Sidon. . . .

I very nearly spoke these thoughts aloud, simply to hear my own voice, but something held me back.

I was *not* alone in that room.

Was it the presence of Artemis I felt? I thought not. Was it the presence of Zeuxidemus, now snoring more loudly than before? No.

Someone else was in the room.

The room was shaped like the pediment, with a high, pointed ceiling that tilted down to either side and ended in dark shadows. Stare as I might, I could see no one, but I became convinced that someone stood in the darkness at the far side of the room. In other circumstances I would have called out and told the other to show himself. But I dared not speak. I could only watch and wait. I held my breath, the better to listen. A hubbub came from the window, the sounds of the sleepless crowd outside—children crying, mothers shushing, men grumbling.

The torch in the sconce was burning low. It would not be long before it went out, and the room would be almost entirely dark, lit only in places by the faint starlight that came from the window. In such darkness, I would be at a great disadvantage—slightly drunk, unable to see, unsure just who or how many were in the room with me, afraid even to cry out. The wisest thing might be to grab the torch by the doorway and run down the steps, hoping that whoever stood in the shadows would not catch up with me, and that I would not trip and break my neck.

I drew a deep breath, stiffened my shoulders, and was about to bolt when a voice spoke from the shadows.

XX

"That was clever of you, to switch the cups. Adroitly done. But you're lucky the priest is so young and unsuspecting, or else he might have spotted the change, and switched them back."

From the shadows, a figure stepped forward. The two of us stood staring at each other, until Samson laughed.

"Go ahead and speak, Gordianus. We're perfectly alone up here—except for your friend Zeuxidemus, who won't stop snoring until daybreak."

I had to cough and clear my throat before I could speak. Even so, I sounded hoarse. "Then I was right, that he put something into my cup?"

"From where I was standing, I saw him do it. He produced a small bottle from his sleeve and poured the contents into the cup intended for you. But you shouldn't take it personally. His intention was pious. He meant you no harm."

"No harm? He tried to drug me!"

"It's not a poison, merely a sleeping potion. So far as I've been able to determine, every pilgrim who's privileged to sleep in this room, at the feet of that statue, is given the same potion. It produces a long, deep sleep—and dreams. There! Do you see how Zeuxidemus kicks his feet and whimpers? For all we know, he's seeing Artemis at this very moment. If you'd drunk the potion, it would be you in dreamland, Gordianus, while the priest sat here sipping wine and watching over you. From the way he keeps whimpering, do you think he's come upon Artemis naked, and she's set the hounds of Actaeon after him?"

"You seem to take this very lightly," I said. "You might wish to adopt a more respectful tone."

"Respectful?"

"Of the goddess." I glanced up at the statue and lowered my voice. "She's standing right here!"

"I am a Jew, Gordianus. I don't worship Artemis."

This struck me as a foolhardy thing to say, standing as we were in the heart of the goddess's sanctuary, in plain sight of the most revered image of Artemis in the world. "Do you think this statue is only a piece of wood, and no such goddess exists?"

"I didn't say that. But whether Artemis exists or not, my god does not allow me to worship her. Nor would I wish to."

I shook my head. "What a peculiar religion, that instructs its adherent to *not* worship a goddess."

"You don't know much about the Jews, do you, Gordianus?"

"There aren't very many of them in Rome."

"But you've been living in Alexandria. There are an awful lot of us there."

"Perhaps so, but for whatever reason, I've had few dealings with your people. Your ways are mysterious to me."

"But isn't that slave of yours Jewish?"

"Now how could you know *that?*"

"I make it my business to know things that aren't my business."

"Yes, Bethesda's mother was a Jew, but she died young. Bethesda was born a slave, and not in a Jewish household. She does remember some of the stories her mother told her when she was little."

"Like the one about Samson the strongman?"

I frowned. "But what are you doing here, Samson?"

"Doesn't every visitor to Ephesus come to the Temple of Artemis?"

"I suspect that very few visitors find their way to this chamber."

"True. I happened to know it was here from a previous visit, and also what it's used for—this rigmarole of seeking a dream-cure at the foot of the statue. I'm a bit of a snoop."

"How is it that you found your way here today?"

"I didn't come here intending to see you, Gordianus. I arrived only an hour ago, on other business. But I was told about this morning's sacrifice, and when I saw you wandering about with the young priest, I figured you'd end up in this room come nightfall. So I snuck up here ahead of you and waited in the shadows."

"But why?"

"Partly from curiosity. I've heard of this dream-cure and the sleeping potion used to bring it about, but I've never actually seen it done. I wondered if my informants were correct. And so they were. Now you're free to do whatever you wish until daybreak."

"Zeuxidemus will sleep that long?"

"If my informants are correct."

"And where would I go?"

"Didn't you come to Ephesus for a specific purpose? If Mithridates plans on holding you in the palace, under careful watch of the chamberlains, this may be your best chance—perhaps your only chance— to go look for that old tutor of yours. Shall we pay a visit to the house of Eutropius?"

My heart leaped. "But the city gates will have been closed at nightfall. How would we get in?"

"There are ways. But before we go, there's someone I want you to meet."

"Here in the temple?"

"Yes. But once we leave this room, you're Agathon of Alexandria again, and mute. It's very likely there are spies planted among the refugees, so keep your mouth shut. Now follow me. I think this torch may last us just long enough to get down the stairs."

I took a close look at Zeuxidemus, to make sure he slept. He no longer whimpered, but instead was smiling blissfully.

As Samson had predicted, the torch lasted just long enough to see us down the stairs, then burned to nothing. We emerged from the shadows of the hidden doorway into the grand interior, which was now dimly lit by a multitude of lamps hung from ornamental stands or set into the wall. The temple was even more crowded than before, for many of the sanctuary-seekers had come inside to sleep. Picking his way between the slumbering bodies on the floor, Samson led me across the temple to the Roman statue of Diana.

A man stood up as we approached. He was not young, to judge by the groans he made at unbending his limbs. He wore a filthy toga too big for his slender frame.

Without speaking, Samson led us to the narrow, secluded space between the statue's pedestal and the wall behind. "This is the young man I was telling you about," said Samson, introducing me to the old man.

"And this," he said, lowering his voice, "is Chaeremon of Nysa."

So this was the father of the two brothers who were houseguests of Posidonius on Rhodes, the man who had stayed loyal to the Romans and as a result had been outlawed and hunted by Mithridates, with a bounty of forty talents for his capture. I wondered for a moment why he wore a toga, since he wasn't a Roman, then realized it must be a sort of disguise, making him indistinguishable from all the Romans around him. Even in this crowd there might be some who would turn him in for the reward. What an irony, I thought—that anyone in Ephesus should put on a toga to save himself.

"Here, both of you, step into the light, so that you can see each other's faces," said Samson. "I'll do what I can to help you, Chaeremon, but if you shouldn't see me again, Agathon can be trusted."

"Who did you say he was?" Chaeremon sounded weak and exhausted, and more than a little confused. Seeing his face more clearly, I realized that he was not so very old—perhaps no older than my father—but his graying hair and beard were unkempt and his face was lined with worry.

"He's called Agathon of Alexandria," said Samson. "A mute who's come to the temple—"

"What good will a mute be to me?"

"This is ridiculous!" I whispered. Samson looked about uneasily, but seeing no one within earshot, he let me go on. "I'm not mute. My name is Gordianus. I'm Roman. And yes, if Samson isn't able to help, I'll do what I can for you," I said, though I couldn't imagine what that would be.

"My sons, Pythion and Pythodorus—you saw them on Rhodes? They're well?"

"Yes. But they worry for you."

"I think Agathon has said enough." Samson gave me a sharp look. "I only wanted the two of you to meet and take a good look at each other. Now that's done, Agathon and I should be off."

Samson took my arm and led me quickly away from the statue of Diana. "You have a great deal to learn, Agathon, about this business of spycraft. No, don't say a word!" he added, seeing the exasperation on my face.

I never wished to be a spy, I wanted to say. *I only wanted to see Antipater again.* I kept my mouth shut and allowed him to lead me out of the temple and down the broad steps, threading our way between huddled bodies.

"We'll stay off the Sacred Way for as long as we can," he said, and proceeded to cut a path across the open temple grounds. Here, too, there were many people about, standing or lying down, some in crudely made shelters and tents. The ground was mostly flat, but in some places uneven, so that we had to go slowly to avoid tripping.

Passing by one tent, I heard a commotion from inside.

"What's this? You have some bread! Where have you been hiding this?"

"Shut up! Do you want everyone—"

"He has bread! Do you hear? This good-for-nothing has been holding out on the rest of us!"

We hurried on. Eventually, the crowd grew thinner. At one point I almost stepped into a trench, but Samson caught my arm. I looked down at the long, black gash in the earth. At first I thought this must be the trench I had seen from the altar, then realized that it couldn't be, since that trench lay in the opposite direction. There seemed to have been a great deal of digging going on in the open fields surrounding the temple grounds.

We drew near the city walls, and finally stepped onto the paved surface of the Sacred Way. The gates were closed, as I had feared, but a small door, set into one of the massive ones and just large enough to admit a single traveler on foot, stood open, with a guard blocking the way. As we drew closer he ordered us to halt, then to step slowly into the circle of light cast by the lamp hung beside him.

"Just keep your mouth shut," whispered Samson. "Stay behind, and follow when I tell you to."

He exchanged a few words with the guard. I couldn't hear what they said. The guard stepped to one side. Samson gestured for me to follow him. As I passed through the doorway, the guard studiously looked the other way. I found myself in the square where I had earlier witnessed the incident of the begging Roman. The shops were all closed and the streets were deserted.

"You'll be wondering how I managed that," said Samson. "I'll only tell you that it wasn't cheap. You can thank Gaius Cassius for providing us a generous allowance for such expenses."

I would have been hard-pressed to find the house of Eutropius on my own, but Samson seemed to know the way, taking narrow, winding backstreets. At last I began to recognize landmarks from my previous visit, and then we stood before the house.

Samson stepped into the shadows and peered up and down the street. There was no one about. "This Eutropius," he whispered, "is he likely to recognize you?"

"I should think so. I saved his daughter's life."

"You exaggerate?"

"Almost never. In this case not at all."

"Tell me more."

"Perhaps another time."

"Who else in the household will know you? Eutropius's wife?"

"Eutropius is a widower. Anthea is his only child."

"And the servants?"

"At least one of them should remember me. Ah, sweet Amestris . . ."

"A Persian girl?"

"Handmaiden to Anthea, the daughter of Eutropius."

"Whose life you saved?"

"Amestris played a part, as well."

"You really must tell me the whole story sometime. But now to the business at hand. The kind of slave assigned to answer a wealthy man's door at night can sometimes be a bit difficult, unless he knows you, or you can convince him you have pressing business. If you were to speak, you'd be recognized at once as a Roman, and that might cause a stir."

"Then I'll let you speak for me. You'll say that an old pupil has come to see Zoticus of Zeugma, a houseguest of his master."

Samson nodded. "If pressed for details, we'll pretend I'm your bodyguard, and traveled with you from Alexandria. The last part is true."

"But not the first."

"Do I not look the part?" Samson flexed his biceps. Like most men with large arms, Samson enjoyed showing them off.

There was an iron knocker on the door, shaped like a fish. Samson let it drop a couple of times, and in short order a peephole slid open. It was too dark to see the eyes that must have peered out, but the voice was that of a grown man.

"State your business."

"An old pupil of Zoticus of Zeugma has come to see him."

"Has he indeed?"

"Zoticus *is* staying here, isn't he, as a guest of your master?"

"I'm not at liberty to say. Perhaps you'd like to state the name of this one-time pupil?"

Samson was about to answer when I pulled him back and whispered in his ear. "The name Agathon of Alexandria will mean nothing to Zoticus, or to anyone else in the house."

"Should I dare to use your real name, then? To a stranger behind a locked door? I fear we haven't thought this through."

The voice from the peephole grew impatient. "If you're just going to waste my time, be on your way. And don't hang about. The master is expecting guests soon—*important* guests. Begone!"

"No, wait!" said Samson. "I believe your master's daughter has a handmaiden called Amestris."

"Again, stranger, I would ask you to identify yourselves, especially if you expect me to answer any questions."

"The man with me once saved the life of your master's daughter, Anthea."

"What nonsense is this?"

"Perhaps you don't know the story, but your master will."

"If you think I'm going to disturb the master by announcing some fellow who won't even give his name, but makes wild claims—"

"Then go tell Amestris. Tell her the man who saved the life of her mistress is here. She'll know who I mean."

There was a long silence, then the peephole slid shut.

We waited so long that I began to wonder if we should knock again. Then the peephole slid open. I heard girlish laughter from the other side. A few moments later the door swung open. I stepped ahead of Samson into the softly lit vestibule.

"You, bodyguard! You'll stay here with me," said the man who had spoken through the peephole, assuming without being told that Samson was a strong-armer like himself. Pound for pound, he looked to be a fair match for Samson.

"And the man I'm guarding?" asked Samson.

"Him I'll hand over to her." The doorkeeper nodded to a figure who stepped from the shadows into the lamplight of the vestibule.

I recognized Amestris at once, but let out a gasp of surprise, for somehow she was not the same as I remembered her. Had my memories misled me, or had some curious magic been worked on her? She was neither more beautiful nor less, but *different.* Younger, I realized. It was as if, in the years since I had seen her, she had grown that much younger instead of older. But that was impossible. . . .

With an expression of impish glee, the girl watched the confused expressions on my face. She laughed and dared to take my arm, a rather bold thing for a slave to do, then pulled me into a hallway beyond the vestibule, away from the doorkeeper's hearing.

"No, Gordianus, I'm not Amestris. I'm her little sister, Freny. Oh, but *you* look exactly as I pictured you."

"You've heard of me, then?"

"The man who saved our mistress? Oh, I've heard *all* about you."

"Whereas I had no idea you existed." I couldn't stop staring at her. The resemblance to her sister was uncanny. It was as if I had stepped back in time to meet Amestris as she must have been when she was barely a teenager.

"You were here in Ephesus so briefly, we simply didn't have a chance to meet. I was only a child then, anyway, and they kept me in another part of the house. But come," Freny said, taking my hand—again, exercising a most unslavelike liberty. "I'll take you to Amestris. We'll surprise her."

"Surprise?"

"I came for you myself and didn't bother to tell her, because she's too busy—oh, you'll see for yourself!"

I allowed the girl to lead me by the hand, through the garden at the heart of the house and then up a flight of steps.

"Of course, I shouldn't be allowing a man, *any* man, into this part of the house, but, well, everyone knows who you are and what you did for the mistress. Oh, and I thought you had traveled off to the farthest ends of the earth and that I should never have a chance to meet you, but here you are!"

"Your sister and mistress speak well of me, then?"

Freny laughed. "Ah, you're modest, as well. Of course they speak well of the brave young Roman who—"

"Oh, not so very brave," I said, simply to interrupt her. She had already spoken my name aloud, and now had identified me as a Roman to anyone who might overhear, though at the moment I saw no one about. "On the occasion of which you speak, your sister was no less brave, and perhaps even more so—being a girl and a slave, I mean."

"Oh, and freeborn males are necessarily more courageous than slave girls?" asked Freny, rolling her eyes. There seemed no end to her cheekiness. "Here we are," she said, stopping at a closed door and gently rapping on it.

"Who's there?" called someone from the other side. Hearing that voice, my heart beat faster.

"It's only me," said Freny. "And a surprise visitor."

"Surprise?"

"You'll see. Open the door, sister!"

A moment later the door began to open, slowly, so that the person on the other side could peek out discreetly with one eye. In that eye I saw at first caution, then a blink of surprise, then a wide-open stare expressing alarm or delight, or both.

The door swung open. Before me stood Amestris.

XXI

She was as beautiful as I remembered.

No, she was more beautiful.

She wore a garment with sleeves that modestly covered her arms and legs, and with a neckline that only hinted at the fullness of her breasts. Her beautiful body, that I remembered so well, was thus hidden, but no matter; this only served to concentrate my gaze on her face. I looked at it as a man looks at a much-loved city when arriving by ship, noting one by one each fondly remembered landmark: the smooth, olive complexion, the sensual mouth, the elegant nose, the dark eyes of Amestris.

"Gordianus!" she whispered. I couldn't tell which was greater, her alarm or delight, but Freny read her sister's expression more adroitly, for she clapped her hands and laughed with joy, and a moment later I was enveloped in the warm embrace of Amestris.

I would happily have remained in that embrace—I began to feel a stirring of arousal almost at once—but a moment later Amestris stepped back, holding my shoulders and looking into my eyes. I had to look up a bit to meet her gaze; I had forgotten she was slightly taller than me. That had made no difference when we had been horizontal together.

"Who is it, Amestris?" called another familiar voice from inside the room.

"See for yourself, mistress." Amestris let go of my shoulders and gestured that I should step inside.

Anthea sat in a chair with her hands in her lap. Clusters of lamps hung from bronze stands to either side of her, so that the brightest light in the room fell upon her pale face and golden hair. Apparently she was in the midst of having her hair attended to by Amestris, for on a nearby table I saw various combs and pins. The arrangement remained incomplete, for some of her tresses were done up and some were not. She sat motionless, but smiled broadly at the sight of me.

When I had last seen Anthea, she had been only fourteen, about Freny's age. Now she must be eighteen, and truly looked like a woman, not a girl. Like Amestris, she was even lovelier than I remembered.

"Gordianus!" she said. "Oh, I would get up to hug you, too, but—well, as you can see . . ." She gestured helplessly to her hair, which apparently was in such a delicate stage that she dared not disarrange it.

She guessed my reason for being there at once. "You've come to see Antipater, of course. Or Zoticus, as we're supposed to call him, since the king insists that he maintain his masquerade."

"Yes."

Her face darkened. "Have you come from Alexandria? That's where Antipater told us he last saw you."

"Yes."

"But why, Gordianus? Do you not understand the situation here in Ephesus? You're a Roman—yet you're not in a toga." She scrutinized the yellow tunic the Megabyzoi had given me. "No Roman is safe here."

"I realize that. Still, I've come to see Antipater."

Anthea sighed. "I fear I have to disappoint you. He's staying here, yes, but no one has seen him since early this morning. Am I right, Amestris?"

"Yes, mistress. Zoticus is not in his room and his attendants don't know where he's gone."

"His attendants?" I asked.

"His two personal servants," Amestris explained, "supplied to him by the royal household. They look after all his needs, which is why we sometimes hardly see him for days. But earlier today I sent Freny to find him, since of course he should be in attendance when our special visitor arrives."

She exchanged a knowing look with Anthea, who raised a pale eyebrow. "Perhaps dear Zoticus wishes to avoid seeing her. As will I, if my hair is still only half-done when she arrives!"

Amestris laughed softly—the sound of that laughter sent a thrill through me—and picked up a comb from the table. "Don't worry, mistress, we'll be done before you know it. And you shall look very beautiful."

"As beautiful as our visitor?"

"I'm sure *she* won't think so!" said Freny. "The master says he's never met such a vain creature—"

"Sister, enough of that!" said Amestris.

"Yes, Freny," said Anthea. "You really must learn to curb your tongue."

Freny put a finger to her lips to show that she understood. Then she commenced chattering again. "But sister, surely you want to visit with Gordianus. Let me finish the mistress's hair. I can do it as well as you, if not better."

"Who's vain now?" said Amestris.

"You know it's true."

"So it is," said their mistress. "Freny is right. Go find a quiet room, Amestris, and spend some time with Gordianus. Freny can finish my hair."

"If you're sure, mistress . . ."

"Go!" said Anthea. She smiled and shook her head, then stopped herself, reaching up to hold in place the delicate arrangement of her golden hair.

Carrying a lamp, Amestris led me down a hallway and into a room that startled me with its familiarity. I had lost my bearings in the house, but now I regained them, for this was the room where I had slept when

I was a guest of Eutropius—the very room where I had lain with Amestris, and known the pleasures of coupling for the first time. Had she led me here to continue what we began those many months ago?

By the soft lamplight, she looked incredibly alluring. Her dress was modest, yes, but fitted her in such a way that the play of light and shadows displayed the contours of her hips and breasts to perfection. The sight of her took my breath away.

At the same time, I felt a stab of guilt, for what would Bethesda think if she were present? I tried to banish this most unRoman thought from my mind. Bethesda was my slave, after all. I was a free man and free to do whatever I pleased in pursuit of pleasure. If Amestris were willing, why should I not begin by kissing her? Looking at her lips, the desire to kiss them was irresistible.

But as I stepped toward her, she stepped back. A coincidence—or did she deliberately avoid my kiss?

"Amestris," I said, "I've thought about you many times since we parted. I've pictured you in my mind, just as you look now—only you look more beautiful than I could imagine."

There was something dismissive in the smile she gave me. Did she think I was merely paying her a pretty compliment? The words I said were heartfelt and true.

"And *you* look just as I remember," she said. "Only . . ." She touched a fingertip to my forehead and traced the small scar. "I don't remember this."

"Oh, that," I said. "It's from a lion I met in the Nile Delta."

"A lion!"

"This is the very fang that caused the scar," I said, pulling the necklace from inside my tunic and showing her the talisman. She touched it with genuine wonder, and looked again at the scar.

Had I been entirely honest, I might have explained the series of events that resulted in that scar, which perhaps were not quite as perilous as she imagined. But if she saw my scar as a measure of manhood and the fang as a trophy, why not? How many men can say they were wounded by a lion's fang and survived to tell that tale?

"The Nile Delta?" she asked. "So you've traveled in Egypt?" She sounded impressed.

"Oh, yes. I've been living in Alexandria. Before that, Antipater and I traveled all the way to Babylon."

"Babylon! My mother told me that our people came from Babylon."

This came as no surprise. Amestris was a Persian name, and so was Freny. Both sisters possessed the elegant features and dark beauty I had seen in such abundance among Persian women.

I proceeded to name some of the other exotic places I had visited, and to recite a few of my more colorful adventures. Again, why not? Not every man can claim to have seen all of the Seven Wonders of the World.

But for all my bragging, the next time I moved toward her, with kissing on my mind, she eluded me again.

"What about you, Amestris?" I asked, realizing all the talk had been about me. Perhaps my boasting had put her off.

"Oh, little has changed for me, Gordianus. But I can't complain. I'm quite happy here in the house of Eutropius, surrounded every day by those I love."

"Ah, your little sister."

"Yes. And Anthea."

"It's good that you have such a close friendship with your mistress. But who is this special visitor you're expecting, the one for whom Anthea feels obliged to do up her hair in some extraordinary fashion?"

"Why, Queen Monime, of course. Did we not say?"

My heart lurched in my chest. Of course, neither Anthea nor Amestris had any way of knowing that I had met the queen, or that if Monime saw me in the house of Eutropius when I was supposed to be sleeping in the Temple of Artemis it would be the end of me. "Why is the queen coming here?"

"I'm not sure. I don't think anyone in the house knows what the queen has in mind, not even the master. A messenger arrived earlier today saying the queen would pay us a visit after nightfall. The household has been in a flurry ever since."

"Has the queen been here before?"

"No, this will be her first visit. The king has been here a few times, though."

"Mithridates himself?"

"Is there any other king? Or King of Kings, as he likes to be called."

"Why should King Mithridates visit Eutropius?"

"Why shouldn't he? The master is one of the most important men in Ephesus. Especially now that the Romans have been driven from power . . ." She hesitated, perhaps thinking such talk would offend me.

"Go on," I said.

"Well, when the Romans were still in charge, the master was always—how shall I put it?—butting his head against a wall. He was never a Roman-hater—you know that from your own experience, Gordianus, for he likes you very much. But he often complained that the Romans were holding back men like himself, independent-minded Ephesians who wanted to put the interests of Ephesus first, not those of Rome. Now that Mithridates has gotten rid of the Roman governor in Pergamon and driven the Romans from power, men like the master are finally in charge."

"I thought the father of Monime was put in charge of Ephesus."

"Yes, that's right, but no man runs a city alone, and Philopoemen is still feeling his way—so the master says. And as long as the king is in residence, all major decisions come directly from him. When the king comes to visit the master, other men come, too—the important men of Ephesus. They have long discussions. They're planning something . . ."

"Planning?"

"Something secret, for often they speak in low voices, careful that the household slaves can't overhear. As if any of us might be a spy!" She shook her head and shrugged, then lowered her eyes. "And I think . . . I think there's another reason the king keeps coming here."

"Yes?"

"A certain someone has caught his eye."

"You mean . . . a girl?"

She nodded. I had a sinking feeling. "Not . . . *you,* Amestris?"

She raised an eyebrow. "Do you not think I could turn the head of a king?"

"No, it's not that . . ." In fact, I could imagine only too well that the king might desire her. My face turned hot.

"No," she said, "it isn't me who's caught his eye."

"Who, then? Oh, no—does he have his eye on your mistress?" Mithridates could have as many wives as he wished. Being newly wedded to Monime would not necessarily stop him from taking Anthea for a wife, as well.

Amestris laughed. "No, he has no interest in Anthea—thank the goddess!"

I sighed, feeling relieved. I had managed to save Anthea from the clutches of one murderous lecher, but saving her from the King of Kings was surely beyond my capabilities. "I'm rather surprised Anthea isn't married by now."

"There *were* marriage plans, for a while. To some rich, powerful Roman. The master wasn't fond of the arrangement; I think the Roman was somehow coercing him. Nor did Anthea much like the man. Then came Mithridates, and *poof!* That almighty Roman disappeared on the next boat to Rhodes, along with the marriage plans. Anthea and I both heaved a sigh of relief. Now it seems that she will never marry."

"Why not?"

"Anthea has decided to be consecrated to the service of Artemis."

"What does that mean?"

"There'll be a ceremony to mark her commitment. Since she'll no longer be available for marriage, the Megabyzoi will pay a kind of dowry to the master. Anthea will live on the temple grounds and perform certain daily duties. And take a vow of chastity, of course."

"To be a virgin all her life?"

"Like the goddess, yes."

"That seems a waste," I said, then saw by the look on Amestris's face that perhaps I had spoken out of turn. Who was I to criticize the religious devotion of Anthea? "But we've strayed from the subject. Who in the household is the king lusting after?"

"Only with his eyes . . . so far."

"Yes, I understand. But who?"

She smiled. "Freny, of course."

"Your sweet little sister? But that's terrible!"

"Is it?"

"What if he were to buy her from Eutropius, and—"

"Buy her? I think the master is more likely to make a gift of her, to ingratiate himself with the king."

"How sad for Freny."

"Sad? On the contrary, I think it would be wonderful."

"How so, Amestris?"

"Think, Gordianus! My sister and I are slaves. We have no marriage prospects, as free women do. Oh, sometimes it works out that a slave can find a love-match within the household, but such a bond can always be severed at the whim of her master. We may have babies, but they're the property of the master, and they can be taken from us. So what does Freny have to look forward to, even from a good master like ours? How much better it would be for her to become the concubine of the king! Then she could live with his other concubines and their children in the luxury of the royal household, and go traveling with the court. Sad? No, this is surely the very best thing that could happen to little Freny."

"I see. Yes, I suppose I hadn't thought about it that way," I said, still dubious. "What does Anthea think about the king's interest in Freny?"

"The mistress and I are of one mind—not only about this, but about most matters."

"What about you, Amestris, and your prospects?"

She laughed. "I think I must be too old now to attract the attention of the King of Kings."

"Then I call him the fool of fools," I said, causing her to gasp. "But that's not what I meant. If Freny should leave, and if Anthea should be consecrated to Artemis—"

"Then I hope to go with her, as her handmaiden, and live with her on the temple grounds."

"Would you also take a vow of chastity?"

"Yes. That way I can accompany her in the rituals she's to perform at the temple, and sleep alongside her in the chambers reserved for the virgin acolytes."

"You would never know the touch of a man again?" I put my hands on her shoulders, then touched her face, delicately framing her smooth cheeks with my fingers. "How beautiful you are, Amestris! How fortunate I was to know you first among all women." I felt her cheeks blush warmly against my fingers. I drew closer to her, looking into her dark eyes.

"I must admit, Gordianus, that night . . . in the cave . . . when we saved Anthea . . . that was the night that truly changed my life."

"Not the next night? The night you came to me in this very room, and the two of us—"

There was a soft rapping at the door. Amestris drew away from me just as Freny stepped inside.

"She's here!" Freny whispered. "Come, sister! You must come at once. Queen Monime is here!"

XXII

There is a certain sound one hears when everyone residing in a great house is suddenly alert and on the move. It reverberates almost like a distant stampede of horses. It is the combined footsteps of every kitchen worker and scrub maid and handmaiden and stable boy and scribe and tutor and every other kind of slave coming from all corners to assemble, in this case, in the large garden at the center of the house of Eutropius.

Why is it customary for the entire household to assemble when certain personages visit the master of the house? I suppose it shows off the wealth of the host—men are often judged by how many slaves they own—but it also serves to spread the mystique of the visitor. For years afterward, and wherever they might go, those who were present at that moment would be able to say, "I saw her with my own eyes. I beheld Queen Monime."

Leaving me behind, Amestris and Freny joined in this orderly rush, as did Anthea, whom I saw from the back as she strode quickly but gracefully down the hallway toward the stairs to the garden. Her hair was indeed impressive, even seen from the back. By some magic of twisted braids and unseen pins it hovered atop her head like a golden cloud.

Perhaps it would have been wiser for me to lock myself in the room where I had been talking with Amestris, but curiosity got the better of me. I, too, wanted to have a look at Queen Monime and her retinue.

Staying in the shadows of the upper landing of the stairway, I had a view of the far side of the garden below, toward the front of the house. It seemed likely that this was where Monime would appear, for the rest of the garden and the surrounding portico were occupied by the assembled household—so I presumed from the sounds I could hear, for though I couldn't see very many of the people in the garden below, I could hear the murmur of their whispered conversations. There seemed to be a great many of them. When I had been a guest in this house, I had no idea that so many slaves were all around me, staying out of sight. Thus it is in such households, where every need of the master and his guests are met, as if by invisible servants. Only when they all assemble in one place does one realize how many human beings it takes to keep such a household running.

The hubbub grew louder, then abruptly diminished as everyone fell silent. Two figures came into view, facing away from me and toward the front of the house. By her golden cloud of hair I recognized Anthea. Though I could not see his face, the man standing beside her had to be her father. Eutropius was also blond, though with a great deal of silver amid the gold.

A tall, white-haired chamberlain appeared, dressed in the regalia of the royal court. His ringing voice compelled the attention of everyone present.

"Her Majesty, consort to the King of Kings, Queen Monime, accompanied by His Eminence, the Grand Magus, and also by His Eminence, the Great Megabyzus, calls upon Eutropius of Ephesus and his daughter Anthea."

One of Eutropius's slaves, obviously chosen for his strong, distinctive voice, stepped forward. "My master, Eutropius of Ephesus, and his daughter, the lovely Anthea, are most honored to receive Her Majesty, Queen Monime, and are humbled by the presence of Their Eminences, the Grand Magus and the Great Megabyzus."

A moment later, the three visitors stepped forward into the soft lamp-light of the garden. Acutely aware that I was wearing a bright yellow tunic, and that even at a distance one of them might recognize me, I stepped back a bit, deeper into the shadows. What sort of visit was this, that brought not just the queen but also the two most powerful religious authorities in the city? Eutropius happened to look over his shoulder, so that I caught a brief glimpse of his face. His expression was nervous, and his posture was very stiff.

There followed a great deal of bowing and other formalities, all of which seemed to have been rehearsed by Eutropius and the household ahead of time. Despite the fact that I had seen all three of the visitors at close quarters, and knew them to be nothing more than mortals like myself, there was something strangely awe-inspiring about the sight of them standing there, with Monime in the middle and the wise men to either side of her.

The queen was considerably shorter than either of her escorts, espe-cially the Great Megabyzus with his towering headdress, but she com-pensated for this with a truly astonishing costume of purple silk shot with gold and silver threads; part of it clung to her body like a normal gown, but there was also a huge, fan-shaped collar of the same fabric that loomed behind her, framing her face and shoulders. Around her wrists and neck she wore bands of gold set with precious stones; the pieces looked as if they had been fitted for a woman twice her size. The over-sized jewelry and the weirdly elaborate costume looked out of place with the simple purple and white fillet of wool that served as her crown, or perhaps their outlandishness was intended to emphasize the crown's simplicity. If the intent of the costume was to draw every eye to the smooth, moon-white face of Monime, it achieved its purpose. She gazed at the household of Eutropius with half-closed eyes and a cryptic smile.

The formal introductions came to an end. Eutropius beckoned to the slave who had spoken on his behalf and gave him some sort of in-structions. Strain as I could, I was unable to overhear what Eutropius said, but from what followed it seemed that he wished to dismiss all the slaves except those who were needed for further service. There was a sound of rustling as the crowd began to disperse. But when Monime saw what was happening, she stepped forward.

"No one is to leave!" she said. Her voice, which had seemed rather small when I met her, filled the garden. The sound of rustling stopped at once. "Let all the household slaves stay where they are."

Eutropius was clearly agitated. "Your Majesty, I don't quite understand. I had thought this visit was to be . . . of a more informal nature."

"Then you were mistaken."

"I didn't expect the presence of Their Eminences—"

"The participation of the Grand Magus and the Great Megabyzus is absolutely essential. I'm surprised the king did not make more clear to you the sacred nature of this visit."

"Sacred?" Eutropius's voice broke oddly on the word, as if he had begun to anticipate something dreadful.

"What could be more sacred, or more serious, than the sacrifice that is to take place in the Grove of the Furies? You *do* know the sacrifice I refer to, and the reason for it?"

"Yes, Your Majesty. But what—"

"You know that the king has delegated to me the sacred responsibility for assembling the proper participants for this ritual?"

"Yes, His Majesty did inform me—"

"And I have been diligently at work toward that end. I am pleased to say that all the participants have been duly selected . . . except for one."

"One, Your Majesty?" Eutropius's voice was so strained I hardly recognized it.

"The most important. The sacrifice herself. The virgin sacrifice."

Eutropius appeared to shrink. His shoulders slumped and his head fell forward. Though I saw him only from the back, I could imagine a look of fear and anguish on his face. All at once I realized what he was anticipating. I let out a gasp and then covered my mouth, fearing I had been heard in the garden. But the attention of everyone present was riveted on the strange drama taking place between Eutropius and the queen. Monime herself was staring at someone in the assembly before her.

I looked at Anthea, standing stiffly upright beside her father. I saw that she had begun to tremble and to clench her fists.

"Anthea!" I whispered, too quietly for anyone but myself to hear.

A virgin was required for whatever ritual was intended in the Grove of the Furies, the ritual to which I had been selected to pay mute witness. But how would I be able to stand by in silence and witness the slaughter of beautiful, innocent Anthea? I had rescued her once from death. To think I could do so again was surely hubris. It seemed a cruel joke of the gods that I would be made to witness the destruction of a life I once had saved.

"Please, Your Majesty," said Eutropius. His small voice was so choked with emotion he could barely speak. He swayed slightly, as if he felt faint. "The necessity of the sacrifice I do not question. It will be essential, if we are to . . . to take the actions desired by His Majesty. But surely there must be some other suitable candidate for this role."

"At every step, I have conferred with Their Eminences," said Monime. "The leading astrologers of the court have also been consulted. What we do, we do not do lightly. Divine will and the aspects of the stars themselves affirm all the choices that have been made."

"But . . . surely you don't need to take my child, my only child, a girl who longs for a pure life devoted to the service of Artemis—my beautiful Anthea!"

Monime threw back her head and laughed.

I heard gasps from the gathered household—what monstrous amusement could the queen find in Eutropius's suffering?

Monime seemed to enjoy the consternation caused by her incongruous laughter, for she let the uncomfortable silence linger, surveying the faces of those assembled in honor of her visit, until her gaze fixed upon someone I could not see.

"You may put your fears to rest," she finally said. "Your daughter, however worthy she might be, has not been chosen for this honor. I pray that the beautiful Anthea will enjoy a long and healthy life in the service of the virgin goddess."

Eutropius released a giddy noise of relief. But next to him, I saw that Anthea continued to tremble, and to clench her hands. Amestris came into my sight as she stepped forward and joined her mistress—a breach of protocol in the presence of the queen, perhaps, but she could not resist offering comfort to her mistress. Or so I thought, at first; but as they drew very close and one put their arms around each other, it seemed to me that that it was Anthea comforting Amestris, not the other way around.

Then I realized what they had already grasped.

Before I had whispered the name of Anthea. Now I whispered another. "Freny!"

"The virgin we have come for is not your daughter, Eutropius," said the Great Megabyzus, stepping forward. "It is one of the slaves in your household. Her name is Freny, I believe."

Amestris let out a choking sob. How I wanted to hold her at that moment! But it was Anthea who held her tightly—not just to comfort her, but also to restrain her, for a number of armed men now appeared in the garden, striding past Eutropius, heading toward his assembled slaves. There was some sort of commotion that I couldn't see, and a moment later the armed men began to lead Freny away.

They did not drag her; their coercion was subtler than that, as one on each side held her by a shoulder and the others formed a tight cordon around her. As the group passed Amestris and Anthea, Amestris frantically reached toward her sister, but Anthea held her back. The two women shook with weeping.

Just before she disappeared from sight, Freny looked over her shoulder. I saw the terror on her face.

"I expected rejoicing in this house, not tears," said Monime in a frigid voice. "Perhaps, Eutropius, you need to explain to your family and slaves just what an honor this is for your house, that one among you should be chosen to take part in a ritual that is essential to the freedom and safety of Ephesus—not only Ephesus, but all the world. The King of Kings will eliminate every last remaining Roman in Asia, and then from Greece, and then from Italy itself, and from every corner of the earth—and the annihilation of the Romans will begin with the blood of this virgin."

The queen turned around and disappeared. The Great Megabyzus and the Grand Magus followed her. The stunned silence was broken only by the sobbing of Amestris and Anthea.

Freny was to be sacrificed in the Grove of the Furies, while I was made to watch in silence.

XXIII

[From the secret diary of Antipater of Sidon:]

Most alarming! Most alarming!

Only now have I realized that a sheet of parchment is missing from the document I have been writing. Someone has taken it.

The sheets are unbound, not yet sewn together into a scroll. Could this single sheet somehow have slipped away from the others, then slid beneath a piece of furniture or into some other hidden spot? Perhaps. But I have looked everywhere. Everywhere! The sheet is gone.

Someone has taken it.

Who? And for what purpose?

It may be that some member of the household of Eutropius has been spying on me. But far more likely is the treachery of one of these servants assigned to me by the royal household. I have always suspected them of serving two purposes, or perhaps even three—to serve my immediate needs, for one, but also to watch and report on me to someone above them in the royal court. If they are serving that second function, they might as well serve a third, to watch and report on any developments that might be of interest here in the house of Eutropius.

Spies and treachery and betrayal! Spies, spies, everywhere one turns! But who am I to complain, since I am just another of them?

If in fact someone stole this sheet, when did they do so? The words were written some while ago, and since I haven't reread that section since I wrote it, the sheet could have been taken at any time since then.

What exactly did I write on that particular sheet? If I could recall, exactly, that might give me some clue as to why that sheet among all the others was taken, and just how incriminating it might be, or how easily it might be misconstrued.

The final sentences before the gap read, "While the king is busy plotting his next military campaign, the little queen and her father wield absolute power over this city. As long as I remain here, I know . . ." Then the gap. Then the text resumes with, ". . . is in an even worse dilemma than myself, it would be the Romans who remain in Ephesus."

Clearly I was expressing my detestation of Queen Monime—I suppose that very sentiment might be read as treason, though I cannot recall exactly what words I used. I believe I went on to express some suspicion about the two servants assigned to me by the royal household—and as it turns out, those suspicions may have been well founded! Did I express some opinion about Eutropius, and his feelings toward both the king and the Romans? I hope I didn't say anything that might get him into trouble. I seem to recall mentioning young Gordianus, who naturally would have sprung to mind, since when I last stayed with Eutropius it was in the company of Gordianus, who of course endeared himself to our host by the brave deed he did on behalf of Anthea.

Oh, how I miss that youth! How clearly I can picture him in my mind. Of course, months and years have passed, and Gordianus is not quite so young now as he was when I last saw him. He is at that age when a youth truly matures into a man. He will look older now. He will have learned a great deal, living by his wits in Alexandria—if indeed he's still there, and hasn't returned to his father in Rome. Or could some terrible fate have befallen him? One hears about the civil war in Egypt, and dreadful riots in the capital. People die in such circumstances, even fleet-footed, quick-witted young fellows like Gordianus. Especially such a fellow, if he makes the mistake of poking his nose where it doesn't belong!

But my thoughts are rambling. It's because I miss him, I suppose. Because I wish we could have parted on better terms, in happier circumstances—

I have just now checked to see that my letter to Gordianus is still where it should be, and, thank Artemis, it is. At least no one has taken that!

(Or letter-in-progress, I suppose I should call it, since I can't seem to finish it and send it to him. I write one draft of the letter, then read it the next day and decide to burn it—but before doing so, I carefully copy the name and the street of the banking house where Gordianus arranged to receive letters in Alexandria, then I start the letter again. Even if I were to finish it and post it, I have no idea whether Gordianus would receive it or not. Is he still in Alexandria? Does the banking house still exist? For all I know, it might have been burned to the ground as the result of some riot.)

So much uncertainty surrounds every thought. It seems to me the world is like an ocean arrayed with endless whirlpools; escape the pull of one, and you'll only find yourself sucked into another. Over our destinies we have no control whatsoever. But if the Fates control every decision made by every mortal everywhere, then what difference does it make whether Rome rules the world or Mithridates does so? Or rather, what difference does it make whether I think that one is good and the other bad?

Now that is most definitely a treasonous statement.

(Another reason I have never finished or sent that letter to Gordianus: it would surely get me into trouble with either the Romans or Mithridates or with both, should someone intercept it.)

But now I will write what I want, for I have taken all my pieces of parchment and my writing tools and what few of my personal belongings I could carry, and I have departed from the house of Eutropius. I think I managed to do so without either of the two treacherous "servants" taking notice—the wily Zoticus is not out of tricks yet!—so I have successfully escaped to the house of another old friend and associate, whose name I shall not mention, lest I get him into trouble should this document fall into the wrong hands. This place is a more humble abode, not as comfortable as the house of Eutropius, but here I feel free of the constant possibility of discovery and exposure. Here, perhaps I can finish my letter to Gordianus, and be done with this rambling confession, if in fact that is what I am writing.

The massacre of the Romans is imminent. A few days ago, the king paid a call on Eutropius, and I overheard His Majesty pronounce the date for the event. (Was I spying on them? This vile habit of skulking and eavesdropping has become second nature to me.) The thing has been very long in the planning—imagine the logistics of killing every one of them all on the same day, in every city under his control. I think it is his wish that the murdering should be done not by soldiers or city guardsmen, or rather not only by them, but mostly by the ordinary people. A deliberate campaign of deriding and belittling the Romans has been going on, making them not only objects of fear and loathing, but also of ridicule. They have been set apart, not only by having been driven from their homes and forced to seek sanctuary, but by such measures as the decree that they must wear the toga— ostensibly so that decent folk can see these thieves and rapists coming and protect themselves.

To set the slaughter in motion everywhere at once, there must be a chain of command running all the way from the king down to important men in each city, like Eutropius, and then down to neighborhood ringleaders and rabble-rousers who can be relied upon, at the appointed hour, to incite everyone around them to pick up stones and cudgels and knives and set about the bloody work.

My blood runs cold at the thought of it. How I dread the coming of that day!

But first, the king must placate the Furies. If that ritual is to take place before the massacre, it must be very soon—

[Here ends this fragment from the secret diary
of Antipater of Sidon.]

XXIV

"We should go back now. Especially if you want to get any sleep tonight."

Sleep was far from my thoughts, though as soon as Samson mentioned it I felt a great weariness descend on me. It was not the weariness of spent muscles but of spent emotions. I had been made to feel more than enough for one day—beginning with the sight of that poor Roman begging for food and being driven from the city, to the sacrifice to Artemis, through my long day inside the temple, to my reunion with Amestris—which by itself would have unsettled my emotions quite enough—and then to the terrible moment when we all watched, helpless, as lovely little Freny was led away, destined for slaughter.

After the queen's departure, Amestris and her mistress rejoined me in Anthea's room upstairs. The two women were so distraught they could hardly speak. I would have held Amestris had she indicated any inclination to allow it, but the two women seemed entirely occupied in hugging and comforting each other, so I stood by and watched them, as mute as the man I pretended to be, unable to think of anything I could do or say that would bring consolation.

There was a knock at the door. It was Samson. I let him in and told the women what I had told the doorkeeper, that he was my hired body-guard. It seemed simpler than explaining the complicated truth.

"How did you find your way to this room?" I asked him.

"Don't worry, I wasn't seen by the queen and her party—I kept well out of sight. But once they departed I decided to find you as quickly as possible. A small bribe to the doorkeeper brought me here."

Anthea looked up from her huddled embrace with Amestris. "A bribe?" she said, stifling her sobs.

"By the prophets, I've spoken out of turn," said Samson, looking sincerely abashed. "Now I've gotten the fellow into trouble."

"Why do you care?" I said, and rather harshly, venting my frustrations on him.

"It's a kind of betrayal," he said. "A bribe is a bond that works both ways, and unthinkingly I broke that bond just now. Do you not see that, Gordianus?" He shook his head. "You do indeed have much to learn about being a—"

"You are about to speak out of turn *again* . . . bodyguard!"

He shut his mouth and cast a glance at the women, looking even more abashed. The long day was beginning to wear on him, too, making him careless.

"But Samson is right about one thing," I said. "I have to leave now." *How I had rather stay, and spend the night with you, Amestris!*, I thought, but the Fates, or Artemis, or some other force—the dreaded Furies?—had decided that such a reunion was not to be.

"But Gordianus, where are you staying?" said Anthea. "You belong here, with us. You haven't even seen Father yet—"

"Nor should I, I think. Please don't tell him I was here." Even as I said the words, I realized how presumptuous they were. What right had I to ask Anthea to conceal something from her father? "I came seeking Antipater, and Antipater isn't here. So on that count, I've failed."

"When we see him again—"

"Yes, tell him I came looking for him. As long as he's alive and well, then I haven't yet failed entirely in what I came to do."

"How can he find you?"

I shook my head. "I can't tell you where I'm staying. Nor can I explain the mess I've gotten myself into." If I began to do so, the tale would lead inevitably to the revelation that I was to witness Freny's death. The sobbing of the two women had finally subsided, and I had no wish to set it off again. "I've traveled here under another name, pretending to be someone and something I'm not. I can't tell you more than that."

"Very well, Gordianus." Anthea's voice was suddenly cold and distant. As I had vented my frustration on Samson, so, I think, she was venting her emotions on me. "If you must go, then go. Perhaps we'll see you again, or perhaps not. Perhaps we'll tell Antipater that you came, or perhaps we won't."

"Mistress, no!" whispered Amestris, her voice hoarse from weeping. "We can't be angry with Gordianus. Not after all that he did for us."

Now it was Anthea's turn to look abashed. "You're right, of course. Oh, my lovely Persian dove is always right!" She touched Amestris's cheek and gazed at her in such a way that I felt a stab of something like jealousy.

Samson tugged at my tunic. I realized I was staring at them and lowered my eyes. "Anthea, Amestris, I'll leave you now."

If I expected a parting embrace from Amestris, I was to be disappointed. She remained where she was, seated next to her mistress—too exhausted and distraught even to give me a friendly farewell kiss, I thought. I desired that kiss from her more than ever. It was not to be.

Samson led me stealthily through the house and past the doorkeeper. The man studiously avoided seeing us, even when Samson pressed a coin into his hand—not part of the bribe, I thought, but guilt money for having betrayed the man's indiscretion to his mistress.

More coins changed hands at the guarded door in the city gate. Samson paid, and I stepped through, but he didn't come with me. I presumed he was headed back to the palace. Or was he headed off on yet another mission, with some purpose unknown to me?

I followed the Sacred Way. The paving stones seemed to glow very faintly, reflecting the pale starlight. In my yellow tunic, I, too, must have seemed to glow. The recumbent forms that dotted the landscape looked more like stones than people, but from either side I occasionally heard a sleepy whimper or a hushed voice asking if I had food or water.

"Don't even ask him!" whispered one voice. "He'll only spit at us, or hurt us."

How I longed to take off the yellow tunic and find myself a toga to wear, and say to them, "I'm one of you. I'm a Roman, too!" But I had no toga, and I didn't dare to speak. I hurried on.

At last I came to the temple steps, so crowded with restless sleepers they were almost impassable. The light of two burning braziers at the top of the steps helped me find my way.

Inside, the floor of the temple was likewise cluttered with sleepers. The flickering light of scattered lamps helped to guide me, but still I became disoriented within the vast interior. Weary and confused, I finally found my bearings and came to the hidden door. Slowly, with each footstep heavier than the last, I made my way up the stairs to the secret chamber in the pediment.

Zeuxidemus was where I had left him, snoring softly at the foot of the statue of Artemis.

I found a coverlet and some pillows and collapsed to the floor. Almost at once I fell into a deep sleep.

My slumber was filled with strange dreams.

I dreamed that I was not asleep at all, but lying awake amid the pillows at the feet of Artemis, with the young priest snoring nearby. Suddenly the goddess above me gave a sigh. She broke from her stiff pose, stretched her back, and shook out her arms. She looked down at me, and then leaned forward. The pendulous, fleshy orbs adorning the front of her body hung above me, swaying slightly, like heavy fruit from a tree.

"Gordianus," she said, in a soft, pleasing voice. "They tell me you've come to ask a favor of me. They say you've gone mute and want your voice back. But you aren't mute at all, are you?"

"No, goddess," I said. It seemed a proper way to address her. "O great Artemis" would be too formal, while "Artemis" alone would be too familiar.

"But there is something you desire, is there not?"

I was suddenly heartsick and filled with dread. "Yes, goddess—that we all should be safe from harm." I meant Antipater, but also Bethesda, and Amestris, and little Freny, and my father back in Rome.

I didn't say their names aloud, but Artemis knew my thoughts. "That would be too much to ask. You must give up one of them, I think."

"Then . . . if one of them dies, all the others will be well?"

"They must all die, sooner or later." She shook her head. The motion caused the dangling orbs to sway, and now they were not fleshy at all, but more like dried gourds. They made a hollow, clacking noise that set my teeth on edge.

"Must Freny die, then?"

"Can you imagine any way that her death might be stopped? I can do nothing to interfere. She is not being sacrificed to me, but to *them*." She made a gesture with one hand, seeming to indicate others who were behind her, out of sight because she blocked the view. By some magic, space itself was bent for an instant, so that I caught a glimpse of the dark things that lurked beyond her—things unspeakably hideous, hungry, and hateful. I heard a slithering of batlike wings and a shrill cackling.

I opened my mouth to cry out, but Artemis put a finger to my lips. "We must not name them," she whispered. "Even to speak their names is to invite their wrath. That is why the poets of olden days called them *Eumenides*, 'the Kindly Ones'—the very opposite of what they are."

The rasp of slithering wings diminished, and the cackling faded. Suddenly we were no longer in the temple, but in a wood beside a stream. The goddess was no longer the Artemis of Ephesus, but Diana as I had grown up knowing her, a beautiful young maiden dressed for the hunt in a flimsy, loose-fitting tunic, tanned and tawny, bare-limbed and holding a bow. A warm breeze sighed through the sun-dappled wood, carrying a sound that came from far away, not the cackling of the Kindly Ones but something nonetheless disquieting, but still so faint and far away I paid it no attention as I stepped away from the goddess, toward the brook, where a little waterfall emptied with a babbling noise into a small pool surrounded by mossy stones. There in the pool stood Amestris, her nakedness lit by beams of sunlight and by glittering flashes of light bouncing off the water—naked as I had never seen her, for when we made love she had come to me by night and departed by dawn. I felt a stab of heartsickness and a desperate longing, for she was more beautiful than anything could be in the waking world. She radiated a kind of beauty that can be seen only in a dream, a beauty that brings pure bliss.

The disquieting noise carried on the warm breeze grew closer, and louder, but with the splashing of the waterfall in my ears I couldn't make it out, and paid it no heed.

I stepped into the water, and realized that I was naked, too. The water was cold around my feet, while the fragrant breeze from the forest was warm upon my arms and legs. Patches of sunlight were all around me, on the mossy stones and on the leaves of the trees, on the splashing water and on the wet, glistening flesh of Amestris. I imagined that we were creatures made of sunlight, Amestris and I, and I longed for us to merge together into a single, pure beam of light. But when I reached out to touch her, she was flesh, and I was flesh, and then I wanted our flesh to touch, everywhere and all at once.

The baying of the distant hounds grew louder.

Then I realized it was not Amestris in the pool, but Freny. Still holding her by the arms, I looked over my shoulder, and saw that Diana, standing on the bank where I had left her, was very angry.

"How dare you gaze upon the virgin naked in the bath?" she shouted. "How dare you touch her?"

"But . . . I only wanted to save her," I said.

The hounds were now very near, and very loud.

"Ha! Save yourself, Actaeon—if you can!" said Diana. "Run, Actaeon! Run!"

The hounds were almost upon us. I could see them in the woods beyond Diana. Freny slipped from my grasp. I looked all around and saw that she had vanished.

I ran. Naked and barefoot I bounded through the woods. Branches and twigs scraped my flesh. Brambles bit my ankles. Thorns stabbed my feet. I ran into a mass of hanging vines, which slithered around me like writhing snakes. I was trapped like a wild beast in a net, and then the hounds were upon me, tearing at me with their claws and their fangs—

"Have mercy on me, Artemis!" I cried. "Have mercy! I beg you!"

Then I remembered the talisman that hung from the chain around my neck, my lucky lion's fang. I laughed aloud with relief, for as long as I possessed it—at least in the dream—no harm could come to me. I reached up to grab hold of it—only to find that it was gone!

I was naked and defenseless against the ravening hounds. Blood spattered my face. Thrashing in agony, I looked around me and saw that the leaves and vines were covered by a shower of blood, as if the sky had opened and poured down red rain. There was so much blood, it could not all be mine. No single mortal could contain so much blood! The rain grew even heavier, flooding the earth. There was such a rush of blood that it swept the hounds away, and the mesh of vines released me, and I found myself awash on the grisly current, wounded and weak and about to drown in a sea of blood—

"By sweet Artemis, wake up! Wake up!" someone said.

It was Zeuxidemus, shaking me awake. Above and behind him loomed the Artemis of Ephesus. The statue stared straight ahead, as stiff and silent as ever, but now silhouetted by bright sunlight.

XXV

Had I spoken in my sleep?

That was the first coherent thought that came to me, as I was gradually released from the clutches of that horrible dream. Had I muttered a name, or cried aloud for mercy? I looked at Zeuxidemus, to see by his face if I had given myself away. He only smiled and sat back, looking relieved.

"You were thrashing and whimpering so much, I feared that . . . well, I've kept watch over other sleepers in this room, but I've never seen anything like it. Usually their dreams are sweet. And usually they've awakened before now."

I sat up, craning my neck. Through the round opening beyond the statue I saw a bit of bright blue sky.

"It's almost noon," said Zeuxidemus. "By rights, I shouldn't have awakened you, because the suppliant is supposed to sleep as long as . . . well, as long as it takes the goddess to come to him. But no one has ever slept this long, or seemed to experience such a nightmare. I was afraid I had . . ."

His voice trailed off, but I knew what he was thinking: had he given me too much of the sleeping potion, making me sleep too long and have the wrong kind of dreams? Instead, unknowingly, he had drunk it, and had awakened from the sleep intended for me. He appeared to be quite alert and well rested, and his expression was very serious, in contrast to the ridiculous state of his hair.

"Well, Agathon? Did Artemis come to you in your dreams?"

I blinked, then nodded vigorously. Indeed she had!

"And? Did she grant your request?"

I looked at him blankly.

"Has she restored your speech, Agathon?"

I opened my mouth. I moved my lips. No sound came out. I bowed my face and slowly shook my head.

Zeuxidemus sighed. "I'm sorry for you, then. The goddess doesn't grant every request. Not even the Great Megabyzus can predict whether she will show favor or not. But take heart, Agathon. This confirms that you're suitable for the ritual in the Grove of the Furies."

He stood up and pushed his hair back, then put on the tall yellow headdress. At once his whole demeanor changed. It is remarkable, how a few articles of clothing can make a man look like he knows what he's doing.

I washed my face, drank some water, and relieved myself—there were vessels for doing this in a little room off to one side—and then Zeuxidemus led me down the long winding stair to the sanctuary.

The floor was still crowded with people sitting or lying down, but not as crowded as it had been during the night. In darkness, those lumps of flesh had seemed hardly human, but by the bright light from the open doors, I could see the faces in the sea of bodies around me. Their despair was jarring. Why did they not speak? By the yellow tunic I wore they must have known I was a suppliant seeking the favor of the goddess, and they were beyond hoping for help from a stranger. Instead, they cowered and cringed as we passed. I looked from face to face, and shivered.

A cordon of spear-bearers awaited us at the bottom of the temple steps. We walked up the Sacred Way at a steady pace, toward the city. As in the temple, the scene that had been disturbing by starlight was even more frightful by daylight. There were thousands of Romans all around me, people of all ages, all wretched, all slowly being starved—deprived not just of food but also of hope. By divine law, the temple and its grounds offered them sanctuary from the wrath of the Ephesians, but unlike the gods these mortals could not live on incense and smoke. It would almost be more merciful if Mithridates would put them out of their misery—

I shuddered, and tried to banish the thought. But if such an idea could occur to me, surely the king had thought of it already, and so had every Roman-hater in Ephesus. They looked on the Romans as pests, as vermin. First we had infested their city, taking all the best things for ourselves. Driven out of the city, now we were infesting and polluting their most sacred and beloved institution, their claim to fame, their very own Wonder of the World, the Temple of Artemis.

As we approached the boundary of the sacred temple precinct, a toga-clad figure suddenly rushed up to one of the spear-bearers in the rear, catching the man by surprise and taking the spear from him. The others in the troop reacted swiftly, turning about and lowering their spears toward the Roman, who assumed a defensive crouch and pointed his stolen spear back at them.

I drew a sharp breath, for I recognized the Roman. It was the man who had come into the city to beg the day before, the man the crowd had pelted with food. The image of his desperate face was burned into my memory. Now his desperation was verging into madness.

"You must give us food!" he shouted. "My child is almost dead with hunger." He glanced at a nearby woman who held a frail-looking boy in her arms. The woman's red hair hung in tangles and she wore a tattered stola. "And someone must come and tell us what's to happen to us. We ask those yellow-robed fools at the temple and every one of them tells us a different story. What does the king intend to do? Does he mean to make slaves of us?"

"He wouldn't dare!" shouted a woman. A crowd had begun to grow behind the Roman wielding the spear.

"What would the monster *not* dare to do?" said another woman.

The captain of the spear-bearers strode through the troops, pushing aside the lowered spears to either side of him until he stood before the crouching Roman, apparently unafraid of the spear in the man's trembling hands.

"You will drop that weapon at once," he said.

"Never!" said the Roman. "Not until . . . not until the king himself comes to speak to us."

"Yes! Let the king come," said a gray-bearded Roman behind him. "Let Mithridates come and explain his intentions. He owes us that much."

"The king owes you nothing," said the captain sternly. "Now I order you again to drop that weapon."

"Or what? You'll starve me to death?" said the Roman, with a demented laugh.

So swiftly it seemed to come from nowhere, the butt-end of a spear swung through space and struck the Roman soundly against the side of his head. At a signal from the captain, one of the spear-bearers had sprung forth, swinging his spear before anyone could stop him.

The Roman went reeling. He fumbled with the spear at first, then dropped it and tripped over it, so that he hurtled headlong toward the spears lowered in his direction. He managed to catch himself just before colliding with a spearpoint, then scrambled back, at last coming to a halt by falling on his backside. The men surrounded him. Two of them took hold of his arms and pulled him to his feet. The Roman struggled weakly against them and began to weep.

The red-faced soldier who had lost his spear retrieved it.

"Hand that to me!" shouted his captain, grabbing the upright spear from the soldier. "You're not worthy to carry it. Now draw the knife from your scabbard and kill this Roman at once."

There were gasps from the crowd. Even some of the spear-bearers were taken aback.

Zeuxidemus spoke up. "Captain, we're still within the sacred precinct. This man has been granted the protection of Artemis. You can't shed his blood here."

"No? How about over there, beyond that marker alongside the Sacred Way, where those men are digging that trench? That's not sacred ground, is it?"

"No, but—"

"Carry the Roman over there," said the captain to his men.

"Captain, you don't intend—but the Roman harmed no one," said Zeuxidemus, following behind the captain.

"Ha! Tell that to the fool who lost his spear, after he's received his lashes for incompetence." He turned to the soldier, whose face was now pale. "But I'll make a deal with you, soldier. If you can manage to kill this Roman cleanly, with a single cut, I'll see that your lashes are reduced by half."

"Captain!" said Zeuxidemus. "Surely for now it would suffice to arrest the Roman, and let some higher authority decide his fate."

"I have all the authority I need, vested in me by the king's decree."

"What decree?"

"The one that forbids any Roman to bear arms, upon immediate penalty of death."

"But the Roman was within the sacred precinct—"

"Where he seized and then brandished a weapon at my men."

"But he was very quickly disarmed—"

"The Roman armed himself in blatant defiance of the king's decree. The punishment must be carried out at once. Should I fail to do so, I would be defying the will of the king. As would anyone who made any effort to thwart this execution."

These last words were clearly meant to silence Zeuxidemus, but he would not be stifled. "The Great Megabyzus himself showed mercy to this man, only yesterday. You were there. Do you not remember?"

"I do. Had that angry crowd been left to deal with this piece of Roman filth then and there—instead of seeing him rewarded by the Great Megabyzus with all the food he could carry—we wouldn't have had to face this unpleasantness today. Now, then—you men, hold the Roman fast, so that your dishonored comrade can dispatch him at once."

Zeuxidemus stood by helplessly, as did I. The Roman crowd, including the man's wife and child, stayed behind the marker by the road. Not one of them dared to step outside the sacred precinct, but many began to weep and cry out as the captive was forced to his knees. The man's wife would have run to him, but others restrained her. One of the soldiers pulled the Roman's head back by a fistful of hair, baring his throat. From the Roman's lips I heard a frantic babble—a curse on Mithridates, a desperate plea to Artemis.

The soldier with the knife strode forward and drew back his arm. With a single motion he cut the Roman's throat. A ghastly sound came from the man's open mouth, then a torrent of blood gushed from the gaping wound, cascading onto his filthy toga. He jerked horribly as the men held him in place, then became still. The man holding him by the hair released his grip, and the Roman's head slumped forward. His eyes were still open, staring lifelessly at nothing.

The man's wife began to wail. She fell to her knees, dropped the child, and began to tear at her tangled red hair.

Zeuxidemus made a noise of dismay. The captain looked at him sidelong and grunted. "How can one of you lot be so squeamish, priest? For the glory of the goddess you can kill one bleating beast after another, until blood clogs the gutters of the altar, yet you blanch to see a man put to death—and a filthy Roman, at that!"

"The man should at least be given the proper rites," said Zeuxidemus in a hollow voice.

"Funeral rites? For this scum?" The captain laughed. "You men, drag his carcass to that trench over there and dump it inside. If any of his countrymen should wish to retrieve the corpse, they can step outside the sacred precinct to do so. Otherwise, he can rot in that ditch and be eaten by maggots."

After this was done, the spear-bearers re-formed the cordon around Zeuxidemus and me. As we strode past the ditch, I glanced at the body of the Roman, lying twisted and crumpled amid the muddy soil. I thought of all the trenches being dug just beyond the perimeter of the sacred grounds, and suddenly imagined them full with corpses—not merely filled but overflowing, heaped with dead bodies. The vision was so startling, so real, I seemed for a moment to glimpse the future.

It was then that I knew without a doubt what Mithridates intended to do with the Romans who had been driven from Ephesus, though how he meant to accomplish such a vast slaughter I could not imagine.

What of all the other Romans still trapped in the cities and villages conquered by Mithridates? They numbered in the tens of thousands. Surely the king did not intend to kill them all, I thought, as we hurried past the trench and on to the city gate.

XXVI

The chamberlain met me as soon as I arrived at the palace. He took me to the dining hall, where I was given a meal of bread and dates, which I consumed like a starving man. Then he escorted me back to my quarters. I was surprised, and happily so, to see no one in the room but Bethesda.

As soon as the chamberlain closed the door, I took her in my arms.

"But where are the other two?" I whispered in her ear.

"Gnossipus and Damianus were given their own room," she said.

"Do you mean we're alone?"

"Yes."

What followed involved no words. My longing for her was as sharp as a nettle, as sweet as honey. The room seemed too small to contain it. There was no piece of furniture or bit of floor or wall against which we did not make love in one position or another. How long this went on, I couldn't say, as time seemed to have fled from that room.

There was a bowl of fruit and a pitcher of water on a small table, and from time to time we paused to eat and drink. Even during these moments of rest, we said little, and I never spoke above a whisper, fearful of being overheard by some listener at the door. We seemed to be alone, but occasionally I wondered if someone might be spying on us through a hidden peephole. What a show we gave them, if that were so! But there was never any indication, afterward, that anyone saw or heard anything that transpired in that room. I think we truly were alone all through that languid morning and lazy afternoon.

From time to time, in the heat of passion, I imagined it was Amestris with whom I was making love; the music of her voice and the beauty of her face were vivid in my memory. But thoughts of Amestris led to thoughts of doomed Freny, and to memories of my dream of Artemis the night before, and I would shake myself and open my eyes and gaze at the woman I was with—no phantom or goddess or memory, but Bethesda, who to my eyes was more beautiful than any other. What a lucky man I was to hold in my arms the treasure I valued above all others!

As the day waned and the dinner hour approached, I told Bethesda, in bits and pieces, and always in a whisper, what had happened to me after she and the others departed from the temple grounds and I was left in the care of Zeuxidemus. When I mentioned the appearance of Samson, her eyes widened ever so slightly. If I sometimes imagined Amestris when I was with Bethesda, did she sometimes imagine Samson, or some other man? As soon as that thought occurred to me, I strove to banish it. Such thoughts never lead to anything good.

When I told her about our visit to the house of Eutropius, I left out Amestris entirely. The doom laid on the young virgin slave of Anthea's—so I described Freny—was poignant enough without including the anguish of her older sister.

"Why always a slave?" was Bethesda's comment. "If her mistress also is still a virgin, would she not be more suitable? Surely the life of the daughter of a powerful citizen is of more value than the life of a mere slave, and so would be more pleasing to those who receive the sacrifice?" I noticed that she avoided mentioning the Furies by name.

"I don't think that's the way it works," I whispered. "If you could have seen the queen's face . . ."

"Describe to me again what she was wearing."

Thus did Bethesda lead me into digressions of more interest to her than to me, interrupting the thought I was about to express: that Monime somehow (through spies?) must have learned of the king's attraction to Freny, and had used her influence to convince the Great Megabyzus and the Grand Magus to choose Freny for the sacrifice. Thus the queen would get rid of the poor girl, presumably with the king himself being forced to watch while the object of his desire was slaughtered. What sort of mortals were this king and queen, to play such games with the lives of others?

Instead of sorting out these tangled thoughts, I was doing my best to recall the details of the queen's clothing when Bethesda interrupted me. "The fortune-teller back in Alexandria!" she said. "She spoke of a virgin, did she not? A beautiful young virgin, in danger. That must be Freny. The fortune-teller also mentioned a sacrifice—yes, I'm sure of it. She even spoke of the wrath of . . ."

"The Furies," I dared to whisper, at which Bethesda made some sort of sign, as if to protect herself from the Evil Eye. What did I recall of the fortune-teller's rant? I had not taken her seriously at the time. Her advice had been to stay away from Ephesus, and I had ignored that advice. What else had she said? Suddenly I heard her voice in my head, almost as if she were in the room with us:

"Blood! Fountains of blood, lakes of blood, a sea of blood! The streets will be filled with rejoicing. The temples will be filled with corpses!"

There was a rapping at the door. I gave a start, but it was only a slave who called through the door that the dinner hour had come.

[From the secret diary of Antipater of Sidon:]

I find myself back at the palace.

Early this morning a royal chamberlain appeared on the doorstep of my ostensible hiding place—obviously not a hiding place at all!—and politely asked to see Zoticus of Zeugma. I must have been followed when I came to this house yesterday, thinking to escape the scrutiny of the king and queen. Or can there be spies even in this humble abode?

When I came to the vestibule of the house, the man told me to gather up all my things, as my presence was requested at the royal palace, where a room would be provided for me. A couple of slaves appeared, to carry my things. Outside in the street, I could see armed courtiers. Was I being invited to the palace, or arrested? Or is there a difference, when the summons is issued by an all-powerful monarch?

"Was it the king who sent you?" I asked the chamberlain. "Or was it the queen?"

"My orders never come directly from either of Their Majesties," he said, and rather condescendingly, as if I were a simpleton. "Be assured I speak with the authority of the royal household."

"So I have no choice but to obey?"

"None at all," he said.

And so I was escorted back into the lion's den, so to speak. The quarters I was given are in the lower story of the house, with the acrobats and other riffraff. Among the scant possessions that the slaves dutifully delivered to my room were my writing instruments and the unbound pages of the journal I have been writing, which are tightly rolled up and kept inside a small leather cylinder, a scroll satchel of the sort Roman schoolboys carry and call, in Latin, a capsa. How could I ever have thought those words were secret? Undoubtedly the servants assigned to me in the house of Eutropius were spies, and have read every word I've written.

These words, too, will almost certainly be read by some spy from the royal household. I can assume that nothing I do is in secret.

It occurs to me that perhaps I should burn these pages, rather than add more words to them. And yet, the only comfort I find in my predicament is to continue recording my thoughts—but for whom? Who is the imaginary reader for whom these words are intended?

Gordianus. Who else?

But he is far from here, in Alexandria, or perhaps back in Rome. By what possible means could these words ever reach him? It is futile to think *that we shall ever be reconciled, or that I could ever make him understand the choices I made. What a fool I have become in my dotage! Truly, Antipater of Sidon has turned into Zoticus, the simpleton poet of Zeugma!*

But there is the knock at my door, letting me know that I may now have the pleasure of dining in the company of tumblers and contortionists. Even the doomed must continue to eat . . .

[Here ends this fragment from the secret diary
of Antipater of Sidon.]

As before, I was allowed to bring Bethesda with me into the dining hall. I had put aside the yellow tunic and put on one of my own.

We arrived just in time to behold the spectacle of Sosipater juggling whatever anyone cared to toss his way. Among those watching him, I saw Gnossipus and Damianus.

Sosipater already had several plums in the air, then someone tossed a fig at him, which he deftly caught and added to the circle of flying objects. More items were tossed to him—a small clay cup, a copper bowl, even a shoe. Each in turn joined the other airborne objects, which seemed to fly of their own accord, swooping up and down, and only by coincidence bouncing off the palms of Sosipater's hands. I had seen street entertainers who called themselves jugglers in Alexandria, but I had never seen anything like this.

Sosipater kept this up for quite some time, making various facial expressions to evoke laughter from the crowd, and even closing his eyes for a while, as if he had nodded off. Then he appeared to grow careless, and with a desperate look on his face he bolted this way and that, seemingly on the verge of dropping everything. But this was only a part of the act, which evoked exclamations of alarm followed by raucous laughter.

He ended the performance by letting the copper bowl land upright in one hand, into which the pieces of fruit fell one by one. The shoe fell into his other hand. As for the clay cup, it landed on top of his head and stayed there, perfectly balanced. I could hardly believe my eyes.

"But what sort of fool walks around with a cup on his head?" said Sosipater. "A cup is not a cap! Here, who needs a cup? How about you, old fellow?"

With his chin, Sosipater pointed toward a man who had just stepped into the room. I was so intent on watching the juggler that I saw the newcomer only from the corner of my eye. I could tell that he had a white beard, but little else.

Somehow, with a toss of his head, Sosipater managed to throw the cup toward the newcomer. The old man was caught by surprise and fumbled the catch. The cup bounced from hand to hand as if it were a hot coal, then fell to the floor, where it broke into pieces.

"You clumsy fellow!" said Sosipater, who now stood with his elbows out and his fists on his hips. Somehow he had made the copper bowl of fruit and the shoe disappear while no one was watching.

Standing next to me, Bethesda joined in the laughter and applause, but I stood like a statue, dumbstruck. The old man who had dropped the cup was Antipater.

Embarrassed and red-faced, he kept his eyes lowered, and didn't see me staring at him from across the room. A moment later, with an exclamation of disgust, he turned around and left the room. When I moved to follow him, a strong hand gripped my shoulder.

"Stay where you are, Agathon," whispered the voice of Samson in my right ear. "Don't go after him."

Why not? I wanted to ask. *For what other purpose am I here, but to find Antipater? Now, at last, I have!*

But I didn't dare to speak, even in a whisper, and as I stared at the empty doorway through which Antipater had made his flustered exit, where a slave was kneeling down to pick up the broken pieces of the cup, my sighting of him began to seem unreal, almost as if I had imagined it. I had glimpsed the old man's face for only an instant. Had I seen what I wanted to see? Even as I began to doubt my eyes, Samson spoke again in my ear.

"Yes, that was Zoticus you saw. But this is not the moment. Later."

I turned and looked him in the eye.

"Later," Samson repeated. "Tonight, I'll come to you." Then he turned his back on me and moved away, joining the crowd that was still laughing and talking about Sosipater's performance.

"What did he want, I wonder?" said Bethesda, who stood to the other side of me and had been unable to overhear Samson's words. Nor could she have recognized Antipater, since she had never seen him. The strained look on my face puzzled her. Her eyes followed Samson's broad back as he moved away from us.

"I'm not sure I trust that fellow," she said.

Nor am I, I thought. But what choice did I have?

XXVII

As soon as we had eaten, we returned to the room. From farther down the hall I heard the sound of a flute being played, and rather badly. I was thankful once again not to be sharing quarters with Gnossipus and Damianus.

As night fell, there was a knock at the door. It was only a slave who had come to light our lamps.

I sat on the bed and waited. Bethesda dozed beside me. We had worn ourselves out with lovemaking that day, and I would have slept, too, had I not been listening for another knock at the door, having no idea when it might come. With Bethesda close to me, I began to feel a stirring of arousal—I had not been drained entirely of desire, after all— but I didn't care to be caught in the act when Samson came, so I let Bethesda sleep, and contented myself with gazing at her by the soft light and gently stroking her long hair.

At last, so softly that I wasn't sure I heard it, there came a rapping at the door. I managed to get up without waking Bethesda. I opened the door. Samson slipped inside.

I sniffed the air, then saw the source of the musty odor that had entered the room with Samson. "By Hercules," I whispered, "what are you wearing?"

His face brightened. "I wondered if anyone would notice," he whispered. "Do you like it?"

Over his shoulders he wore a woolen cloak that fell a little past his waist. There were catches in front, but he left them undone. What could there be for anyone to like about such a garment? By the feeble light of my last burning lamp, the color appeared to have faded to a dull, reddish brown. The garment looked well-made, but the fabric was visibly worn and tattered in several places. It also had an odor, like the musty smell of a trunk that hasn't been opened for a long time.

"It suits you," I said, simply to move on to more important matters.

"Does it? Why, thank you. Can you imagine where it came from?"

I sighed, frustrated at the time and breath being spent on something so trivial. I wrinkled my nose. "From a tomb, perhaps?"

"Ha! Yes, it does have a bit of a smell, doesn't it? It could use a good airing. But you're not far off. It didn't come from a tomb, but from a treasury. While you no doubt spent the day making love to that beautiful creature on the bed—"

"How could you know that?" I snapped.

He shrugged. "A lucky guess. Anyway, while you were doing that, I was finally allowed to have a look at the Jewish treasury seized at Cos, or at least what's left of it. The hoard is being kept in a storehouse on the waterfront, surrounded by a small army of guards. No one would dare to break in. The guards are mostly there to watch one another, I think, and make sure no one carries anything off—"

"That's wonderful news," I said. "But what about—"

"Indulge me, Gordianus. We have a bit of time to kill. They're not ready for us yet."

"*Who* is not yet ready for us? Do you mean . . . Zoticus?"

"Patience, Gordianus! Now where was I? Oh, yes, I was finally allowed to have a look at the treasure, with several of the king's courtiers as well as a number of armed guards watching me the whole time. Well, not surprisingly, a substantial portion of the treasury has already been carted off to be sold piecemeal, or else melted down to make coins."

"How could you tell what was missing?"

"From the ledger, of course. A very careful list of every item in the treasury was kept both at Cos and in Alexandria. Oh, there were all sorts of gold and silver vessels, and candelabra, and candlesnuffers, and jewelry, and coins, and other items precious more for their history than for their intrinsic value. The whole collection should have filled a room about three times the size of the one we're standing in now, but at least half the hoard was gone. That tells us two things."

"Is one of those things about Zoticus?"

"Patience!" he said. "The first and most important thing it tells us is that King Mithridates never intended to return the treasury intact to the Jews of Alexandria."

"Might he have done such a thing?"

"As a grand gesture, yes. It was a possibility much hoped for by the Alexandrian Jews. The king could have said he seized the treasury from Cos only because it would be safer elsewhere, and then, at some later date—perhaps arriving in Alexandria either as an ally or as a conqueror—imagine what a magnificent gesture that would make, to publicly restore to the Jews of the city the treasury they had thought was lost. Mithridates would have won the trust and good will of Jews everywhere, not just in Egypt but in all of Asia and Judea. But clearly, that was not his intention."

"And the other thing the liquidation of the treasury tells us? Is it about Zoticus?"

"We'll get to him, never fear. No, the other thing it tells us is that Mithridates has need of that wealth, or else he would have left it intact for his own use later. No matter how loyal they may be, armies have to be paid. They have to be fed, too, and properly equipped. It's all very, very expensive. Running a royal household is also expensive, especially for a king as extravagant as Mithridates. You heard about the sum he was willing to pay Philopoemen, just to make Monime his mistress? Fifteen thousand pieces of gold! Simply on a day-to-day basis, imagine the cost of feeding and clothing all the courtiers and chamberlains and slaves—even the lowliest slave has to eat, and cannot go naked—and then the expense incurred every time the household moves from one city to another. It staggers the imagination."

"I suppose it does," I grudgingly admitted. "But when will—"

"So the precious treasury built up by generations of Jews in Egypt, buying and selling, saving whatever they could, year after year, surviving intact even when one Ptolemy threw another off the throne and heads rolled at the palace in Alexandria—half of that treasure is already gone, spent by Mithridates in a matter of months. Even so, I did manage to get my hands on a few items—"

"You were allowed to take some of the treasure?"

"Only a handful of items—literally a handful, or two, I should say, for I was allowed to take no more than I could carry, and each item I selected had to be approved by an assessor from the palace. The agreement was that I could take only items of historical or religious significance, things particularly precious to the Jews of Alexandria. Naturally, I grabbed the most expensive-looking objects I could find. Oh, you won't believe your eyes when you see the jewel-encrusted cup they let me walk away with. That required some special pleading, but I wore them down at last. I told them it was a thousand-year-old drinking cup, presented as a gift to King Solomon by the Queen of Sheba."

"Is it?"

"Who can say? But I tell you, the emeralds and rubies alone must be worth a fortune! That was the biggest prize, but I also left with some very nice pieces of silver. Still, compared to the entire treasure as listed in the ledger, I walked out with a mere pittance, only the feeblest gesture of goodwill from the looter to the looted."

"And the cloak you're wearing? That came from the treasury, too?"

"Ah, yes!" He looked down and touched a bit of the frayed hem to one side of his broad chest. "Well, there it was, lying amid some other pieces of cloth—elaborate wall hangings with golden threads and such—and I said, 'May I take this, as well, so as to have something to wrap around the cup and the other items?' The assessor hardly glanced at it, and when I held it closer, so that he could take a better look, he turned up his nose."

"It has a smell, Samson. Like something from an old person's house."

"Does it? Well, at any rate, he let me take this cloak as well. It worked nicely as a sort of sack to carry the other items."

I nodded. "So you've achieved one of your main objectives. The Jews of Alexandria sent you here to assess whatever remained of their stolen treasure, to negotiate for its return, and, failing that, to retrieve whatever token restitution Mithridates might offer."

"Yes. Exactly."

"Congratulations, Samson. But I, too, came here with an objective."

"Ah, yes. To see your old tutor again."

"I could have run after him earlier this evening, when I saw him in the dining hall—"

"And take him by surprise? Have him call out your real name, and then wait for you to answer? Cause any passersby to wonder how the two of you might know each other? No, Gordianus, that would never do. You realize that."

I took a deep breath. "Yes. But when—"

"So you don't think the cloak flatters me?"

"No!" I said, raising my voice, then biting my tongue.

"Is it too small for me? Perhaps it would look better on you." He began to pull it off. "If I were to offer it as a gift—"

"Samson, no more talk about this old cloak! Will I see Antipater tonight?"

He looked at me shrewdly. "Antipater, you say?"

"I mean . . . Zot—" I stammered awkwardly on the Z. "Zoticus—of course."

"Of course. Zoticus, Antipater—well, we all seem to have more than one name, don't we? Except for that beauty." He smiled at Bethesda, who slept on her side with her hands folded beneath her head, too exhausted to be awakened by our hushed conversation.

I looked at her peaceful face and shook my head. "I should never have brought her here. What a situation I've landed us in! I should have thought of some other way, or simply stayed in Alexandria. But I was selfish. I wanted to come, and I wanted her with me. I didn't want to be parted from her . . ." I was saying more than I should. I had already let slip Antipater's true name. "Please, Samson. No more jesting. I want to see Zoticus. If he's here in the palace, I want to see him now."

Samson saw that my patience was exhausted. The smile vanished from his face. He nodded, and seemed about to speak when we heard a gentle rapping at the door. Bethesda turned in her sleep, but did not wake.

Samson cracked the door to peer out with one eye, then opened it just enough for the visitor to slip inside. It was not Antipater. The man was much younger, and slender, with chestnut hair. With a start, I realized it was Zeuxidemus, dressed not in his yellow robes but in a plain tunic and with his hair neatly combed.

I was so surprised I almost spoke, but caught myself. Samson saw my consternation. He smiled. "It's all right, Agathon—Agathon, I say, because it will be simpler if we can all stick to one name, though we no longer have anything to hide from Zeuxidemus. You can speak, Agathon."

Never had I trusted Samson less, and never had I needed to trust him more. A priest of Artemis was in the room, and Samson seemed ready to give me away, if he had not done so already. At last I found my tongue. "What does this mean? Why have you let this man into the room?"

"Things are moving very fast now," said Samson. "Almost too fast for even me to keep up. As of yesterday, you had every reason to keep your secrets from Zeuxidemus. But today, all that has changed. Zeuxidemus has been vouched for, at the very highest level."

"The highest level of what?"

"I understand your confusion, Agathon. But everything will soon be made clear to you—what is being asked of you, and what is being offered."

I didn't like the sound of that. "Something tells me this bargain will be lopsided."

Samson cocked his head. "Indeed, it will be. What will be asked of you is as nothing compared to what may result."

"What is that?"

Zeuxidemus spoke. "A chance, however slim, to save the lives of many people. Tens of thousands of people."

"I came here to save only one."

"You may yet be able to do that, as well," said Samson.

"Something tells me there's a risk involved."

"Yes," said Samson. "A terrible risk. But then again—no. None at all. If you accept what we offer, and things do *not* go precisely as we hope, then yes, you will almost certainly die. But if you don't accept the role we offer, we shall expose you as a fraud, and then you will most certainly die, without question."

The hairs stood up on the back of my neck. What was this talk of dying? I had been thinking only of somehow helping Antipater—if indeed he needed my help—and then contriving some way to get Bethesda and myself out of Ephesus, perhaps by relying on Samson, who seemed to understand every situation and had access to money and other resources from Rome. The idea that I might be killed—indeed, would probably be killed, no matter what, as so starkly stated by Samson—had not been in my mind.

The two of them saw the look on my face. They looked at each other.

"Will they be coming here?" asked Samson.

"No. Too risky," said Zeuxidemus. "We'll go to them."

Samson nodded. "I see you've changed out of your yellow robes. A good idea. Less conspicuous that way."

"Yes, but I'll also have less authority to override anyone who questions us."

"A headdress does give one perquisites," said Samson.

"You, on the other hand, might wish to take off that . . . what is that thing you're wearing over your shoulders, anyway?"

"Oh, this?" Samson touched the frayed hem of the cloak and smiled. I gnashed my teeth at the prospect of being made to endure the same conversation again. "Let him wear the old cloak if he wants to," I said. "If we're going somewhere, why don't we get started?"

Zeuxidemus raised an eyebrow. "He really can speak, can't he? But by Artemis, that Roman accent! I hear accents like that every day, from all those Romans at the temple, but it's a bit of a shock, hearing such a thing under this roof."

"His accent isn't as bad as some," said Samson in my defense.

Zeuxidemus looked dubious. "It's pretty thick. Say something else, Agathon."

"I'll call down some curses on you in Latin, if I don't get some answers soon."

Zeuxidemus pursed his lips. "Yes, I suppose we should go. That lamp is almost burned out. No point in the three of us standing here in the dark."

"What about Bethesda?" I asked.

"The girl?" said Zeuxidemus. "Don't worry. She's quite safe here. Leave her sleeping."

"Will I be back before she wakes?"

"If you come back at all," said Samson.

XXVIII

[From the secret diary of Antipater of Sidon:]

To be mocked and made a fool of by that creature Sosipater! I surely can fall no lower. So here I sit, brooding and hungry and alone, unwilling to set foot in that dining hall as long as the juggler is holding court. Why am I back in the palace? What does the king want from me? Or was I brought here at the queen's behest?

I wonder sometimes what would have happened if I had not hearkened to the call to serve Mithridates, had not faked my death, had never left Rome. Would I have been happier? Probably not, for Italy was plunged into a miserable civil war shortly after I left, and with the rise of Mithridates it is hard to imagine that Greek poets (or any other Greeks) are very popular in Rome nowadays. And had I not taken the course I chose, I would not have seen the Seven Wonders, watching young Gordianus grow from a boy into a man along the way. So it must be with any fork in the road of life, that either way may lead to joy and tribulation, and both will end at the same place.

I had thought that serving the king as court poet was to be my destiny, the capstone to my career. I would be celebrated not only for my poems in honor of the king, but for the risks I had taken and the dangers I had braved. All my secrets I would proudly reveal, and Antipater of Sidon would be famous as the poet who cheated death, who traveled the world as a spy, who witnessed the rebirth of the Greek world at the side of King Mithridates. Instead I am like a Titan forced into a tiny box and barely able to move. I cannot speak my own name, much less recite my poetry. I feel no inspiration to make a new poem. I am an old man and not long for this world. Is there not one last useful, meaningful thing I can do before the end?

But there, I hear someone knocking at my door. This cannot be good. But I suppose I cannot ignore it . . .

[Here ends this fragment from the secret diary
of Antipater of Sidon.]

Zeuxidemus led us by a circuitous route that took us upstairs, then kept to the shadows of a square portico that surrounded a courtyard open to the sky, then headed down a long hallway and up another flight of stairs. Few people were abroad at this hour. Guards stood outside some of the doorways, but we saw them only at a distance.

I was hopelessly turned around by the time we halted at a door where Zeuxidemus made a peculiar knock, apparently using some sort of code, for this was followed by a rapping from inside the room, at which Zeuxidemus knocked again, and then the door swung open.

We stepped into what appeared to be a storage room. Even palaces must have places to put the mops and buckets and spare furniture. Several lamps illuminated the room, but the stacked crates and other contents were so jumbled that much of the space was in deep shadow, including the face of the man who must have opened the door, for he appeared to be the only person present.

The light did illuminate his feet, however, and I could see that his Corinthian-style slippers were made of very finely tooled leather. "Look at a man's feet if you want to determine his station in life," my father had taught me. Even in disguise, a rich man will seldom forego the luxury of wearing fine shoes, and these looked quite expensive. His tunic was plain, but well-made. Though his face was in shadow, by his silver hair and his spotted, gnarled hands I judged him to be in his seventies.

"This is the fellow?" he asked, indicating me. He spoke Greek almost like a native, but not quite. His accent, and the way he held himself, made me sure he was a Roman, even though he was not wearing a toga. But then, neither was I.

"This is the fellow," said Samson. "If I introduce him as Agathon of Alexandria, you'll laugh when he opens his mouth, so we might as well call him Gordianus."

The man nodded. "I knew your father, young man, back in Rome. Not well, mind you, but my path and that of the Finder crossed from time to time, over the years." His Latin accent became more pronounced as soon as he said the word *Rome*. "I am Publius Rutilius Rufus."

"The consul?" I asked.

"Why, yes, though that seems a lifetime ago. You were no more than a child the year I was elected."

"I was five," I said. "That was the year my father made me memorize all the consuls of Rome, beginning with Brutus and Collatinus. The list ended with you and your co-consul, Gnaeus Mallius Maximus."

"Ah, well, the world has taken many a turn since then, and most of them for the worse. I understand you're quite well traveled for a fellow your age."

"I've been to Babylon and back."

"And seen all the Seven Wonders. Yes, Samson told me a few things about you. You live in Alexandria."

"For the last few years, yes."

"Perhaps that makes you a bit of an outsider in this struggle between Rome and Mithridates, since Egypt has thus far stayed out of it."

"Agathon of Alexandria is an Egyptian, but I'm not," I said. "I was born a Roman citizen and I remain one, no matter where I may live. I'm every bit as much a Roman as you, Consul."

"More than I, some would say. The conviction that resulted from my trial imposed only a fine. My enemies didn't manage to strip me of my citizenship and exile me from Rome, as they would have liked. But I left Rome anyway, in disgust, and I'll never go back. I'm in voluntary exile. My enemies say that I've renounced my citizenship."

"Have you, Consul?"

"Absolutely not! I may regret but I'll never renounce being Roman. Like you, young man, I was born and will always be a Roman, no matter that I can no longer bear to be in Rome."

"You find Ephesus more bearable?"

"For the moment."

"Does King Mithridates know that you're here?" I asked.

Rutilius laughed. "Do you think I snuck into the palace? No, the king brought me here."

"As prisoner or guest?"

"With a king, I suppose a man can never be entirely sure until he tries to leave; but I'm being treated as a guest. I am even, about certain matters, the king's advisor."

"His advisor? Then you've turned against Rome and thrown in your lot with Mithridates." Why had Samson brought me to this traitor? What purpose could the consul and I have in common?

"It's not quite that simple, young man," said Rutilius.

"Surely a man must be with Mithridates and against Rome, or vice versa."

He turned so that the light revealed his face. He looked neither calculating nor exasperated, but only rather weary. "In the first place, Gordianus, the war perpetrated by Manius Aquillius was illegal and without the authorization of the Roman Senate. A true patriot would oppose such a war; had I been in Rome, I would have spoken out against it. But once hostilities commenced, as a Roman, even a Roman in exile, I could not favor the king's cause over Rome. I did not take up arms or involve myself in espionage for either side. Then I found myself in territory captured by Mithridates. I hoped the king would overlook me, that I would be of no interest to him. But no, the king knew exactly who and where I was, and summoned me to his presence. Perhaps, Gordianus, you've heard about the punishment inflicted by the king on Manius Aquillius, another Roman of consular rank? Yes, by your face I see you have. I feared that a similar fate awaited me. As a Stoic, I prepared myself for death—and a most unseemly death at that.

"But the king is neither a fool nor a fanatic. He knows that not all Romans are the same. I settled in this part of the world because I have so many friends here, far more than I have in Rome. And why is that? Because of my humane conduct and upright dealings when I was a legate here. I stood up for the locals when Roman businessmen and bankers sought to squeeze every denarius from them—the conduct that got me into so much trouble back in Rome. When I entered the throne room, instead of chopping off my head, Mithridates threw his arms around me. He asked me to join his court and to advise him—never on military affairs, mind you, but only on matter of jurisprudence."

"Jurisprudence?"

"Conquering a kingdom is one thing. Administering it is quite another. Courts must be created. Honest judges must be found. Laws must be drafted."

"Like the proclamation that all Romans must wear the toga?" I asked. "You seem to be in violation of that decree, Consul."

Rutilius pursed his lips, but did not respond.

"Or the decree that any Roman in possession of a weapon will be killed on the spot?" I asked.

"Ah, yes. Zeuxidemus told me about today's . . . unfortunate incident."

"Very unfortunate indeed for the Roman who had his throat slit, not to mention his starving wife and child, who had to witness such a thing."

"You would help that man's family, if you could?" asked Rutilius.

"Of course I would."

"Good. That's why we're here. We all agree that the slaughter of innocents must be prevented."

"What slaughter? Which innocents?"

Rutilius looked at Samson. "He doesn't know?"

"I'm not sure what Gordianus knows and doesn't know," said Samson.

"I know the king is planning some sort of ritual. There's to be a human sacrifice, meant to appease . . ." I had caught Bethesda's superstitious dread, and hesitated to name the Furies aloud.

"We all know to whom the sacrifice will be made," said Rutilius. "But do you know why the so-called Kindly Ones must be appeased? And not merely appeased, but won over, made to take the side of the king against his victims—"

"*Victims?*" I asked.

The consul cocked his head, not understanding my emphasis on the word.

"You didn't say *enemies*," I said. " 'Take the side of the king against his enemies'—that would mean the Roman legions. You said *victims.* You're talking about those Romans who've taken sanctuary at the Temple of Artemis. Mithridates intends to kill them."

Rutilius nodded. "And not only those Romans, Gordianus. In a single day, at a prearranged time, Mithridates plans to slaughter every Roman left in Asia. We are speaking not of thousands, but of many tens of thousands. All at once."

I had known that something of this nature was afoot, but I had not imagined the scale of it. "How could such a thing be done? Does the king have enough soldiers in every town, every village—"

"The killing will not be done by soldiers," said Rutilius. "Oh, in some instances, soldiers may lead or initiate the slaughter, and they'll surely be called on to help dispose of the bodies, but most of the killing will be done by ordinary men and women, roused by the leaders of their communities to such a pitch of hatred that they'll take up whatever weapons they possess—stones and sticks, if they have to—and murder every Roman they see. Men, women, children, the old—all of them. The next morning, there won't be a Roman left alive in any part of the kingdom. It will be as if everyone woke up, and the Romans had simply vanished."

"Except for the blood on the temple steps," I said. "And the stench of the dead."

"The blood will have been mopped up. The corpses will have been burned and buried, or taken to sea and dumped for Poseidon to swallow," said Rutilius.

"Rome will never forgive such a slaughter," I said. "The Senate and the people will demand vengeance."

"Vengeance against whom? The killing will have been done not by armies but by ordinary people."

"Then Rome will take vengeance on the people," I said.

"And kill every person in Ephesus, and every other city that takes part in a massacre?"

"Yes. Kill or enslave them. Consul, you know that Romans never forgive, and they never forget. How many generations did the war against Carthage last? How many times did old Cato end every speech by saying, 'Carthage must be destroyed'?"

Rutilius sighed. "I actually heard one of those speeches, when I was a boy."

"And in the end, Cato got his way, though he didn't live to see it. Carthage *was* destroyed, and all her people slaughtered or sold into slavery. This massacre won't be the end of Roman oppression; it will only be the beginning, because Rome will never stop until every city that takes part is punished. You know what I say is true, Consul. A massacre of the Romans will be a disaster for the people of Ephesus."

Rutilius bowed his head. "What you say is true, Gordianus. All the more reason that we must do something to stop this massacre."

"But how?"

"Before the slaughter takes place, Mithridates must seek to appease the Kindly Ones. He will do so by sacrificing the virgin you spoke of, this girl called Freny. But such sacrifices are rare—so rare that the Grand Magus and the Great Megabyzus were at pains to determine exactly how and where it should take place, and were sometimes at odds with each other. The king thought to perform the ritual quickly and be done with it, but there was one delay after another as various requirements had to be met, including the participation of certain 'witnesses,' such as you. While the ritual was repeatedly put off, planning for the massacre carried on, so that now the king is hard-pressed to offer the sacrifice before the massacres are committed. Only a handful of men across the kingdom know the exact date for the massacres—I do not—but it must be very soon now."

"So the sacrifice will take place, and poor Freny will die, and then . . . the massacre of the Romans," I said. "But how are we to stop any of this from taking place?"

There was a rapping at the door. It was gentle, but it startled me even so.

The consul's face brightened. "Once all of us are here, the situation shall be made clear to you, Gordianus."

"'All of us'?"

After an exchange of coded knocks, the consul indicated to Zeuxidemus that he could open the door.

A tall, slender man stepped inside, dressed much like Rutilius in a plain tunic and good shoes. For a moment I didn't recognize him without his yellow robes and headdress. It was none other than the Great Megabyzus. His long, gray-streaked hair was pulled back from his face and tied behind his head. Without his priestly robes and the severe expression that went along with them, he looked quite ordinary. He gave me a faint smile of recognition.

Another man followed him into the room, a graybeard who furtively ducked his head so that I couldn't see his face. At last he looked up, and our eyes met. He looked as if he might faint from astonishment.

It was Antipater.

XXIX

Antipater stared at me with his jaw hanging open. Slowly, the deep furrows of his brow turned upward and his gaping mouth formed an uncertain smile.

"Gordianus!" he whispered.

"So the two of you *do* know each other," remarked the consul, "just as Samson said."

A part of me longed to embrace Antipater. Instead, I took a step back. In the small room, I could retreat no farther.

"I don't understand," I said. "What is the Great Megabyzus doing here? Isn't he the very man we're hiding from?"

"Perhaps I should speak," said Samson, "since it was I who brought us all together. And I'm the only one here who knows the true name of everyone in the room."

The six of us stood roughly in a circle. I looked from face to face, beginning with Samson to my left hand, and then to Zeuxidemus, who stood closest to the door, then to the newcomers Antipater and the Great Megabyzus, and finally to Rutilius.

The Great Megabyzus flashed a wry smile. "Even I have a name. I suppose, in these circumstance, I might as well use it. When I take off my robes and headdress, my family and friends call me Kysanias."

Samson gave Kysanias a respectful nod. "Except for me, every man here, in one role or another, will take part in the sacrifice at the Grove of the Furies—yes, let's use their true name, and no more talk of 'Kindly Ones.' This long-delayed sacrifice will take place . . . ?"

"Tomorrow night, an hour after sundown," said Kysanias.

Samson nodded. "If the sacrifice goes well, then the massacre of the Romans will follow very soon thereafter. We assume that the date for the massacre has already been set, since such a thing must necessarily require a great deal of planning. No one in this room knows the exact date—not even Kysanias—but we know it must be very soon. Therefore—"

Antipater cleared his throat. In a thin, rasping voice, he said, "I believe that I know the date."

I was so pleased to hear him speak that I hardly heard what he said. The sound of his voice made me smile. Antipater possessed a highly trained voice, as skilled as that of any orator or actor, capable of many inflections, for a great poet must be able to speak in the voice of a young girl or an old crone or a heroic warrior, or even a god, and no poet was a more versatile reciter than Antipater. Yet, ironically, his own voice, his normal speaking voice, was rather high and not entirely pleasing to the ear. Still, just to hear it made my heart beat faster. No matter how strange the circumstances, I was at last gazing at Antipater in the flesh and could see that he was indeed alive, if not looking as well as I had hoped. Was it the harsh light of the lamps, casting shadows across his furrowed face, that made him look so haggard?

It was only from the startled reactions of all the others that I realized what Antipater had just said. I stared at him as I spoke. "Teacher, is this true? You know the date of the massacre?"

He stared back at me. Surrounded by the others, we could hardly react to the sight of each other in a normal way, and certainly could not say all that needed to be said. When Antipater spoke, I felt like laughing and crying at once, for here was the eloquent poet, never at a loss for words, seeming to stumble over every sentence.

"It was in the house of Eutropius . . . I've been staying there . . . instead of the palace—but the king would visit . . . talk of the killings to come . . . and Eutropius was given a part to play, you see, whether he liked it or not . . . one of the few men in all of Ephesus to be told . . . and now this awful news about that poor slave girl from his house! How many times did Freny wait upon me, and how many times did I look at her beaming young face and take heart, despite my troubles? But never mind that—yes, I know the date, for I happened to overhear it—oh! I have hardly been able to sleep since then . . ."

Rutilius shuddered with frustration. "Who *is* this jabbering fellow?"

"To the royal court," said Samson, "he was introduced as Zoticus of Zeugma, a little-known poet and retired tutor."

"Yes, yes," said the consul, "I've seen him across the room at royal banquets, but who *is* he, and why is he here?" Zeuxidemus and Kysanias also looked interested in hearing the answer.

Samson looked to me and cocked an eyebrow.

I cleared my throat. "This man . . . this man was my tutor when I was a boy, back in Rome. I was very lucky to receive instruction from him. My father could never have afforded to pay his usual fees. There was some bond of friendship between the two of them . . . and a bond also grew between us, between pupil and teacher. So strong a bond that when he did a most unusual thing, and pretended to be dead—being so bold as to attend his own funeral!—I went along with the deception, and so did my father. That is how he came to take the name Zoticus of Zeugma."

"So this is the man with whom you saw the Seven Wonders?" asked Rutilius.

"Yes. We traveled many miles, across seas and forests and deserts, and saw many things. We met many people. But while I was distracted by beauty and pleasure, Zoticus . . . Zoticus was up to something else. He was acting as a messenger and spy for King Mithridates. And I never knew—until we parted ways in Alexandria. That was three years ago.

Not a word did I hear from him, or about him, after that—no letter, no news. Until just a few days ago, when a document arrived in Alexandria addressed to me. A piece of parchment taken from some larger document—an excerpt from a sort of diary, perhaps. . . ."

Antipater made a fist and put it to his mouth. "The missing page!" he said. "It was sent to you! But by whom? And how did they know where to reach you? Oh, dear—the letter I kept writing and never sending, addressed to you. They must have copied your name and the banker's address from that." He seemed on the verge of tears.

"We have strayed from the purpose of this meeting," said Kysanias. "And we have very little time. Tell us at once, young Roman: Who is this man?"

I drew back my shoulders. I stood with my chin up and my arms bent in a particular way, assuming the posture learned by every young Roman when he becomes a man. I felt almost as if I wore a toga, for the weight and the folds of the garment become second nature to those who are taught to take the stance of a dignified Roman citizen. "This man, whom I was proud to call my tutor and traveling companion, is better known to most of the world—the parts of the world that speak Greek, anyway—as the greatest of all living poets. Surely you know his name, Consul."

Rutilius looked confounded. "But . . . no!" He shook his head and stared at Antipater, who seemed to shrink under such intense scrutiny. "I knew the man by reputation, of course, but I never met him. When he died, I was too busy preparing for my trial to attend the funeral, though everyone else did. You can't mean to say . . ."

Zeuxidemus stood back a bit from Antipater, gazing at him with a mixture of curiosity and wonder. "Do you mean to say that in our midst, all this time, without anyone knowing—"

"The king knows who I am," said Antipater. "So does the queen— or she knows my name, anyway. About poetry I suspect she knows very little."

"Yes," I said, answering Zeuxidemus. "This man is Antipater of Sidon."

Though they had already guessed, still I heard small gasps from the consul and the two priests. Such is the power of fame. Antipater seemed to grow a bit—especially when, under his breath, Zeuxidemus recited the famous line, " 'But the house of Artemis at Ephesus, of all the Wonders Seven. . . .' "

"What an unlikely group this is," said Kysanias. "A Roman consul in exile . . . a Jewish envoy from Alexandria . . . a young Roman pretending to be a mute Egyptian . . . two priests of Artemis . . . and—of all people, living or dead!—Antipater of Sidon. But I take it we are all desirous of the same end: to somehow avert the mass slaughter of the Romans. Agreed?"

Kysanias looked at each of us in turn. Each of us nodded, and said aloud, "Agreed."

I added, "And I would prevent the death of Freny—if I could. . . ."

"As would I," said Kysanias, very quietly. "To stop the massacre, once it commences, will be impossible. So many people are already so eager to do away with the Romans, it will take very little to set them into action, and once that's done, there will be no stopping them."

"What are we to do?" I asked.

"The slaughter must be stopped before it can begin," said Kysanias. "The sacrifice in the Grove of the Furies must go awry. If the sacrifice is spoiled—if the Furies have not been appeased—then Mithridates may yet be turned from this course."

Kysanias paused for a long moment, so that we could all appreciate the gravity of what he had just said. The highest priest of the world's greatest temple to Artemis was suggesting that we—himself included—should deliberately pervert a sacred ritual calling upon the most dangerous and terrifying forces known to mankind.

"If we do such a thing . . ." Rutilius seemed hesitant to speak the thought aloud. "Might we not turn the wrath of the Furies on ourselves?"

"We must weigh that possibility against the appalling magnitude of the act we are trying to avert," said Kysanias. "If in the end the Furies and all of Olympus are on the side of Mithridates, if this massacre is sanctioned by the gods, then any attempt to avert it will fail, and we must suffer for our hubris. But who here, in his heart of hearts, does not believe the slaughter is uncalled for—terrible in itself, and a blight upon the cause of Mithridates? People given sanctuary in the Temple of Artemis will be dragged out and killed. Blood will be shed on sacred ground, not only in Ephesus, but in cities and temples all over the kingdom. I cannot believe such a thing accords with the will of Artemis.

"I believe that each of us here is an instrument of the Fates, for how else did we all arrive from distant points to come together at this very time and place? You, Gordianus—do you not feel that you were guided here for a purpose greater than you imagined? Pretending for your own reasons to be mute, you became the mute witness whose presence was required for the sacrifice."

"But . . . as you say, my muteness is a pretense. I meant to fool mortals, not gods! And certainly not . . . the Furies. At every moment I feel I'm hanging by a thread—"

"Exactly so—a thread woven by the Fates!" Kysanias nodded, his eyes wide with excitement. "The ritual requires a mute witness, and none was found until you, yet you are not genuine. So when the ritual takes place, it will already be compromised, by your presence in place of a genuine mute witness. Surely that is a sign that the ritual is intended to fail. The sacrifice will go awry, and Mithridates will be put off, afraid to proceed with the massacre."

Rutilius looked doubtful. "It's hard to imagine the king being afraid of anything."

"Mithridates is a mortal like any other," insisted Kysanias. "In the Grove of the Furies, he will sense a power greater than himself. He can be made to feel fear."

"Your Eminence," I said, "I understand what you say about the twisted path that led me here. But Samson says we're all to play a role in the sacrifice." I looked at Rutilius. "What is *your* role, Consul?"

He shrugged. "Mithridates wants a Roman to witness the sacrifice, preferably a Roman of high rank, to see that the massacre has been divinely sanctioned. I will be that Roman."

Antipater bristled. "You claim to be merely a witness? I overheard you outside the king's door, plotting with Metrodorus the Rome-Hater, discussing how best to dispose of the bodies."

Rutilius sighed. "Like everyone else here, I'm playing more than one role. Yes, I know something about the planning of this massacre. It might be argued that I even, to some extent, helped to plan it—but only so that I might stop it. How better to avert this mad idea than by discovering all I could about it? Toward that end, you see me here. It was Samson who felt me out, acting on behalf of the deposed Roman governor in Rhodes. I will *not* become an agent of Rome against Mithridates, but in this single instance I will do what I can to foil the king's intentions. And you, Antipater—are you also taking part in the sacrifice?"

"So it seems. The king decided that a poet should witness the sacrifice. Who else would he choose but the world's greatest living poet? But as I was trying to tell you, earlier—"

"I wondered why the king insisted that the poet be a man I'd never heard of," said Kysanias. "I should have known there was more to this so-called Zoticus of Zeugma than met the eye. Again, we see the hand of the Fates!"

"Or the hand of Samson," I said. "And you, Your Eminence? And Zeuxidemus? Are you of one mind about this?"

Kysanias put his hand on the younger priest's shoulder. "Zeuxidemus is pure of heart, as he has demonstrated many times, by words and deeds and by his devotion to the goddess. He is the only one of my fellow Megabyzoi with whom I have shared my true feelings about this matter. As for me . . . this all began when the king called the Grand Magus and me into his throne room and revealed to us in strictest confidence the massacre he was planning. How his eyes shone, how his voice quavered with excitement!

"I was taken aback. So, to his credit, was the Grand Magus. We suggested alternatives. To rid himself of the Romans, could His Majesty not strip them of all property and send them into exile? Or if he preferred a harsher punishment, might he not enslave them? No! He was insistent that they be killed, every one of them, even the women and infants. But it had occurred to him that dark forces might arise in response to an act of such magnitude.

"By various means, the Grand Magus and I determined that the Furies must be placated, and that only the sacrifice of a virgin would suffice. Only one person could carry out the sacrifice—myself.

"In my many years as a Megabyzus serving Artemis, I have slaughtered hundreds, perhaps thousands of animals. Never have I been squeamish. The glimmer of awareness in the animal's eyes in the moment before it dies, the slicing of the blade into the flesh, the gushing of the blood, the thrashing of the victim—I have exulted in these things, for they serve the greater glory of Artemis. And yet . . .

"As I contemplated the act required of me—the slaughter of a young girl, by my own hand . . . the prospect haunts my dreams. Every night I see myself in the Grove of the Furies, standing at the altar, with the girl restrained and helpless before me. She struggles against her bonds, she cries out through the gag in her mouth—and that is a good thing, for with an animal sacrifice the docility of the victim is a sign of submission to the deity, but with a human sacrifice, the greater the struggle, the better.

"The knife is in my hands. The moment comes. I look into her eyes. I raise the blade—and the moment that follows is so horrible that I wake in a cold sweat. Even now, thinking of it, I feel a chill. My stomach tightens. My hands shake—do you see?"

Kysanias help up both trembling hands.

"A sign from Artemis. These hands are dedicated to her service, and see how they shake at the very thought of what I'm being called to do? I must not do it. I will not! You must all help me. We must find a way to stop it. In doing that, we may stop the greater slaughter that is to follow."

A grim silence followed his words, as we all looked from face to face in the flickering lamplight.

Antipater opened his mouth to say something, but I spoke first. "What about you, Samson?" I asked.

"Me?"

"You brought us all together. But why? What is your purpose?"

"You know why I came here, Gordianus: to recover what I could of the stolen treasure of the Jews of Alexandria." He shrugged, and fingered the hem of the old cloak he had taken from the treasury.

"But that doesn't explain why you brought us all together. Why do *you* want to stop this sacrifice and avert the massacre of the Romans?"

"You know the answer to that, Gordianus. My mission was in part funded by Rome and Rome's allies in Rhodes. To the extent that I accepted their help and money, I'm obligated to do whatever I can to further their interests. Surely, stopping the slaughter of tens of thousands of innocent Romans is something Posidonius and Gaius Cassius would want me to do."

"You have no religious qualms? You fear no punishment for impiety or hubris?"

"As I told you before, Gordianus, I am a Jew. I don't worship Artemis. Nor do I fear these Furies you all regard with such awe. At any rate, I have no part to play in the sacrifice. Tomorrow night, you won't see me in the Grove of the Furies."

Antipater stamped his foot and gritted his teeth. I thought he was vexed by Samson's impiousness, until he spoke.

"You must all be quiet! You must let me speak. I know the date for the massacre. I know, because I overheard the king give instructions to Eutropius, telling him the day and the hour. It's sooner than you seem to think. It will happen two days from now—the day after tomorrow!"

XXX

There was a stunned silence.

"But that means . . ." Zeuxidemus furrowed his brow.

Kysanias shook his head. "Impossible! Without placating the Furies, the king cannot proceed with the massacre. What if the ritual goes badly? If the killings have been arranged to take place the very next day, there'll be no way to stop them—no way to send the organizers a message. Winged Hermes couldn't travel that fast!"

Rutilius looked at Antipater. "You're absolutely certain of this?"

"It's not something a man would forget," said Antipater. "I've been counting the days, dreading what's to come."

"Impossible!" Kysanias repeated.

"No, it's all too possible," said Rutilius. "It's just like Mithridates, isn't it? The man has never been afraid to take a risk. While the date for the sacrifice was repeatedly postponed, the date for the massacre was firm. Now the one will take place on the very eve of the other. Mithridates is gambling that the sacrifice will go well. He thinks himself so favored by the gods, how could it go otherwise?"

"The hubris of the man!" said Zeuxidemus.

Kysanias raised his hand. "We are not here to speak against the king. Our purpose is to stop the king from making a terrible mistake."

"But Your Eminence, don't you see? We can't stop it now," said Zeuxidemus. "No matter what happens in the Grove of the Furies, the massacres will take place the next day, everywhere at once."

"Perhaps . . . not everywhere," I said. "Might we avert the massacre here in Ephesus, at least?"

Kysanias considered this. "Yes. If we can contrive to spoil the sacrifice, and the king is made to fear the consequences, then he might at least put a stop to the killing here. The Romans in Ephesus might be saved, and the sanctity of the Temple of Artemis preserved. That would be . . . no small accomplishment."

"But much smaller than we hoped," said Rutilius. "What of the Romans in Pergamon and Adramyttion, in Caunus and Tralles? What of all the temples that will be profaned in those cities?"

Zeuxidemus bowed his head. He was weeping.

Kysanias put his arm around the younger priest. "This is . . . a disappointment. But we mustn't be deterred from our purpose. If only one life can be saved, is that not worth our efforts?"

"Only one life?" I whispered. I was thinking of Freny, remembering her smile and her laughter, and also the look of terror on her face as she was taken from the house of Eutropius. "I still don't understand. Who will disrupt the sacrifice, and how?"

"Who?" said Kysanias. "*We* must do it—the five of us in this room who will be there. As to how . . . that is what we must decide."

"Can't you simply refuse to conduct the sacrifice?" I asked.

Kysanias shook his head. "I've already postponed it as long as I could—too long, as it turns out, since now we've lost any chance to save the Romans beyond Ephesus. I can't call off the sacrifice altogether."

Antipater spoke up. "Your Eminence spoke of the ritual going awry. How might that happen?"

"A crack of lightning at the right moment would do the job," said Kysanias. "But I don't suppose we can manage that. Likewise, if certain birds were to be seen atop the tall cypress trees that encircle the sacred space around the altar; but that, too, is beyond our control. If the victim were discovered to be a hermaphrodite, or not a virgin—but the girl has already been examined."

"Her virginity could be taken from her," said Rutilius, raising an eyebrow.

"The man who did that would be flayed alive," said Kysanias. "And such a rape would most certainly summon the wrath of the Furies."

"I don't suppose we could contrive to leave her alone with the king for an hour?" I asked. "I believe the only reason Freny was chosen was because the queen discovered the king's desire for her. Now Freny has been put beyond his reach. He'll never have the girl . . . and neither will anyone else."

"That would be rich," said Rutilius, "if we could trick Mithridates into taking the virginity of his own virgin sacrifice! But I don't see how that could be accomplished."

"I think we should return our thoughts to the ritual itself," said Kysanias, "and the means at our disposal to disrupt it."

"And somehow keep our heads, into the bargain!" said Antipater. "What about an uncanny voice?"

"A voice?" asked Kysanias.

"The way your voice changed just now, when you spoke to us so firmly, put me in mind of it. In my long lifetime I've heard of a number of sacrifices and other religious ceremonies being interrupted by uncanny voices—voices from the sky, or out of the earth, or from an animal's mouth, that sort of thing."

Rutilius nodded thoughtfully. "I, too, have heard of this phenomenon. An uncanny voice . . . but how might we achieve such an effect, and in such a way that the sacrifice would be spoiled? It's too bad there's not an actor among us, or a theatrical manager. Those people know all sorts of ways to fool the eye and ear."

"In my experience," I said, "the men who manage temples can also be rather skilled at creating illusions." I looked at Kysanias, who looked back at me shrewdly. "And while we may not have an actor among us, we do have the world's greatest living poet."

We all looked at Antipater. He drew back his shoulders, like a man who had been issued a challenge. Once again he seemed to grow larger, and several years fell away from him.

"I have an idea," I said.

It was almost dawn when I returned to my room. I crept into bed, thinking Bethesda was asleep. But an instant later she twined her arms and legs around me, pulling me tightly against her.

"I thought something terrible might have happened to you," she murmured.

I was so weary, I thought I would fall asleep at once. My consciousness faded even as my body responded to her touch. Our lovemaking was ferocious and dreamlike. I fell asleep not knowing where my body ended and hers began.

At some point reality ended and dreams began, for the woman in my arms became, in some gradual, inexplicable way, not Bethesda but Amestris, though I could not have said in what way she changed. Indeed, when I pulled back for a moment and looked in her eyes, it seemed to me she was both women at once. The goddess Artemis spoke to me then, saying, "You have only ever coupled with one woman, and this is her in your arms."

"Is she a goddess then, that she assumes so many different guises? Is she you, goddess?"

"She could never be me, because I am forever a virgin," said Artemis. She laughed like a girl. I recognized that laugh—yes, it was Freny! Then Freny stopped laughing, drew her arms to her sides, and became as rigid as a statue. I saw that coils of rope held her arms to her sides. She struggled against them but couldn't move. Then she was on her back, faceup, being carried by several men toward an altar already covered with blood. I saw that she was gagged and unable to speak, but she looked at me frantically, pleading with her eyes.

I woke with a start.

The sun was up. Bethesda sat in a chair across the room, dressed in the yellow tunic I had worn the day before. The color flattered her smooth, dark skin and long black hair. She was gnawing at a piece of bread.

"Are you hungry?" she asked. "This morning they brought us food." She gestured to the small table beside her, where a tray was heaped with bread, fruits, and nuts. "You're not to leave the room. There's a man outside to make sure you don't. He says they'll bring more food later, though it seems to me there's plenty here already. Then, in the late afternoon, they'll come for you. To take part in this ritual, I gather. They won't let me go with you. I'll have to stay here."

I opened my mouth to speak, but she put a finger to her lips, then gestured to the door, indicating that the guard might overhear. She rose from the chair and came to the bed, then put her ear to my lips.

In a whisper, I told her what had happened the night before, and what I hoped would happen that night. She didn't interrupt me, but occasionally she pulled back and gave me a skeptical look, or made some scoffing noise. Were our plans really so full of holes that an Alexandrian slave girl could see through them? It occurred to me that the six of us crammed together in that stifling storage room had descended into a kind of mutual madness, and the scheme we had concocted was not just deranged but doomed.

By the harsh light of day, were the others all coming to the same conclusion? But there was no way we could meet again before the time for the sacrifice arrived. There could be no more revising or rehearsing. I saw no choice but to go through with what we had planned. Either that, or let the sacrifice take place as Mithridates intended, watch Freny die, and leave the Romans of Ephesus to their fate.

"Once it's all over," I whispered, "and as soon as it's safe to do so, Samson will bring you to me." That was the plan. But what if everything went wrong? "If that's not possible . . . for some reason . . . then you're to go with Samson anyway. He promises to keep you safe."

"I'm to be his slave?" Her voice rose sharply. She caught herself, looked toward the door, and clamped her mouth shut.

"Absolutely not!" I whispered. The idea made my face hot. "But you may have to pretend to be his slave, or his wife, or whatever, in order to get away from Ephesus. Once you're back in Alexandria, he's to take you to Berynus and Kettel. They'll know what to do."

"Then I'm to be the slave of the two eunuchs?" Her voice rose again.

In fact, as I had told Berynus and Kettel before I set out, with the banker who handled my money and my mail I had left a document with instructions that Bethesda was to be manumitted after my death, and to inherit whatever money I had stored up. Could she make a life for herself as a free woman in Alexandria, without resorting to crime or prostitution? Perhaps, especially if she could find the right man to marry her. I didn't like to think about that, and I saw no need for her to do so, either. I wasn't going to die, was I?

I whispered the words aloud to her. "I'm not going to die, am I? So you need not worry about becoming someone else's slave. I'm only saying that if . . . if Samson is not able to bring you to me . . . then you're to go with him, and do as he says."

"You trust Samson, then?"

"Yes. I think so," I whispered, thought it still seemed that more about Samson had been kept hidden from me than had been revealed.

She sighed, and with a faraway look on her face she muttered, "I suppose there could be worse men to become my new master. . . ."

Did she *like* the idea of becoming Samson's slave? My face grew hot again. No, she was only teasing me. Yes, that must be it, I told myself.

[From the secret diary of Antipater of Sidon:]

What a relief it is, to be back in the palace, staying with the royal household. No sooner had I stepped foot inside than I felt a great weight drop away from me. I was like a lost sheep returned to the fold—yes, exactly so, and if I am a sheep, then Mithridates is the shepherd. Of all the mortals of his generation, what better shepherd has appeared to lead mankind? (Note: remember this metaphor as material for a possible poem—the king as shepherd, the poet as wandering lamb.)

I admit that I have been torn by doubts since joining the royal household.

I was shocked by the execution of Manius Aquillius. I chafed against the king's insistence that I remain Zoticus of Zeugma. I was suspicious and fearful of his beautiful queen. But now I see the light of his wisdom. Like a lighthouse, the King of Kings towers above the rest of us, not only illuminating our way, but also able to see much farther than the rest of us. We must learn to trust his wisdom, even when we are too shortsighted to discern the path he sees ahead. (Yet another metaphor worthy to be worked up in verse! "How like the Pharos is the King of Kings, towering high above us. . . .")

How I look forward to taking part in tonight's ritual! What an honor it was for me to have been chosen by the king! And after that, very soon, we shall see the last of the Romans in our midst. Then the king will be free to carry the war to the enemy . . .

But now I must rest, and ready myself to play my part in tonight's events.

[Here ends this fragment from the secret diary
of Antipater of Sidon.]

XXXI

I spent much of that day sleeping. I badly needed the rest, having had so little the night before.

Late in the afternoon, the chamberlain came for me. "Wear whatever you like," he said. "You'll be properly dressed for the ritual after the bath."

"Bath?" asked Bethesda, reading the quizzical look on my face.

"Of course you must be cleansed before the ritual. There are boys who will bathe you. Unless your slave usually bathes you? In that case, you may bring her along. But she can't wear that yellow tunic. It wouldn't be proper."

The two of us dressed in the clothes in which we had arrived, then followed the chamberlain to a small, beautifully tiled room, all in shades of dark green and blue. If I had been expecting a proper Roman-style bath—something I had not had in days, and had begun to crave—I was to be disappointed. Here there were no pools in which a man could submerge himself, but instead only a simple drain in the floor, tiled benches along the walls, strigils of various shapes, flasks of aromatic oils, several pitchers of water of various temperatures, and cloths for drying myself. After we were left alone, I stripped, allowed Bethesda to apply the oils to every part of me, then stood while she scraped the oil off using whichever strigil had a blade best shaped for that part of my body.

Since we had been left alone, and there was plenty of oil and water, I did the same for Bethesda. I realized I had never bathed her in such a way, paying such close attention to every part of her. The act was erotic, to be sure, but also strangely calming, and somehow somber, since this might be the act that marked our final moments together. If so, the Fates were kind to allow this last act to be so intimate, and of mutual service to each other. I dared not speak, lest someone overhear, but no words were needed. I had never felt closer to her.

Once cleansed, we rinsed each other first with warm water, then with cold. Enough of the oil clung to the skin to leave us supple and gleaming and lightly perfumed. As I gazed at Bethesda, who stood before me wearing nothing, I wondered how I could ever have confused her in my dreams with Amestris, or with any other woman, since Bethesda was the most beautiful of all. I should have liked to simply stand there, staring at her, but she quickly dressed, not wanting the chamberlain to come upon her while she was naked.

When the chamberlain returned, he brought me a dark tunic that reached below my knees and covered most of my arms. He insisted on dressing me himself. I think this was so that he could check to see that I had been sufficiently cleaned. "Your slave did an excellent job. She seems to have bathed herself as well," he noted, not realizing that it was I who bathed her. "She'll be taken back to your room now, and you will follow me."

Another chamberlain was waiting at the door. He nodded to Bethesda, then led her away. She gave me a last glance over her shoulder. How I longed to speak her name!

The chamberlain led me in another direction. It was the hour of dusk, when preparations are made to light the lamps. Servants were kindling fires, carrying torches, and pouring oil into vessels. The hours of daylight were done. The hours of darkness had begun.

I was led to a large courtyard where several litters were waiting, all shrouded with black curtains. The chamberlain indicated that I should step into one of these, and I found myself once more in the company of Gnossipus and Damianus. Like me, they wore dark tunics. They sat side by side, while I sat across from them.

The deaf man gave me a grunt of welcome. Gnossipus raised an eyebrow. "Is that you, Agathon?"

The interior was so plush with pillows and cushions that I had to search to find a hard wooden surface on which to rap my knuckles. I did so twice.

"Ah, so it *is* you, Agathon. Often I can recognize people by their smell, but we've all been scrubbed clean and perfumed with the same scented oil, so we all smell alike. Here we are, the three of us, off to do whatever it is the king requires. I find it rather exciting, don't you?"

I rapped my knuckles twice. *More exciting than you know,* I thought. As the litter was lifted from the blocks, my heart began to race.

All night Antipater and I had practiced what we planned to do. But would I have the nerve? Would Antipater? We were to act on a signal from Kysanias. Would the priest carry through with our plans, or would his courage fail him?

The curtains remained closed as we set off. I could see nothing outside the litter. As the last light of day receded, the interior of the litter became so dark that I was almost as blind as Gnossipus.

"I wonder where we're headed?" he said. "I mean to say, I know we're off to the Grove of the . . . Kindly Ones . . . but I don't know where that is. Do you?"

I knocked once. With so much else to discuss and rehearse the night before, I hadn't thought to ask Kysanias the location of the grove. With the curtains closed and darkness all around, I had no idea in what direction we were headed. At some point, from the sounds outside, I was certain we passed through a city gate, but Ephesus had several gates, all leading in different directions.

Gnossipus began to hum tunelessly. "They wouldn't let me bring my flute," he said morosely.

Damianus began to shift nervously in his seat. Unable to hear and with only darkness around him, it was no wonder he began to feel unsettled. I realized that I was shifting about uneasily, too, and grinding my teeth.

The journey seemed to last a long time.

At last we came to a halt. I felt the litter settle onto blocks. The curtains were drawn back. A figure holding aloft a torch silently beckoned for us to step out. The light of the flames revealed the face of Zeuxidemus, though he was dressed not in yellow but in a dark tunic not unlike the one I was wearing. So were all the men around him. Among them I recognized some of the Megabyzoi and Magi who had examined me naked, including the Grand Magus and Kysanias. Their clothing was so dark that it was hard to tell one from another, but that was intentional. A man does not approach the Furies dressed in such a way as to call attention to himself.

Leaving the litter-bearers behind, and led by a few among us bearing torches, we walked a short distance, stopping at a low wall made of rough-hewn stones. There was a break in this wall, beyond which a gravel path led to a circle of towering cypress trees. In the darkness, it was hard to judge the diameter of this circle. The tall, slender trees stood so close together that they formed a sort of wall. Whatever might be inside that circle of trees could not be seen.

The night was very still. There was no sound except that of footsteps and the crackling of torches. A company of spear-bearers approached; these were the king's private bodyguards, clad in armor and helmets that gleamed in the torchlight. They escorted a small group dressed in the same dark tunics as the Magi and Megabyzoi. Among the approaching faces illuminated by the flickering light I saw those of Antipater and Rutilius.

At the head of this company was a man who would have stood out even if he had not been wearing a fillet of purple and white on his head. Mithridates stood taller than even the tallest of his bodyguards, and his black tunic did not conceal the breadth of his shoulders and the brawniness of his arms and legs. Though the night was warm, he wore a cloak as well, just as Kysanias had predicted, saying the king always wore it for important occasions—the purple cloak of Alexander the Great, taken from the Egyptian treasury at Cos. The gold embroidery on the cloak caught the light, further setting him apart from the rest of us.

The king's face was clean-shaven, showing his powerful jaw. Torchlight picked out strands of silver amid the long hair combed back from his face. His strong features were those of a man who looks his best in middle age. His mouth was grim but his eyes glittered with confidence.

The only other monarch I had ever seen so close at hand was the recently deposed King Ptolemy, back in Egypt. Two men could not have been more dissimilar. If King Ptolemy was the fattest man I'd ever seen, Mithridates was one of the fittest, and certainly the most formidable. Seeing him in the flesh, I despaired for his enemies, including Rome.

I despaired for myself, as well, for this was the man we were conspiring to deceive. Even at a glance, I saw that Mithridates was no man's fool. What had we been thinking? I remembered the scoffing noises Bethesda had made as I described our scheme. I felt light-headed. A trickle of sweat snaked its way down my spine.

Next to the king, so much smaller that she seemed almost a child, was the queen. Monime was swathed in black silk. Her body merged into the darkness, so that her red-gold hair and pale round face seemed almost to levitate, as if attached to nothing beneath.

I glanced at the others in the king's company. Besides Antipater and Rutilius, I recognized the young Prince Ptolemy, who stood near Monime. The golden cobra of his uraeus crown, with its ruby eyes, glittered in the light. Why was he being included in the ritual? Did the king think of the kidnapped prince as part of his household? Or, since he wore a crown, was Ptolemy present as a royal representative of Egypt, despite his father's fall from the throne?

There was also a man I took to be Metrodorus of Scepsis, the so-called Rome-Hater, one of the king's closest advisors. Kysanias had described the man and told me a little about him the previous night, saying Metrodorus would be the observer around whom we must be most careful, because of his famous ability to remember every detail of everything he saw and heard. Metrodorus had perfected his memory with a method of his own invention, based somehow on the divisions of the zodiac. I wished I could have met him under other circumstances. My father had taught me some simple tricks of memorization, but what might Metrodorus be able to teach me?

Also near the front of the company was a man I assumed to be Monime's father, Philopoemen. As Episcopus of Ephesus, he carried a staff with a gold knob at the top to show his authority as a royal over-seer. I looked at him only for an instant, because I suddenly saw two men farther back in the group, hidden in the shadows until that moment.

The two men stood out for very different reasons, one on account of his size—he was even taller than the king, indeed quite possibly the largest man I had ever seen—and the other because, unlike everyone else, he was dressed in white. The giant had a gaunt, grim face and yellow hair, and held a chain linked to an iron collar around the Roman's neck—for the other man was most certainly a Roman because he was wearing a toga, and not just any toga but one with a broad purple stripe, marking his status as a promagistrate authorized to wage war. This had to be the captured Roman general, Quintus Oppius, and his keeper was the giant called Bastarna. Kysanias had told me these two might be present, the king's bully leading the king's pet Roman on a leash. Standing out because of his toga, was Oppius meant to attract the attention of the Furies and call down their wrath on his fellow Romans?

Kysanias stood before the opening in the low stone wall. We gathered before him in a semicircle. He addressed us in his deep, commanding voice. "We have arrived at the Grove of the Furies. This stone wall marks the perimeter of the sacred precinct. Except for the sacrificial knife and ax in my hands . . ." Kysanias held them upright, so that the blades glittered in the torchlight. "Except for these, no weapon of any sort can be allowed beyond this point. If you wish your bodyguards to accompany you, Your Majesty, they must lay down their arms."

"That will not happen, Your Eminence," said Mithridates. "These men keep their arms at all times."

"Then they must remain outside the wall," said Kysanias. In his voice I heard no quaver of doubt or hesitation, and took heart. Might we succeed, after all?

"Very well," said the king. "These men will stay here. Except for Bastarna. I want the Roman dog to witness the sacrifice, and someone has to hold his leash. Lay down your weapons, Bastarna."

The giant made a grumbling noise, but obediently unbuckled the sword and sheathe from his belt and removed several other small knives and bludgeons from his person.

"Does any other man here have a weapon?" asked Kysanias. "If you wish to enter the grove, you must lay it down now. Any weapon present during the ritual is likely to provoke the rage of those we are here to placate." Kysanias looked at Mithridates as he said these words. Even in Alexandria people knew the story of the concealed blade that Mithridates had used to kill an unsuspecting rival in full view of both their armies, pulling it out of a hiding place next to his genitals after both men had professed to be disarmed.

Kysanias continued to stare at the king. Mithridates gazed back defiantly, but finally reached into his clothing and pulled out a dagger. The silver handle glittered with jewels. He handed it to the captain of his bodyguards.

The man took the dagger reluctantly. "Your Majesty should not go unarmed into a place where his bodyguards cannot follow."

"But if every other man present is unarmed, there will be no danger," said Mithridates. His eyes swept across the semicircle of listeners, and for an instant he looked straight at me. Another trickle of sweat worked its way down my spine.

The king's gaze eventually came to Monime. They smiled at each other, as if at some private joke, and then Monime reached into the folds of black silk and pulled out her own bejeweled dagger, a smaller companion to the one carried by her husband. Mithridates took it and handed it to the captain, who now held a royal dagger in each hand and did not look happy about it.

"Let us enter the grove," said Kysanias, turning around and leading the way. We followed in single file down the gravel path. No instructions were given; everyone seemed naturally to fall into place. The king went first, with the members of his retinue following, except for the bodyguards, who stayed behind. Then came the Megabyzoi and the Magi, except for Zeuxidemus, who stayed back to usher us so-called witnesses before him. Damianus led Gnossipus by the hand. I followed, with Zeuxidemus behind me.

I glanced back at him. His eyes glittered with excitement. "Have courage!" he whispered.

Yet at that moment, walking toward the black circle of towering trees, my courage reached its lowest ebb. My knees wobbled. My mouth turned dry. The earth tilted beneath me. What madness had possessed me, that I had abandoned the safety of the eunuchs' house outside Alexandria to come to this godsforsaken spot?

I reached to my breast and clutched the lion's tooth hanging there. "Cheelba, give me strength!" I dared to whisper.

When I had first looked at the circle of cypress trees, I had seen no place to enter, but there was such a place, a sort of tunnel that had been cut in the dense foliage, just high enough and wide enough for a man to step through. The king had to lower his head, and the light-bearers had to stoop low and carry their torches with outthrust arms. Bastarna the giant had to stoop very low, yanking the Roman general behind him. Except for Zeuxidemus, I entered last of all.

The circle inside the cypress trees was larger than I had expected. It seemed almost as if we had stepped through a magical barrier, that so much space should exist inside a circle that looked so much smaller from the outside. The diameter of the circle was perhaps equal to the height of the surrounding trees. In such a space, there might have been room for a small temple, but there was none. Nor did I see any sort of shrine or any statue or image of the Furies. There was only a large altar in the very center of the space, which appeared to be crafted from a single piece of dark red marble. We did not encircle the altar, but gathered before it, so that our party filled less than half the circle.

The night before, Kysanias had described the space to us and we had worked out how and where each of us should stand. I went to one side of the altar, along with Gnossipus and Damianus. Kysanias went to the other side of the altar, with the Grand Magus next to him. The others gathered at the foot of the altar, with the king and queen foremost. Behind the royal couple stood their retinue, including Antipater and Rutilius, the Magi and Megabyzoi, Ptolemy and Bastarna and the rest.

I gazed up at the circle of starry, moonless sky beyond the treetops. It seemed to me that the circle of trees formed a vertical tunnel, a portal between the night sky and the underworld. What might emerge from such an opening?

Stands for holding torches were set to either side of the altar, near the head, so that one of these stands was not far behind me, and another not far behind Kysanias. All of the dozen or so torches were set into these stands.

The sacred space seemed somehow to enfeeble the torches. They had burned brightly outside the grove, but now began to flicker, providing a fitful, unsatisfactory light.

"We could have done with a few more torches!" muttered the squinting Grand Magus.

It was no accident that only a dozen of the Megabyzoi and Magi carried torches. There should have been twice as many. Kysanias had taken charge of this detail, deliberately limiting the number of torches so that we might have the advantage of semidarkness from the start. The torches were also smaller and more short-lived than the more long-lasting torches normally used for a nocturnal ritual.

When everyone else was assembled, the sacrifice was brought in.

It was just as I had seen in my dream: Freny was naked, with her arms bound to her sides and her mouth gagged, carried by six men. The bearers laid her on the altar and then quickly withdrew. Freny writhed in terror and looked up at the faces around her. When her eyes met mine, she furrowed her brow, at first confused, and then, for one brief instant, hopeful. Then the Grand Magus and Great Megabyzus began reciting an incantation in unison, and I saw the hope die in her eyes. She shut them tightly, like a child refusing to acknowledge the unbearable reality of what was about to happen.

XXXII

"Alecto, we dare to speak your name!" said Kysanias.

"Your name means 'never-ending, unceasing,'" said the Grand Magus.

"Megaera, we dare to speak your name!"

"Your name means 'bitter, grudging.'"

"Tisiphone, we dare to speak your name!"

"Your name means 'vengeful, violent.'"

While the priest and the wise man recited their litany, Freny writhed on the altar. Mithridates stared at her intently, gritting his teeth. Next to him, Monime gazed at Freny's helpless suffering with a smile of smug satisfaction.

"We call on you, we name the unnameable, we say aloud your names!" said Kysanias. "You were born from the blood that gushed from the wound that unmanned Uranus—Uranus who was made seedless by the child of his seed, Kronos—Kronos who set in motion the passage of time—time which puts an end to all things save the gods—"

Standing at the altar next to Damianus and Gnossipus, across from

Kysanias and the Grand Magus, I grew more and more light-headed. The Grove of the Furies began to seem unreal. Surely no such place existed, and the moments I was experiencing were outside of time, a weird and frightful illusion. I felt oddly detached, yet at the same time on the verge of panic. I tried to breathe deeply, but couldn't seem to catch a breath. It was as if my body had forgotten how to breathe.

The air around me was as thick as water. Objects seen at a distance seemed horribly close, as if just beyond my nose—the iron collar worn by Quintus Oppius, the ruby eyes of the cobra in Prince Ptolemy's crown, the gold knob atop the royal staff held by Monime's father. At the same time, the people surrounding the altar seemed very distant, no taller than a finger seen at arm's length.

I would never be able to do what had been asked of me. It would not be possible. I would not be able to move, much less—

"You dwell among the dead in Tartarus," Kysanias was saying, "but we call you forth from your home to receive this sacrifice. Hear the prayer of this mighty king—this king whose coming was foretold by dreams, visions and oracles—portents and prophecies that seek fulfillment—fulfillment that may only come with *the wrath of the Furies*—"

That was my cue.

When I was a boy, and Antipater was my occasional tutor, he and my father decided that it would be a good thing for me to speak in public, reciting some bit of poetry I had learned before an audience of other boys and their fathers.

The prospect terrified me.

I had never done such a thing before. Nor had I any desire to do so. Was it not enough that I should learn the words of Ennius, or Homer, or Hesiod, or Sappho? Why must I speak them aloud, by memory, in front of other people?

Because, my father said, oratory was the birthright of every Roman.

The Republic had been born from the spoken word, for action was always preceded by will, and will was shaped by the spoken word. The better a man could speak, and the larger his audience, the greater his chance to shape the world around him, rather than helplessly be shaped by the world.

But why recite the words of some dead man? Because, Antipater said, it was from the poets, especially the Greek poets, that we learned that speech could be not only persuasive, but also sublime, achieving a beauty and perfection approaching the divine.

For a month, every day Antipater drilled me, and every day I dreaded the coming of that occasion.

I was not the only boy to speak that day. Others came before me. While I awaited my turn, I became light-headed and hardly able to breathe. Objects near at hand seemed far away, and distant objects attained a horrible nearness. I knew that I would never be able to do what was required of me. I would stand babbling and stuttering before my audience, unable to speak, and I would melt, like a wax table in the hot sun, while my father and Antipater and the others looked on, aghast.

But that was not what happened.

When called upon, I rose from my seat. Like some automaton, propelled by a mechanism outside my own volition, I walked to the dais and mounted it. I turned to face the audience. I opened my mouth, and the words of Anacreon came out . . .

> *"It irks me that Eurypyle, so glamorous,*
> *For boorish Artemon has cravings amorous . . ."*

The listeners looked at me intently. They did not look aghast, but quite the opposite. Antipater smiled. So did my father. When I came to the lines,

> *"But now the son of Artemon appears*
> *In a chariot, with gold rings in his ears,"*

some in the audience laughed out loud, and their laughter was like wine to me. I felt a novel sensation of power, as if I held them all in the palm of my hand.

By the time I came to the final line, I did not want my turn to end. I would gladly have recited another poem for them, and another. But I stepped aside and let the next boy mount the dais.

That day I had a very small taste of the thrill that actors must feel on the stage, and politicians on the podium. My father was right, and so was Antipater. To speak in public must surely be the most powerful thing a man can do, and also the most sublime. . . .

We never know, later in life, what childhood lessons we will call upon. That night, in the Grove of the Furies, I called upon that long-ago experience.

The memory gave me comfort and strength. I *would* be able to do what had been asked of me. I would do it for Freny. I would do it for all the Romans who had taken sanctuary at the Temple of Artemis. Why, I was not even being called upon to speak, only to stand before an audience and—

"*The wrath of the Furies!*" Kysanias repeated, daring to look straight at me across the altar, despite our prearranged agreement that we would not look each other in the eye.

All night, Antipater and I had rehearsed. He devised the words, then drilled me over and over until I knew them by heart. Now the time had come.

Moving stiffly, I stepped back, then strode to the head of the altar. Here, as Kysanias had told me there would be, I saw a small wooden platform attached to the altar. Stepping onto it, I stood tall enough for everyone in the grove to see me, or at least to see my shadowy form. The torches in the stands to either side and slightly behind me had gradually burned lower and lower. As if they were alive and hungry, black shadows were swallowing the light.

Freny was directly below me, her feet pointing away from me. She stared up at me. We saw each other's faces upside down.

"Mute witness!" Kysanias cried. "Why have you left your place?"

I kept my head lowered. "Best to start with your mouth unseen," Kysanias had advised the night before, "in case at the beginning you and Antipater are not in perfect unison."

But our beginning was perfect. I felt Antipater's touch on my back. While all eyes were on me, on the opposite side of the altar he had successfully scurried unseen behind Kysanias and the Grand Magus, to take up a spot just behind me. Even as I mouthed the first word, I heard it spoken. Though I had heard it the night before, the voice that spoke was so strange it set my hair on end—a voice neither man nor woman, perhaps not even human. It was the rasping, guttural, grating voice of a Fury—as imagined by Antipater, not only the world's best poet, but also the best reciter of poems.

"Who carelessly calls upon us?" demanded the uncanny voice that seemed to issue from my mouth. "Who dares disturb us?"

"What is this?" whined the Grand Magus, squinting up at me. "Does the mute witness speak?"

I raised my face a bit. Everyone in the grove was looking at me, but from the way they squinched their eyes and stared I knew that not one of them could clearly see my face, because the light from the torches was in their eyes. It was the same effect the fortune-teller in Alexandria had used on me, by sitting below a window that cast light in my eyes.

I had the advantage of the light, which illuminated the crowd before me. The people farthest away faded into the encroaching darkness, but at the back of the group I could clearly see the towering figure of Bastarna. Much closer, at the foot of the altar, stood the king and queen, with Philopoemen to one side of them and Prince Ptolemy to the other. Their faces expressed surprise and alarm.

I moved my lips but did not speak. The voice came from elsewhere.

"Who summons Alecto? Who calls upon Megaera? Who invokes Tisiphone?"

From the corner of my eye I saw the Grand Magus squinting up at me. He suddenly started back, as if touched by something hot. Across from him, Gnossipus clutched at Damianus—the one person in the grove who could not hear the uncanny voice. The deaf man alone was immune to the wave of uneasiness that passed though the group. As one sees a gust of wind set tall grass to shivering, so I perceived this growing distress in those before me.

"It is the King of Kings who calls upon you," said Kysanias, with a tremor in his voice. He sounded genuinely fearful. He held up the ritual knife and ax. "He offers this sacrifice."

Again the uncanny voice spoke, seeming to come from my lips. "The thing you seek cannot be given! The blessing you beg for can only be a curse! No man should summon what no man can control!"

One of the torches, already burning low, suddenly went out. Then another torch went out, and another. The grove grew darker and darker.

Someone in the group cried out, as if he had been stabbed or bitten. Another man screamed. These cries came from Rutilius and Zeuxidemus, doing what they could to spread panic in the others.

"What's that?" cried the Grand Magus. "There, in the trees!"

One of the towering cypress trees had begun to shake, hard enough to break twigs and small branches. Then the tree next to it shivered, and then the next, as if some unseen, unearthly force was at work in the Grove of the Furies, moving from tree to tree. The shivering, crackling trees produced an eerie sound, as if ghastly beings hissed and groaned.

Another torch went out. There were more cries of panic.

"Why is it so dark?" shouted Mithridates, his voice breaking. He clenched his fists and looked over his shoulder. More than ever, Monime's pale face and coppery hair seemed to levitate, disembodied. Her eyebrows were raised above staring eyes and her mouth was open in a perfect circle. Next to her, Prince Ptolemy looked strangely thrilled by the mounting confusion.

I concentrated on my task, for the uncanny voice had more to say—cryptic prophecies of unending punishment, hissing threats of unearthly torment. The uproar of the group rose to such a pitch that Antipater's voice was almost drowned out. The trees around us continued to shudder and sway.

"I see them, in the trees!" cried the Grand Magus. He no longer squinted but gazed up in awe. What did he think he saw with those wide-open, nearsighted eyes of his?

"I see them, too!" yelled someone in the crowd. It sounded like Rutilius.

"It's the Furies! They're here!" This was Zeuxidemus, who then produced a blood-curdling scream.

At that moment, by pure chance, something actually did flitter above our heads. I think it was a bat. Mithridates must have glimpsed it, for he suddenly ducked and pulled Monime close to him, clutching her tightly. In that instant I saw what very few—perhaps no one— had ever seen: a look of utter panic on the face of Mithridates.

"I see their eyes, in the trees! I see their wings!" This cry, surprisingly high-pitched and with a strange accent, came from Bastarna. By the light of one of the few remaining torches, I could see the giant's face. His expression was one of sheer terror. He had shortened the chain held in his fist, doubling it over several times as if to make it into a weapon. Quintus Oppius was forced to stand on tiptoes, clutching at the iron collar around his neck. His tongue was out and his face was dark red.

Bastarna stiffened. He shut his eyes and whimpered—then screamed like a little girl.

The squealing giant looked so ridiculous, I couldn't help myself. I laughed.

Even as I helplessly laughed I felt a quiver of panic, thinking I had ruined everything. But because I tried to stifle it, the laugh came out as a blubbering bark. The sound was so bizarre, so horrifically out of place, it must have seemed yet another manifestation of the uncanny voice, for it caught the attention of everyone in the grove. They flinched at the sound, and grimaced, and stared at me, aghast.

Antipater gave me another poke. "Darkness comes!" cried the uncanny voice, while I mouthed the words. "We bring upon you darkness and death and destruction!"

Only two torches still burned. They sputtered and went out.

"Everyone will be staring at one of those torches, craving the light," Kysanias had predicted. "Their eyes will be dazzled, so that when the torches go out they'll be as blind as Gnossipus. Close your eyes for a moment, Gordianus, so that when you open them, you'll be able to see by starlight."

There was a sharp cracking noise. Severed near its base, one of the trees directly behind Kysanias swayed and then began to fall into the circle, toppling toward the altar in the center. Kysanias grabbed the Grand Magus and shoved him out of the way. Damianus did the same for Gnossipus, who cried out in confusion.

Below me, Freny could see the dark silhouette of the towering tree falling straight toward her. She screamed into her gag and writhed wildly from side to side.

This was the most critical moment. My instinct was to run from the falling tree, but if I were to save Freny, this was the only chance.

I stepped off the wooden platform. The altar, carved from a single block of marble, was also hollow. When I kicked aside the platform on which I had been standing, a door was revealed. The door opened to an empty compartment within the altar. This space, Kysanias had explained, was now used only for the storage of sacrificial utensils, but it had originally been intended for hiding the animal to be sacrificed, which could thus, under the right circumstances of darkness and distraction, be produced as if from nowhere—a typical example of the chicanery used by priests to awe their congregants.

With all my strength I took hold of Freny's shoulders and pulled her toward me, off the altar and into my arms. Holding her tightly, I fell to my knees and scrambled inside the hidden chamber.

As soon as we were inside, the door was closed behind us, and the concealing platform was pushed back in place by Kysanias. We were in absolute darkness.

There was a tremendous crash as the midsection of the tree struck the altar and splintered into pieces. The altar lurched as if there had been an earthquake, but the marble did not crack.

Freny struggled against her bonds and squealed into the gag.

"Quiet!" I whispered in her ear. "Trust me, Freny."

She grew still, but her body remained stiff and wary in my arms, like a frightened bird.

Only vaguely could I hear any noises from outside. It was impossible to know what was being said or done.

My work was finished. I had only to lie very still, keep Freny quiet, and wait until one of the others came for us.

Unless the enraged Furies came for us first.

XXXIII

In that dark, tomblike chamber, Freny and I lay side by side for what seemed to be hours.

For a while I heard muffled, indistinct noises from outside. Then the noises stopped, and there was only silence.

Eventually I dared to speak, but only in a whisper. I explained to her what had happened, and what I hoped would happen next. We would have to be patient. If we were to push open the door, and someone should see us, all would be lost. We had to wait until one of the others came for us.

Moving awkwardly and in darkness, I managed to undo her gag and the bonds constraining her arms. Then I fell into a sort of stupor. My performance as the embodiment of Antipater's uncanny voice had depleted all my resources. I was exhausted.

Time seemed to grind slowly to a stop. The air became thick. The darkness was absolute. I began to wonder if we might already be dead, slain by the Furies, and this was to be our afterlife. Had we arrived in Tartarus, here to dwell in blackness forevermore?

Perhaps I slept for a while, and this notion of Tartarus was only a dream. In such a place it was hard to tell whether I was awake or not.

At last I heard the noise of the door being opened, and a shaft of light entered the compartment. It was the faint gray light of the hour before dawn, but to my light-starved eyes it seemed bright. At the same time a small gust of fresh air entered the chamber. I sucked it in, and realized how foul the air had become inside that tomblike space.

Stiff and blinking at the sudden light, and gasping for air, I managed to crawl backward out of the chamber. Freny, more nimble than I, quickly followed. Samson averted his eyes from her nakedness and handed her a simple tunic and a pair of shoes. She quickly dressed herself, and then the two of us managed to stand, blinking at the predawn glow that revealed the aftermath of our night in the Grove of the Furies.

The tree that had fallen lay broken into two parts on either side of the marble altar, bisecting the circular space. We three were alone in the grove.

"Your performance last night was quite amazing," said Samson.

"So was yours," I said, "far beyond what I expected." For it was Samson, acting alone, who had shaken the trees and caused one of them to fall. "How exactly did you do it?"

He smiled. "Last night, while you and Antipater were going over your lines, I slipped out of the palace and came here, to have a look at the place."

"By yourself?" said Freny, staring up at him wide-eyed. "You dared to come to such a spot in the dead of night, alone?"

"Young lady, I am a Jew," he said. "This place is not sacred to me. I have no fear of these so-called Furies. I looked at the grove purely as a theatrical venue, and asked myself: what is there to work with, and what sort of effects might be achieved? As I circled the grove, from the outside, it occurred to me that if a man were strong enough, he might be able to run from tree to tree, leaping inside them and giving them a good shaking. I practiced doing so, and by breaking a few branches here and there I was able to clear a sort of path which allowed me to run from tree to tree, making each one shiver. Then I thought, what if, ahead of time, one of the trees was nearly severed, near the base, and then, when the time came, given a very hard push—"

"But how did you manage to cut through the tree trunk?" said Freny.

"I used an ax I found in that storage compartment inside the altar, where you've been hiding."

I shook my head. "You used a consecrated ax from the altar of the Furies to cut down one of the sacred trees in the Grove of the Furies." The brazen impiousness of such an act made my head spin. "I think we should leave this place as quickly as we can."

"At once," said Samson. "If you're strong enough to walk," he added, looking at Freny. "If not, I can carry you—"

"I'm not a weakling!" said Freny, with a laugh. She looked very slender and delicate by the soft morning light, but her laughter was strong and clear, and to hear it brought joy to my heart.

"Where are we going?" I asked, for this next step had been left undecided the night before.

"To the Temple of Artemis," he said. "With all that's happening, we decided that would be the only safe place for us all."

"So the massacre has been called off?"

His face darkened. "The thing we hoped for . . . was not accomplished."

"But why? What went wrong?"

"Come with me now. Hurry! We'll have plenty of time to talk about it when we reach the temple."

"But surely that's the last place we want to be."

"Trust me, Gordianus."

"Where is Bethesda?"

"She's already there, waiting for us. Follow me."

On shaky legs, I followed Samson out of the Grove of the Furies. It was first necessary to climb over the fallen tree, and then to duck through the tunnel-like entrance surrounded by foliage. Once we stepped beyond the stone wall that marked the sacred precinct of the Grove, I had no idea where we were, and saw no landmarks by which to orient myself. The land around us was a mixture of woodland and meadows, misty in the early light.

By what route we made our way to the Temple of Artemis I cannot remember. Perhaps the vividness with which I remember what came later that day somehow blurred my memories of what came before. I know that we didn't go through the city. At some point I saw the temple ahead of us, and the thousands of Romans who crowded the temple grounds.

"Samson!" I hissed, taking his arm. "If this is the day, and the thing is to happen, we have to warn them."

At that moment the captain of a troop of armed men took notice of us. The soldiers were patrolling the perimeter of the sacred precinct.

"Who are you and what's your business here?" asked the captain.

"We're pilgrims, come to worship at the temple," said Samson.

The captain scrutinized him. "What sort of accent is that?"

"Alexandrian Greek," said Samson. "The purest form, handed down from Alexander himself."

The captain laughed. "You Alexandrians, always full of yourselves! But if you wish to worship Artemis of Ephesus, you might want to wear something nicer than that." He indicated the faded old cloak that Samson insisted on wearing. "Anyway, this is not a good day to visit the temple. Come back tomorrow."

"But I have an appointment with the Grand Megabyzus."

"I'm sure you do!" the captain scoffed.

Samson produced a rolled-up piece of parchment, undid the yellow ribbon tied around it, and showed it to the captain. The man examined it for a moment, then handed it back.

"The Grand Megabyzus himself! Well then, I suggest you get inside the temple and find him, quickly. In fact, my company will escort you, to make sure these Roman scum don't give you any trouble."

"That's not necessary—"

"I insist."

The troop formed a cordon around us. As we strode toward the temple I looked at all the people around me, longing to cry out to them, to warn them of what was about to happen. But I said nothing.

As we approached the temple, I saw a strange thing. The round window in the pediment through which one could see the statue of Artemis was black, as if some sort of curtain or screen had been drawn across it from inside.

The temple steps were covered with refugees, many of them still asleep. They stirred and scrambled out of the way to let us pass. The troop came to a halt at the temple entrance.

"Stay here, men," said the captain. "I'll be back shortly."

He handed his sword to his second-in-command and then escorted Samson, Freny, and me into the temple, hailing the first of the Megabyzoi he saw and telling the priest to fetch the Great Megabyzus. When the man balked, the captain told Samson to produce the document. The priest raised his eyebrows as he read it, then quickly went off to find the Great Megabyzus.

The interior of the temple was dimly lit. Only a few lamps were burning, and the weak morning light from the doorway did little to dispel the shadows. While we waited, I looked around us, at all the unsuspecting refugees lying huddled in sleep or milling about. Again, I longed to warn them, and again I said nothing.

A few moments later, Kysanias appeared, dressed in his yellow robes and towering headdress. He surmised the situation at once.

"Thank you, Captain, for escorting this party into the temple."

"My pleasure, Your Eminence," said the captain, who then looked sidelong at Samson. "So the letter was genuine! If it had been a fake, I was going to cut the heads off of all three of you." He turned about and went to rejoin his men outside.

I spoke in a whisper. "Your Eminence, we have to warn—"

"Say nothing!" Kysanias said through gritted teeth. "All of you, be silent and follow me."

I did as he said. I was beginning to feel light-headed from hunger and queasy from dread. He took us to the hidden stairway that led to the upper room, locking the door behind us. Up, up we trudged. My legs were like lead.

When we stepped into the room inside the pediment, Freny gave a cry of joy and rushed into the arms of her sister.

"Amestris!" I said, then saw that Anthea was there as well. "But how did the two of you come to be here?"

"Do you forget, Gordianus, that I'm in training to become a hierodule, a lifelong servant of the goddess?" said Anthea. "And of course Amestris goes wherever I go."

"Yellow becomes you both," I said, for they were dressed much like the Megabyzoi, but without the headdresses.

I was staring at Amestris and Freny, and beginning to feel a bit jealous of their long, loving embrace, when someone behind me produced a polite cough. I turned about and saw—

"Bethesda!"

The next moment she was in my arms, never mind that Romans and their slaves do not display mutual affection in public.

"Samson told me you'd be here," I said.

"He brought me here from the palace while it was still dark."

"What a busy night he's had," I said, and laughed at the pure joy of holding her—and then started back and gaped, slack-jawed, as the statue of Artemis dominating the room slowly began to turn. It was as if she heard us speaking and was turning around to look at us.

"But how—?"

Kysanias saw my wonder. He looked a bit chagrined. "That's Zeuxidemus, in the chamber below us, turning the crank. It's merely mechanical, Gordianus, not miraculous. Even though we've covered the round window so that the goddess will not have to witness the thing about to happen, I thought it proper that she should turn her back upon the proceedings, as well."

Kysanias walked past the pedestal of the statue, to the sheer black curtain that covered the window. Bethesda and I followed him. From outside, the curtain would appear solid black, but from the relative darkness of the room we were able to see through it, as if through a thin veil of smoke. Outside, the Roman refugees were beginning to wake up.

"Samson says we failed," I said. "He says the massacre will take place, in spite of all we did."

"That's right," said Kysanias with a sigh.

"But how can that be? What did we do wrong?"

"Once you were inside the altar, you couldn't hear what was said?"

"Not a word. Only murmurs."

"Then you didn't hear the argument between myself and the Grand Magus and His Majesty?"

"No."

Kysanias stiffened his jaw. "There was a great deal of bluster and bravado from the king—exactly what you might expect from a famously fearless man who's been badly frightened. I told him that the sacrifice had failed and the portents were against him. But the Grand Magus had a different explanation. According to him, since the sacrificial victim had vanished, that meant the Furies had taken her—that they had accepted the offering, indeed were so very pleased with her that they wished to take her whole and unharmed. I protested and pointed out the apparitions in the trees. The Grand Magus agreed that we had seen the Furies unleashed, but against the Romans, not the king. Their appearance proved that they were eager to oversee the massacres today. When I continued to object, the king silenced me. The Grand Magus told him what he wanted to hear, you see. The king accepted every word the Grand Magus said and refused to listen to me."

"But what about the words of the uncanny voice?"

"They became lost in the argument. The king and the Grand Magus remembered them one way, I another. I turned to Metrodorus, knowing he must recall every word that was spoken, but the Rome-Hater had an inexplicable lapse of memory and refused to back me up."

"Then we failed," I said.

"Not entirely. You saved the girl."

I looked at Freny and Amestris across the room, still embracing. I turned and gazed through the black scrim at the Romans outside.

"Only one life, compared to so many. The life of a single slave, compared to so many Roman citizens—"

"How is one life any more or less valuable than two lives, or three, or a thousand?" asked Kysanias. "All lives begin and all lives end. There is no scale upon which to weigh the value of one life against another, or one life against many lives. You did what you could, and thanks to you, Freny is still alive and her sister is filled with joy. Whatever Freny does from this moment on, however she affects the lives of everyone she meets, will owe something to you."

I sighed and looked outside again. "How soon will it begin?"

"Very soon, I suspect. First there is to be—"

"Gordianus!"

I turned to see Antipater. Apparently he had just emerged from a hole in the floor, for the trapdoor was still open and Zeuxidemus was following him through the hatchway.

"I'm so relieved to see you!" Antipater threw his arms around me. "I feared you might suffocate inside that altar."

"Where did you come from?" I asked.

"From the room below. I wanted to see for myself the mechanism that turns the pedestal upon which the statue stands. It's simple, really, but I was surprised that a single man could turn it so easily. Very clever. But not half as clever as you, my boy. I'm told that your performance last night was flawless. You truly looked possessed. Young Zeuxidemus tells me he almost wet himself, watching you mime the lines I spoke."

"I never said that!" protested Zeuxidemus.

"Antipater is known to take poetic liberties," I said. Suddenly I was very hungry. "Is there anything to eat?"

"We have bread, water, and wine," said Zeuxidemus.

"Have you any of that sleeping potion?"

Zeuxidemus cocked his head. "Why do you ask?"

"Freny had a restless night. She needs to sleep. And after the horror of what was done to her, I don't think she needs to see yet more horror. It would be a blessing if she could sleep though the day, never hearing or seeing what's about to happen."

"You speak wisely," said Kysanias. "Those who sleep in this chamber do so with the blessing of Artemis. I'll see to it that Freny receives the wine we give to dreamers. Perhaps you should drink some of that wine yourself, Gordianus."

"No. For better or worse, I'll stay awake, if I can."

"As you wish. Brace yourself."

XXXIV

I was given bread and water. Freny was given bread and wine. I watched her fall asleep in her sister's arms amid the cushions at the foot of the pedestal, where I had watched Zeuxidemus sleep before.

Amestris continued to hold her sister for a while, then gently extricated herself. She saw me watching her and came to me. Bethesda was elsewhere, and so was Anthea, so that Amestris and I had a moment to ourselves.

"Thank you, Gordianus, for saving her."

"My reward was the look on your face when we came in the room."

Her eyes glimmered with tears. "I was heartbroken when they took her. Now I have to say good-bye to her again."

"It's decided, then, that she has to leave?"

"Freny can't stay in Ephesus, or anywhere else in the kingdom. Can you imagine what might be done to her if Mithridates or Monime ever saw her? No, she'll go with you when you leave. Samson promises to look after her. We have freeborn relatives in Tyre who might take her in."

I nodded, then touched her arm. "What about you, Amestris?"

"Me?"

"When I decided to come to Ephesus, I hoped I'd see you again. I've thought of you often since . . . our night together. When I finally did see you, the other night—it ended so wretchedly, with the queen's visit. But before Monime arrived, there was something you said to me. I can't get it out of my mind. It was about meeting me, the first time—you said it changed your life. If you have such feelings for me, Amestris, then perhaps. . . ."

She narrowed her eyes and looked at me with something between a grimace and a smile. "Oh, Gordianus, you lovely man! I think you misunderstood me. Yes, that night when you and I saved Anthea did truly change my life, because that was the first time I knew what love is."

"Oh, Amestris—if things had gone differently . . . If Antipater and I hadn't left Ephesus so quickly . . ." I cast a sidelong glance at Bethesda, who was across the room, eating a bit of bread and talking to Samson.

"Gordianus, I think you still misunderstand. That was the night I realized I was in love, and always will be—with Anthea."

"With . . . Anthea?"

"Of course. I'm in love with Anthea, and she's in love with me."

"But . . . she's a freeborn woman."

"Yes, just as you're a freeborn man. And are you not in love with a slave?"

"I . . ."

"I should have thought that our love was obvious to you, from the way we talk and touch, just as your love for Bethesda must be obvious to all who meet you."

"I hardly think—"

"Anthea and I will live together here at the temple of the virgin goddess, where Anthea's virginity is greatly prized. Only virgins can perform certain rituals of purification—and after what is about to happen, there will be a great deal of pollution, requiring much purification. But—did you hear that?" She turned her head sharply, toward the round window with its black screen.

We all heard the noise—all except Freny, who was soundly asleep. Without saying a word, everyone in the room gathered before the black curtain and gazed out the round window. Bethesda stepped beside me. Without a thought for what others might think, I took her hand in mine.

"That sound," said Samson. "Like a roar. What is it? Where does it come from?"

"It comes from the theater, I think," said Zeuxidemus.

"Yes, it's the sound of many voices," said Kysanias. "Criers ran through the city at daybreak, calling everyone to the theater. His Majesty will have staged some sort of spectacle for the people—something to rile them up and get their blood boiling. That captured Roman general probably had a role to play; the king will have humiliated him in some horrible way, if he hasn't killed him. I was supposed to attend and give my blessing, but I refused. I told His Majesty that my place today must be at the temple and nowhere else. Whatever happens here, I must bear witness, as high priest of the goddess."

"They're chanting something," said Antipater. "My ears are not what they once were. I can't make it out."

"'Death to the Romans,'" I said. "They're chanting, 'Death to the Romans,' over and over."

I felt a knot in the pit of my stomach as I peered though the black cloth. If I could hear the chant, then so could the people below. I saw a sudden flurry of movement, as if an ant bed had been poked with a stick. Those who still slept were quickly roused. People began to rush this way and that, with nowhere to go, for beyond the sacred precinct were the trenches that had been dug, and beyond the trenches a ring of soldiers had encircled the entire area. Their upright spears had the appearance of a spiked fence.

Suddenly, responding in unison to a shouted command, the soldiers all lowered their spears at once, pointing them inward.

The crowd panicked. People ran toward the temple. From below us, I could hear the stampede of feet on the temple steps as they rushed inside. But the ring of spear-bearers did not advance. They stayed where they were.

Then, like a river pouring through a broken dam, the citizens of Ephesus flooded though the gate and came rushing down the Sacred Way toward the temple. I could no longer make out a chant. I heard only a great roar that grew louder and louder. By the time the mob reached the sacred precinct, the sound was deafening.

"Oh, sweet Artemis!" whispered Anthea, touching her lips. "It's going to happen."

The mob carried knives, axes, cudgels, chains, ropes, and bags full of stones. Without hesitation, they fell upon those Romans who had not fled into the temple and set about killing them.

I had seen men die in public before, at gladiator shows in Rome. My father had allowed me to attend a few such spectacles despite his own dislike for them, because I had begged to see them. After seeing a few, I had seen enough. What I saw that day in Ephesus was a little like seeing death in the arena, as I watched from a safe distance while blood was spilled below me. The ring of soldiers were the audience, as they held their line and looked on, cheering. But the killers were not gladiators. They were ordinary people, and their victims were unarmed men and women and children, all savagely slaughtered without mercy.

I saw old men beheaded, children stoned to death, and women staked spread-eagled to the ground and raped. I saw a man cut in two with an ax. I saw men wrap a baby in a bloody toga, throw it against the ground, and then stamp on it.

Those of us watching from the veiled window frequently turned away, sickened and overwhelmed. I think only Kysanias stayed at the window without flinching, forcing himself to witness all that happened below.

Suddenly, by her tangled red hair and tattered stola, I recognized the widow of the Roman I had seen put to death for seizing a spear. Burdened by the frail child she carried and unable to reach the temple in time, the widow sought refuge at the altar. A group of a dozen or more women fell on her, dragging her from the altar. They held her down, tore off her clothing, then ripped out handfuls of her hair. They kicked her repeatedly, then forced her to watch while a man picked up her child by the feet, swung him around and around, and then smashed his head against the stone altar.

The man threw the limp corpse aside, then shouted, "Should I do the same to the Roman bitch?"

"Not yet," shouted one of the women. "Let her weep over her dead darling for a while, then we'll come back and finish her off. You can have a go at her if you want."

That was when I turned away from the window and stopped watching.

But I heard what happened next. Having killed almost every Roman in sight, the mob rushed into the temple. The huge open space of the sanctuary seemed to magnify the screams below us as the Romans were dragged outside, then murdered on the temple steps.

I sat on the floor, slumped against the statue's pedestal. Bethesda huddled beside me. I was so exhausted that I fell asleep despite the screams.

It was a dark, uneasy sleep. I dreamed that I was still awake, standing at the window, watching one scene of horror after another, longing to look away but unable to turn my head or close my eyes. Behind me, the statue of Artemis wept. The Furies, flitting on their batlike wings above the killing field, mocked Artemis with doglike barks, grinning to show their fangs and watching all that happened with eyes like glowing coals.

[From the secret diary of Antipater of Sidon:]

Thank Artemis! Gordianus has finally fallen asleep.

The poor boy should have taken a sleeping potion like Freny and slept through the massacre. Now he will have these sounds and images in his head forever.

I will force myself to watch until the very end. I did everything I could to support the king against the Romans, and now I must see the result.

I think I am not long for this world, anyway. Not just because I am an old man, but because I have no more poems in me. My last verses were those I recited aloud in the Grove of the Furies, while Gordianus pretended to speak—before a royal audience, at last! But those words fell on deaf ears. They created a brief sensation, but did not achieve the desired effect. The ritual was interrupted and the sacrifice aborted, but the massacre was not averted. My most ambitious poem was a failure.

These are my last written words, upon this page. Not a poem, not a confession, not an indictment—merely the final scribblings of a man who fancied himself the world's finest poet, who saw a great deal of the world, who played spy for a while, who came to sorrow in the end. But the sight of you has given me a last moment of joy, Gordianus.

Two nights ago, we were reunited, but our meeting was not exactly a reconciliation—we hardly spoke about the long silence between us, and my hasty departure from Alexandria, and the fact that I deceived you for so long. Circumstances were pressing, and we had no time to speak of all that. But in a way what happened was better, at least for me. We trained our thoughts on a single goal and collaborated on a joint enterprise, devising the words to be spoken by that "uncanny voice," going over them again and again so that we would both know them by heart. We were like tutor and pupil again—except that in this effort we were equal partners, and working toward a selfless objective, the saving of so many innocent lives. I hope that is how you will remember me, as a poet who used his talents in a noble cause, at least at the end, and not as a skulking spy who tricked an unsuspecting Roman youth.

I give these words to you, Gordianus. They are for your eyes and for no one else's. When you are done reading them, burn them, lest they be found on your person and get you into trouble.

Looking through what I have written, I see that a few more pages have gone missing. Monime's minions must have rifled through the pages and stolen a few more. Why did they take a certain page and send it to you, Gordianus? For surely it must have been Monime who lured you here. But why?

I think the queen was determined to destroy me, or rather, to have her husband destroy me, but first he had to be turned absolutely and irrevocably against me. Had she merely shown him this or that incriminating page from my journal, he might simply have laughed it off—the King of Kings has no fear of mere words. But if she could succeed in luring my Roman protégé to Ephesus, and catch the two of us in the act of conspiring against the throne, Mithridates could be convinced to kill us both. It was a good thing you played your part so stealthily, Gordianus, and kept your mouth shut. You came to Ephesus and actually met the queen—and she never knew who you were, or your connection to me! Had you been exposed as a Roman and my pupil, Monime would have told the king that I was a double agent and that you were my Roman handler, and that would have been the end of us.

What a creature the queen is! If she had her way, you and I would have been flayed alive—and little Freny would have had her throat cut, just to spite Mithridates.

What I have seen today is the last straw. Not only has my muse been silenced, but any partisanship I felt for the cause of Mithridates is done with. When I imagine that such slaughter is happening not only here but also in cities all over the kingdom, I am sickened.

I have left intact, among these pages, the one I wrote two nights ago, in which I pretended to praise the king and his cause and look forward to the sacrifice. You will understand that I wrote that passage knowing it might very likely be read by one of Monime's spies, or for all I know, a spy of the king, and it was my intent to put the hounds off the scent. I state this explicitly lest you think that passage was in any way sincere, and that I might have been thinking of betraying you at the last minute.

Even as I write, the killing continues. Words have always been my servants and friends; they desert me now. There are no words to describe this horror. Zoticus of Zeugma is rendered speechless—as mute as Agathon of Alexandria.

[Here ends the secret diary of Antipater of Sidon.]

XXXV

Eventually, there was no one left to kill.

As darkness fell, bonfires were lit. The people of Ephesus made their way back to the city. The ring of soldiers remained in place to prevent any survivors from escaping under cover of darkness.

I woke early the next day. The black curtain had been removed from the round window. I looked out to see that a thick morning mist covered the plain. The altar was barely visible, a block of marble that seemed to float in the dense fog.

"This is our best chance," said Samson. "The mist will hide us from the soldiers. If it extends up the river, it will also be hiding the ship that's waiting for us. And if the ship's captain agrees to cast off in this fog, we can sail downriver unseen, all the way to the sea."

Those who were leaving with Samson included Freny, Bethesda, Antipater, and me. Anthea and Amestris would accompany us as far as the ship.

We said our farewells to Zeuxidemus and Kysanias. They were good, decent men. Ephesus would need such men, I thought, when the Romans came to exact vengeance, as sooner or later I knew they would.

We descended the stairs. The interior of the temple was deserted except for a few Megabyzoi, assisted by hierodules, who had already begun the work of purifying the sanctuary. Clouds of incense sweetened the air.

The temple steps were covered with corpses and blood. Freny trembled at the sight. Her sister guided her down the steps.

Our progress across the misty ground was a series of rude surprises, as the swirling fog parted to reveal one horrifying scene of death after another. To have watched the murders from afar was one thing; to see the staring, lifeless bodies lying twisted and broken at my feet was another. Was this the misty realm of Tartarus, where the Furies dwelled? Were they watching us even now?

Then an all-too-human voice called out, "Halt! Stay where you are."

A small troop of soldiers appeared. Their captain looked us over. "What are you people doing here? Only men sanctioned by the king are allowed to scavenge the bodies. Did you not hear the royal decree read yesterday at the theater? It forbids anyone from looting the corpses, upon immediate penalty of death."

"The king seems awfully fond of decrees with immediate penalties of death," muttered Antipater. "So much for Greek notions of judges and trials and juries!"

The captain frowned. "What's the old man saying?"

It was Anthea who answered. "Can you not see by my yellow gown that I'm a hierodule from the temple? These pilgrims from faraway lands arrived yesterday to worship the goddess. They were trapped in the temple overnight. I was sent by the Great Megabyzus himself to escort them from the sacred precinct."

The captain gave us another look. "Yes, I see. I'll escort you, then—"

"There's no need," said Anthea. "I know the way."

"Very well. But you should know that there's no longer a cordon around the area. If any of the Roman scum did get away from us, they'll be pretty desperate. Be careful. But if you do meet one of those filth, that fellow looks big enough to take care of you." He indicated Samson, who responded with a nod but kept his mouth shut.

We pressed on.

I knew we had gone beyond the boundary of the sacred precinct when I saw long trenches to either side of us. Several layers of bodies had been piled into the trenches, but I saw no diggers nearby. Freny had begun to weep. Then I heard something, and shushed her.

It was a muffled cry. "Help me!"

"Where is it coming from?" I whispered.

"From the trench over there," said Samson. "Here, help me."

I shuddered at the thought of digging through corpses. Then Antipater, standing next to me, fell to his knees. He was clutching his chest.

I dropped to my knees beside him. "Teacher, what's wrong?"

His face was ashen. He grimaced.

I heard the muffled cry again, but louder now, as Samson, working alone, uncovered the man who was calling for help. As I continued to stare at Antipater, wondering what was wrong with him, the man stumbled out of the trench. I glanced at his filthy, bloodstained toga, then saw his face.

"Chaeremon of Nysa!" I whispered.

Antipater continued to grimace and clutch his chest. He gasped. "This is the end of me!"

"No, Teacher!" I whispered.

"Give this man my tunic."

"What are you saying, Teacher?"

"He can't be seen wearing that toga. Give him my clothing. Cover me with his toga . . . and leave me here."

"No, Teacher, you're coming with us!" I said, with a catch in my throat.

"Do you not see, Gordianus? The Fates have given me a last chance . . . to do something worthwhile. Give this man my clothing . . . so that he may go with you safely. And take for yourself . . . the pages I carry with me."

"What pages?"

He struggled to reach inside his tunic. He pulled out a leather cylinder.

"But, Teacher, I can't leave you here."

He fell to his side and began to gasp for breath. I wept.

"What does it matter . . . where my body lies?" he said, his speech slurred as if he were drunk. I put my ear to his mouth and strained to hear him. "Let them bury me here . . . with the Romans. Do I not already have . . . a funeral monument . . . in Rome . . . from the *first* time I died?" He made a sound that might have been a laugh, then a long sigh issued from his throat, and then there was silence.

While I stood by, trembling and fighting back tears, Samson removed Antipater's tunic and gave it to Chaeremon. The man appeared to be unscathed, despite the bloodstains I had seen on his toga, but he was badly shaken. He removed his toga and laid it over Antipater, like a shroud.

Chaeremon had just finished putting on Antipater's tunic when we heard footsteps approaching. Out of the mist, the troop of soldiers reappeared.

Their captain looked at us for a moment, then laughed. "You lot, again! This fog is so thick, either you're walking in circles or we are!" He scrutinized us more closely, and his eyes came to rest on Chaeremon. Did he remember Antipater's face, and realize that someone new had been added to our party? Or did he simply see an old man in a tunic?

At last he took his eyes off Chaeremon and waved to his men to keep walking. "Be on your way," he said to us. "May the goddess guide you safely through this infernal fog!"

Thus did the gift of his tunic, the final act of Antipater, save the life of Chaeremon of Nysa, a loyal friend of Rome, and the only known survivor of the Ephesian massacre.

We hurried on, leaving Antipater behind.

We crossed the misty landscape. We saw no more bodies, and encountered no more soldiers. At last we came to the river, where a boat was anchored alongside a short pier.

Samson conferred with the captain, then told us there would be a brief delay while the ship was made ready to sail.

Still stunned by the death of Antipater, I sat on the pier with my legs dangling over the side, my feet not quite touching the water. A blanket of swirling fog floated a few feet above the river. The sight was strangely beautiful.

I opened the *capsa* Antipater had given me. The first piece of parchment I pulled out happened to be the very last he had written. Seeing my name, my eyes fell on the sentence, *I give these words to you, Gordianus.*

I looked through the other pieces of parchment. Some pages appeared to be missing. From my tunic I pulled out the piece that had been sent to me. I found the place where it belonged.

Blinking back tears, I read the final entry of his diary. My mind was slow, so that I had to read some sentences more than once to make sense of them. But no matter how many times I read it, his idea that Monime had sent the stolen page to me—to lure me to Ephesus as part of some plot to bring down Antipater—made no sense. Surely the queen could have done away with Antipater more easily than that, given the power she wielded in the royal household.

As I pondered the mystery—who sent the page to me, and why?— another solution occurred to me. The more I thought about it, the more sense it made. Of course, I would never be able to prove it. . . .

And then, out of the mist—literally—came the embodiment of my conjecture. I thought I must be hallucinating, until Samson, standing nearby on the pier, gave a start.

"Who are those three?" he asked in a low voice. "And what in Hades are they doing here?"

"I know who they are," I said, quickly rolling the pages and slipping them back into the *capsa* as I stood up. "The one in the middle, at least . . . because I was just thinking about him."

Even without his cobra crown, I recognized young Prince Ptolemy. He was dressed in a common tunic, as were his two servants, but his shoes were exquisite. Each of the servants carried a heavy-looking sack slung over his shoulder. The prince smiled a bit uncertainly as he stepped onto the pier. Looking behind me, I saw that Bethesda and the others

had drawn closer together, and that Samson stood before them, holding a knife in one hand.

"You may put aside that weapon," said the prince quietly. When
Samson didn't respond, his voice became stern. "I have asked you nicely.
Now, as a prince of Egypt, I order you to do so. Are you not an Alex-
andrian, subject to the House of Ptolemy?"

Samson hesitated for a moment, then put away his knife. "What are
you doing here, Your Majesty?"

"I've come to sail away with you."

Samson cocked his head. "But how . . . ?"

"I think I know how the prince followed us here," I said. "These two
servants are the same two who were assigned by Monime to look after
Antipater. Am I right?"

"They are!" said Freny. "I recognize them both."

"You are indeed correct . . . Gordianus of Rome," said Prince Ptolemy.

"But their true loyalty is to you."

The prince nodded.

"And despite Antipater's attempts to elude them," I said, "one or the
other of them never let Antipater out of his sight. Thus you knew where
Antipater went, when he fled the house of Eutropius. And you knew
that last night he was in the Temple of Artemis. And this morning, by
some feat of stealth, you managed to follow Antipater and the rest of
us through the mist."

He nodded again. "And at a distance I witnessed his death. Alas!
The world has lost a great poet. I had hoped your old tutor would be
with us on this journey, so that he might amuse us with his verses."

"But how is it that you're free to go where you wish?" asked Samson. "The king never allows you to leave the palace."

"The whole city, including the palace, has been in an uproar, day
and night, ever since the massacre commenced. I took advantage of all
the confusion to slip quietly away. I had help to do so; these two are
not the only servants in Mithridates's household who are secretly loyal
to the House of Ptolemy. Still, even with my loyal minions covering

for me, sooner or later the queen will realize that I've gone, so I suggest we cast off at once."

"Taking you with us was not in my plans," said Samson.

"If it's payment you require, that can be arranged." The prince gestured to the sacks carried by his two servants. "I managed to bring along a few personal items—rings and bracelets and other such trinkets."

"I wouldn't consider taking payment from you," said Samson.

"You show wisdom. One day, I shall sit on the throne of Egypt, and when that happens, I shall not forget those who helped me in my time of tribulation."

Without his fancy robes and ruby-eyed cobra crown, Ptolemy looked no different from any other plump-cheeked teenager. It was hard to imagine him ruling Egypt, but stranger things had happened.

"There's something I want to know," I said. "Was it you who sent me that page from Antipater's diary?"

He nodded. "After my servants showed me the page, I told them to send it to you."

"Why?"

"I thought it might lure you here, Gordianus of Rome. And so it did."

"For what purpose?"

The prince sighed. "Luring you here was only one of many, many small schemes I've hatched in the days since I was captured. All the other schemes came to nothing, but this one . . ." He smiled. "It so happened that these two servants, assigned by Monime to spy on Antipater, were actually loyal to me—*my* spies, if you will. They secretly read his diary and reported back to me. It was clear that Antipater had lost enthusiasm for the cause of Mithridates, and that he especially disliked Monime. How might his discontent be turned to my advantage? When I discovered that Antipater had a young protégé in Egypt—a Roman no less—my interest was further piqued. What mischief might occur if I could lure that young Roman to Ephesus, and reunite him with the disgruntled poet?"

"You merely wanted to make mischief?"

"Mischief creates opportunity! When a prince finds himself without power, making mischief and sowing discord may be the best he can do, along with biding his time. Many a Ptolemy has learned that lesson over the centuries. So—how to bring Gordianus of Rome to Ephesus? I couldn't write to you myself—any such letter might be intercepted—but it occurred to me that that particular page from the diary might do the trick. And so it did. And the mischief created has borne fruit beyond my wildest expectations—for here am I, and there is the ship to take me away from this infernal place."

I thought about this, and looked at the *capsa* in my hand. "Other pages from the diary seem to be missing. Antipater himself noticed."

"Yes, there were certain comments he made about Egyptian politics—about my father and uncle, and even about myself—that I prefer no one should read. So I had those pages destroyed—as I suggest you do with the pages that remain. One never knows what further mischief they might spawn."

I looked at the others on the pier, including Freny. "How did Monime learn of the king's attraction to Freny—from the two servants watching Antipater?"

"Yes. They had to report *something* back to the queen, to make a pretense of being her spies in the household. A tidbit like that seemed harmless enough."

"Yet it almost got poor Freny killed!"

He nodded. "But you managed to prevent that. What a show you all put on the other night! Mithridates almost wet himself, and his vile bitch of a queen nearly fainted from terror."

"I thought you liked Monime."

"Like her?" He made an ugly face. "I loathe her! Oh, yes, I made a pretense of being her crony, her comrade, her cozy confidant—all the while trembling inside with disgust. She and her father are the worst sort of upstarts, crude commoners pretending to be royal. They're nobodies, with no manners and no breeding. Cousin Mithridates is bad enough, but Monime . . ." He made a retching sound.

The captain called to Samson that the boat was ready to sail.

Samson looked at the prince for a long moment, then stepped aside and indicated that the rest of us should do likewise, so that Ptolemy could board first. As he walked up the pier, from somewhere in his tunic the prince produced his cobra crown and fitted it on his head. A shaft of sunlight pierced the mist and fell upon the sparkling ruby eyes.

Samson boarded the vessel. He helped Chaeremon step aboard. I boarded next, then helped Bethesda onto the ship.

On the pier, with much weeping, Anthea and Amestris said their last farewells to Freny. At last she came aboard, and the ship cast off. The two women stood on the pier, waving. I gazed at the face of Amestris for as long as I could. Then the fog thickened, and I saw only two spots of yellow that gradually disappeared in the mist.

XXXVI

"Will we stop at Rhodes?" I asked.

"That was my plan," said Samson, "but according to my informants in Ephesus, the king's navy has already blockaded the island. We'll have to steer well clear of Rhodes."

We were a day out of Ephesus, sailing on the open sea under a cloudless sky. Freny and Bethesda were nearby, dozing under the warm sun. Prince Ptolemy, stricken by seasickness despite the calm waters, was somewhere belowdecks, attended by his two servants. Chaeremon, still wearing Antipater's tunic, stood at the prow, gazing at the sea.

"So there'll be no reunion for Chaeremon and his two sons on Rhodes?"

"Not yet."

"Will we head straight for Alexandria, then?" That was my hope.

Samson shook his head. "I'm not sure about that. Amestris asked me to take Freny to Tyre. And I have some business in Jerusalem. To get there, we would land at Joppa."

"Isn't that where Perseus rescued Andromeda from the sea monster?"

"So the Greeks say."

I stared at the sea for a while. "Why go to Jerusalem? I thought you were an Alexandrian Jew."

"A Jew is a Jew, Gordianus. Every Jew has a reason to visit Jerusalem."

"What is your reason?" Once again I realized how little I knew of Samson's true agenda.

"I want to make an offering at the Temple."

"Which one?"

"There is only one Temple."

"What sort of offering? One of those precious items you retrieved from the stolen treasury?"

"Perhaps." He fingered the hem of the old cloak he insisted on wearing. "Did I ever tell you that one of my ancestors fought for Alexander the Great?"

"No. I wasn't aware there were Jews in Alexander's army."

"Oh, yes. Alexander himself visited Jerusalem, and my ancestor fought for him all the way to India and back."

We stared at the sea.

"What was in that *capsa* Antipater gave you?" asked Samson. "Some final poems from the world's greatest poet?"

"No. There were no poems. Only a sort of diary."

"Still, the world might want to read it. There must be an audience for anything that came from the hand of Antipater of Sidon. You could hire scribes to copy it, and sell copies to rich Romans who like to appear cultured. I'm sure the Library at Alexandria would want a copy."

I shook my head. "I don't think it would enhance Antipater's reputation. Also, he makes references to people and events that might yet do harm to someone, as this war between Mithridates and Rome continues. No, I think Antipater's diary must remain a secret—though it would be hard for me to burn it, as he asked me to. It's too precious to me."

"By all means, don't burn it! So many precious things are lost to fire, and decay, and flood, and even to hungry insects." Samson smiled. "I have a secret, too."

"*You,* Samson? Imagine that!"

"Now that we're safely away from Ephesus, on the open sea, where no one can overhear, I think I shall tell you."

"Please do."

"But you must promise *not* to tell Prince Ptolemy."

"I promise."

He paused for a long moment. "This cloak that I'm wearing, the one that came from the treasury of the Alexandrian Jews at Cos . . ."

"Yes, what about that smelly old thing?" I asked, though to be fair, the fresh sea air had done much to clear away the musty odor.

"This is the cloak of Alexander the Great."

Samson looked at me, expecting a response, but I only stared back at him, speechless.

"It was for *this* that I traveled to Ephesus," he went on, "so that the cloak would not be claimed by Mithridates, or lost, or thrown away."

I frowned. "But . . . Mithridates was wearing the cloak of Alexander when we saw him in the Grove of the Furies. He found it in the treasury of the Ptolemies at Cos."

Samson shook his head. "No, that cloak is a fake. A decoy. *This* is the true cloak."

I shook my head. "That can't be right. After he died, the cloak of Alexander was claimed by his general Ptolemy, who became king of Egypt and handed it down to his descendants."

"True enough, but a few generations back, one of the Ptolemies became so short of money that he sold the cloak to the Jews of Alexandria. The sale was kept secret. The king had a replica made, and put it in the Egyptian royal treasury at Cos, even as the real cloak was stored in the Jewish treasury there. When Mithridates laid his hands on both treasuries, we thought the cloak was surely lost. Then we realized he was making a show of wearing the false cloak, which meant the real cloak might still be among the other items from the Jewish treasury. To anyone who didn't know what it was, the cloak might appear worthless. It might even be tossed out with the rubbish. We had to save the cloak of Alexander the Great. And I did!"

Samson slipped it from his shoulders and held it aloft, so that it fluttered in the gentle sea breeze.

I looked at the thing in wonder. Presumably it had once been purple, but had faded to a dull, reddish brown. It looked old and ugly, whereas the cloak Mithridates had worn, though old, had a certain austere beauty. Why was one cloak any more valuable or sacred than the other, simply because it had touched the person of a certain long-dead mortal?

And what did it mean, that my travels with Antipater had taken me to the Seven Wonders spread across Alexander's empire, and that I had been living in the city named for him, and that the sarcophagus of Alexander the Great had played such a large role in my adventure with the raiders of the Nile—and now, without my knowing it, the cloak of Alexander had played a role in this episode? For without Samson, whose true mission was to reclaim the cloak, my trip to Ephesus would surely have turned out very differently. I seemed to be living somehow in the shadow of Alexander the Great.

Bethesda and Freny saw the cloak held aloft. Wondering what Samson was up to, they came to join us.

Suddenly, the gentle sea breeze became a gust. The cloak went flying from Samson's grasp and fluttered out to sea.

Samson stared at the cloak, his eyes wide and his mouth open. He cried out something in Hebrew—Jehovah was mentioned—and then dove overboard. He disappeared under the waves for a moment, then resurfaced, sputtering and flailing his arms. The cloak had landed in the water a few feet away from him. Samson paddled desperately toward it. Several times it eluded his grasp, but finally he grabbed it.

"Man overboard!" I cried. The captain heard me and began to circle back.

"I have it! I have the cloak!" Samson shouted to us. "But . . . I can't swim!"

"Neither can I!" I shouted. I looked about frantically. The sailors were all busy. Prince Ptolemy and his servants were belowdecks. Chaeremon was too frail to go in the water. Freny was too small, and Bethesda was no better at swimming than I was.

I gazed at Samson as he struggled to stay afloat, fearing he might disappear at any moment.

Then something seemed to bump him from beneath the waves, buoying him up. I watched in amazement as two chattering dolphins took turns keeping him afloat. I had heard stories of dolphins rescuing drowning men. I never thought I would see such a thing.

"Master!" cried Bethesda. "Those are the same two dolphins we saw on the way to Ephesus!"

I shook my head and laughed. What peculiar notions Bethesda sometimes had. Who could tell one dolphin from another?

And yet . . .

Kysanias would probably see the hand of Artemis at work in Samson's rescue. Samson himself had cried out to Jehovah, which I presumed to be the name of his jealous god. Bethesda seemed to think the two dolphins were benevolent guardians, following our journey.

What did I think?

The life I had hoped to save in Ephesus had been lost, but another life had been saved.

The woman with whom I first knew bliss had not been pining for me ever since, but had found true love with another woman.

I had learned that my voice was precious to me. I would never be mute again, even if to speak was to put myself in danger.

Had the Fates steered me to Ephesus, as Kysanias believed, or was the world ruled by chance—and mischief? I touched my lucky lion's tooth and gazed at the sparkling waves at the far horizon, and wondered where my life would take me next.

CHRONOLOGY

Great Pyramid, and then to Alexandria. Antipater soon leaves, but Gordianus remains in Egypt.

90   Gordianus acquires Bethesda.

89   War begins between Rome and King Mithridates of Pontus. In 89 and 88, Mithridates has massive successes in Asia Minor and the islands of the Aegean.

88   Mithridates takes the island of Cos, seizing the Egyptian treasury there and taking the son of King Ptolemy X hostage.

       23 March (Martius): Gordianus turns 22. The events of *Raiders of the Nile* commence.

       Civil war breaks out in Egypt; King Ptolemy X flees Alexandria and his brother seizes the throne.

       Mid-year: the events of *Wrath of the Furies* commence.

AUTHOR'S NOTE

(This note reveals elements of the plot.)

The central event of this novel—the simultaneous massacre in 88 BCE of every Roman in Asia Minor—actually occurred. Confusingly, modern historians call this event the Asiatic Vespers or Ephesian Vespers.

Why "Vespers"? French historian Théodore Reinach coined the phrase "Vèpres éphésiennes" in his 1890 biography, *Mithridate Eupator, roi de Pont.* The name echoes that of a later massacre, the so-called Sicilian Vespers, the sudden slaughter of all the French on the island of Sicily, which commenced as church bells were ringing vespers on Easter Monday, March 30, 1282. That bloody purge is vividly described by Steven Runciman in *The Sicilian Vespers: A History of the Mediterranean World in the Later Thirteenth Century* (Cambridge, 1958):

> To the sound of the bells messengers ran through the city calling on the men of Palermo to rise against the oppressor. At once the streets were filled with angry armed men, crying "Death to the French" ("*moranu li Franchiski*" in their Sicilian dialect). Every Frenchman they met was struck down. They poured into the

inns frequented by the French and the houses where they dwelt, sparing neither man, woman nor child. Sicilian girls who had married Frenchmen perished with their husbands. The rioters broke into the Dominican and Franciscan convents; and all the foreign friars were dragged out and told to pronounce the word "ciciri", whose sound the French tongue could never accurately reproduce. Anyone who failed the test was slain. . . .

Note that a French accent gave the victims away, just as Gordianus's accent would have given him away in Ephesus.

Our details about the massacre of 88 BCE are equally vivid. The Roman historian Appian catalogues the atrocities (*Mithridatic Wars*, 22–23, Horace White translation):

These secret orders Mithridates sent to all the cities at the same time. When the appointed day came calamities of various kinds befell the province of Asia, among which were the following:

The Ephesians tore fugitives, who had taken refuge in the temple of Artemis, from the very images of the goddess and slew them. The Pergameans shot with arrows those who had fled to the temple of Aesculapius, while they were still clinging to his statues. The Adramytteans followed those who sought to escape by swimming, into the sea, and killed them and drowned their children. The Caunii . . . pursued the Italians who had taken refuge about the Vesta statue of the senate house, tore them from the shrine, killed children before their mothers' eyes, and then killed the mothers themselves and their husbands after them. The citizens of Tralles, in order to avoid the appearance of blood-guiltiness, hired a savage monster named Theophilus, of Paphlagonia, to do the work. He conducted the victims to the temple of Concord, and there murdered them, chopping off the hands of some who were embracing the sacred images.

Such was the awful fate that befell the Romans and Italians

throughout the province of Asia, men, women, and children, their freedmen and slaves, all who were of Italian blood. . . .

Almost five hundred years later, the lament for the slaughtered continued. Augustine of Hippo (*City of God*, 3.22, Marcus Dods translation): "How miserable a spectacle was then presented, when each man was suddenly and treacherously murdered. . . . Think of the groans of the dying, the tears of the spectators, and even of the executioners themselves."

How great was the slaughter? Valerius Maximus (*Memorable Deeds and Sayings*, 9.2.3) and Memnon (*History of Heraclea*, 22.9) speak of 80,000 dead. Plutarch (*Sulla*, 24.7) nearly doubles that number, citing 150,000. Cicero, who mentions the event in more than one oration, speaks only of "many thousands" (*Manilian Law*, 4.11).

The date of the massacre is a vexed question. A. N. Sherwin-White ("The Opening of the Mithridatic War," *Miscellanea di studi classici in onore di Eugenio Manni*, vol. VI, Rome, 1980, pp. 1981–95) dates the massacre to late 89 or early 88 BCE, but this novel places the event in the middle of 88 BCE, the latest time allowed by Ernst Badian ("Rome, Athens and Mithridates," *American Journal of Ancient History* 1, 1976, pp. 105–28).

The horrific death of Manius Aquillius is described by Appian (*Mithridatic Wars*, 21) and by Pliny (*Natural History*, 33.14). Was Manius Aquillius really forced to sully his name with a pun, proclaiming that he was crazy? As comedians often say nowadays, "I couldn't make these things up." Regarding this question, my thanks to Jona Lendering at Livius.org for his explication of the Greek text of Appian at *Mithridatic Wars*, 21. On another question to do with Manius Aquillius, my thanks to Gaylan DuBose for his translation of the Latin text of Granius Licianus, *History of Rome*, 35.

The story of Bouplagos, who rose from the dead, and the raving Roman general comes from Phlegon of Tralles's *Book of Marvels* (pp. 32–37 in the translation by William Hansen published by Exeter Press in 1996).

The case of Publius Rutilius Rufus ("the Roman without a toga") is examined by Gordon P. Kelly in *A History of Exile in the Roman Republic* (Cambridge, 2006). Gossip that Rutilius was somehow complicit in the massacre is reported, but rejected, by Plutarch (*Pompey*, 37).

Mithridates's seizure of the Jewish treasury on Cos is reported by Josephus (*Antiquities of the Jews*, 14.7). Mithridates's acquisition of the cloak of Alexander the Great is reported by a somewhat skeptical Appian (*Mithridatic Wars*, 117).

The whereabouts of Prince Ptolemy (Ptolemy XI by modern reckoning) after his abduction on Cos are largely mysterious, but we know that he escaped from Mithridates because he later appears as a client of the Roman dictator Sulla, who managed to put him on the Egyptian throne—if only very briefly. The maddeningly jumbled threads of Ptolemaic genealogy were brilliantly untangled by the late Chris Bennett at www.tyndalehouse.com/egypt/.

Was a virgin sacrificed in the Grove of the Furies? The little we know is from Julius Obsequens, *Book of Prodigies*, 56, which can be found in volume XIV of the Loeb edition of Livy. (Thanks again to Gaylan DuBose for his help with some perplexing Latin.) I discovered this rather enigmatic prodigy—which was to give me the title and fulcrum of my plot—while reading (and rereading) Adrienne Mayor's splendid biography of Mithridates, *The Poison King* (Princeton, 2010). My battered copy of this book has dog-ears, highlighting, and scribbled notes on virtually every page.

The first epigraph that precedes this novel (from the *Eumenides* by Aeschylus) is from the Herbert Weir Smyth translation, now in public domain, as revised by Cynthia Bannon and Gregory Nagy. The full text can be found at www.uh.edu/~cldue/texts/eumenides.html. The second epigraph, from Cavafy's poem "Darius," is from the 1923 translation by George Valassopoulo. All other verses in this book are my own (sometimes rather loose) translations.

My thanks to my editor, Keith Kahla, for his invaluable feedback, to my husband, Rick Solomon, for his insightful comments, and to my agent, Alan Nevins, who went above and beyond the call of duty in recent months.

Lastly . . . what about those cherries? In the very first novel of the series, *Roman Blood* (1991), the thirty-year-old Gordianus used cherries as a simile to describe Bethesda's lips. It was pointed out to me that cherries were not introduced in Rome until fourteen years later, when the cherry trees brought back from the Black Sea region by Lucullus created a sensation. To fix the perceived anachronism, those cherries became pomegranates in later editions of *Roman Blood*. To put the matter behind me, I wrote a short story called "The Cherries of Lucullus," and in the Historical Notes to the collection in which that story appears, *A Gladiator Dies Only Once* (2005), I disclosed the papered-over anachronism in *Roman Blood*. But now, in recalling the youthful travels of Gordianus, I discover that he first encountered cherries in 88 BCE—well before his return to Rome and the events of *Roman Blood*. Perhaps in some future edition of that book, the pomegranates will become cherries again, bringing full circle the never-ending quest for a perfect text.